Finding Todd

Escaping the Past: Book Four

by

Suzie Peters

First Published in 2018
by GWL Publishing
an imprint of Great War Literature Publishing LLP

Produced in United Kingdom

ISBN 978-1-910603-42-0 Paperback Edition

GWL Publishing
Forum House
Sterling Road
Chichester PO19 7DN

www.gwlpublishing.co.uk

Dedication

For S.

Chapter One

Todd

The guy standing in the arrivals hall looks bored to death. I guess he's thirty, or thereabouts. He's probably just under six feet tall, well-built, with short reddish-brown hair and stubble. He's holding up a card with my name printed on it, but he's looking around and doesn't notice me until I'm right in front of him.

"You looking for me?" I ask him.

"If you're Todd Russell, then yes." I'd hardly be asking the question, if I wasn't... I just look at him until he nods, holds out his hand to me and says, "I'm Adam Harris." I shake his hand and he turns away. "Follow me," he says over his shoulder.

"Where are we going?" I ask.

"My car... the car park."

"I got that. I mean where are you taking me?"

"Oh. Paddington Green Police Station."

"Okay." I kind of wish he'd said a hotel, so I could freshen up, but I guess cops like us aren't allowed such luxuries, no matter which side of the Atlantic we work on.

"Andy – that's my boss – wanted to brief you and Holly as soon as you arrived." He keeps talking as we get in the elevator.

"Who's Holly?"

"You'll be working with her."

"I will?" I know I'm going undercover, although I don't know in what capacity yet, but no-one's mentioned a second role... or a female officer taking it. I hate working with people I don't know, and I'd like a heads up. "What's she like?" I ask.

"No idea, mate." He turns to look at me, smiling. "Never even met her."

"Excuse me?"

"She only transferred to CID a week ago... and then promptly went on holiday."

"Great."

"Yeah." His smile becomes a grin. "Rather you than me."

We exit on the fourth floor and as we approach a black Volvo, he pops the trunk, and I load my case inside.

I've only just climbed into the passenger seat, when my phone rings. I check the display. It's Grace and I can't help but smile.

"Hey, Grace," I say, connecting the call.

"Hey yourself," she replies.

"You're up early."

"George woke me. I've just finished feeding him."

"Thanks. I needed that image in my head," I tell her and she laughs.

"Where are you?"

"Just leaving Heathrow, on my way into, um... Paddington?"

"Okay. And why didn't you tell me you were going to England? I could have given you all kinds of tips for places to visit."

"I'm working, Grace. I won't have time for sightseeing."

"You might."

"I doubt it."

"Then I could have helped you out with my useful guide on how not to annoy the British. Matt and Luke make use of it all the time."

"That's because they're both real annoying. I'm not." She really laughs this time. "Okay... you can calm down now. It wasn't that funny. How is that husband of yours?" I ask, and Adam coughs. I guess he thought I was talking to my girlfriend, or wife. Now he probably assumes I'm talking to my mistress... If I wasn't so tired, I'd be tempted to have some fun with this.

"Matt's fine. He's still asleep."

"And the wedding?" I can feel Adam's eyes on me as we exit the parking garage. He's really confused now.

"It was lovely." She yawns.

"Is George asleep again yet?"

"Yes."

"Then go back to bed. It's only just after six-thirty with you; and it's Sunday. You can get another couple of hours' sleep yet."

"But Matt said we won't hear from you for a while."

"No, you won't."

"Oh." She sounds upset.

"You'll live."

"We'll miss you."

"I'll be home soon." I keep my voice as reassuring as I can.

"Take care of yourself, won't you?" I guess it didn't work. She sounds upset, *and* concerned now.

"I'll do my best."

"And say hello to London for me." That's better. She sounds a little more optimistic.

"Of course."

We say our goodbyes and hang up. Adam keeps looking at me. "That was the wife of a friend of mine," I tell him, because I don't have the energy to play games with him. "She's British." To me, that's enough explanation. It's all he's getting, anyway. Matt's more like a brother than a friend, but Adam doesn't need to know that.

He steers us onto the freeway... or motorway, as the Brits call it. "Good, it's not too busy," he says. Looks busy enough to me, for a Sunday morning.

I'm just about to say so, when my phone rings again. This time, it's Luke. I pick up.

"Hey," I say to him.

"When were you gonna tell me?" he replies by way of greeting. He sounds a little pissed with me.

"I didn't want to take the edge off your day."

"So you just left?" He seems offended.

"No. I told Matt and Will. They did explain, didn't they?"

"Yeah, Will did. But you didn't say goodbye."

"No."

"And we won't hear from you while you're there?"

"No. I'll be turning my phone off later today… You won't be able to contact me."

"Will said this could be dangerous… the job you're doing." His voice softens at last.

"It's a possibility. I'm hoping it won't be though."

"Take care of yourself, man."

Everyone keeps saying that. It's kinda hard to know how to reply. "Sorry I missed the end of your wedding." It's a reasonable change of subject.

I can hear him smiling. "You missed the main event."

"I don't want to know about that. What you and Megan get up to in your own time—"

"Not that," he says. "Will and Jamie got engaged."

"You're kidding me." I didn't see that coming… not for a while yet, anyway.

"No, I'm not. This means you're the last single man standing."

"It's a badge I'll wear with honor and pride," I tell him.

"Until some beautiful brunette comes along and steals your heart…"

"It's never gonna happen… not to me."

"We all said that. And look where we all are now."

"Tied down?"

"Happy," he says. I know he's right. My three best friends are all happily married, or engaged – evidently – and settled with incredible women, who a lot of men would kill to be with. I'm not envious. It's not something I want. I made my decision about that years ago and I don't intend changing my mind now. Not for anyone.

"Speaking of you being happy," I say, "why are you calling me at this time of day? I thought you and Megan had a swanky suite at the Boston Harbor. Surely you've got better things to be doing the morning after your wedding than talking to me."

"Megan's still asleep… I kept her up late last night." I can hear him smirking.

"Once again… I really don't need to know that."

"I'll wake her in a while. We're due to leave in a couple of hours…"

"For Italy?" Luke's planned a surprise honeymoon trip for them. Matt, Will and I knew about it, but Megan had no idea… and still doesn't, if things have gone to plan. It was the best-kept secret of the whole wedding.

"No, just to go home and relieve Will and Jamie of babysitting duties. We leave for Italy this evening."

"And Megan still doesn't know?"

"No. I'm gonna tell her on the way to the airport."

"Well… have a great time."

"We will."

"And give Megan and Daisy a hug from me," I tell him.

"Okay."

"I'll be in touch when I can… And I'm sorry I didn't tell you."

"You're forgiven. But only if you get back here safe and sound… and soon."

"I'll do my best."

"You'd better…"

After I've hung up, I notice Adam's looking at me again. "That was a friend of mine," I explain. "He got married yesterday. I had to duck out of the end of his wedding to catch my flight."

"Oh… so that's why you couldn't come over on Friday?"

"Yeah. I wasn't missing the wedding."

"Good for you," he says. "But Andy wasn't too pleased about that."

I glance across at him. "Do I look like I give a fuck?"

He grins at me and changes lanes.

"I'm Andy Reed." The guy holds out his hand to me and we shake. He's a little taller than Adam, but a couple of inches shy of me. He has cropped brown hair, is clean-shaven and is wearing the smartest suit I've ever seen on a cop. "It's good to meet you," he adds. "Come into my office."

I follow him, dragging my suitcase along behind me, and he closes the door once we're both inside. "Leave that in the corner," he says, nodding to my case, and I do. "We just need to wait for Holly."

He sits behind his desk and indicates the two chairs in front of him. I take the left hand one.

"She's not here yet?"

"No. She was due to land at about the same time as you. Her flight was coming in from Pisa. She's been on holiday... or vacation, I suppose you'd say."

I'm confused. "Then why didn't we wait and pick her up?"

"Because she left her car in the long-stay car park. It would have been pointless."

"Oh, I see."

He glances at his watch. "I don't know where she is," he says. "She wouldn't have had to go through immigration, just passport control, and that shouldn't have taken too long." He huffs out a breath. "We'll give her a little longer."

"She's new, isn't she?"

"Yes. Very."

"And you chose her for this assignment...?"

"Because she's the only female officer I've got who's suitable," he says.

I find it hard to believe a woman who's only worked in criminal investigation for a week, and has spent all of that on vacation is the most suitable person he's got. I think my skepticism must show.

"I've only got two other women in this department," he explains. "One is nearly forty. She's good at her job, but for what we need, she's not right. The other is pregnant – very pregnant. She goes on maternity leave at the end of the week." He leans forward, resting his chin on one upturned hand, and he opens the file on his desk. "I've read through your case notes," he says.

"And your killings match ours?" I ask. I guess it's a dumb question. They wouldn't have bothered to fly me all the way over here if they didn't.

"Yes." He doesn't look up. "In every way."

"There's been nothing in the press at home. We've deliberately kept it quiet. So it can't be a copycat," I add.

"No. I discussed that with your captain." He raises his head and stares at me. "Interesting man."

"That's one word for him." We exchange a smile. Carpenter has been my boss for the last two years. He's the main reason I'll be resigning as soon as this case is over and done with. The man's an idiot. He's gonna get someone killed one day soon, and it's not gonna be me…

"How's this going to work?" I ask him. "The undercover element, I mean…"

"I think we'll wait for Holly to arrive, then——"

Before he can finish his sentence, there's a knock on his door.

Holly

I know I shouldn't complain. I've had a week away in Italy. I spent four days and nights in Florence, and the rest of my time in Pisa. It was stunning. I'd like to go back there one day, in happier circumstances. It wasn't the holiday I'd planned; not even remotely. But it was a holiday – and I needed it. What I hadn't expected was the text message I got on Friday afternoon from my new boss, Andy, asking me to cut short my holiday and fly home. I was just looking into changing my ticket, when I got a second message, telling me not to worry… that I could catch my scheduled flight, and if I could get into the office by twelve today, that would be great. Well, it would be a bloody miracle, considering I didn't land until eleven, had to get my baggage, get through customs, collect my car from the long stay car park, which was a fifteen minute bus ride away, and drive from Heathrow to Paddington – which even on a Sunday takes nearly an hour. So, not a chance, Andy.

This time yesterday, I was having a panini and a glass of chilled Pinot Grigio at the Tower House in the Via Santa Maria... and today I'm driving down the A40 behind a removals lorry. The comparison is almost enough to make me smile and I haven't done that in a long time – not even during my holiday.

It's when I'm parking that I remember why I bought such a small car... You can park it pretty much anywhere and I find a spot easily. I suppose it also helps that it's a Sunday and less busy than usual.

I check the time on my phone. It's nearly a quarter past one. I don't imagine Andy is going to be too happy that I'm over an hour late, but I haven't even stopped to go to the toilet, let alone to grab a coffee, which I desperately need.

Whatever's so important that I have to come in on my Sunday off, I'm sure it can wait another few minutes while I just visit the Ladies' on my way to Andy's office.

As if my day wasn't perfect enough, I discover that my period has just started. It's a day early, and I rummage in my bag for a sanitary towel. I've got one, thank goodness, but I know there are none at home. I'll have to go shopping anyway when I've finished here, so I can pick some up then. While I'm washing my hands, I check my appearance in the mirror. I've seen worse. Okay, I've also seen better – but not usually in my own reflection. I hope Andy doesn't mind that I'm wearing jeans and a casual blouse, and no make-up...

"Tough," I whisper to myself. "He's on my time today. He can take it or leave it."

Once I'm finished, I go along the corridor to his office and knock twice.

"Come in," he calls.

I open the door and a man, who's been sitting in one of the chairs in front of Andy's desk, gets to his feet and turns to face me. He's enormous. He must be at least six foot three, with short, light brown hair and eyes the colour of milk chocolate. He's got dark stubble on his square jaw and, as he takes a step towards me, his mouth opens into a wide smile of brilliant white teeth. His leather jacket fits tightly across his broad shoulders and muscular arms… and I need to stop staring at him and pay attention to what Andy's saying.

"Holly…" Andy also stands. "Nice of you to make it." I ignore the sarcasm. It's not worth biting. I'll only lose. "Holly King, this is Todd," he says by way of introduction. "Todd Russell." The giant offers his hand and I take it. His grip is strong.

"Hi," he says. "Pleasure to meet you." He has a deep, yet soft, velvety voice with a pronounced American accent.

"You're American." I state the blindingly obvious.

"Yes, ma'am." He smiles again. I can't help but giggle. That's odd… I've gone from not smiling in weeks, to giggling like a schoolgirl, just because a handsome, tall, muscular American smiled at me. *Grow up, Holly.*

"They pay us to notice things like that," I tell him.

"Well, if it's anything like back home, they don't pay you enough."

"Amen to that."

"Okay," Andy says. "Enough of the mutual self-pity society. Come and join us, Holly." Todd waits until I'm seated before sitting down again himself. "Todd's come over from Boston," Andy explains.

"Oh?" I look from one to the other of them. "Is this why you needed me to come back early?"

"Yes," Andy replies. "Sorry about the mix up. We were trying to get Todd over here on Friday evening, but he couldn't make it, so there seemed little point in getting you to cut short your holiday in the end."

"Sorry for messing you around," Todd says, looking at me.

"You didn't." I look up at Andy. "I still don't understand why I'm here…"

"You're going to be working together – on a murder case."

The room starts to spin, just a little. "I'm sorry," I say, "did you say 'murder'?" I thought I'd be making the coffee and pushing paper around for weeks… maybe months, and I'm about to be put on a murder case, on what is effectively my first day?

"Yes."

"But… Are you sure you've got the right person. You do remember I've only just started here, don't you?"

"Yes," Andy says. "And normally I wouldn't even consider giving you a case like this to work on, but I've got no choice." Well, I suppose at least he's being honest.

Todd turns in his seat to face me. "There have been three double homicides in Boston since Christmas," he explains. "They're all exactly the same in terms of the way in which they're carried out, the manner in which the bodies are left, and so on. There was one the day before Christmas Eve, one in the middle of January and one in late February. Then it went quiet. I've been working the case, but haven't been able to find any leads. I'd started to wonder if our guy had given up... lost interest."

"Right," I say. "But what's that got to do with us?"

"We had an identical murder here," says Andy. "The bodies were found in the early hours of Friday morning, although we think the killings took place on Wednesday night, or early Thursday morning."

Todd looks up. "I wasn't told that," he remarks. "I was told the murders happened on Friday morning... we've already lost four days, then..."

"I did inform your captain of the details," Andy replies.

"Yeah, well he didn't pass that on." Todd looks angry.

Andy turns back to me, shaking his head, then continues, "Because of the nature of the killings, and the fact that one of the deceased was an American, from Boston, it didn't take us long to put our murders together with the ones in Todd's precinct. And his captain and our Superintendent decided he should come over here..."

"Seems sensible," I say. "But I still don't see why I'm involved?"

Todd looks at Andy. "You haven't really explained it to me either," he says. "All I was told is I'm going undercover. I didn't know anyone else would be involved." He glances across at me and smiles apologetically. I shrug my shoulders. I don't blame him for being doubtful about me – *I'm* pretty doubtful about me too.

Andy takes a deep breath and stares down at the open file in front of him. He doesn't make eye contact with either of us. "All the people who've been murdered were couples. They all frequented a particular club which has branches all over the world, but for our purposes, we're only interested in the Boston and Mayfair branches… especially the Mayfair one, since that was where our couple had been on the evening they were killed… last Wednesday." He glances up at Todd as he says the last word, like he expects him to say something.

Todd ignores Andy's emphasis on the day and leans forward. "Each of the couples in Boston had also visited the club there on the night they were killed. We've interviewed all the other guests, the members, all the staff, visitors, even the suppliers… everyone. We couldn't find a damn thing."

"I know," Andy says. "I've read the files. Your case notes are very thorough."

"So?" Todd says, again ignoring Andy's compliment.

"So, we're going to have you two pose as guests… as a couple…"

Todd lets out a long sigh. "You're kidding me, right?" Andy shakes his head. "I'd assumed you were sending me in to work in the club, behind the bar, or something…"

"You couldn't find out anything when you interviewed everyone. What makes you think that going undercover as an employee would work any better? You'd have to establish who you think it is, and then earn their trust… it could take months, and in that time, they could kill again. And if it's a guest – a member – who's responsible, you might never even get to meet them."

"And you think this plan is better?"

"We've set you up as members. Whoever it is targeted an American in London. Out of all the members he could have chosen, he went for an American—"

"He?" I interrupt, picking up on what they've been saying. "How do you know it's a he?"

Todd and Andy exchange glances. "Tell her," Todd says. "You're asking her to do this. I'm not. She has a right to know."

"The women," Andy says, looking from Todd to me. "The women in each case… they were all raped."

"And?" Todd says. "Tell her everything."

Andy glares at him. "They were raped… and sodomised."

"Sodomised?" I say quietly.

11

"Yes. You know… anal sex."

"I know what it means, Andy. I'm not *that* stupid." I think about what he's said. "Before or after death?" I ask.

"Before," Todd replies.

I feel very cold all of a sudden, but my mind is racing. "I still don't see how that guarantees it's a man," I say.

Andy stares at me. "Want me to draw you a picture?" he says.

"No. But couldn't it be a woman, or more than one person, forcing the male partner in the couple to perform those acts on the female?"

"We thought of that," says Todd. "We did DNA tests on the semen. It didn't match the male partner… not in any of the cases."

I turn to him. "And nothing showed up on the DNA database?" I realise the ignorance of that statement just as the words are leaving my lips, but I can't stop myself from saying them in time.

"Do you think we'd all be sitting here if it had?" Andy says.

"Cut her some slack," Todd barks at him, then turns back to me. "No," he says calmly. "Nothing at all."

"And what does he do to the male partner?"

"Do you really want to know? Whatever happens, it won't affect you."

"Yes, I want to be fully aware of what I'm getting into."

"Okay. Show her the pictures," Todd says to Andy, leaning back in his seat.

Andy turns over a few pages, then pulls out some photographs and, without even glancing at them, hands them to me. I look down and it takes me a moment or two to realise what I'm seeing – or what I think I'm seeing – and then I can feel my stomach churning, the bile rising in my throat. I put my hand across my mouth.

"Sorry," I manage to say and I run from the room, bolt down the corridor and clatter through the door to the Ladies'. I just make it into a cubicle before I empty the meagre contents of my stomach.

My walk back to Andy's office is shaky, to say the least. When I get inside, Todd gets up and comes over to me.

"Sorry," he says.

"You did warn me." I look up at him. His eyes are filled with concern. "I'm fine," I tell him, lying through my teeth. I feel anything but fine, and I'd still be in the Ladies' if it wasn't for the fact that I know I've got nothing left to be sick with… I've been sitting on the floor of the toilet cubicle for the last ten minutes, retching.

"Come and sit back down," he says, stepping to one side.

I notice that the photographs have been put away again. I'm grateful for that. I've never seen so much blood, so much mutilation. I don't even want to think about it, let alone look at it again.

"Is this really the best idea you guys can come up with?" Todd asks, sitting down beside me. "Sending us in as bait?"

"It's not my idea," Andy replies. "Your captain agreed it with my boss. I've had very little say in the matter. But, on the whole, I do agree with them."

"I still don't see why I can't go into the club undercover on my own," Todd says.

"I've already explained. It'd take too long; it's too unreliable. Our man isn't looking for a single American barman, or waiter, or bouncer; he's looking for an American couple – clients of the club."

"Er… I'm not American," I manage to murmur.

"Todd is. Remember… I said only one of the victims in our case was American. The woman was British."

"But how do you know the killer's looking for an American at all? That could have just been random."

"We don't think so," says Todd, with some reluctance. "The members concerned had only just joined the London club the week before. There aren't many American members. It seems a bit contrived to single them out."

"I suppose so." I turn back to Andy. "Do I have a choice?" I ask.

"Yes. You can say no, if you want to."

"And what'll happen then?"

"We'll have to re-think things. I've got no-one else here who can do this, but I might be able to get another female officer from another station to come in and take your place. It'll take me a little while to find someone."

"And in the meantime, he could kill again?"

"It's a possibility."

I nod my head. "I just can't see how we're going to pull this off," I say, almost to myself.

"Why not?" Andy asks. "Todd knows the set-up of the clubs. He's got experience of working undercover. You'll really just have to turn up and watch; keep your eyes open and let him be heard and seen. Let him make himself obvious as an American."

"I understand that. What I mean is, won't the killer follow us, at some point, check us out, and realise that Todd goes back to a hotel, and I go to my flat…"

I look at Andy. He's staring at me. "No," he replies. "You're going to have to act like a normal couple all the time. Well, at least when you're in public. Behind closed doors, you can do whatever you want… Todd won't be staying at a hotel, Holly. He'll be staying with you."

Oh, will he now? "Um—" I don't even get to start my sentence, let alone finish it.

"And how do you know that's convenient for Holly?" Todd interrupts, sitting forward in his chair again. "Does she have space for me? Does she have a husband, or boyfriend?" He turns to me. "Sorry," he says. "I'm talking about you like you're not here."

"Go right ahead," I say turning to Andy. "Have you considered that it might not be okay with me? Or are you just going to ride roughshod over my private life?"

"We both know you live alone now," he says, having the decency to look a little embarrassed. "And we also both know you've got a big enough flat."

"And what if Holly doesn't want me living at her place?" I like the fact that Todd's concerned about how I'll feel, although I doubt Andy's going to pay any attention.

"The budget won't stretch to renting you the kind of place that people who frequent this club would be living in," Andy says.

"And Holly's apartment fits the bill?" He turns to me. "Sorry, but I know what cops earn, at least back home. I can't imagine it's that different over here."

"Don't apologise," I say to him. "It's nice to have someone fighting my corner for a change." He keeps his eyes on mine for a moment, a furrow appearing on his brow, then turns back to Andy.

"Holly's place is just fine. When you get back there, you'll see what I mean," Andy says, smiling.

"Okay," Todd replies. "But what about if this guy decides to do his research and finds we're living in an apartment that belongs to a cop?"

"He won't," I say.

"He might," Todd argues. "He's thorough."

"No. You misunderstand. I mean he won't find that my flat is registered to me. According to the Land Registry, it belongs to my father's company. Unless he decides to really dig deep, he won't find out anything that way."

"See?" says Andy, with an annoyingly triumphant gleam in his eyes. "It's perfect."

Chapter Two

∞

Todd

Perfect? It's the most stupid, reckless, dangerous, dumb idea I've heard in my life. And I've heard some dumb ones.

Holly's seemingly as mystified as I am by his idea of what qualifies as 'perfect' in this setup. I look across at her. I've been doing a lot of that. Ever since she walked in, just over an hour ago, I've found it hard to keep my eyes off her. She's tall – I'd say around five foot nine; slim but not skinny, with long, long legs. Her dark brown hair is styled in what I think would be called a 'messy bob', which falls just below her chin line. She's turned toward me now and it's hard not to notice her soulful blue-gray eyes and the fact that, even though she's not wearing any make-up, she's got a glow to her soft, delicate skin... although right now, she's so pale, she's white – probably because she just went and threw up in the Ladies' Room.

I'm intrigued by her. And I'm never intrigued – it requires too much concentration. Something's obviously happened to her – quite recently I'd say. Andy said she lived alone 'now', which suggests she didn't before; and then she made a comment about liking having someone fighting her corner. I'm guessing someone's hurt her – and she's not over it yet. I don't like the idea of her hurting, but it's that unusual thought that brings me to my senses, stops this weird need I keep having to go to her, hold her and ask her what's wrong, and reminds me why I like to keep control *and* why I don't do relationships... they're complicated. Not to mention, getting caught up in dumb and dangerous assignments like this one has the potential for a high cost – to me and anyone involved with me. I don't want that responsibility.

"Are you okay with these living arrangements?" I ask her. I'm not sure I am. I've lived on my own for over ten years and I've never lived with a woman before, except my mom and sister – and they don't really count.

"We're not being given a huge number of options, are we?" she says. She just about manages a smile, but it's real half-hearted. Seems like she's about as thrilled as I am.

I turn back to Andy. "Does the Mayfair club keep the same opening times as the one in Boston?" I ask him.

He opens the file again, flicks forward a few pages and looks back up. "They're open Mondays, Wednesdays and Fridays, nine pm until two am."

"Is that it?" Holly asks. "They don't believe in working too hard, do they?"

"With the amount they charge for membership," I tell her, "they don't need to." I turn to Andy again. "The one in Boston opens on Saturdays as well."

"They may have had trouble getting a licence to be open at the weekend," he says. "Or they might make more money during the week anyway... who knows?"

I face Holly again. "If you're okay with it, I suggest we go back to your place, get something to eat, get a good night's sleep and spend tomorrow going over the case notes. We can visit the club tomorrow evening and have a quiet look around." I've got a feeling her first visit is going to shock her. I don't think she'll notice much of any great importance, and I'll probably spend most of the time watching her, making sure she doesn't give us away. The second visit is when we'll really start working. I don't tell Andy this.

"Tomorrow?" she breathes. "So soon?"

I lean toward her. "You'll be fine," I tell her.

Andy gets up. The meeting's concluded. "You'll liaise with Adam," he says. "And please tell me you didn't bring any weapons with you."

"No." I want to tell him I'm not stupid.

"Good," he says. He reaches into his desk and hands me a mobile phone. "Adam's details are programmed into that," he says. "Only he and I have the number. Call him after you've been to the club. Set up regular times to contact each other and keep your personal phones switched off."

"I know," I try to keep the impatience out of my voice. "It already is."

"I think he was talking to me that time," Holly says.

Maybe he was, but I'd have made sure she didn't do anything to jeopardize the assignment.

He puts his hand back in his drawer again and pulls out a folder, handing it over to me. "This contains everything you'll need, including your club membership," he says to me, locking eyes for a moment. "It's just the basic package."

"I'm glad to hear it," I tell him. We sure as hell don't need the upgraded membership. "And no-one at the club knows about us?"

"No. No-one. Good luck," he says, shaking my hand just before I grab my case from the corner of the room. "Stay in touch with Adam. We'll be waiting to hear from you."

We ride down in the elevator together.

"Is he always such an ass?" I ask her.

"I don't really know. This is my first day."

"I know that, but I got the impression he knew you."

"He knows *of* me," she explains. She's got a reputation? Is that good? I wait, hoping she'll elaborate. "He's a friend of someone I used to go out with," she says, looking away. So that's what he meant about her living alone.

"I see. This other guy, I'm guessing he's a cop too?"

She turns to me. "Yes."

"He works here?"

"No. He's based at Westminster." She looks real sad. We need to change the subject. I don't like it when she's sad. This is really odd. When have I ever been overly bothered by something like that in the past? I shake my head… What's wrong with me today? I guess this must be what jet lag does to you…

"How does Andy know about your apartment being suitable?"

"My ex invited him and a couple of other friends over during the last World Cup. England won the match, I guess that made it memorable." The elevator door opens and I let her out first. We go through the main entrance, down the steps and around the corner, and she stops by the smallest car I've ever seen.

"This?" I say.

"What do you mean 'this'?" she asks.

"Just that I think we're going to have to rip out the front seat, and I'll sit in back."

She looks up at me. "I admit, it'll be a squeeze."

"A squeeze? I've got my suitcase as well…"

"A tight squeeze." She smiles. It's a small victory over her earlier sadness, but I'll take it.

"The trunk?" I ask.

"The boot, you mean?"

"I guess." I'm starting to wish I'd asked Grace to give me some translation tips.

"My bags are in there," she says.

"So we've got the back seat…"

"Yes," she says. "I'm sure it'll be fine."

"I admire your optimism." I realize pretty quickly that once we get my case onto the back seat, it's not going to come out again in a hurry. "Hold on a second," I say. "I need to get my tux out. I'll have to get it cleaned before tomorrow night."

"Seriously?"

"Yes, seriously. I was at a wedding yesterday. Is there anywhere—"

"On a Sunday afternoon?"

"I'm asking the impossible, aren't I?" I literally threw my tux into my case last night. I dread to think what it looks like now.

"No, you're not, but we can't do it today. There's a dry cleaner's not far from my flat. They do a same-day service. If we drop it off first thing tomorrow morning, they'll get it back to us in the afternoon."

"Great… So I haven't got to unpack my case in the middle of the street then?"

"Well… if we can't get it in the car, you might have to. You could put your clothes in the car, and leave the case here."

"You're joking, right?"

"Not really." She smiles up at me. Two smiles in a couple of minutes… I'm on a roll here.

"I'll get my case in, don't worry," I tell her, trying to ignore the way my stomach just flipped over when her eyes lit up.

"Just don't damage my car."

It takes us a while, but we manage to get the case in eventually. "See… not a scratch in sight," I say. "Now we've just got to get me in as well."

"Hang on," she says and bends over, leaning into the car, giving me a perfect – and I mean perfect – view of her ass. My cock hardens at the sight… and, in fairness to me, it is a fantastic sight. She adjusts the front seat, moving it back as far as it'll go, then she stands again. "Do you want to give it a try?" she offers. I can think of a million and one things I'd like to try with her… and none of them have anything to do with her car. A little self control would be good here. I'm normally really good with that, so why can't I seem to manage it today? *Christ, this is fucking weird.*

I climb into the car. She was right… it's a squeeze, but I can fit in and I close the door. Holly goes around to the driver's side and gets in. "See?" she says. "It's not so bad."

I laugh out loud. "I never thought I'd empathize with a sardine, but I'm really getting that whole crammed into a tin can feeling."

"Did you just call my car a tin can?" She looks at me, her eyes narrowing, but her lips twitching upward.

"I wouldn't dream of it," I say.

"Good," she replies, starting the engine. "I'd hate to make you get out again."

"I'm not sure I can."

She pulls out of the parking space and heads down the street, taking a right at the end. It's the middle of a Sunday afternoon and there isn't that much traffic.

"How far away do you live?" I ask her.

"Why? Are you worried you'll get stuck in that position?"

"It's a strong possibility."

"It'll take about ten minutes," she says, then she slaps her hand on the steering wheel. "Except I need to go shopping. Damn."

"Well, we're not gonna fit another thing in this car," I tell her. "Can't we go back to your place and drop off our bags first?"

"Yes. And we can walk to the supermarket," she says. "Or I don't mind going by myself while you rest, if you like. I feel like I've been sitting down all day."

"I'm happy to come with you," I reply. "We're supposed to be a couple, remember?"

"And couples do *everything* together, do they?"

"I don't know... you tell me." Oh shit, I wish I hadn't said that... a shadow crosses her eyes, and just for a moment, she looks sad again.

"In my experience, no, they don't." Whoever the guy was that hurt her did a good job.

"Well, I think we should go together. I can carry the bags, and I could do with the walk... that is, if my legs ever work again."

"You're determined to make a drama out of this, aren't you?" She glances across at me and her lips curl upwards again.

"Absolutely I am."

She's right, it doesn't take long to reach her apartment and she parks up behind a large, red-brick building.

"How old is this place?" I ask her, as I extricate myself from her car.

"I think it was built around 1900, maybe a little after," she says. "But don't worry, the plumbing and electrics are very twenty-first century."

I smile at her across the top of the car. "I'm relieved to hear it."

I retrieve my case – it's easier to get out, than it was to put in; Holly gets her bags and we go over to a back entrance. Holly puts a four-digit code into a security pad and opens the door, then we go down a short corridor and into an elevator, which takes us up to the third floor.

"I've got a spare key," she says, as she opens the door to her apartment. "I'll let you have it later... and the code for the outer door is 9872."

"Okay. Thanks. I guess it might be useful to be able to get in… if I go out on my own."

She holds the door open and lets me pass through, into a long, narrow hallway. It's painted in white, with a pale gray carpet, and a huge mirror further down on the right hand wall, which makes it seem lighter and larger than it is.

She puts her bags on the floor. "You'll be in here," she says, opening the door to my right.

The room has the same color scheme of gray carpet and white walls, with a king size bed, and two nightstands, one on either side. The bedding is white, and the only splash of color comes in the form of a dark purple throw over the foot of the bed. There's a large built-in closet with mirrored doors to my left.

"I hope it's okay," she says. "There's space in the wardrobe for you to put your things."

"It looks great." It does. It looks really comfortable.

"Leave your case in here," she says, "and I'll show you around."

"Thanks." I dump my bag at the end of the bed and take off my leather jacket, throwing it on top.

Across the hall from my bedroom is the kitchen, which is very sleek and luxurious, with black shiny cabinets and a white countertop. There's a six-ring gas hob, with a wide oven beneath.

"Oh, while I think about it, I'll just show you how the tap works," she says.

"We have those in America too, you know," I reply.

"I'm sure you do," she replies and goes over to the sink. I stand and watch, folding my arms across my chest. "For cold water, you turn the lever to the left and lift," she says.

"How novel," I reply, noting that she pronounces 'lever' differently, with more emphasis on the first 'e'.

Her eyes narrow as she looks back at me. This time she's not smiling.

"For hot water, you turn to the right."

"Do you know… I think I'd have worked that out all by myself… It might have taken me a while, but…"

"Right," she snaps. Whoa… her tone's changed. I think I just made her mad. "You're the detective. Look around the kitchen. You tell me what's missing." She turns and leans back against the sink and she folds her arms too. The action pushes her breasts up and, for a moment, I'm distracted. It's only a moment though, before I drag my eyes away and look around. There is literally nothing on the countertop. Not a thing.

"You don't even have a kettle?" I've learned something from Grace in the few months I've known her. The British are obsessed with tea and, unlike us Americans, they believe the water must – at all costs, on pain of excommunication – be freshly boiled, ideally in an electric kettle. "I know you British are obsessed with tea," I continue, "so how do you boil water?"

"Like this," she says, and she unfolds her arms, turns back around and lifts and lowers a plunger at the base of the tap, then twists it to the right and boiling hot water comes out of the faucet, creating a cloud of steam.

"Clever," I say, walking over and standing beside her. "And I apologize for being facetious."

"You're forgiven. Just don't get it wrong and stick your hands under the boiling water by mistake."

"I won't."

She presses on the door under the drainer and it pops open, and it's only now that I notice there are no handles on any of the units. "The dishwasher's here," she says. "And the fridge-freezer is over here." She walks to the tall unit behind us, opening it in the same way. "Except my fridge and freezer are both pretty empty." She looks embarrassed.

"Which is why we're going shopping," I say.

"Yes."

I follow her back out into the hallway. "That's my room," she says as we pass a door on the right, although she leaves it closed, and on the left, opposite, is the bathroom. There's a break from the monotone colors of the rest of the apartment in here. The tiles, which cover the floor, walls and ceiling are cream. There's a large jacuzzi bath, and a separate walk-in shower.

"Do I need a faucet… sorry, tap demonstration in here?" I ask.

"No. It's all pretty self-explanatory."

The final room, at the end of the hallway, is the living room. Although the walls are the ubiquitous white, and the gray carpet is ever-present, there is more color here, provided by a large, deep sofa in a bright blue which is in the middle of the room, facing a modern fireplace that's set into the wall. Above this is a huge TV screen and in front of the sofa, is a long, rectangular coffee table. Against the wall to our left, is a small, square dining table, with two chairs. There's a bay window on the far wall, letting in the sunshine.

"It's a lovely room," I tell her.

"Thanks," she says. She checks her watch. "It's only just gone three. We've still got a couple of hours before the supermarket closes. Do you want to freshen up... have a shower, get changed... or would you rather go and do the shopping first?"

"Maybe shopping first? Get it over with."

"I'm glad you said that."

Holly

The supermarket's busy, but then it always is at this time on a Sunday. It's like everyone forgets the shops aren't open all day long, and suddenly realises there's something they really can't live without. In my case, it's food... food and sanitary towels.

I'm wheeling a small trolley through the fruit and vegetable section.

"What do you want to get?" I ask Todd.

"I don't know. What do you like?"

"I like most things, really."

"So do I."

This is ridiculous. We'll be here all day at this rate. "Well, how about we buy a microwave lasagne, and get some prepared salad, and a bottle of wine." Especially the bottle of wine.

"Um… okay."

"You don't sound convinced."

"That's because I'm not."

"I'm tired. So are you. Can we do proper cooking another night? We can come back tomorrow and get something a little more tempting." Is it me, or do I sound like I'm pleading, a little pathetically?

He looks down at me, his brown eyes penetrating mine just for a moment. It's almost like he can read my mind. "Go get whatever else you need to buy," he says gently. "I'll deal with tonight's dinner and I'll catch you up."

I can't refuse that offer. "Are you sure?" I ask.

"Absolutely. See you in a minute." I leave him by the mushrooms and go first to the feminine hygiene section. I'd like to get this out of the way before he reappears. I grab a couple of packs of sanitary towels, then head for the bakery department and put some bread and croissants into the trolley. In the dairy section, I add milk, butter and some cheese and eggs. I've already managed to hide the packs of towels. This is working well. Now I can dawdle a bit more… I know I'm out of olive oil…

I've smiled more in the last few hours since meeting Todd than I have in the last five weeks. That doesn't mean I'm not still hurting, or that I've forgotten the pain. But I don't want him to know know how sick and tired I am; how lonely, rejected, angry, heartbroken and disappointed I feel. I particularly don't want him to know that I've been sleeping in the spare room – the room he's going to be sleeping in – since the night it happened, but that now he's here, I've got no choice other than to use my own bed again… and I don't want him to know how much that scares me. Trying to put a brave face on it is exhausting, when all I want to do is curl up in a ball and cry… as if I haven't already done enough of that.

"You said you'll eat anything, right?" Todd appears from behind me, just as I'm picking up some foil and clingfilm from the shelf.

"Yes, pretty much." I look down at the armful of groceries he's carrying. "What have you got there?"

"Chicken, salad, lemons, tomatoes, garlic… I don't know. I'm jet lagged. I was just grabbing things in the end." He grins at me and leans over, gently dropping the items into the trolley. "I do need yoghurt though," he says.

"Yoghurt?" We pronounce it differently. He emphasises the 'o' more than I do.

"Yes, yoghurt." He tries saying it my way, smirking… and I just have to smile… again.

"Come with me." I steer us back to the dairy aisle and he chooses a carton of greek yoghurt.

"And do you have wine vinegar?" he asks.

"Yes. I think so."

"Perfect," he says. "Now, we just need a bottle of actual wine… not vinegar."

"Oh, we definitely need a bottle of wine."

We choose a Fleurie. It should be quite light, and I'm not in the mood for a heavy wine, or a hangover.

"Are we done?" Todd asks, looking at the trolley.

"I think so. We should probably have made a list."

"That sounds a bit organised."

"You don't like organised?"

"For work, yes. At home… not so much."

"Well, if we've forgotten anything vital, I'll blame you then."

"I'm sure there's nothing we can't live without until tomorrow," he says, and takes the trolley from me, steering it towards the checkouts. "If you're the more organised one, you can pack," he adds as he starts unloading everything onto the conveyor, while I go to the other end and start talking to the most chatty salesperson I've ever come across in this shop. We've just finished discussing how good the weather is, considering it's only the beginning of May, and how her husband and son have gone camping for the weekend, when she passes my sanitary towels to me. So much for keeping them hidden. I sneak a quick glance back to Todd, but he's disappeared. *Where the hell has he gone?*

"You'll need to slow down," I tell her. "My… my partner has disappeared on me."

"That's men for you," she says, just as he comes jogging around the corner of the aisle, carrying a carton of ice cream. He must have a sweet tooth… like me.

He adds the ice cream to the rest of the shopping and comes to help me pack. "Sorry," he says. "I realised I'd forgotten something."

"Ice cream?"

"Not just any ice cream… Ben and Jerry's Chocolate Fudge Brownie ice cream. It's a necessity."

"If you say so."

"I do."

We finish packing and we wrestle over who's going to pay, but he gets his card into the chip and pin machine before I can.

"You can pay next time," he says, inserting his pin number and taking back his card. He grabs all the bags and we start walking.

"I can carry something," I say to him.

"That's not how it works, not where I come from," he replies. "If my mom saw me walking along the street, letting a lady carry the groceries, she'd roast me alive, after she'd skinned me and marinated me."

"I like the sound of your mother."

"She's an amazing woman." He doesn't say anymore and we walk in silence until we get back to the flat, where we unpack the shopping together, so he knows where everything goes.

"That took longer than I thought," he says. "It's nearly five o'clock."

"Do you want to shower?" I ask him.

"I'd love to. I don't even want to think how long I've been wearing these clothes. Is that okay with you?"

"Of course. Go ahead. I'll make some coffee for when you come out. There are towels in the bottom of the cupboard in the bathroom."

"Thanks."

He goes down the hallway, and I retreat to the living room, where I switch on the television for a while… Anything to avoid my bedroom.

I get up when I hear the water stop in the bathroom, and go along to the kitchen. As I hear the bathroom door open, I call out to him, "How do you take your coffee?"

"Black, no sugar," he says. I turn round on hearing his voice, a little closer than I'd anticipated. He's standing in the doorway, a towel wrapped low around his hips and I feel my mouth dry as my eyes drift up his body. He looked good with clothes on; he's utterly flawless without them, his chest and stomach hard and chiselled. He raises his arm and runs his hand across his now clean-shaven jaw and through his damp hair and I notice, along the length of his forearm, a tattoo in the form of a series of Chinese letters, in two lines. "Sorry I've been so long," he says. "Your shower's great. I'll just get dressed and I'll be out in a minute," he says.

"That's fine," I manage to say, dragging my eyes away from him. "I'll leave your coffee here and I'll go for a shower myself. Make yourself at home."

"Okay, thanks," he replies and walks away. I don't look up. I don't want to see how good his back view looks. Well, I do… but I'm not going to.

I rest my hands on the work surface and draw in a deep breath. I've never seen such a gorgeous man in my life… *He's here on business, Holly, and even if he wasn't, why would he want you?* He's almost certainly got a girlfriend, or a wife at home. Men who look that good aren't single. Besides, I'm not looking for anyone… not any more. I can't do that again.

That was a really good shower. The one in the hotel in Florence was okay, but in Pisa, it lacked pressure. So, I've been looking forward to getting back to my own power shower for a few days. I dry off and pull on my cream coloured silk robe, and wrap a towel around my hair, then leave the bathroom and am about to cross the hallway to my bedroom, when I hear a voice coming from the kitchen. Todd's singing. He's singing quite well. Well enough for me to recognise the track, anyway. I creep along the hall to the kitchen door and peek inside. He's standing by the work surface, wearing black jeans and a dark grey t-shirt, with half the contents of the fridge spread out in front of him, and a pair of earphones in his ears. He's managed to find a mixing bowl and whisk, and a chopping board and a couple of knives, by the looks of things. I stand and watch him for a moment, until he turns, and suddenly becomes aware of me.

He pulls the earphones from his ears, and I'm not sure which one of us is more embarrassed.

"Sorry," he says. "I thought I'd make a start on dinner. You did say to make myself at home."

"No… it's absolutely fine." I pull my robe slightly tighter around me, holding it closed at my neck with one hand. "I'll go and get dressed." I start to move away, towards my bedroom, but then turn back. "Bruce Springsteen…"

"Yeah," he says. "You like him?"

"Yes."

He smiles. "A woman with taste."

"*Born to Run*… It's one of my favourites."

"I'm surprised you could recognise it. I think I was probably murdering it."

"No. It was good."

He's staring at me and my mouth has turned to dust again. "I'd better get my hair dried," I say, and move out into the hallway.

"Okay," he calls after me. "There's no hurry."

I close the door behind me and lean back against it, staring at my bed… and if I needed a wake-up call – the equivalent of a cold shower – this is it. The image is still seared into my brain… their bodies locked and writhing, him lying between her raised legs, pounding into her, her arms around his neck, her fingers laced into his hair. The sound of their moans, grunts and sighs still fills my ears. I shake my head to try and clear it. How the hell am I going to sleep in here tonight?

I dry my hair and pull on faded jeans and a long pale pink shirt, rolled up at the sleeves. I check the mirror and wonder briefly if I should put on a bra… but I don't normally wear one at home and I want to relax. I twist and turn a little. It's fine… I'm sure he won't be able to see anything.

I go back out again, and into the kitchen.

"What can I do to help?" I ask him.

He turns and looks at me for a moment. "Nothing," he says. "I told you at the grocery store, dinner is my treat tonight." He pulls forward a couple of wine glasses that he's obviously found in the cupboard above the sink, and pours us both some of the Fleurie. "Cheers," he says, handing one to me.

"Cheers," I echo, and take a sip. It's very fruity and light, exactly what I wanted. I put the glass down again, but he picks it up and gives it back to me.

"Go sit down," he says. "Put your feet up."

"That feels wrong," I tell him, even though I'd quite like to take him up on his offer. My back's aching, and I've got slight cramps.

"Why?"

"Because you're my guest."

"I'm intruding into your private life for the purpose of getting the job done. That hardly makes me a guest."

"You're not intruding." I don't add that I haven't got a life anymore, private or otherwise.

"Well, I am grateful that you're letting me stay here. It helps with the case," he says, leaning back against the work surface. "We need to catch this guy, Holly." He's suddenly serious.

"I know." I remember I promised to give him a spare key, and I squeeze past him.

"Where are you going?" he asks.

"I've got to give you that key," I tell him.

"Now?"

"I'll forget." I open the drawer and take out the key, handing it to him. He puts it in his pocket.

"Thanks," he says, and takes a gulp of wine. "Now... go sit."

"How about if I lay the table first?"

"If you must, but then sit. I'll only be about another twenty minutes."

Dinner is exceptional. He's marinated the chicken breasts in a little of the wine and olive oil, with garlic and herbs, then chargrilled it, and served it with a mixed salad, and a dressing made with yoghurt, lemon juice, olive oil, garlic, and white wine vinegar. I know this because I asked him.

"So, your dad owns your apartment?" he asks half way through the meal.

"Yes. Well, his company does, anyway. He's semi-retired now, so he doesn't need it."

"He used to live here?"

"During the week, yes."

"And at the weekends?"

"My parents have a place near Arundel."

"Where's that?" He tops up the wine.

"It's in West Sussex."

"You make it sound like that should help." He smiles.

"West Sussex is a county. Arundel is a small town, I guess about fifty miles outside of London," I tell him. "It's fairly near the south coast."

"Okay. And you grew up there?"

"Yes."

"What's it like?"

"Arundel?" He nods. "It's quaint. It's a market town, full of antique shops and restaurants. Oh, and there's a castle."

"A real castle?"

His enthusiasm makes me smile. "It's about a thousand years old."

He stops chewing. "A thousand?" he repeats.

"Yes."

"Bet their plumbing's not as good as yours." He grins.

"I've never tried it."

We finish eating as I tell him more about the castle and the Catholic cathedral that also dominates the town, and then he offers to clear the table.

"Now that's really not fair," I tell him. "You cooked."

"And you can choose us a movie to watch, while I take these things out to the kitchen," he suggests.

"You trust me to choose a movie?"

He studies me for a moment. "Yeah… I think so," he says.

Chapter Three

Todd

I don't think she's deliberately trying to tempt me. In fact, I don't think she even realizes that when the light is at the right angle, the blouse she's wearing hides pretty much nothing. I can see she's not wearing a bra, and that her nipples have been erect since the moment she walked back into the kitchen from her bedroom. I'd like to think that's because of my presence and not because she's feeling cold. I'd like to think I'm having a similar effect on her to the one she's having on me.

Sitting across from her at dinner was torture and delight, in equal measure. She's so good to look at, I really wouldn't want to be anywhere else, but I've got to keep my head in the game and stop letting it wander, which it's starting to do with an unusual regularity. I've also got to stop imagining her without that blouse, with my hands on her firm breasts, or those perfect, full lips around my cock. *What's the matter with me?* I need to stop being so easily distracted and focus on what she's telling me.

"I'll have a look through the movie channels," she says and gets to her feet, stretching her back and rubbing it with her hands. Ahh… so I was right. I know the signs… I've seen them many times before.

"I won't be long," I tell her. "By the way, the only thing I really hate is horror."

"So do I," she says. "So we'd never have been watching that anyway."

"Good." I start stacking the dishes, and she takes the wine glasses and goes over to the sofa.

Once I've cleared away, stacked the dishwasher and tidied the kitchen, I grab the tub of ice cream from the freezer, and two spoons from the cutlery drawer, and go back into the living room.

"I thought we could have this," I tell her, sitting down next to her.

Her eyes light up. "That's just what I need," she replies, and I hand it to her. I know I won't get much of it, but that's fine. I didn't really buy it for me anyway.

She's paused the picture on the television and I can't tell what we're going to be watching. "What's the movie?" I ask, as she peels the film from the top of the ice cream carton and places it on the table in front of us.

"Casino Royale," she says.

"David Niven, or Daniel Craig?" I ask, handing her a spoon.

"Daniel Craig, of course."

"Why 'of course'?"

"Because he's a great James Bond." She offers me the ice cream first, but I shake my head.

"After you," I say and she digs her spoon in. "You think he's better than Sean Connery?"

"Yes," she replies, placing the spoon in her mouth and holding it there for a moment, closing her eyes and savoring the rich chocolate flavor. The look on her face is something else… I've seen a lot of women eat before, and it's never had any effect on me, but there's something about Holly… the way she holds that spoon between her lips… it's pure eroticism. It's entrancing, and the only distraction is my cock pressing uncomfortably hard against my zipper. When she opens her eyes, I'm still staring at her. "Sorry," she says, "I should press play before stuffing myself with ice cream."

"It's no problem," I tell her. I could happily watch her eat all night long, if she's going to look like that. "I fully appreciate a woman's need for ice cream transcends everything else."

"No," she replies, picking up the remote and pressing play. "A woman's need for *chocolate* ice cream transcends everything else."

I lean over and take a spoonful, rolling it around my mouth until it melts. "And we mere men must never forget the distinction. There are times of the month when only chocolate will do…" *Shit*. I really didn't mean to say that. It's a little personal. She turns to look at me, raising an eyebrow. On the screen, Bond is busy beating the crap out of some guy in a men's room, with a view to earning his 'license to kill', but I'm only vaguely aware of that. I shrug, then explain, "I'm a detective, as you pointed out earlier… you were rubbing your back after dinner and I couldn't fail to notice the items you picked up in the grocery store… Individually, the evidence is inconclusive, but taken together, there's only one conclusion a guy can draw."

"So it would seem," she replies. "And you learned this invaluable piece of information about chocolate ice cream from… your wife? Your girlfriend?" Is she fishing? I'm not sure, but oddly, I kind of hope so. I kinda like the idea that she might be interested. *Why the hell would I want her to be interested? I normally end relationships at the point when women get interested…* Still, I guess I got personal, so she's entitled to ask, whatever her motives.

"I don't have a wife," I tell her. "I've never been married."

"And a girlfriend?" She's still staring at me.

"Not at the moment." I don't add that it's been months since I last dated anyone. I've been so absorbed with this case since before Christmas, I haven't had time for women.

She digs into the ice cream again. "Then how did you get to be so knowledgeable?" she asks.

"I have a sister, Vicky. She's a few years older than me. I learned at an early age that chocolate, hot water bottles, a little patience and TLC, can work wonders."

She stills, with the spoon in her mouth once more, and my cock twitches, just as she pops the spoon out. "Your sister's a lucky woman," she says.

I laugh. "I doubt she'd agree. I could also be a pain in the ass when we were growing up."

She offers me the ice cream again. "Please eat some," she says, "or I'll eat it all myself."

"So you want me to save you from yourself now?" I ask.

She nods her head. I oblige, and after a few more mouthfuls, we decide to put it back in the deep freeze before we both over-indulge. Holly takes the carton back to the kitchen and, when she returns, we settle down to watch the movie properly, each sitting at either end of the couch.

"I'm surprised you chose an action movie," I say after a while.

"Why?" she replies.

"I don't know… I just assumed you'd go for something romantic, or a comedy, maybe."

She looks across at me. "I'm not in a romantic mood," she says, "or a funny one."

"Oh, okay." That sure told me.

"Sorry," she says, huffing out a breath. "That was rude."

"No, it wasn't."

"Yes, it was."

"Okay, have it your own way." I turn and smile at her. "But you're entitled to watch, or not watch, whatever you want."

In the light from the TV, I can see her eyes start to glisten. Hell, is she gonna cry? And if she does, what should I do? All my instincts are telling me to hold her, but I don't even know her…

"I only broke up with my boyfriend a few weeks ago," she says. "It's still a bit raw."

"I see. This is the guy from work?"

"Yes," she whispers.

"I'm sorry."

"Don't be," she adds.

Whoever the jerk was, he must've been mad to give up being with a woman like her.

I just about manage to stay awake for the end of the movie, but then tiredness takes over. I've been up for so long, all I want to do is sleep.

"I'm gonna have to go to bed now. I'll see you in the morning," I say to Holly, as I stand.

"We can't be up too late tomorrow," she says, switching off the TV. "We've got to take your suit to the dry cleaners."

"You don't have to get up early, just tell me where it is and I'll deal with it."

"It's fine," she says. "We'll go together. They're only around the corner anyway."

"Okay, if you're sure." I pause in the doorway. "Goodnight."

"Goodnight," she replies. She's still sitting on the couch, staring at the blank screen.

"Are you alright?" I ask.

"Yes… yes, I'm fine." She doesn't look fine; she doesn't sound fine either, but I can't keep asking.

"Okay," I say and I go down the hallway to my room.

I think it can only have taken me a few moments to drop off to sleep, because I remember getting into bed, putting my head on the pillow, turning over, and nothing else after that. Now, though, I'm wide awake. Something startled me a few minutes ago… a noise from somewhere in the apartment. It's still dark outside, so I check the time on my phone. It's ten after one, which means I've only been asleep for a few hours, even though it feels like much longer than that. I listen intently… but there's nothing, so I turn over and close my eyes, just as I hear the sound again.

I sit up in bed, then get up. I'm never gonna be able to go back to sleep if I don't find out what it is.

I open my door quietly and peer down the hallway. The apartment is in darkness and I stand still, listening for the sound once more… There it is. It's coming from Holly's bedroom. I move along the hall until I'm standing outside her door. Now I'm here, I can make out the sound more clearly. She's crying. No, she's sobbing… really sobbing.

Part of me thinks I should just go back to my room and leave her to it. She won't appreciate me getting involved. I take a step back, just as lets out a longer, more plaintive cry. To hell with it… I knock on the door and wait. She doesn't reply, so I knock again.

"Holly?" I call out.

"Yes?" Her reply is choked.

"Can I come in?" I ask. She doesn't answer, so I gingerly open the door and poke my head inside. I look at the bed first, which is still made; it doesn't seem like she's even sat on it, so I glance around the room. She's sitting in a chair by the window, her knees pulled up to her chest. She's wearing short pajamas, with a strappy top, which in this light, look as though they're made of a silky material. I go in, but leave the door open, and walk across to her, just as she looks up.

"Sorry," she mumbles, sniffing, "do you need something?"

She's playing the host... now? "No. But I think you do."

She shakes her head. "I'm fine," she says. "I'm sorry I woke you."

"You're not fine," I tell her. "Are you in pain? Do you want some painkillers, or a hot water bottle, or something... Let me help you."

She looks up at me, tears still rolling down her cheeks, and my instincts are still telling me to hold her, to see if I can make it better – whatever 'it' is.

"It's not that," she says.

"Well, whatever it is, it won't get any better if you don't get some sleep." I hold my hand out to her. "And you won't get any sleep sitting there. C'mon," I say, "you need to get into bed."

She shrinks away from me. "I can't," she whispers.

I crouch down beside her. "What do you mean, you can't?"

"I can't sleep in here." She looks across at the bed. "In that bed."

Okay... This is odd. "Why not? It's your bed, isn't it?"

"Yes... that's the problem."

I'm too tired for riddles. "I don't understand," I say.

"I haven't slept in here since the night I threw him out," she says.

"Him being your ex?" I ask.

"Yes... J—Jason." She chokes again, on his name this time.

"Then where have you been sleeping?"

"In the guest room."

"Where I am?"

She nods her head.

Her reaction seems a little extreme to me. Just because they broke up, I don't really see why she doesn't want to sleep in the bed they once, presumably, shared. She can't avoid it forever.

"I can't face it," she says, sniffing. "Every time I look at the bed, I can still see them."

Did I just hear that right? "Do you say 'them'?"

"Yes. I was working night shifts, but I wasn't well, so I came home around midnight…" I know what's coming and I want to hold her even more now. "I found them together in our bed. He was… I mean, they were…"

"It's okay," I tell her, "I get the picture." *What a jerk. What a stupid, stupid jerk.* I stand up again and hold out my hand. "Come with me," I say.

"I can't."

"Yes, you can." She stares up into my eyes and I nod my head. "It'll be okay."

She places her hand in mine. Her skin is feather soft but I manage not to rub her knuckles with my thumb. I pull her to her feet and lead her out of the room and down the corridor to my bedroom.

She pulls me back, just as we get to the doorway.

"What are you doing?" she says. "I'm not sleeping with you."

I turn to her. "I know. I'm not suggesting that." Even I've got a little more sensitivity than that. I let her enter the room first, which she does, but then she stands still, her free arm bent across her chest, all defensive. I don't blame her. I let go of her hand and go across to the bed, pulling back the covers. "Get in," I tell her. Even in the dull moonlight coming through the open blinds, I can see her shake her head. I come back and stand in front of her. "I'll go and sleep in your room," I say, "if that's okay with you. Or I can sleep on the couch, if you prefer." She looks up at me, her lip trembling.

"You'd do that?"

"Of course I'd do that. I don't mind where I sleep."

"You can sleep in my bed," she says, managing a very slight smile. "You won't fit on the sofa."

"Thanks. Now, let's get you into bed." I go back across the room again and this time she follows and climbs under the covers. I pull up the comforter and she snuggles down. "Sleep well," I say. "I'll see you in the morning."

I walk over to the door and am just about to close it behind me when she calls out, "Todd?"

I turn and poke my head back around. "Yeah?"

"Thank you," she says.

"You're welcome. Now… sleep."

I'm lying in her bed, surrounded by her things and, although I noticed how great she looked in those silky pajamas, especially those incredible long legs of hers… the thing I can't stop thinking about is her eyes, overflowing with tears – which is hardly surprising, I guess, considering what happened.

I may have never done the whole 'love' thing, but I do understand it. It's because I understand it so well, because I've seen it at close quarters, that I've never done it. I saw what happened to my mom and I don't want to be responsible for doing that to anyone… ever. At the same time, though, I've never cheated. When I'm dating a woman, I date her, and no-one else, until one of us dumps the other, usually because, although I've made it clear I don't want a relationship, she still wants more than I'm prepared to give.

I turn over onto my back and think about how it must have felt for Holly to be cheated on. She must've loved the guy a lot to be so tormented by his actions. I take a deep, deep breath and try to fight the unwelcome feeling that's growing in my chest.

I know exactly what the feeling is, even though I've never felt it before… It's jealousy. I'm jealous of the guy she loved enough to let him hurt her. And I've never felt it before, because I've never cared enough about a woman to warrant it… Until now, that is. *Damn. How the hell did I let that happen?*

Holly

It's only when I wake up that I realise the impracticality of Todd's suggestion. Yes, I slept; I slept really well, and I know I wouldn't have done that in my own bed… but all my clothes are still in my room… where he is currently sleeping. And his things are in here. I've been using my room as a glorified dressing room for the last few weeks… This is never going to work.

Why can't I just accept that Jason was a bastard – *is* a bastard – and move on? Why do I have to keep going over and over the events of that night… and the weeks leading up to it, trying to work out why he did that to me, and where I went wrong?

The knocking on the door brings me back to reality.

"Come in," I call, sitting up a little.

"Hi." Todd peeks in through the crack in the door. "I didn't wake you, did I?"

"No, I was already awake."

"Good." He comes into the room and, once again, I'm distracted. He's wearing shorts… and nothing else. He must've looked like this when he came into my room during the night, but I didn't notice then… which just goes to show how upset I was. How could I have missed this? I have to fight to pull my eyes back up to his face, and judging by the smile on his lips, he's noticed me taking in the scenery, which is mortifying… almost as mortifying as what happened last night. I feel like there's a theme to my behaviour around him. "We're going to need to work something out," he says.

"Are you talking about your clothes being in here, and mine in there?" I nod towards my bedroom.

"Yeah."

"I know… it's a little impractical. I was just thinking that."

"We'll figure it out. I'll just grab a few things for now," he says, "and head for the shower… unless you want to go first?"

"No, that's fine. I'll make some coffee and shower after you."

He smiles. "That'd be great. I don't normally communicate until I've had at least two coffees."

"So I should think myself lucky then?"

"Not sure I'd call it lucky," he replies, going to the chest of drawers.

"I am." I sit forward, pulling my knees up and resting my arms on them. He turns to face me, his head tilting to one side. "Thanks again for last night."

He shrugs. "Don't worry about it," he says.

"You were very kind. I'm grateful."

"Really, Holly, it's fine." He turns back around and gathers his clothes, going over to the door again. "See you in a minute… with coffee." He grins.

I wait until I hear the shower turn on, then sneak back into my room and grab my robe, some underwear, jeans and a top, some socks and my trainers. I put everything in the spare room, except my robe, which I pull on, then I go into the kitchen and make a cafetière of strong coffee, taking one cup back into my room and leaving it beside the bed for Todd. My own coffee, I take into the spare room, and I sit on the bed, waiting for him to finish.

He doesn't take long and, as he comes out of the bathroom, I call out that his coffee is in the bedroom.

"Thanks," he calls back. "You're a lifesaver." I quickly finish mine and then go into the bathroom to shower.

By the time I've finished, finger dried my hair and dressed, he's in the living room, standing by the window. He's wearing jeans and a white shirt, with the sleeves rolled up. I notice the tattoo again as he raises his arm and waves his cup at me. I've seen most of his body now, and this appears to be the only bit of ink he's got. I'm intrigued as to what it means.

"I poured myself another coffee," he says. "I hope you don't mind."

"Not at all. Was it still warm enough?"

"Yes, thanks. Did you want one? I can always make some more…"

"No, thanks, I'm fine." I check my watch. "It's eight-thirty," I tell him. "We should go."

"Sure," he says, swallowing down the last of his coffee. "I'll just grab my tux." He goes along to the bedroom, returning a few moments later, with it folded over his arm.

"Hold on, I'll get a bag for you to carry it in." I fetch a shopping bag from the kitchen, he drops his suit into it, and we set off.

"Whose wedding was it?" I ask once we get out onto the street.

"Sorry?" he asks, seemingly confused.

I point to the bag he's carrying. "The suit… the wedding… whose was it?"

"Oh," he says, "a friend. A very good friend. I was a groomsman."

"That's different to being the best man, right?"

"Yes." He smiles down at me. "You still stand up with the groom, but you have lot less responsibility, thank goodness. I guess it's like being bridesmaid, as opposed to maid or matron of honour."

"So, you were a bridesmaid?" I try to hold back the laughter that's rippling beneath the surface.

"I've been called many things," he says, "but never a bridesmaid."

"There's a first time for everything," I tell him.

He looks down at me, his eyes darkening, as we turn the corner at the end of the road. "Yeah," he says, suddenly serious. "It seems there is." I have no idea what he means by that.

The dry cleaners is the fifth shop along, and we're there before I even have time to think about his words or the look he just gave me. I make the arrangements to have his suit cleaned, using their express service, and to have it delivered to my address by five pm, and Todd pays them.

When we leave the shop, as I turn for home, he grabs my hand, then quickly lets it go again, like I burned him. "Let's go out for breakfast," he says, running his fingers through his hair. "My treat."

"You bought dinner last night. If we go anywhere, it'll be my treat."

"My idea… my treat."

"Then we'll go home."

"Dutch?" he says.

"Okay." I smile at him. "You talked me into it. This way." I turn in the opposite direction and take him to a café down the street. It's warm enough to sit outside and we order. I have smoked salmon, scrambled eggs and toasted brioche; Todd has pancakes, maple syrup and fruit. We both order coffee.

"This reminds me of Italy," I say. "Just a little, anyway. I had breakfast outside in a café like this every day."

"You went on your own?" he asks, leaning forward and looking at me, his elbows resting on the table.

"It wasn't meant to be that way but, yes." He tilts his head to one side again. He seems to do this when he doesn't understand… I'm learning that. "Jason and I booked the holiday together about four months before we broke up. After what happened, he at least had the decency to cancel his ticket. I still felt like the break, so I went on my own. I needed time to work things out."

"And did you?"

"I thought I had… until I got home again, as you gathered from last night. I—I thought, you see, that he'd suggested the holiday because he wanted to propose. How dumb was I?"

"You weren't dumb," he says gently. "You were deceived. That doesn't make it your fault. How long had you been seeing the guy?" he asks, running a fingernail along the grain of the wooden table.

"Just under three years. I thought…" I want to say that I thought Jason loved me, but I can't get the words out.

He looks up at me. "I get it," he says, and turns away again.

I wonder if he does. I wonder if he understands what it's like to question every single thing I've thought of as a certainty for the last three years of my life, including my own feelings…

The waiter brings our food and we start to eat.

"So, do you like travelling?" he asks.

"Yes, I do."

"Where have you been?"

"Oh… France, Austria, Italy, Greece… I spent a few weeks in India one summer. And I've been to America, just the once."

"Was it once too often?" he asks, smiling across at me.

"I'm not sure I went to the best place…"

He puts down his fork. "Why? Where did you go?"

"Las Vegas."

He sits for a moment, staring at me. "Hmm. I wouldn't have thought Vegas was your kind of place."

"It wasn't."

"Then why did you go?"

"I didn't choose the destination."

His smile fades. "Don't tell me..."

I can feel my shoulders slump. "He booked it as a surprise last autumn. In reality, it was because he wanted to go. It had nothing to do with me. He'd have been better off going with his friends, or by himself, for all the time we spent together..." I let my voice drift. Did I really just say all that out loud... to a man I've known for less than twenty-four hours?

He continues to stare for a long while, then says, "You'd like New England, I think."

"Would I?"

"Yeah, I think you would." He picks up his fork and starts eating again. "I thought we'd have breakfast out," he says between mouthfuls, "because we've got to spend the day working... going over the file, getting used to our aliases..."

"We've got aliases?" I interrupt, swallowing my mouthful so quickly, I choke.

"You okay?" he asks. I nod my head.

"I just wasn't expecting aliases," I tell him when I can speak again.

"We're undercover," he says. "We can't go in as ourselves."

"So what are our names?"

"I have no idea. It's all in that file Andy gave me. I thought we could spend the day getting to know our new selves, becoming familiar with our backgrounds... then we'll need to eat early tonight and get over to the club for nine."

"It only opens at nine... shouldn't we aim to get there a little later? Once things liven up a little."

He gives me a look that I don't quite understand. "Not tonight," he replies, stabbing a blueberry with his fork. "Tonight is just about looking around, getting a feel for the place. When we go back on

Wednesday, we'll maybe get there a little later... We'll see how it goes tonight."

On the way home, we stop at the mini-market and pick up a few things for dinner, and we're home again by ten-thirty. I make us more coffee and we sit on the sofa. Todd has brought the file from the guest bedroom.

He sits beside me and opens it up, pulling out some pages that are stapled together in the top left hand corner. He nods his head as he reads.

"Okay," he says. "It seems you're Holly and I'm Todd."

"Not great aliases, then," I reply.

"Using our real first names can be advantageous sometimes. It avoids us making silly mistakes. We have different last names." He stops and looks inside the folder again. "Thank God they remembered..." he says, taking something out and holding it in his clasped hand, before putting the file down again.

"What?" I ask.

"We're married, evidently."

"We are?"

"Yes. We're Mr and Mrs Sanders." He opens his hand and reveals two white gold bands, one slightly larger than the other. "Let's hope they got the sizing right." I take the smaller ring and place it on my finger. It's a little loose, but it's okay. Todd's fits perfectly.

"Okay," he continues, "we met on holiday in the Bahamas, five years ago. You moved out to the States when I proposed, a year later, and we've been living in New York since then, but we've just moved to London, at the beginning of April. Our third wedding anniversary will be on September 17th."

"Do we need this much detail?" I ask.

He looks across at me. "Sometimes. It can help to have a back-story. Even if we don't use it, it can be beneficial if we feel like there's something behind the façade."

"You've done this before, haven't you?"

45

"Not quite like this," he replies. "I've always gone undercover on my own." He's still staring at me. "And I'm usually armed," he adds.

He hands me the papers and I start to read. They've set up fake birthdays, e-mail addresses, work places, phone numbers…

"Why so much?" I ask.

"That's what I meant when I said 'sometimes'. In this case, there's more than usual. It was all needed for the membership," Todd explains. "They wouldn't have wanted to give the club any of our real details… except our first names."

"I see." I notice his fake birthday is given as October 12th. "When's your actual birthday?" I ask.

"It'll confuse you if I tell you," he says.

"I'm not that easily confused."

"It's July 28th."

"So you're a Leo?"

"Yes. What are you?"

"According to this… Actually, I don't know what the star sign is for June 10th."

"Neither do I," he says. "What are you really? When's your actual birthday?"

"The 30th of August."

"So you're a… Virgo?"

"Yes."

"Well known for their shyness, devotion and loyalty."

"And their pickiness." I smile. "Whereas Leo men are…?"

"Generous, stubborn – really stubborn – arrogant, passionate…" His voice drops down a note on that last word and then he leans towards me. "And domineering." I feel a pulse radiate through my body, making me shiver and, for a moment, I can't take my eyes from his lips, which are only inches from mine. If he leant forward, just a little further…

"We should…" I manage to say at last, although I have no idea how I intended to finish that sentence.

"Yeah, we should," he replies, leaning back again.

I hand him the papers and he puts them on the coffee table. "I'm going to ask a stupid question." I'm desperate to take my mind off the thought of how soft his lips might feel.

"Go ahead," he replies, twisting so he's facing me.

"Surely, all we need to do is find someone who was either a member or employee of the club in Boston between December and late February, and who's now based over here."

"Sounds easy, doesn't it?" he says, smiling.

"You've thought of that already…"

"Yeah we did. So did Andy. You're right, of course. But the problem is that still gives us a lot of people to look at. This chain of clubs move their personnel around a lot. They don't like the clients to see the same faces too often; it keeps the experience fresh."

"I don't understand. What do you mean 'experience'?"

"It's one of the reasons they can charge so much for membership," he says. "You'll rarely see the same act twice."

"Act? Um… What kind of clubs are we talking about here?"

"They're adult clubs, run exclusively for couples," he says.

"You mean sex clubs?" I know my voice has dropped to a whisper, but I can't help it.

He keeps his eyes fixed on mine. "Well, yes and no. Probably not in the way you're thinking of. It's a little more sophisticated than a strip joint… insofar as a place like this could ever be called sophisticated. There are rooms for sex… to watch, and to participate. And there are rooms where you can just sit and enjoy a drink with like-minded people."

"Like-minded people?"

He nods his head. "People who want to add a little something to their sex lives."

"By sharing it with complete strangers?"

"Not necessarily. The couples can choose their level of membership. The basic level entitles you to use the bar, watch the main shows and visit private rooms. You can upgrade to have more intimate, individual shows, and hook up with other members, by mutual consent."

"Hook up?" Does he mean what I think he means?

"Have sex, Holly." He does.

"And our membership…?"

He smiles. "Don't worry, we've just got the basic package."

Thank God… although even that sounds daunting.

Chapter Four

∽

Todd

Hell… I was only about two inches away from kissing her. I could have just leaned in and taken her, and I wanted to. I really wanted to. And, if I'm being honest, I think she wanted me to as well; at least for a moment, until she came to her senses. Thank God she's sensible. I seem to have left my senses – as well as my detachment, and my self-control – somewhere in the middle of the Atlantic. I'm supposed to be focusing on the job, on finding the killer and keeping her safe, not thinking about her eyes and her smile, her giggle… and how it would feel to get her underneath me, pinned to the bed, with those long legs wrapped around me…

She's lying back in the corner of the couch now, looking confused and vulnerable. "Holly?" I say and she focuses on me again. "Are you okay with this?"

"I have to be, don't I?" she replies.

I was worried about taking her into the club before, but now – knowing what I know about her past, that her hurt is still so fresh, and seeing her reaction to what the club is about – I'm more than worried.

"Can I ask you something?" she says.

"Sure, go ahead."

"How were they killed?"

Damn. I really hoped she wouldn't want to know this. "You've seen the photographs."

"Yes, and I saw a lot of blood, and mutilation, but I want to know exactly what was done to them."

"Why?"

"Don't you think I have a right to know?" she asks. "You told Andy I did."

I can't argue with that. "Yes, but it won't help," I tell her. She continues to look at me. "Okay," I say and I take a deep breath, moving a little closer to her. "The male victim was tied to a chair, bound by the wrists and ankles. We think he was then made to watch the… the assault on the female victim, which we believe took place, in each instance, over a period of about two hours. She was then strangled…"

"Using what?" she asks, her voice steady and quiet.

"His bare hands," I tell her. I swallow. "After that, the male victim's penis was cut off, and placed in his mouth, and then he had his throat cut."

"It was done in that order?"

"Yes."

"Dear God, no." She's pale, her eyes wide with fear.

I move closer still, and take her hands in mine. "Look at me, Holly." She does. The expression in her eyes makes my chest hurt. "I won't let anything happen to you. Do you understand? No-one's going to hurt you… or me for that matter." I smile at her. "There's a certain part of my anatomy I'm quite attached to. I've got no intention of being separated from it."

She tries to smile, and almost succeeds; she gets halfway there. "He's sick," she says. I like the fact that she hasn't pulled her hands away.

"Yeah… he is."

"I think I need more coffee," she adds.

"Good idea."

There isn't much else she needs to know about tonight, nothing that can't wait until a bit later, anyway, so when she brings the coffee back, I decide to change the subject.

"What are we going to do about the sleeping arrangements?" I ask her.

"I don't know," she replies.

"Why don't I move my things into your room, and you can just come in and get whatever you need when I'm in the shower – like we did this morning. It's not practical for you to move all your things into the guest room. I might not be here very long." That thought makes me sad and, just for a second, I see that reflected in her eyes. At least I think I do. Maybe it's wishful thinking.

"I suppose…" she says. "It's not a good long-term solution, is it?"

"How do you mean?" I've already said I might not be here for long.

"I can't sleep in the guest room forever. I need to move back to my own room at some point in my life."

I think for a minute. "What about if we switched the beds over?" I suggest.

"You mean put my bed in the guest room and vice-versa?"

"Yeah… we could move the furniture around in your room as well, so the layout's different. Then you wouldn't see the same image when you walked in there."

"I suppose it might work," she says.

"Well, think about it. In the meantime, I'll move my things when I get changed for tonight. That way, I won't have to keep disturbing you."

"And what about me disturbing you?"

"Don't worry about it. It's your apartment, Holly."

My tux is delivered back just before five and a little after that, Holly starts making the dinner, and I take the chance to move my clothes from her guest room into her bedroom. I'm happy to live out of my suitcase, which I put on the chair by the window.

She's made us pasta with a rich, spicy tomato and garlic sauce, shaved parmesan and crusty bread.

"This is good," I tell her, twirling the spaghetti onto my fork with one hand.

"I've never been very good at that," she says, watching me.

I smile at her. "Like a lot of things in life, it's down to practice… well, practice and wrist action." What is it about her that makes me flirt like this? I've never really flirted before, not like this, and especially not so obviously – not ever.

"Wrist action?" she smiles back. "I would have thought it had more to do with how you use your fingers…" Her gaze moves from my hand to my face, locking with my eyes, and staying there. She's flirting back, I'm sure she is. The innuendo here is obvious – at least it is to me.

"Those too," I say. "You can do a lot with your fingers."

"Really?" Her eyes light up. It's not just me feeling the electricity between us. I know it isn't.

I lean toward her. "Yeah… really," I whisper and I hear her exhale. Damn, I'm so hard right now, it hurts. Her mouth opens just a fraction and I can see her tongue, and I'm tempted to walk around the table, haul her to her feet and kiss her.

"What does your tattoo mean?" she asks, and I'm brought back to earth with a bump.

"Excuse me?"

"Your tattoo… What does it mean? Isn't that something I'd know, as your wife?"

I guess she has a point. But I've never told anyone. Not even my friends know what it means, although I guess that's because it's about them. I put down my fork and push up my sleeve just a little.

"The top line says 'Blood makes you related'," I tell her.

"And the bottom line?"

"That says 'Friendship makes you family'."

She looks at me for a moment. "Your friends matter to you." It's not a question, but a statement.

"Yes."

"More than your family?"

"I don't have a problem with my family, but you can choose your friends. They stick around because they want to, not because they have to."

"You obviously have very special friends," she says quietly.

"Yeah, I do. I'll introduce you, one day." *What the hell…* I've never done that before. Not once, in all the years I've known the guys, have I ever brought a woman into the group.

"I think I'd like that," she replies softly, and she smiles again. And I know I'll do it.

I'm ready before Holly, because it's easier for her to have access to all the clothes in her bedroom, being as she still hadn't decided what to wear. So, I've changed into my tux and am sitting in the living room waiting for her. The cab's ordered for eight forty-five and it's only eight-fifteen, but there's one more thing I need to run through with her before we leave. I've waited until now, because I didn't want to give her time to back out, or freak out.

Finally I hear her bedroom door open and after a moment, she appears in the doorway.

"How's this?" she says, looking at me.

"It's... it's great," I tell her.

"Except it isn't. I can tell from the tone in your voice."

I stand up and she stares at me. She *really* stares at me and her eyes roam down my body and back up to my face again. "What's the matter?" I ask.

"Nothing," she replies, her voice a little croaky. I smile, remembering her looking at me in just the same way this morning when I came into her room before my shower, and last night, in the kitchen. Even though I'm fully clothed in my tux, she's still looking and I can't help it if that makes me feel good... I can't help it if all I can think about is getting out of these clothes as fast as possible, pushing her back against the wall and... "What's wrong with my dress?" she asks, shattering my dream.

I go over to her. "If we were going out for dinner, it'd be perfect," I tell her truthfully. She's beautiful. She's put on a little make-up and the way her lips are shimmering makes them look even more kissable than they usually do. Her dress is dark blue, and fitted and it's got short lace sleeves and finishes just above her knee. It's classically stylish and suits her perfectly. "But it's too... too conservative for where we're going. Have you got anything a little... shorter?" I ask tentatively.

"Shorter? I'm not going there to sell myself."

I laugh. "No, you're most certainly not. If you were, I'd make damn sure I was the only one buying." Her eyes shoot up to mine. "But you need to look the part."

"What part is that?" she asks, more softly.

How do I put this? "The part of an enlightened, liberated woman… who also happens to really enjoy having sex with her husband… outside of the privacy of their own home?" That last bit sounds bizarre, even to me.

"I didn't even know such people existed until earlier today," she says, thinking for a moment. "I'll see what I can do. Give me five minutes."

She disappears again and I sit back down and pick up a magazine from the coffee table. I don't hear her come back into the room until she speaks.

"Better?" she asks.

I look up and I can't breathe. At the same time, my cock hardens against my zipper. "Much," I manage to croak out.

"The problem is," she says, "which shoes?"

"What are the choices?" I ask, happy to be distracted from the low-cut black, beaded dress that comes down to the middle of her tanned thighs. It's made of a stretchy material that's clinging to her body and making it real difficult to focus on anything except how great she looks. She holds up her hands, with a pair of shoes in each.

"There's these," she says, holding forward a very sensible looking pair of flat pumps. "Very good for running away from potential murderers. Or there's these." She switches hands, showing me a pair of sandals with a heel that's probably four inches high. My cock twitches again as I imagine her wearing those, with her legs over my shoulders, while I'm buried deep inside her…

"Personally," she's saying, "I think the flat ones would be the best choice."

I get up and pull down my jacket as far as it'll go, hoping to God that it, together with the dim lighting will hide my obvious erection.

"The heels," I say, walking toward her.

"Really?" she replies. "You don't think I should be prepared…"

"To run?" I finish her sentence just as I come to stand in front of her. "No, Holly. You don't need to worry about running." I look down at her and her mouth drops open just a fraction. "No-one's gonna get close enough to you that you'll need to run away from them. I'll be with you. All. Night. Long." She sighs out a breath. "Nothing's gonna happen to you, I promise. Okay?" She nods her head. "Go put on the heels." She stares at me for a moment longer, then turns and goes back along the hallway.

By the time she comes back, the cab's arrived and we have to leave. I really need to explain this final element of the evening to her, before we get to the club. We climb in the back of the taxi and I lean forward, giving the driver the address and telling him not to get us there until ten after nine, even if he has to drive around a little to achieve it. He shrugs his shoulders and nods his head. I close the partition window and sit back.

"I need to speak to you," I say to Holly. She turns to look at me, twisting in her seat, so her dress rises up, revealing even more of her silky, tanned thighs. Could my cock get any harder? I have a horrible feeling I'm gonna find that out during the course of this evening.

"What about?" she asks.

"Tonight. There's one thing I've not mentioned before."

"What's that?"

"The way we'll have to behave when we get inside the club."

"How do you mean?"

"We're meant to be married," I tell her. "We can't go in and act like we barely know each other."

"No," she says.

"This will make more sense when we get there," I say, "but, I'll have to do certain things to you, if we're going to look the part."

"Like what?" Her eyes have widened, but I think it's with fear, rather than the desire I'd like to see in them.

"Don't panic. We'll just need to look like we're enjoying ourselves and are intimate with each other."

"So… what will you do?"

I smile across at her. "I hadn't got a plan in mind. I was just going to wing it. I'm warning you now, so you don't act surprised when I touch you. And ideally so you don't slap me." I grin at her.

"I see," she says, and she manages a smile. "And… and do I need to do anything to you?" she asks.

"No," I say, because as much as I'd like her to, I don't want it to be at the club. When… if… no, hopefully, when she does touch me, I want that to be somewhere very private… very private indeed. "I can make this look authentic. You just have to give the impression you're enjoying what I'm doing."

I give her a moment. "And I need to apologize, Holly. This isn't the way I want things to be between us." Her shoulders seem to drop. Does she think that means I don't want her? To hell with that… I move a little closer to her. "I want to be with you, Holly, but not here… and not like this."

She twists her head toward me, her eyes widening. "Y—you want… to be… with *me?*"

"Yes. Of course I do." I lean into her. "But I'm sorry it has to be like this."

Holly

He wants me? Seriously? That look in his eyes, the way his voice drops down a note when he's saying those things to me… it makes me want him too. I'm not altogether sure how he manages to look even better in a suit than he does half-naked, but he's done it. And seeing him like this, makes me want to find out how his body feels, as well as how it looks; to explore his skin, discover his lips, his tongue… Oh God… He's leaning closer still and the scent of his body wash, is enticing. I can feel myself falling… But I snap back to reality, just in time. This is just a sexual, hormonal reaction, nothing more. It's a response to a beautiful, sensual man, and to what Jason did to me; a desire to prove myself sexually attractive, rather than a cast-off. Well, who needs that? Who needs the pain and heartache that'll follow when Todd lets me down too?

How do I know he'll let me down? He's a man, isn't he?

We arrive a few minutes later, neither of us having said anything else. Todd climbs out of the taxi, helps me step down onto the pavement and pays the driver. The building we're in front of looks like any one of many Mayfair houses; four stories high, plus the basement, with two steps up to the black painted front door. Todd rings the doorbell, and the door is opened by a large man in a suit and bow tie, who holds out his hand, into which Todd places our membership card. The man scans it through a hand-held device, looks up, smiles, hands back the card and stands to one side.

"This way, please," he says, waving his hand. We enter the impressive hallway. "It's your first time here, I believe," he continues, guiding us to a set of doors on our left.

"Yeah," says Todd, laying on his accent a little thick. "Although we've used your club in New York."

"I see." The man couldn't sound less interested if he tried. He opens the doors and lets us pass through into a large room, with a bar at one end. There are leather sofas, chairs and low glass tables set around the room. The walls and carpet are off-white, the furnishings grey and black. "Please, make yourselves comfortable," the man says. "Feel free to use the facilities in the main suite upstairs, when you're ready, and the private rooms on the second floor. The third floor is restricted."

"Thanks," Todd replies and guides me further into the room, towards a sofa in the corner. "Let's sit," he says, smiling down at me. I do as he says and a waiter appears beside us. "Two glasses of champagne," Todd says.

"By the glass, we have a Bollinger Rosé, a Louis Roederer, or a Veuve Cliquot," the waiter replies.

Todd turns to me. "Which would you prefer, darling?" he asks.

"The Bollinger for me, please," I say, trying to sound as though I order it every day, and being called 'darling' by him is perfectly routine.

Todd looks back to the waiter. "And I'll take the Veuve Cliquot," he says. The waiter leaves, and I lean toward Todd.

"And who's paying for that?" I ask him, my voice barely audible.

"The first drink each night is free," he replies. "It's part of the membership."

"So we're on mineral water from here on?"

He smiles down at me. "You bet we are." He takes hold of my hand and, keeping his eyes on mine, kisses my palm; the sensation sends tiny shocks through my body, most of which seem to end up in the pit of my stomach and, to stop myself from asking him to do that again, I take a look around the room.

There are three other couples, seated at different tables. Two of them are middle-aged, but the other pair are probably younger than us; I'd say in their early twenties. None of them seem like the sort of people who'd indulge in a place like this, but I suppose you can't tell what a person's like in private just by looking at them. My thoughts are interrupted by the return of the waiter, carrying our glasses of champagne on a silver tray. He places them before us and it's only then that I notice Todd's still holding my hand. He doesn't let go, even when he passes me my drink and we clink glasses.

I take a sip and lean a little closer to him. "This isn't what I'd expected at all," I whisper.

"In what way?" He puts his glass back on the table and turns to face me, moving nearer still, as though we're having an intimate conversation.

"It's more… tasteful," I say, still keeping my voice quiet.

"Really? You think so?"

"Yes."

His lips twitch, just a little. "Be careful," he murmurs softly. "Watch how you react, and take a closer look at the pictures on the walls."

I glance around the room again, taking another sip of my champagne, and let my eyes settle on the photograph which is on the wall behind Todd's head. It takes me a moment to register what I'm looking at. The image is in black and white. It's grainy and looks as though it's been taken at the height of a summer's day, with a venetian blind off to one side, creating a striped effect on the body of a naked woman, lying prone on a bed. She has one hand between her legs, the other behind her head. I turn and look at the photograph on the wall next to the bar. The style is the same, but this time, the woman is standing naked, her hands on her breasts, tweaking her nipples. My eyes wander… They're all the same, or similar.

"You're blushing," Todd says, smiling.

"That'll be the champagne," I reply.

"If you say so." He picks up his own glass and takes a drink. "Still think it's tasteful?"

"I suppose it could be worse." I keep my eyes fixed on the table in front of us.

He chuckles. "Yeah, it sure could."

We finish our drinks and Todd stands, then leans over, his mouth next to my ear. "Show time," he says, then straightens and I let him pull me to my feet, and lead me back out into the hallway and up the stairs.

At the top, there's a set of double doors, with a suited man standing guard outside. He holds out his hand as we approach and Todd gives him our membership card again. He scans it in exactly the same way as the man at the front door, then hands it back to Todd and, without a word, opens the door behind him, and we pass through.

Inside, the lighting is dim and it takes a moment or two for my eyes to adjust. When they do, I stand still, stunned. The room is huge – I imagine it was originally two rooms, which have been knocked through into one. Around the walls are booths, in some of which are couples, in various states of undress, kissing and fondling each other. Regardless of what they're doing, most of them are also watching the scene in the centre of the room, where there's a raised stage and it's to here that my eyes are drawn. There's a low bed, on which a woman is lying. A man is kneeling between her raised and parted legs, and he's inside her, moving back and forth rapidly… Their groans and cries fill the room and no matter how hard I try, I can't drag my eyes away from the sight before me. It's like I'm back in my own bedroom, watching my life disintegrate all over again.

Chapter Five

Todd

Shit. She's frozen. We're only just inside the door and she's gone like a statue on me. I tug on her hand, but she doesn't budge. I pull a little harder, but with no result. So, I move behind her, put my arm around her and maneuver her to my left, quite forcefully, toward the third booth along, which I've already noticed is vacant. Her legs and arms are stiff and moving her is hard work. It'd be easier to carry her, but that would look even more odd than this does. I sit her in the corner of the booth and lean across in front of her, blocking her view of the room.

"Holly," I say as loudly as I dare – which is quite loud, considering the amount of noise coming from the stage, and the couples either side of us, as well as the background music. She finally focuses on me. "Get a grip," I tell her. "You're meant to want this; you're meant to enjoy it. Try acting like it."

"How?" she mutters, and I see her glancing over my shoulder again, tears in her eyes. It's brought it all back to her. Jason and the other woman… *Damn.*

I place my hand on her cheek and turn her face toward mine. "Look at me," I say. She does. "Just relax. Try not to think about what they're doing."

"How do I do that?"

"Let it wash over you." She swallows hard. "I'm sorry I was rough with you," I tell her.

"It's my fault," she mutters, the tears welling again.

"No it's not." I lean back a little and glance around, just in time to see a guy in a suit approaching us. He's probably just here to keep an eye on things, make sure no-one breaks the rules, or does anything outside their membership boundaries, so I can't imagine he's going to say anything to us. I'm pretty sure they couldn't care less whether we have wild sex, make out, or sit here and write out our grocery shopping list, as long as we've paid our fees; but I don't want to attract the wrong kind of attention, especially as I've told them we're regulars at the New York Club. "Someone's coming," I whisper in her ear. "I'm going to touch you... I'm sorry, but I have to."

She nods her head and I put my hand on the outside of her thigh, moving it upward to her ass, pulling our bodies closer together. At the same time, I lean down and start to kiss her neck. Kissing her lips would be too much – for both of us – right now. Her skin is soft and delicate, her scent intoxicating. She grips the front of the seat with the hand that's between us and brings the other up, letting it rest on my shoulder. *Good girl.* I fondle her gently through her thin dress, while tracing a row of kisses from her chin to her ear. "You're doing great," I whisper when I get there, and I nuzzle into her. Her head rocks back, exposing more of her neck and I lick a delicate line down to her shoulder. At that moment, I hear and feel her sigh, and then a loud moan escapes her lips. Um... that's not really necessary for our little performance. No-one can hear us. My already hard cock presses even further into my zipper as she groans again and shifts slightly, arching her back and moving a little closer. She may not like everything else that's going on in this room, but she's turned on by what I'm doing to her, and that thought brings a smile to my lips.

From the noises behind me, I'd say the couple on the stage are getting near the end of their act. I stop kissing Holly's neck for a second and glance up at her. Her eyes are closed, and the look on her face is one of undiluted desire. It could be part of our own show, but I really hope not. I wish I knew.

The position we're in is no good. I need to be able to see what's going on in the room. I think about it for a minute... Yeah, there should be enough stretch in her dress for what I've got in mind. I move my mouth back to her ear. "I'm going to sit you on my lap for a while, okay?" I whisper. She hesitates for a moment. "It's just so I can see the room better. Nothing's gonna happen," I tell her. I pull back and look at her. "I promise." She nods her head. "Just stay where you are," I say, "I'll move you." And I sit back in the seat so I'm facing into the room. Then I lift her and turn her, so she's facing me, and I sit her astride me, on my lap, keeping one hand behind her. The dress is fine. Her ass is covered. I reach up and bring her head down to mine, my mouth next to her ear again. "I'm so sorry about this, Holly," I say to her. "Just grind into me, a little."

"Like we're…?" She leans back, her eyes wide.

"No, but like you want to; like we're building up to it."

She pauses, just for a second, then shifts forward so her core is against my erection, and starts moving her hips, achingly slowly, and for a moment, I can't breathe… again. I can feel her heat along the length of my cock, so she has to be able to feel me, but there's damn all I can do about that. I guess we've both found out how hard I can get…

I pull her head down to mine again. "I need to be able to see the room," I tell her. "Just lean back again and keep doing that, but move a little to your left and ignore everything I do." She gives an almost imperceptible nod of her head and does exactly what I've said, resting her hands on my chest. I watch her for a moment, then I let my head rock back just a little, my eyes half closed, like I'm somewhere approaching heaven. I am, but I'd rather be doing this naked, in her apartment. I take a moment to bring myself back to the task in hand, and then start to register the rest of the room, twisting my head. Most of the booths are occupied, and all with couples who are doing a lot more than we are. I've never believed our killer is a client, so I focus on the members of staff instead. There are four waiters, standing around expectantly, in case anyone wants to order drinks, and three suited guys, like the one I saw earlier; and the performers, who are just leaving the stage, both now wrapped in robes – which seems a little ridiculous considering they were just writhing naked on the bed. The guys in suits move around all the time, so they'd have the best chance of listening out for accents, but then the waiters take orders from people too. There again, I suppose anyone with access to the membership list would be able to find out the nationality of the guests. I wonder who has access? It's a question I need to get Adam to ask the management. It might narrow the field a little.

A new couple walk onto the stage and remove their robes, placing them on a chair beside the bed. I look away; I've got no interest in what they're doing.

Holly is still moving on my lap and, despite my concentration on our surroundings, I'm going to have to stop her soon, before I don't remember how to; because there's no way anything's happening between us here. I open my eyes fully and place my hands either side of her face. "We're done in here for tonight," I tell her.

"What should I do?" she asks, still rocking gently back and forth on me.

"Nothing," I say, smiling up at her. "I'll handle it."

I lift her to her feet, then get up myself and take her hand. One of the suited guys opens a door at the side of the room and, as we pass, he says quietly, "Natasha will greet you upstairs."

I give him a nod and a smile, and let Holly go through the door first.

"That was—" Holly starts to say, as a couple appear from our right. It's the performers who left the stage a few minutes ago, now fully clothed. I grab Holly and push her up against the wall, my hand behind her head, my arm blocking their view of our faces as I lean in close to her.

"Shhh," I hiss, my mouth almost touching hers. The performers ignore us and pass through the door we've just exited, which strikes me as odd. I'd have thought they'd have either gone home, or gone down to the bar. Once the door closes, I pull away from Holly. "Sorry... again," I say. "Did you see who that was?"

She shakes her head, a little breathless. "I didn't get the chance."

"It was the couple who were on the stage when we arrived," I whisper, taking her hand and guiding her up the stairs.

"And you recognized them?" She turns to look at me. "With their clothes on?"

"I was looking at their faces, Holly." I smile at her. "Nothing else."

"Hmm." She stops. "Why would they be going back in there?" she asks.

"Good question. I was just wondering exactly that… Maybe they like to watch too." Holly pulls a face, like she still can't believe any of what she's seeing.

We carry on up the stairs, until we reach the top, where there's a small desk, with a blonde woman sitting behind it. She lights up like Christmas when she sees us, her eyes grazing over me, and ignoring Holly.

"I'm Natasha," she says. "Can I see your membership card?" Her voice is deep and husky. In a previous life, before I met Holly – so anytime before yesterday lunchtime – I might have called it sexy. Hell, I might even have been tempted…

I hand over the card, and she lets her fingers dwell on mine for longer than is necessary. *Seriously?* She scans the card, again, and then reaches into a drawer in her desk and brings out a key. The fob it's attached to is made of carved dark wood, in the shape of a bow tie… the club's logo.

"Third door on the left," she says, throatily, and nods down the hallway to our right.

"Thanks, ma'am," I drawl out, making sure she's heard the accent.

"You're American?" she says. I can't ignore the opportunity. Our killer's a man, but he may get his information from anyone working here.

"Sure am." I grin at her.

"Where from?"

"Oh… I live here now," I say. "But I'm originally from New York."

"I love New York," she says.

"Me too." I do my best to lower my voice and make it sound sexy. "Have you visited there often?"

"Just the once. It's beautiful."

"I know." I give the blonde a smile just as Holly tugs my hand. "Be seeing you," I say, and I let Holly pull me away and down the hallway to the door the blonde indicated.

Once we're inside with the door closed, Holly turns on me. "When you've quite finished flirting…" she says, her arms folded across her chest. "We're here to work."

I smile down at her. "Now, now, Mrs Sanders. There's no need to be jealous."

"I'm not bloody well jealous," she splutters, her cheeks reddening. It's all I can do not to laugh: she's real cute when she's mad. I move toward her.

"I wasn't flirting," I say, losing the smile with a little difficulty. "I was acting, to the best of my abilities. I was just letting her know how American I am and that we're living here, and not on vacation, in case the killer is using her to get his information."

"Oh," she says, letting her arms fall to her sides. "Sorry. I didn't realize." I take her hands in mine, holding them between us.

"Don't worry about it. I don't really do flirting. Not like that... It's not my thing." I tell her.

"Really?" I can't blame her for being surprised, considering I've taken every opportunity to flirt with her since yesterday.

"Well, I don't normally. But even if I did, why would I need to flirt with her?" I look deep into those soulful eyes. "When I can flirt with the most beautiful woman I've ever seen."

She raises an eyebrow, her head tilted to one side. She seems to do that when she's confused and doesn't want to let on.

"I'm talking about you, Holly."

"Me?" she breathes, her mouth open, her eyes wide.

"Yes, you."

Holly

He's staring deep into my eyes and I can't drag mine away. I don't even want to try this time, I just want to fall into his, and keep falling until he catches me. And after the way he's been this evening, he will catch me; I know he will. I'm almost certain he won't let me down, even though he is a man. Whatever else has happened tonight, something's definitely changed between us. And I think he feels it too.

"But… I'm not beautiful," I manage to say at last.

He frowns. "Whoever told you that?" he asks.

"Pretty much everyone."

"Then they're all wrong."

"I suppose it depends what you're comparing me with. Compared with the back end of a bus, I do okay. Compared with little miss blonde flirty pouty-lips out there… well…"

He leans in even closer, and I stare at his mouth. "I don't make comparisons. Ever. You're beautiful, Holly. Period. And that's *not* me flirting, by the way." He grins.

I swallow hard and notice him looking at my neck. I wonder for a moment if he wants to kiss me there again… I'd like it if he did. I'd more than like it. I wish he…

He blinks a couple of times and pulls away from me. I immediately miss his closeness and wish he'd come back, but I take the opportunity to calm down a bit and glance around the room. It's small; but then how big does a room need to be, when the only furniture in it is a bed, with a sofa at the end?

"What are we supposed to be doing in here?" I ask, turning back to him. My eyes instinctively drop down to his erection, which is still visible, even now. I've been able to feel it against me while I was sitting on his lap. I know it's long… and very hard. What I don't know is if it's got anything to do with me, or if he was just turned on by the sights and sounds in the room…

He notices the direction of my glance and smiles. "Officially, having fairly hot sex I guess, because we're more restrained than some of the other people here, and we want some privacy." His smile fades. "Unofficially, we're not going to be doing anything," he adds. "Except sitting around for an hour or so."

"Why? We could just leave, couldn't we?"

"No. We need to make it look realistic. They need to think we're in here having a great time."

"Okay… but an hour?" Jason never made love to me for an hour. Twenty… maybe thirty minutes at most, including the foreplay. But then did Jason ever 'make love' to me? And why am I thinking about making love in the first place? I know the answer to that, even if I don't want to admit it.

"Well, we could make it longer," he smirks. "Maybe two would be more realistic…"

"Two? Two hours?" I'm suddenly breathless. Just the thought makes me tingle.

He moves close to me again, our bodies almost touching. I can feel the heat radiating from him, and scorching into me.

"After what you were doing to me downstairs… hell, I could stay in here with you all night and still want more… much more." I feel myself blushing. Surely he doesn't mean that. "I'm sorry if I embarrassed you," he continues.

"The whole evening has been one long embarrassment," I tell him. "To which of my many humiliations were you referring?"

"It was more my humiliation than yours," he says. "I'm referring to my rather obvious… um… arousal." My mouth forms an 'O' shape, but no sound comes out. "I apologise if you found that difficult."

I look down, focusing on his shirt buttons. "I didn't," I whisper. "I found it flattering." And then I remember his arousal might have had nothing to do with me at all. "Sorry… I mean…" I stammer, suddenly, looking up at him again. "Of course, your reaction… it was probably because of what was going on around us, which is quite natural, and has nothing to do with me… I mean, why would it? I'm—" He brings a finger up and presses it onto my lips.

"It was because of you," he says firmly. "Entirely you." His voice has dropped to a low whisper that makes me tremble. Again, he stares at me for a long moment, before moving away. I clear my throat. We need to get back to talking about something else… anything will do.

"How… I mean, why and how do people watch things like that?"

"It takes all sorts," he says, shrugging and moving over to the bed, where he sits down.

I remain standing. It seems sensible to keep a little distance between us, especially when one of us is on a bed.

"Yes, but having sex is such a personal, intimate thing, why would you want to share it?"

"I don't," he says, quickly. "But the acts are all put on anyway. None of it's real."

"Are you sure?" He looks up at me.

"Of course."

"It seemed pretty real to me."

"Well, it's real for the guy," he says, not taking his eyes from mine. Try as I might, I can't stop looking at him either. "But the women are all faking it."

"How on earth can you know all this."

"Well… Because the guy can't fake it. He's hard, obviously… and he always pulls out before he comes. I guess so the audience know it's for real and don't feel cheated."

He's so matter of fact. "How can you be so sure about the women though?"

"You can tell," he says.

"You can?"

"When a woman's faking it? Yeah…" He stops talking and his stare intensifies. He's tilting his head to one side again. "Well, I always thought I…" His voice drifts off.

"You thought what?"

"I thought I could tell when a woman was faking it… until tonight, that is," he says, getting up.

"Has it happened to you often?" I ask, trying not to smile.

"Twice," he says, looking embarrassed. "I was much younger, I was in a bad place, and I was very drunk, both times… and I'm making excuses now, aren't I?" I grin at him. "I wasn't at my best," he says, smiling.

"And you knew… they were faking?" I ask.

"Yeah… it was so obvious, even with all the booze." I'm not about to ask how he knew. I don't want that much detail about his sexual history.

"So what did the woman on stage do to make you doubt your convictions?"

"She didn't," he replies. "That was you."

"Me?" What's he talking about?

"Yes." He takes the two steps needed to stand right in front of me. "Were you faking it, Holly?"

Faking what? "I'm sorry, what do you mean?"

"Earlier, when I was kissing your neck, you moaned. Was that just part of the act? Were you faking that, or was it real?"

"You heard me?"

"Yes, I heard you. Was it real?" he repeats, with just a hint of desperation in his voice.

"Does it matter?" I'm playing for time.

"Yes, it matters… to me."

I take a deep breath and let it out slowly. "It was real."

Chapter Six

Todd

Pulling away from her is getting harder every time I do it. I've never wanted a woman, or spoken to a woman, or shared any part of myself with a woman like this before. I'm used to having complete control over the relationships I get into, so I can dictate their course, what we do – or more importantly, don't do – and how and when they end; that way I can keep my barriers intact… and keep emotions out of the picture. But with Holly, it's all so different. I don't know what it is about her, but I want to let her in. I want to let her see the real me… the me I've never shown any woman before. This is very new, kinda weird, really exciting and, if I'm being honest, a little scary…

As I let the thoughts roll around my mind, I start to feel a whole new kind of warmth inside, which starts in my chest and spreads outwards.

"I'm sorry if it bothered you," she says at last, and I realize that, as well as moving away from her, I've been silent for quite a while.

I turn back to her. "It didn't… well, it did. But only in a good way." I check my watch. We've not been in here half an hour yet. To hell with it. I need to get her out of here before I do something we both regret, because this is not the right place for anything to happen between us. I turn around, and pull back the sheet on the bed, crumpling it up, then I toss the pillows around, leaving one on the floor, and the other halfway down the bed, before I grab her hand. "C'mon, we're going." I need to get her home.

"But it hasn't been an hour yet. I thought you said…"

"I know. I don't care about that anymore." I smile down at her. "Besides, it's my reputation that'll get shot to pieces."

"What does it matter? It's all pretend anyway," she says.

"Not to them it isn't. They think we're for real. But like I say, it's my reputation…" I open the door and let her out, following behind and taking her hand again, once I've locked it. As we walk slowly down the hallway, I notice the blonde looking up at us, and I adjust the zipper on my pants and whisper in Holly's ear, "Just go along with what I say… and giggle."

She looks up at me.

"Why giggle?" she asks.

"Because I like the sound." I smile at her and I wiggle my eyebrows. She lets out a laugh, bringing her hand up to her mouth. She's so fucking sexy… and what's weird is, she doesn't even seem to know it.

When we reach the desk, I hand the key back to the blonde.

"Thanks," I say to her. "My wife was in a *very* accommodating mood tonight." Holly places her hand on my chest and rests her head on my shoulder. I kiss the top of her head. "C'mon, beautiful," I say, "Let's get you home. I think I owe you."

"Hmm… so do I. Twice, I believe," she murmurs gently and my mouth opens slightly. The little… "And I intend to collect," she continues, her voice low but just loud enough for the blonde to hear.

"We'll see you again?" the now wide-eyed Natasha says as we head to the stairs.

"Oh, yeah," I say over my shoulder. "We'll be back. We'll be back real soon."

It takes a few minutes to hail a cab and when we're sat in the back, I turn to Holly.

"Twice?" I say, grinning. "Twice… in less than half an hour…?"

"You were worried about your reputation," she smiles back. "Now Natasha thinks you're some kind of sex God."

"I don't care what she thinks… well, I do, but only insofar as it affects the case." I stare at her. "Twice…" I mutter, shaking my head. Holly smiles, then turns and looks out the window and I try to calm down. It's not working... mainly because, now I've thought about it, I know I could easily take her twice in half an hour... and keep going. I don't think I'll ever get enough of her.

I glance across at her. She's turned away from me and, for the first time, it occurs to me that she might not want me... I get a sharp pain in my chest and try to dismiss the thought, because I can't accept that I'll never have her. I just can't... I swallow hard. We've gotten kind of carried away tonight and, for the time being at least, I need to try and concentrate – focus on the case.

The cab drops us at her place and, as we go up in the elevator, I take off my jacket and undo my tie and top two buttons. Holly lets us in, shutting the door and slumping back against it, her eyes closed. "Thank God that's over with," she mutters, kicking off her shoes. She looks sexy as hell, but she also looks real vulnerable. Fuck the case, and fuck concentration... it's seriously overrated. I drop my jacket and step over to her. Resting one hand on the door by her head, I bring the other up and rub my thumb along her bottom lip. Her eyes pop open and find mine.

"You were amazing tonight," I tell her.

"Yes... I did spectacularly," she replies, her voice laced with sarcasm. "Apart from nearly giving us away by behaving like a scandalized nun, then getting jealous, oh, and let's not forget talking too much when we came out of the room. Yes, all in all, I did brilliantly."

I move closer placing my feet either side of hers. I can feel her body against the length of mine and I'm hard again in an instant... and I don't give a damn if she knows it.

"Stop beating yourself up," I say quietly, my thumb resting on her chin. "You were nothing like a nun – scandalized or otherwise. I should have realized how difficult it would be for you. I should have warned you. That was my fault, not yours." I lean a little closer. "I like that you were jealous," I whisper, smiling, "and from the perspective of our characters, it makes sense that you would be. I'm supposed to be your husband. You'd have every right to object to me flirting, so there was nothing wrong with that. And, as for talking when we came out of the room… how were you to know anyone would appear?"

"You did."

"No I didn't. I just happened to see them before you did. I've done this before, Holly. More times than I want to think about."

She stills and takes a deep breath, her breasts pressing into me, and I lean down, my lips so close to hers I can feel her breath mingling with mine.

"What did you mean?" she whispers.

"When?" I ask, the tips of my fingers caressing her neck.

"Just now, when you said…" Her breath catches. "When you said you should've realized how difficult it would be for me tonight."

"I meant seeing the performers, like that. It was bound to remind you…" She stiffens and a shadow crosses her face just before tears well in her eyes and her head drops. Shit. I've lost the moment and I think… I think I've lost her. *Please don't let it be for good.* That thought brings a really sharp pain to my chest, where all that warmth had been building… Things changed for us tonight; well, they did for me, anyway… but can they have changed *that* much? Can I really be falling in love with her? So soon? Is that even possible? I guess it has to be…

Does any of that matter though, when she's still so clearly in love with Jason. I take a step back, then bend and pick up my jacket from the floor. As I straighten and turn, she reaches out and grabs my arm.

"Do you want a coffee?" she asks.

What have I got to lose? My sanity? I lost that hours ago… or maybe yesterday, when she walked in the door of Andy's office. *Was that really only yesterday?* My heart? Oh… she's already stolen that. Entirely.

"Sure," I say. "I'll just change." She breathes out – like a sigh of relief. "You okay?" I ask.

"I think so. I—I don't know." She looks up at me. God, she looks so lost. "I'll make the coffee." She pushes herself away from the wall and pads, barefoot, down the hallway to the kitchen.

Changed into jeans and a white t-shirt, I join Holly in the living room. Two cups of coffee are on the table in front of the sofa, where she's already sitting in the corner, her legs tucked up under her. I want to pick her up and put her in my lap, but not so she can grind on me again, just so she can sit there and I can hold her, let her rest her head on my chest, while I stroke her hair... Instead, I sit at the other end of the couch and pick up the coffee nearest to me. "Thanks," I say, taking a sip.

"We have to go back again, don't we?" she asks.

I set my cup down again. "Yes. On Wednesday." I turn to her. "I know you don't want to, but it should be easier this time around. You'll know what to expect. I deliberately kept this visit short, just so you could see what it was all about, and so I could have a look around."

"You mean we'll have to stay longer next time?"

"Well, it depends what happens, but yeah, probably."

"In that room?"

"Which one?"

"The one with the stage."

"Yes." I wonder if it's the room, or what we were doing there that bothers her. I need to know... and not just for the investigation. "What's the problem with it?" I ask outright. "Was it the room... or what we were doing?"

"It was the room," she says straight away, which is a relief, although she doesn't look at me. "Well, not the room itself. It was seeing the people on the stage, and the other guests. It made my skin crawl. I just don't understand why they want to be there."

"Neither do I," I tell her and I move a little closer to her. "You're sure it was nothing I did? Nothing I made you do, that made you feel uncomfortable. You have to be honest with me, Holly. We have to go back, but if you need me to do things differently, you have to tell me."

She looks up. "I preferred it when I had my back to the room," she says. "When I was on your lap, I didn't have to see and I didn't have to think about what was going on then."

"Okay," I tell her.

"But that's not very helpful to the investigation, is it? I'm hardly earning my keep, am I, if I just sit there?"

"Who says? I can't get into the club without you. It's really helping me to have someone to bounce ideas around with... You're more than earning your keep. Don't worry about observing at the club, I can watch what's going on."

She dips her head slightly, although her eyes stay focused on mine. "How did you do it?" she asks quietly.

"Do what?"

"Stay so calm... so detached."

She thinks I was detached? I move closer still; she's like a damn magnet. I reach out and let my hand rest on the side of her face, my thumb rubbing her cheek. "I can detach myself from the room, the people, what they're doing to each other, the noises they're making, the atmosphere," I tell her. "I can do that quite easily. That's the job." I lean toward her. She's not doing a damn thing, and it's like she's pulling me in. "What I'm struggling with, is you."

"Me?" she whispers. "Why?"

"It doesn't matter how professional I try to be, what I can't do is detach myself from you," I murmur quietly. "I'm finding that real hard."

"D—do you need to?" she mutters, and hope flares inside me, just for a second.

"I don't know... do I? You tell me."

"I don't understand," she says.

"If you're still hung up on Jason, then yeah... I probably should detach myself from you, for both our sakes." Although Christ knows how I'm gonna do that. "Getting involved won't be real healthy for either of us," I add.

"And if I'm not... hung up on him?"

I almost can't breathe. "If you're not," I manage to whisper, "then just tell me. Just say the words to me, Holly. Tell me you're over him. Tell me you want us to be together, that you trust me not to hurt you. Because I won't, you know... I'll never hurt you." Our eyes are locked for what feels like forever, as I wait... and wait. *Tell me you trust me, Holly, please.*

75

"Everything changed tonight, didn't it?" she says eventually. It's not what I hoped she'd say, but it's better than, 'I'm still in love with Jason,' so I'll take it for now.

"Yeah, it did. I feel like there's a different path ahead of us," I tell her. "I don't know where it's taking us, and I really don't care. The only thing I need to know is, are we going down it together?"

The tears are still welling in her eyes. I'm not sure if that's good or bad. "More time," she whispers, a little incoherently.

"You need more time?" I ask. She nods. "Then you got it," I say, and I move forward, putting my mouth next to her ear. "I'll wait," I murmur and I feel her hands come around behind my head, holding me close to her. "I'll wait, baby."

I've never waited for any woman in my life... I've never had to. I know that sounds arrogant, but that's not really how I mean it. If I've found a woman attractive, but they haven't been interested, or available, I've just moved on. Not looking for love or long term relationships means you don't get hung up on one person, so waiting for them to want you doesn't really come into it. Until now. As I climb into her bed, in her room, on my own, I remember how I felt at the club... and how I've felt since I met Holly. I've hardly been able to think about anything else... I've wanted to get her naked, to see her, touch her, taste her, hold her down and bury myself deep inside her. And I still want all of that, but I want so much more. I want all of her. I want to care for her, I want to make her smile, and keep her safe. I want to love her with everything I've got, and the thought of putting my needs to one side and waiting for her doesn't bother me in the least. The thought of her still pining for Jason... yeah, that bothers me. That bothers me a lot. And she's got to really be over him if we're gonna stand a chance.

She's got to need me, and want me enough, to leave him in the past. She's got to believe in me, and put her faith in me, and know I'll never do anything to hurt her. And I guess I've got to show her that she can do all that, so she'll come to me and say the words I need to hear. It'll happen, I know it will. Her eyes, her reactions, her body, they all tell me that. It's just a question of waiting for her brain and her heart catch up.

In the meantime... well, I'm gonna prove to her that I'm worthy of her trust... and that I'm worthy of her.

∽

Holly

Most of the time, when I'm with Todd, I feel as though choosing to be with him would be the easiest, most obvious decision in the world. He makes me feel more alive than I've ever felt; more wanted, more needed. We have fun together, we laugh, we tease, we flirt... And he wants me in a way I never would have thought possible; his words, his touch, they set me on fire and I crave them, like chocolate... I guess that makes me a molten puddle of melted chocolaty goo for about ninety percent of the time. I've never wanted anyone, or anything more. He's like a drug. I never had any of this with Jason... never.

But therein lies the problem. The ten percent. The one and only thing that makes me hesitate. Memories of Jason keep creeping in, like at the club, or when I'm in my bedroom, or just at odd times of the day, when something reminds of me what he did, and then I think that Todd could so easily do that to me too. I trusted Jason, I'd known him for years, and he cheated, he lied, he betrayed me in the worst way possible. I've known Todd a matter of hours and he's asking for that same level of trust... Todd could lie and cheat; he'd probably even do a better job than Jason. He's used to working undercover, used to pretending to be someone he isn't. How do I know this is for real? Trusting him feels like such a big step, and if he did cheat... if he did betray me, he'd break so much more than my heart.

I wake up late, having spent a restless night, going over everything in my head, until I was so confused I knew I wasn't getting anywhere. At around four this morning, I reached the decision that I want to be with Todd. But then, if I'm honest, I think I already knew that anyway.

How could I not want to be with someone who makes me feel like he does? Making that decision felt like a weight off my mind, for about thirty seconds, because then my brain was then crowded with doubts, and 'what ifs', which occupied me for another hour, until I finally drifted into a fitful sleep. I already hated Jason for what he did to me, for the betrayal, and for making me feel second best… I hate him so much more now, because he's tainted my perspective of Todd – well, of all men, really – and made it so hard to trust again and, although I know that's not fair, I can't help it.

I climb out of bed and open the bedroom door. I can hear Todd talking, his voice coming from the living room and I move quietly along the hallway. He's standing by the window, his back to me, the phone that Andy gave him pressed to his ear. His hair looks damp and he's wearing jeans and a black t-shirt, which shows off his broad shoulders and muscular arms, and I can't deny that part of me wants to go over and lean against him, rest my head on his back and tell him how much I want him… except I know me *wanting* him won't be enough for either of us. He needs me to tell him I'm completely over Jason. I think I could do that. But I need to be able tell him I trust him completely, that I'm ready to move forward with him, and that I believe in him, that I believe there can be an 'us'. That's got to come from me… that's what he wants, and it's what we both need…and that's the hardest part. I stand in the doorway and, despite the temptation of his gorgeous body, his strong arms, his molten chocolate eyes, and his captivating words, my feet won't move; so I guess I'm not ready yet.

"Drop it over this morning," he's saying, "or get it delivered, and we'll take a look, but I'm not convinced." He turns and his eyes catch mine and light up, a smile spreading across his lips. "Yeah, I get that," he continues, "but the opportunities aren't there. The set-up's all wrong." He pauses, still watching me. "Speaking of that," he says, "I need you to ask the management at the club a question. I want to know who has access to the membership lists, and how often they're updated, and by whom. Can you find that out for me?" He waits again. "Thanks. And you'll bike over that information…? Okay. I'll call you tomorrow morning, eight o'clock again."

After he's hung up, he turns the phone off and drops it onto the sofa. "Hi," he says, his voice gentle, like silk brushing over my skin. I shiver… He's managed that with just a single word. He moves towards me, stopping a couple of feet away, his hands in his pockets. "How did you sleep?" he asks, keeping his eyes on my face.

"I've slept better," I tell him honestly.

"Me too," he says.

He looks tired and I want to collapse into his arms, let him hold me, let him tell me he can make everything okay again, and let myself believe him. Instead, I ask, "Was that Adam?"

"Yeah," he replies.

"Shall I get coffee?" I ask.

"Sure." He follows me down the hallway, and it's at this point that I remember I'm only wearing thin, short pyjamas, and I'm sure he's getting a good view of my behind. I should really have put on a robe, but I didn't think. I can hardly duck back into the bedroom room to put it on now; he'd think I felt uncomfortable around him, and I don't… I feel precisely the opposite. I feel so comfortable with him, it's like I've known him all my life, rather than just a couple of days. If only I could stop judging him by Jason's standards, things would be so much easier.

I go into the kitchen and Todd stands in the doorway. "He's sending over the membership list," he says.

I look up. He's got his arms folded and he's leaning against the door frame, watching me, a broad smile on his lips. "What?" I say. "What's funny?"

"Nothing's funny," he replies. "I just like looking at you."

"You do?"

"Isn't it obvious?" His smile becomes a grin and he moves across the kitchen, until he's standing in front of me.

"I don't know… I guess." I smile up at him.

"Well, I do," he says, and reaches into the cupboard behind me to fetch down the cups. If he's trying to be irresistible, he's doing a very good job of it. He hands me the cups. "You were making coffee, I believe…"

"Y—Yes." God, I'm stammering now. "Why do we need the membership list?" I ask, turning my back on him, so I can make the coffee, and regain my composure – just a fraction of it anyway.

"It's an idea Andy's had," he says. "It's pointless, but I've said we'll look into it."

"What's the idea?"

"One I'd already considered months ago… that the killer is a member of the club."

"And that's pointless because…?"

He leans back on the work surface beside me. "Well, aside from the fact that these clubs are for couples and I believe our killer works alone – even if they use someone else to get their information – I just don't see how a member could find out the nationality of the victim in the London club. It doesn't make sense to me that a staff member would give up that information to a guest."

"So you think it's an employee?"

"Yes. But Andy's insisting we check out the London membership list and compare it to the one for the Boston club, which I've got on my laptop."

"It'll give us something to do, I suppose."

He leans in, his arm touching mine. "Do you think we'll get bored then?" he asks.

I look up at him. His eyes are alight, his lips curving upwards. "No," I whisper. "No, I don't."

I've just finished dressing, and I'm making the bed when the doorbell rings, but Todd calls out that he'll answer it, and then a moment later, knocks on my door.

"You decent?" he asks.

"Yes," I reply.

"That's a shame," he says, opening the door. He's carrying a manila envelope. "A courier just dropped this off," he continues. "Shall we get some breakfast and then start work?"

"Okay."

"We could have those croissants you picked up at the store," he suggests.

"Sounds good to me."

"I'll go warm them up. I guess we'll need to go shopping again, won't we? We're gonna need something for dinner tonight... Unless you'd... let me take you out." He actually sounds nervous.

"I'd like that," I tell him, because it's the truth. "But we'll still need to go to the supermarket. We've got nothing for lunch, and we're nearly out of milk."

"We can take a walk down there later this morning," he says. "We'll need a break by then." He moves to the door, then stops and turns back. "You're sure about dinner?" he asks.

"Yes, absolutely sure," I say. He smiles and, without replying, goes out into the hallway.

"Look... there." I say, leaning forward and gently tapping the screen of his laptop with my pen. "Eric and Rachel Watson. Their names are on both lists." We've been at this for over an hour, and I think we're both a little word-blind.

He grabs his pencil and underlines the names on the paper list, putting a star next to them as well. "So that's one couple," he says, leaning back and stretching his arms above his head. "Out of all these names... Not that I think it means much. If anything, I think we should be guarding them, not watching them."

"You think...?"

"They're American." He shrugs. "Our guy seems to like Americans."

"Or hate them," I add. "When did the Watsons join the Mayfair club?"

Todd checks the list. "Ten days ago. But it's a temporary membership, just until the end of the month. See... the address they've given is in Boston. They must be here on vacation, I guess." He looks at me and neither of us say what we're both thinking. This couple could really be in danger.

I lean back in my chair. "Do you think it would help us identify the killer if we could work out why he's targeting your compatriots."

"Yeah, it would. But where do we start?" he says. "His reason could be anything..."

He has a point. "We'll need a photograph of this couple," I say. "If we're going to keep an eye on them."

"Yeah. I don't think they've got anything to do with the killings," he says. "But we need to watch them. I think tomorrow night, we'll try and keep tighter observation on the waiting staff, and the security guys as well; see if any of them react differently to Mr and Mrs Watson... assuming they're there, of course." He checks the time on his computer. "I'm not supposed to turn on my phone... Can I use your landline?" he asks.

"Of course."

"I've got to call the States... Is that okay?"

"It's fine. The phone's in the kitchen." He gets up and goes down the hallway, returning a couple of moments later, carrying the handset.

"You're going to think I'm an idiot," he says.

"I doubt that very much. What's the problem?"

"What's the code for the US?" he asks. "I've never had to dial it before..." He smiles down at me, looking a little awkward.

"You add a one at the beginning," I tell him.

"Thanks," he says and starts dialling. He waits for a minute, stepping over to the window and looking down the street. "Hi," he says into the phone. "Yeah, yeah, I know it's early... Well, if I'd waited for you to get into work, I'd still be here in three hours' time... I guess you've got no incentive to get in early, have you? I'm not there to make the coffee for you..." He laughs, then waits for a moment, listening, and turns to face me. "No," he says, "it's good. I like it here. I like it a lot." The tone of his voice has changed and I can feel my cheeks redden. "Something like that," he says into the phone. "Oh, knock it off," he continues, then takes a deep breath. "When you've finished with the jokes, I need you to do something for me." Again, there's a pause. "I need you to get hold of all the information you can, including photographs, of Mr and Mrs Eric Watson." He comes across to the table, checking the list. "Her name's Rachel." He scrolls across the list and reads out their address. "I need that today, I'm afraid… sorry," he adds. "Send it to my work e-mail, can you? I'm not collecting from my personal one at the moment." He waits for another minute or two. "And if you need to get in touch, call me on this number. I can't turn on my cell while I'm here." There's another pause. "Yeah. Thanks." He looks at me again. "I don't know," he says. "It'll take as long as it takes, I guess." They say goodbye and he hangs up, putting the phone down on the table.

"I assume that was someone you work with?" I say as he sits back down again.

"Yes."

"A friend of yours?"

"A colleague. There's a difference."

I lean forward, resting my elbows on the table, my chin on my upturned hand. "Tell me about your friends," I say to him.

"My real friends?"

"Yes."

"There's Matt," he says, mirroring my position, so we're only a few inches apart. "I met him when he was at college. I'd been at the Academy for about six months by then. After a while, he introduced me to Luke, who's his business partner… and then there's Will, who's Luke's brother."

"And they're all the same age as you?" I ask.

He smirks. "I'm the oldest," he says, "by a year or so. Matt and Luke are the same age. They're both thirty-two, which I guess makes Will twenty-nine. It was his birthday a couple of days ago."

"So you're thirty-three?"

"Yes."

"Thirty-four in July…"

"You remembered." He seems surprised.

"Of course." I look at him. "And which one just got married?" I ask.

"That was Luke. He married Megan; she had their baby back in March. Matt got married a little over a year ago, and he and his wife, Grace, have just had their first baby too."

"And Will?" I ask.

"He got engaged at the end of Luke's wedding, evidently. I missed that part, because I had to leave early to catch my flight over here."

"And they're all happy?" I don't know very many really happily married people.

"They're all damn delirious." He laughs.

"You're not jealous of them, are you?" I ask.

"No," he says and he leans forward a little further so our mouths are almost touching. "I've found my own kind of happy right here."

"You're happy here?"

"God yeah…" He pauses, and runs his fingertip along my lips. "I'd rather wait for you, Holly, than be with anyone else."

Chapter Seven

∽

Todd

I found this restaurant on the Internet while Holly was making lunch, and made a reservation. It's a family-run Italian place, just around the corner from her apartment, with a really nice atmosphere. I think the candles, mis-matched chairs and photographs of old movie stars help, although I've hardly been able to drag my eyes away from Holly since we got here. She's wearing a knee-length white cotton dress, and just a touch of make-up, and in the candle-light, she's completely bewitching.

Holly's ordered chicken in a wild mushroom sauce and I've got strips of sirloin steak cooked with peppercorns and cream. I'm gonna need to find a gym if I keep eating like this, or I might go for a run in the morning... Still, it tastes really good. We're sharing a bottle of Valpolicella, which goes well with the steak.

"Do you like white wine as well as red?" Holly asks, as she takes another sip from her glass. We've only drunk red since I've been here.

"I probably prefer red," I reply, "but I'll drink white."

"You're not a wine snob, are you?" She's smiling.

"Hell, no." I smile back.

"So you'll drink anything?"

"Well, I wouldn't go that far... What about you?" I ask. She tilts her head to one side. "Red or white?"

"I like them both."

"Just not in the same glass?"

She laughs. "Not at the same time, no."

We both take a mouthful of food. Watching her eat is a really sensual experience… and a distracting one. It's not quite as distracting as the sight of Holly's ass in her skimpy pajamas this morning. Damn… just thinking about that makes me bone hard – again. I stare at her across the table as she takes another mouthful, totally oblivious to the effect she's having on me. That's one of the things I love most about her: she has no idea how sexy she really is…

"Tell me about your family," she says, catching me off guard. I don't often talk about them, but I know what she's doing… or I think I do, and I don't mind one bit. I think she wants to know more about me and, after our conversation last night, after I've asked her to trust me, I guess she's entitled.

"I've got one sister," I tell her.

"Any brothers?"

"No. It's just me and Vicky… well, and my mom, of course."

"And you said Vicky's older than you?"

She remembered that too. "Yes. Three years older. She lives just outside of Atlanta."

"Georgia?" It's a question and I nod my head.

"I'm impressed, considering I didn't even have a clue where West Sussex is. She married the owner of a big electronics company down there. Well, it's a big electronics company now; it wasn't when she married him." I laugh, just a little.

"What's funny?" she says.

"I was just remembering how my parents reacted when she came home from her second year in college and announced she was getting married… to a guy she'd known less than a month."

"They weren't happy?"

"My dad wanted to lock her in her room and go find the guy… with his gun." That brings a smile to my face.

"But he didn't… obviously."

"No. She talked them round." She could always do that to get her own way.

"So, she was at college in Atlanta?" Holly asks.

"Yeah. I've got no idea why she chose to go there, but she did."

"And she met him there?"

"He wasn't a student, they met at a function, or something… spent the weekend together and that was it. She was in love." I stare across the table… I guess Vicky and I do have something in common, after all. We both fall hard, and fast, it would seem

"Do you see much of each other?" she asks, bringing me back to the here and now.

"I go down there once or twice a year. She's got three kids, so it's easier for me to travel than her. And… and my mom lives down there now too." She looks at me. "My dad died nearly thirteen years ago…" I stop talking.

She's finished eating and puts down her knife and fork, reaching across the table for my hand, which I put in hers. "I'm so sorry," she says, with breathtaking compassion.

"It's okay," I reply, even though it isn't. "When the dust had settled, my mom decided to move to Atlanta, to be nearer Vicky."

Holly keeps her eyes focused on mine. Although she doesn't say anything, I think she understands how much that rankles… even now… especially given what went on at the time.

"Your dad must've been quite young," she says, still holding my hand.

"He was fifty… a couple of months shy of his fifty-first birthday."

"That's no age."

"No." I know she wants details. It's hard. I've only ever spoken to one other person about this, and that's Matt. He got me through those weeks after my mom moved away. Without him, I'd never have stayed on at the Academy. I'd have drowned at the bottom of a bourbon bottle. But, I'm asking Holly to trust me… That's a two-way street. "He was shot," I tell her. Her fingers tighten around mine. "It was a drive-by. Wrong time, wrong place."

She leans forward. "You don't have to tell me," she says. "Not if it's too—"

"It is," I say, not letting her finish. "But I still want to tell you."

The waiter comes and removes our empty dishes. He asks if we want dessert, but we both shake our heads and agree we'll have coffee instead. He goes away again.

Now the table's clear, I pull our hands into the center and rub her knuckles with my thumb, watching the movement, back and forth. "He was working nights. I was at my apartment when I got the call from one of the sergeants in his precinct…"

"He was a policeman too?"

"Yeah… sorry, didn't I mention that?"

"No."

"Oh. Yeah, my dad was a beat cop. A damn good one. The kind of cop kids look up to, you know?" She nods her head. "He was the whole reason I joined the force. I'd only been at the Academy a short while when he was killed." I pause for a moment. "He never pulled his gun, in nearly thirty years… not once." The irony that he died by the gun has never been lost on me.

The waiter brings over our coffee. "So you got a phone call…" she prompts, once he's left us alone again.

"Yeah. It was about three in the morning. Derek – he was the sergeant who called me – he told me to get round to my mom's and he'd meet me there. I knew before I got there what he was going to tell us. Dad was killed instantly."

"I'm sorry," she says.

"It was tough," I tell her.

"It still is, isn't it?" Our eyes meet again.

"Yeah."

Outside, it's really chilly. "When did it get so cold?" I say. "It was warm when we got here,"

"That was over two hours ago," Holly replies, and gives a little shiver. She didn't bring a coat, so I take off my leather jacket and hold it out for her to put on. She looks up at me, then turns and puts her arms in the sleeves, letting me pull the jacket onto her shoulders, where I keep my hands on her just for a moment. She nestles back into me. "Thank you," she mutters, then turns around to face me. "Won't you get cold though?"

"Not any more," I say, smiling down at her. She leans into me and, taking her hand, we walk back to her place.

It doesn't take as much time as I'd like it to, and before long, we're back at the apartment.

I let Holly go in first, then close the door behind us and she switches on the light in the hallway, then turns to me. "Thank you for a lovely evening," she says.

"My pleasure," I tell her, because it was.

"Would you think me really boring if I went straight to bed?" she asks, shrugging off my jacket and handing it back to me.

"No, of course not."

"I'm really tired." She looks up at me. "And I imagine we'll have a late night tomorrow?"

"Probably."

"I thought so."

"I'll say goodnight, then." She goes to walk away, but I grab her hand and pull her back. "Thanks for listening," I say.

"Thanks for telling me."

I bring my hand up and rest it on the side of her face, then lean down and kiss her gently on her other cheek. "You're easy to talk to," I tell her, then let her go, and move along the hallway to my – well, her – bedroom.

"You can use the bathroom first, if you like," she calls after me.

"Thanks," I say and let myself into the bedroom. I close the blinds, switch on the bedside lamp and then go across to the bathroom, returning a few minutes later. I strip off my clothes, putting them in a pile by the chair, then bend over my case to find some shorts. I've just put my hand on them and am pulling them out, when I hear the door open behind me.

"Oh bloody hell!" I hear. "Oh... um... shit... I'm so sorry." I'm already laughing at her reaction as I grab the shorts, before covering myself and turning toward her. Holly's standing in the doorway, staring, her cheeks flushed. "I'm... I'm..." She's flustered beyond words, her eyes raking over my naked body, the shorts just about covering my growing erection, while she's trying to back out of the room. This is hilarious.

"What do you need?" I ask her, hoping she'll say she needs me, although I think that's highly unlikely.

"I… um… I can't remember."

I laugh out loud again and go across the room, standing in front of her. "Well, let's see if I can help you." I take her hand and pull her back into the room. "Let's see… was it nightwear?" I ask, but she shakes her head, her eyes fixed on my chest now. "Clean clothing?" I take a step closer. "Underwear?" I whisper. I'm not playing fair. I know I'm not, but this is fun.

She shakes her head again. "It can't have been that important," she says. "I—I'll leave you to get undressed. I mean… dressed…" She turns and flees, closing the door behind her.

I've just pulled up my shorts when she knocks on the door. "Come in," I call.

"Are you decent?" she asks.

I go over and open the door. "I wouldn't have said 'come in' if I wasn't," I tell her. "I think you've had enough shocks for one night."

"It wasn't a shock," she says, getting embarrassed again. "I just wasn't expecting you to be in here. I thought you were still in the bathroom."

"It doesn't matter, really it doesn't."

She swallows, her eyes dropping to my chest again, and then snaking lower. I like that she enjoys looking at me. It's entirely mutual, believe me. Even with clothes on, she's beautiful.

"I remembered what I came in here for," she says. "I need a new pack of cleansing wipes. They're in a box in the wardrobe."

I stand to one side and let her in, and she goes over to the closet, retrieving a plastic packet and coming back to me.

"Goodnight," she says, still not looking at me. "I promise not to disturb you again."

I grab her hand, just as she's about to leave, and pull her back. "Holly," I say quietly, "you can come in here whenever, and however, you like. And I don't mind what I'm wearing." I smile at her. "I don't mind what you're wearing either." I put her hand to my lips and kiss her fingers. "Just do whatever makes you comfortable... I'll go along with it."

She's staring at my mouth, her own open, just a fraction. "Todd... I—" She's interrupted by the landline ringing and looks up at me. I let go of her hand. "I'd better get that..." She seems flustered, although I'm not sure whether that's because it's late to be getting a call, or because of what we've been doing, and saying... I hope it's the latter.

I'm not even remotely tired now. I'm wide awake. I might even sit up and watch a movie, and I might see if Holly wants to join me. I'm just about to grab a t-shirt, because I think she's been embarrassed enough for one evening, when she reappears in my doorway, holding out the phone. She looks upset.

"What's wrong?" I ask her.

"It's for you," she says, offering me the handset.

I take it from her and put it to my ear. "Hello?" I don't take my eyes from Holly.

"Hi." It's Chris. Holly stares at me for a moment, then walks away. What's wrong with her?

"What's up?" I say into the phone, following Holly out of my room. She's gone into her own and closed the door. What just happened? I'm so confused.

"Nothing... well, maybe nothing. I've e-mailed over the information on the Watsons, but I just found out something else. I thought I should run it by you."

"Okay, what have you found out?" I lean back against the doorframe.

"They've only been married a couple of months..."

"And?" I can't see why this is important.

"And it was a real whirlwind romance. They met just after Christmas, and got married on Valentine's Day."

"How romantic. What's your point, Chris?" I want to end the call... I need to find out what's wrong with Holly.

"Before they were married, Mrs Watson dated one of the employees of the club."

All of a sudden, Chris has my full attention. "Who?" I ask.

"One of the bar staff... A guy named Dylan Murphy."

I'm trying to work out if this is even relevant. "Okay..." I'm still thinking. There's one detail that will make all the difference... "Where's this Dylan Murphy now?" I ask.

"He's still here, in Boston."

"Then I can't see it's relevant. We're looking for someone who's here in the UK."

"Like Mrs Watson?" Chris says.

"Yeah, but none of us think the killer is a woman."

"And Mr Watson?"

"Only came on the scene after the first murder."

"Are we sure about that?" I guess it's possible the Watsons have gained access to the membership list through this Murphy guy... it still seems a bit far-fetched to me. But then I've never gone along with the idea of our murderer being a member of the clubs.

"I don't know, Chris. You tell me?" I say. "Is there a connection between Eric Watson and the clubs before Christmas... before the first murder?"

"I don't know."

"Well, can you check it out and let me know?"

"Sure. I'll call you."

"Okay... just not tonight."

Chris laughs. "Why? Are you busy?"

Yes. "No. But it's late here."

"Hmm. I believe you."

"Goodnight, Chris."

I hang up, and wander along to the kitchen to plug it back into the charger. The light's still on in Holly's bedroom and I knock on her door. She doesn't reply, so I knock again. "Yes?" she calls.

"Can I come in?"

"Okay." I open the door and peer inside. She's sitting on the bed, still wearing her white dress, with her back to me. I take a couple of steps into the room.

"Holly?"

"Yes?"

"What's wrong?"

"Nothing." Well, that's bullshit; something's wrong.

"Are you mad at me?" I ask her.

She turns to me, glaring. "Why would I be mad at you, Todd?"

"I guess that's a yes, then," I reply. "What did I do?"

She takes a breath, and turns away. "Nothing," she says. "You just acted like every other bloody man…"

"I'm sorry?"

She looks back at me again. "Is it genetic?" she asks.

"What?" Is what genetic? What does she mean?

"Lying… cheating. Is it something men are just born to do?"

"Holly… I've got no idea what you're talking about."

She gets up and comes over to me, standing just a foot away from me. "Oh, really?" she says, her eyes alight with anger. "You've been telling me you'd wait for me… wanting me to believe in you… wanting me to trust you—" Her voice cracks, and she swallows hard. "And all the time, you've got a partner back at home."

"Are we talking about Chris?" I ask her, trying to stay calm.

"Of course. How many women do you have waiting for you then?"

"None."

"Stop lying to me, Todd."

"I'm not."

"Get out!" she yells.

"What?"

"I said, get out!" She pushes me away and I let her. I go toward the door, but stop on the threshold, looking back at her. She's really mad…

"Holly," I say quietly, "I'm guessing Chris told you she's my partner?"

"And I suppose you're going to tell me she isn't?"

"No… I'm not. Chris *is* my partner." Even from here I can see the tears forming in her eyes. "There's no need for you to cry, Holly. I'm not in a relationship with Chris. She's a detective," I explain. "She's my partner at work and has been for six months, since she transferred to Boston P.D."

"I—I'm…" Holly stutters, but I don't want to hear what she's got to say, not right now. I can't handle hearing her say Jason's name, and I know she will, because that's why she's being like this… Because he cheated, she thinks I'm gonna cheat. She thinks I'm just the same as he is.

I need some time alone before I can safely deal with any of that.

I turn away and close the door softly behind me.

∽

Holly

What have I done?

As if it wasn't humiliating enough that I barged in on him virtually naked, I then accused him of lying, and cheating… just because his work partner called up to speak to him. What the hell is wrong with me?

I pace the floor for a while. It doesn't help, but it's better than sitting staring at the wall. I feel like such an idiot. I *am* an idiot. How could I have said all those things to him?

I can't leave it. I have to speak to him – to clear the air, if nothing else. What's the worst that can happen? Well, I guess he could be angry with me… but I deserve that.

I go along the hallway to his room and knock on the door.

"Yeah?" he calls out.

"Can I come in?" I ask.

"Sure."

I open the door. He's lying on his back on the bed, his arms behind his head. He's still just wearing his shorts and I stand in the doorway, feeling a little wary.

"I—I wanted to apologise," I mutter. "I was horrible to you. We're not even together, and I accused you of cheating on me… I'm just being completely irrational. I don't know what's wrong with me."

"You don't?" he sits up, swinging his legs over the edge of the bed. He seems surprised.

"No."

He sighs deeply. "Well, I do…" He pats the bed beside him. I hesitate, just for a moment, then go over and sit down. "Want me to explain it?" he offers. His voice is so gentle and kind, considering I just literally threw him out of my bedroom.

I look up at him and nod my head. "Yes, please."

"Okay." He pauses. "You're still seeing Jason everywhere," he says, looking around the room. "He's here in your apartment. He's at the club, he's in every couple you see, in every guy you meet, including me. I know he hurt you, Holly… He hurt you badly, but you've gotta let go, or he's gonna ruin your future, as well as your past."

"I know."

"Chris really is just my work partner," he continues. "We work together, that's all. Her name's Christina Jefferson, she's twenty-eight, comes from Detroit, and moved to Boston to be near her fiancé, who's some hot-shot advertising exec, or something. They're getting married early next year…"

"You don't have to explain."

"Yeah… I do." He moves closer so we're almost touching. "I need you to understand," he says. "I'm not interested in Chris… not in that way. She called because she'd come up with a possible lead. Mrs Watson used to date a guy who works at the Boston club. I don't think it'll come to anything, but she's checking out a few things for me. She's gonna call back when she's got something."

"Oh God…"

"What?"

"I was really abrupt with her. She must've thought I was so rude…"

"Well, if she did, she didn't say anything to me. She probably didn't notice… You've gotta remember, Holly, she's used to working with me. Abrupt is pretty much my middle name."

"I can't see why… you're not abrupt at all."

He leans into me. "Not with you, I'm not."

"I'm so sorry for doubting you, Todd." I can feel tears pricking behind my eyes.

"Don't be sorry. I don't want that. I just want you to trust me." I look up at him. "Please?"

"I want to," I whisper. He pulls me into his arms, and I let him. "I honestly do. It's just so hard…"

"I know." He kisses my hair, stroking it gently, and I really do wish I could just let go of the memories and let him in.

He's talking to Adam again when I get up and, this time, I manage to switch my brain on sufficiently to put on my robe before leaving the bedroom. Last night, he held me for a while, rocking me gently on the edge of his bed, before showing me back to my room. We didn't kiss, but he held me again, standing on the threshold of the bedroom, before we said goodnight. It felt good to be in his arms, nestled against his chest… safe.

I join him in the living room and sit on the sofa while he finishes his conversation. He's already dressed again, in jeans and a pale blue shirt. I'm still struggling to decide whether I prefer him with, or without clothes. He looks good naked, but somehow clothes just hang so well on him. I don't think I've ever been around a man who's so… masculine.

He finishes his call, puts the phone in his back pocket and sits down beside me.

"Good morning," he says, staring at me.

"Hello. Did you sleep okay?"

"I slept fine," he says. "What about you?"

"Not too bad." I did get off to sleep eventually, after I'd spent ages going over everything that happened last night. I still felt uncomfortable about my behaviour… and, if I'm being honest, lonely without Todd's arms around me.

He looks at me for a moment, like he knows I'm hiding something.

"Is everything okay?" he asks. I nod. "Holly?"

I take a deep breath. "I still feel embarrassed about last night."

"Please don't. There's no need. I really just want us to go back to how we were before…"

"Am I forgiven?" I ask him.

He takes my hands in his.

"Nothing to forgive," he says. "It was a misunderstanding, that's all... And just so you know, Chris won't be calling again for the time being. She e-mailed me with the results of her additional inquiries. It seems it was all for nothing."

"What was it about anyway?" I ask him.

"She thought Mr Watson might be our killer and he might be getting the intel from the guy his wife used to date."

"Seems a bit far-fetched."

"That's what I thought, but I got Chris to check it out anyway. There's no connection – nothing that fits."

"So we can rule the Watsons out?" I ask him.

"As suspects, yes. We'll need to watch them though." He's still holding my hands. "And while we're talking about the club... I've been thinking..."

"Oh?"

"We might have a problem. Well, maybe... I'm not sure..."

"What kind of a problem?"

He grins. "First, I'm going to have to ask you a personal question."

"Okay..." after last night, I can't disguise my uncertainty.

"Do you have another short, sexy dress?"

I wasn't expecting that... "I'm not sure it's sexy, but I've got one more short dress."

"Can I see it?"

"Now?"

"You don't have to put it on. Just let me have a look, if that's okay."

"It's in the wardrobe in your... well, my bedroom." I get up. "Follow me."

"I don't mind waiting out here," he says.

"You've got your clothes on," I say. "I think it's safe for me to be in there with you."

He stands and puts his hands on my hips, leaning forward. "Don't be too sure about that," he whispers. "These clothes... they're not glued to me. They do come off, you know... damn fast."

I swallow hard and the increasingly familiar pool of heat settles at the pit of my stomach. This is much better… I prefer it when we're like this with each other, and judging from the look in his eyes, so does he. He smiles down and me, then takes my hand and leads me down the hallway to the bedroom, where he lets me go.

"Let's have a look," he says, standing at the foot of the bed, with his arms folded across his chest.

I go to the wardrobe and pull out my only other cocktail dress. It's deep blue, and very tight, a bit like the black one, but it's even shorter coming down to the top of my thighs and there's no stretch to this one; it's strapless, fitted and unforgiving. I've never really liked it. I turn and hold it up to him. His eyes widen.

"Wow!" he says. "And you weren't sure it was sexy…"

"You haven't seen it on," I tell him. "A lot of dresses look better on the hanger."

"Not this one," he replies.

"Why did you want to see it?" I ask.

"Because we're definitely gonna need to go shopping."

"Why?"

"There's no way on earth I'm letting you wear that to the club tonight, and you can't wear your black dress again either. We're supposed to be a wealthy couple from New York. You wouldn't wear the same outfit twice – not on two consecutive visits, anyway."

"And what's wrong with this dress?" I hold it up again and look at it, both back and front. "I mean, I know it's short, but isn't that the point?"

"Not entirely. Bring it here," he says and I do, stepping closer to him. He takes it and holds it up against me. It finishes about three inches above the dress I wore on Monday. "Just as I thought." He hands it back to me.

"I don't understand."

"Okay… I'll go outside for a minute. You put it on and I'll show you what the problem is." He goes across to the door. "Call me when you're ready." He grins. "I promise not to come in before that."

"Haha. Very funny."

"I try," he says, smiling as he closes the door.

I take off my robe and pyjamas, keeping on my knickers. The dress doesn't need a bra. I pull it on, zip it up and call out to Todd, who comes back in immediately. He must've been waiting right outside the door.

He stops dead, his eyes dragging hungrily up and down my body. No man has ever looked at me like that. Ever. "You thought it looked better on the hanger?" he asks. "You were so, so wrong." That pool of heat just lit up like a flame. He walks across to the bed and sits down. "Come here" he says and I go over and stand in front of him. "Tonight, at the club... you want to sit on my lap again, right?"

"I'd prefer it, yes. I really don't want to watch what's going on in the room."

"That's fine," he says softly. "I understand that. So, let's try it out... with you in your dress that you think looks better on the hanger." He looks down to his lap. "Go ahead."

"Now?"

"Yeah."

I step forward, and raise one knee onto the bed beside him. And I immediately understand the problem. The dress is so tight, the only way I'm going to get on his lap is to hitch it up, leaving my bottom exposed.

I lower my leg, step back and look down at him. "I can't," I tell him.

He stands and, because I'm right in front of him, our bodies are literally touching. "That's not strictly true," he says. "You can, but I'm not going to let you. Not in the club, where other people – other men – can see you. That's not happening."

"But, how did you know?"

"I didn't... I guessed. You struggled with finding a dress on Monday, and you've worn longer skirts, or jeans, out of choice. I guessed this kind of dress, and the one you wore on Monday... they're not exactly your thing, are they?"

"Jason bought them for parties we had to go to. He liked me to wear short skirts... the shorter the better..."

His eyes darken a little. "And you went along with that, even though you felt uncomfortable?"

I don't answer him. I don't want to admit that I was always scared of losing Jason, so I went along with *everything*... and then lost him anyway. I lower my eyes and stare at Todd's chest. There's a long pause, then I feel his finger beneath my chin, raising my face to his. What I see in his eyes is breathtaking...

"Don't ever do that, Holly," he whispers. "Don't let anyone else dictate what you wear, or how you behave, or who you are. Even if you don't have anything else, you have the right to be yourself." He lets go of me and steps away, although his gaze is still intense. "We'll go shopping, and I'll buy you a couple of dresses for tonight and Friday. They won't be your style, they won't be what I'd like to buy you, but you'll be decent, and no-one... no-one," he growls, "will get to see your ass." He smiles as his mood lightens again and he goes over to the door. "I'll make breakfast while you shower. Then we can go out."

The club is a little busier tonight, which makes me even more relieved we went out and bought the two dresses we picked up. It took us ages, mainly because the type of dresses my character would wear would be skin tight and skimpy, and impractical for our purposes, so that's not what we wanted at all. Equally we didn't want a pretty, flowing dress with a full skirt, because while it's more feasible for me to move in, it's all wrong for the club. Eventually, after trying six shops, we found two low-cut, mid-thigh, wrap-around dresses, with spaghetti straps, one in red, the other in black. I tried one on and came back out into the shop, and Todd stood with a broad grin on his face. I couldn't try sitting on his lap in the shop, obviously, but there's plenty of leg room for me to move around, so I think it'll be okay. He clearly thought so too, because he bought them, and then took me out for lunch.

I've drunk my champagne a little quicker tonight, probably because I know what's coming and my nerves are on edge. Todd and I spent an hour or so this afternoon looking through the information that Chris sent over to him last night. It seems Eric Watson works for a music publishing company. His wife has no current employment. He's thirty-five, she's six years younger. They're not a bad looking couple and, once again, I'm left wondering why they frequent the club. Todd spent ages studying their photographs… I looked at them, but I won't be the one facing the room. They're certainly not in the bar.

"You ready?" Todd asks.

I nod, just once. "Frankly I'd rather have my teeth extracted, but I'm guessing that's not an option."

"I'll be with you," he says and pulls me to my feet, leading me from the room. As we're climbing the stairs, I can feel myself tensing up and he pulls me to a stop and into a hug. "Try and act normal," he says into my hair.

"Here?" I mutter back.

"I know it's difficult," he whispers. "When we get in there, just look at me. Ignore everything else. Okay?" I nod again, and he releases me, smiling, before we continue on our way up the stairs.

At the top, we go through the security procedure again, before the door is opened. I don't need to look at anything to know the couple on stage are reaching the climax… and I mean climax… of their performance. If Todd's right and the woman is faking it, she's doing a really good impression of someone having a mind-blowing orgasm. I stare at Todd, but the noises from the couple on stage are distracting, to say the least. He glances around the room for a moment, then looks back at me and pulls me over to an empty booth on the right hand side of the room, opposite where we sat on Monday. He lets me sit down first and motions that I should move to the back of the booth, facing into the room, but he keeps his eyes locked with mine as he joins me and leans across in front of me, pretending to kiss me, our lips almost touching.

"Just give it little while," he says, "and I'll lift you onto my lap." He reaches up and cups the side of my face with his hand, rubbing my cheek with his thumb. "Don't take your eyes off of me."

That's an easy request to follow. He looks as lovely as ever, and his eyes are melting me from the inside out.

"When you're on my lap," he says after a couple of minutes, "can you lean forward onto me, so I can watch over your shoulder?"

"You're going to watch the show… while I'm on your lap?"

He leans back as the noise in the room quietens down a little and I imagine the performers are leaving the stage. "No," he whispers. "I'm going to look around the room." He bends forward and kisses my cheek very gently, then murmurs, "I'm sorry, baby," and I melt a little more.

He shifts in the seat, so he's leaning against the back of the booth and then lifts me onto his lap, just like he did on Monday. And all of a sudden, his eyes widen and his mouth opens… and then a slow smile settles across his lips. He places one hand behind my neck, pulling me close, and the other on my backside, which he rubs gently.

"Okay," he whispers into my ear. "We're fine at the back; the dress covers everything."

"Good," I murmur back to him, pretending to nuzzle his neck… except I'm not really pretending that hard.

"The front, on the other hand…" I can hear his smile and I manage to glance down between us, where I see the black wrap-around dress gaping wide open, revealing my very sensible cotton 'period' knickers. "Don't panic," he says, as if he knows I'll try and adjust my skirt. "I promise not to look."

"You already did," I say quietly, although I can't help but smile myself.

"Yeah," he admits, "but only a little bit." He's still grinning, but then I feel him tense against me. "Time to start moving," he says. "You okay?" I nod my head and shift forward against him. I can feel his erection against me… right against my sex, and I let my head fall onto his shoulder as I start to rub myself along his length, flexing my hips back and forth. I know from doing this on Monday, it's going to be arousing… His cock is so hard and, at this angle, it seems to touch just the right spot… I know it's going to take every ounce of self control I've got not to come. I hear him exhale a long breath and wonder if he feels the same.

He keeps his hands where they are: one holding my bottom in place, the other caressing my neck, but I can feel his head shifting as he looks around the room. After a few minutes, he moves my head to the other side of his, I assume so he can get a different angle of the room. Then I feel his muscles tighten around me.

"They're here, aren't they?" I whisper into his neck. He nods his head. "It's gone quiet," I murmur.

"There's nothing happening on the stage right now," he says.

"Do you want to lift me off for a while, then?" I ask. *I need a break, before I explode.* "It might look odd if this is the only thing we do all evening."

"You sure?" he asks. I nod my head. "Just be careful where you look," he says, and places his hands on my hips, moving me off of his lap and back onto the seat beside him. He immediately straightens my skirt as he leans over, like he's going to kiss me, but stops short, his lips almost touching mine. "They're in the second booth along, on the opposite side," he says. "But they're being a little… active. Speaking of which… Sorry." He looks down at me and his eyes are filled with remorse.

"It's alright," I whisper, and he places his hand on my thigh, where the skirt splits, then moves his head down, kissing my neck gently, before going lower, but now only just brushing his lips against my skin as he reaches the tops of my breasts. Even with this featherlight touch, it's all I can do to keep my eyes open, but I manage to spot the Watsons in their booth. Todd wasn't kidding. Mr Watson is sucking his wife's nipples, alternating between one exposed breast and the other, while his hand is between her legs, her skirt having been pushed up around her waist. She's not wearing knickers and, from the movement of his hand, even in this dim light, it's fairly obvious what he's doing, and I'm wishing I hadn't looked now. Todd moves back up so he's blocking my view.

"You okay?" he asks. I nod. "You went real tense." Did I? I hadn't realised.

"Sorry," I mutter.

"Don't be." He caresses my cheek with the backs of his fingers. I glance over his shoulder and see three people coming onto the stage; two men and a woman. "What's wrong?" he says. How does he know?

"The—the performers," I manage to say.

"They're back?" he asks.

"Yes."

"Okay. I'll move you." He sits back in the seat and looks at the stage. His expression doesn't alter at all, as he lifts me back onto his lap. "I'm gonna start watching the employees now," he says in my ear.

He keeps my head still with his hand and I can feel him shifting his gaze as the members of staff move around the room. After a few minutes, he suddenly stops and moves me back onto the seat again. "We've gotta go," he says, getting to his feet. He reaches out for my hand. "Straighten your dress." There's an urgency to his voice, and I quickly tidy myself up and let him lead me from the room via the main door. Once outside, I realise that the Watsons must have left a few moments before us and are heading down the front stairs towards the entrance. We follow, a little way behind and watch them get into a taxi. We wait for a short while, then Todd hails one for us, giving the driver my address.

"No-one followed," he says once we're under way.

"No. Did anyone even pay them any attention?"

"Not especially. No more than the other members, anyway. We'll come back on Friday, but I need to hear from Adam about who has access to the lists, otherwise we're just watching people for the sake of it."

Once we get back to the flat, I let us in and close the door, then turn to him.

"Thank you," I say quietly.

"What for?" he replies, looking confused.

"I realised tonight, watching the Watsons, that you've been going easy on me in the club. You haven't done, or asked me to do, anything like as much as you could have done."

He takes a step closer. "Do you seriously think I'd do anything like that… anything like all the things I really want to do with you, in front of other people, in a place like that?" he asks.

"No. But I realised tonight when I saw them, how… I don't know… considerate, you're being."

He places his hands on my hips and walks us backwards until I hit the wall, then he moves his hands up, putting them either side of my head. "I don't know what you're used to, Holly… I have no idea how you're used to being treated, but for me this isn't just physical. I want to get to know you. I want to spend time with you." He pauses for a moment. "One day, when you're ready, when you're sure about us, I want more… I want a *lot* more. But when that happens, it'll be private, between us, and not for anyone else to see – or even know about." He takes a step back. "I know you're still trying to adjust… I know you need more time, and that's okay with me. But can I just tell you that I'd never ask you to do anything that made you feel uncomfortable. I'd never take you anywhere you didn't want to be, and then ignore you, I'd never put you in a short dress just to suit my tastes." He runs his hand down the side of my body, touching the dress, and me through it. "Going to the club, and this outfit… that's all for the job, nothing else, you know that, don't you? If you're comfortable in flannel pyjamas, or old jeans and baggy jumpers, that's fine by me. You're the sexiest woman I've ever met, Holly… which is made obvious by the fact that I seem to get hard just being in the same city as you. You never have to dress up for me, or be anything you don't want to be. Ever."

I wonder if he means all that, or if he's just saying it to make me feel better. I want to kick myself for being so cynical, but it's hard to believe anything anymore, no matter how much I want to. And I really want to.

"You're tired," he says. "Why don't you put on those flannel pyjamas, I'll find us a movie and we'll finish that chocolate ice cream?"

"Um… I don't actually possess any flannel pyjamas."

He smiles down at me "Okay, then improvise. Just wear whatever's comfortable."

I join him in the living room, wearing short cotton pyjama bottoms, with a t-shirt, and no bra. He told me to wear what was comfortable, and this is comfortable. The tub of ice cream and two spoons are on the coffee table and, as I sit down, he turns to me, smiling. He's still wearing his black trousers, but he's taken off the jacket and tie, and unbuttoned the top of his shirt.

"Being as you've spent almost the entire evening on my lap," he says, "how about you come over here and we'll watch the movie together? I think we know each other well enough by now, that we can stop sitting at opposite ends of the couch, don't you?"

I nod my head and he turns, putting his legs up on the sofa, and parting them, so I can move between them and lie back on him. He hands me the ice cream tub and a spoon, keeping the other for himself, then presses 'play' on the remote.

"What's on?" I ask.

"Skyfall," he says. "I came in after the first ten minutes, so I paused it. Are you in a Bond mood again?"

"Yes, that's fine."

I open the ice cream and offer it to him, but he tells me to go ahead, so I take a spoonful and snuggle down, feeling his erection prodding into my back. I smirk just a little.

"What's wrong?" he asks.

I twist and look up at him. "I think we might be in the same city again…" I say and he laughs.

"Oh, baby, I've been there since you walked into Andy's office three days ago," he says, and he pulls me up his body, his arms coming tight around me. "Now, can I have some ice cream, or are you planning on eating it all?"

Chapter Eight

❦

Todd

We're walking back from the dry-cleaners, hand-in-hand, having arranged to have Holly's dresses, my shirts and my tux cleaned and returned tomorrow morning. I haven't been able to stop thinking about last night, though. Telling her how much I want her, that she's different… that she's special… that was important. I know I didn't quite phrase it that way; I know I didn't tell her that I've never wanted or even thought about wanting any of those things with anyone else, but I hope she got the message. And then, breaking down a barrier and having her cuddle up to me on the sofa was amazing. What was even better was she fell asleep on me. I know that sounds odd, but I liked the fact that she felt comfortable enough to do it.

Once I realized she was asleep, I managed to get out from under her without waking her, and lifted her up into my arms. Then I carried her to the guest room, put her into bed, and kissed her goodnight – on the forehead. Despite the temptation, I didn't kiss her perfect lips. I want her awake, willing, breathless, when I kiss her for the first time. She murmured something incoherent, and I left her to sleep.

This morning, she thanked me for putting her to bed. I liked that too. I liked the fact she didn't query if I'd done anything. It makes me feel like maybe – just maybe – she's starting to trust me.

"What are we going to do today?" she asks, as we get into the elevator at her apartment.

"When I spoke to Adam earlier, he said he's got a list of people who have access to the membership details," I tell her. "He was going to e-mail it over to me. We can check it out… and then I was wondering if you want to move the furniture around in your bedroom; and swap the beds over?"

"We could do," she replies, letting us into the apartment. "But we're not doing anything until we've had a coffee."

"Do you want to make it while I check my e-mails?"

"Okay. I'll bring it through." She goes into the kitchen and I head for the living room, where my laptop is charging. I set it up on the table and check my messages. Sure enough, there's one from Adam, confirming that the Watsons' movements are being monitored now. I asked him to keep them under surveillance when I spoke to him first thing this morning… at least they should be safe when they leave the club, which takes some of the pressure off. We still have to watch them on the inside, but I don't feel so worried about them now.

There's an attachment to his message, which I open. It's a substantial list of people who have access to the membership details… probably with more than thirty names on it. Alongside each name is their role within the club, and they vary from the security men, to the performers, and even the bar and kitchen staff – which seems a little odd to me. I'll need to check that with Adam tomorrow morning. Why would the performers and background staff need to have access to the list? Unless it's not that they *need* access but just that the management aren't particularly good at keeping things from their employees, and pretty much everyone and anyone who works there has access. I'll ask him in the morning when I speak to him. I'm not really sure there's much to be gained from Holly and me spending any time on this until I've spoken to Adam. I close the lid on my laptop. Holly's taking longer than usual with the coffee, so I go along to the kitchen to see what's holding her up.

As I enter the room, it's like my whole world stops turning. She's on the floor, crumpled in a heap, clearly distraught, tears pouring down her cheeks. I go straight to her, sliding onto my knees.

"What is it?" I say, pulling her straight into my arms. She comes willingly and I sit back on the floor, bringing her onto in my lap, my back against one of the cabinet doors, her head on my chest. "Tell me Holly, what's wrong?" I notice then that she's clutching the phone. "Did someone call?" I ask her. She nods her head. Is this something to do with Chris again? Surely we got over that, didn't we? She knows my relationship with Chris is entirely professional… "What's happened?" I ask her. "Speak to me…" I'm getting desperate. I can't stand seeing her like this… It actually hurts. She presses a couple of buttons on the phone and hands it to me. I put it to my ear and listen:

"Holly, it's me. I've been trying to call your mobile since the weekend, but it's permanently turned off. I don't see the point in having a phone if you're never going to switch it on. If this is you trying to avoid talking to anyone because of what happened with Jason, you need to grow up. Shit happens to all of us. We don't all shut ourselves away and sulk. Anyway, I'm just reminding you that it's dad's birthday party this weekend. Don't let mum down. You have to be there. She'll only ask why if you're not, and we don't want to upset either of them, do we? And don't forget to bring a decent dress for Saturday evening… it's black tie. You might not have a boyfriend to dance with anymore, but that's no reason not to make an effort. I'm sure one of dad's friends will take pity on you and spin you around a few times. See you Saturday afternoon."

The line goes dead and I realize I'm clutching the phone so hard my hand's hurting. That has to be Holly's sister; from the conversation, there's no other interpretation. I didn't know she had a sister; she's never mentioned one before. I wonder why? I hand her back the phone.

"Your sister?" I manage to say eventually, once I know I've got full control of my voice and it's not going to come across as angry. I'm not mad at Holly; I'm raging at her sister for leaving her a message like that. Vicky can be selfish, but she'd never speak to me in that way.

"Yes." Holly's calmed down just a little while I've been listening to the message. She's at least capable of speech now.

"She's…"

"A bitch?" she finishes my sentence for me, thank goodness, because I wasn't sure what I was going to say.

"I didn't want to say that about your sister, but yes."

"Oh, she's a lot more than just a bitch. She's a manipulative, cheating, lying, scheming, double-crossing bitch."

"Okay… so, not your favorite person, then."

"You don't have a brother, so it's hard to explain."

I'm confused. "What does me not having a brother have to do with anything?"

She ponders for a moment. "Are any of your friends close enough to be *like* a brother?" she says.

"Yes… Matt. I mean, we're all close, but I'm probably closest to Matt. Why?"

She looks up at me. "Do you like me?" That's an odd question.

"Um… yeah." I hold her close. "I like you a lot." Now is not the time to tell her I think I'm in love with her… It's too soon and I'm not even sure where she's going with this. It's all a bit random.

"Well," she says, "try to imagine that our relationship was more advanced than it is. Imagine we lived together."

"I don't need to work too hard on that," I tell her, smiling. "We kind of are living together…"

"Right…" She's very matter-of-fact. "But imagine we lived together… and shared a bed."

"I think I can manage that," I reply. It would be my idea of perfect.

She takes a deep breath. "And now imagine how you'd feel if you came home from work unexpectedly one night because you weren't feeling well, and found Matt in our bed… having sex with me…" Her voice fades, and the penny drops.

"You mean… you mean the woman Jason had in your bed was your sister?"

She nods her head. "How would you feel?" she asks.

"If it was Matt… and you?" I can feel my blood boiling at the thought – and it's only hypothetical.

"Yes."

"I think I'd probably want to kill him."

"Not me?"

"No. I'm fairly sure I'd break up with you, but I'd want to kill him. The betrayal by a brother – or sister – it's more... much more."

"I know. It is. I can't forgive either of them for what they did, but if Jason was telling the truth about how it happened, I can get much closer to forgiving him than I can her."

I'm not sure I like the idea of her forgiving him so easily. "What do you mean?" I ask her.

"When they finally realized I was in the doorway, Ellie was just lying there, all satisfied and grinning—"

"Wait a second..." I interrupt her, "are you telling me you came in, found them having sex in your bed... and just stood there and watched them finish?"

"Yes."

"You didn't say anything, or do anything to stop them?"

"No. I was kind of frozen to the spot... and then I turned away. I couldn't bear to look at them..." She stops speaking, then snuggles down into me. "Jason jumped out of bed and came after me..." she continues, her head bowed, her fingers playing with one of my shirt buttons. "I'd gone into the living room. He told me she'd come here, and thrown herself at him."

"Oh... And he couldn't get out the way before she landed?" I say.

She manages a half-laugh. "It would seem not. But that's fairly standard behavior for Ellie. Even when we were little, she always wanted what I had... and she'd do whatever she had to do to get it."

"And now she's leaving you messages like that?" I say.

"That's Ellie for you."

"Not that it matters, but is she older or younger than you?"

"She's four years older. She's just turned thirty-one a couple of months ago, and I'll be twenty-seven in August."

"And will you go?" I ask her. "To the party?"

"I have to," she replies. "It's my dad's sixtieth birthday weekend. It's been planned for months. I'd forgotten all about it, what with Jason, the holiday, starting the new job... and the investigation." I notice I'm not on that list of distractions. I'm not sure if that's good, or bad.

"And she'll be there?"

"Yes."

"Will he?"

"Who?"

"Jason."

"No."

"They're not still together then?"

"Um… no. She didn't want him… not really. She just didn't want me to have him. She thought I was happy, though… and that wasn't allowed. That's how it's always been… If Ellie's not happy, no-one else is allowed to be happy, especially not me."

"Ellie's a piece of work."

"Except everyone thinks she's wonderful.".

"Really?" I'm stunned. "Can't they see her for what she is?"

"No. She has a way with people. She always manages to say the right thing at the right time, she tells people what they want to hear. It's all completely superficial, of course, but people can't see that. It's not a gift I have…"

"Bullshitting people, you mean? No, I don't think you have that 'gift'." I turn her so she's facing me, still in my arms. "That's not a gift, Holly. Lying to people so they'll like you isn't something to aspire to." She looks up at me. "This party… it's all weekend?"

"Yes."

"Do you want me to come with you?" I ask her. "I know I'm not invited, but hearing your sister's message, having me there might prove… well, useful." Also, I'm not sure I want her to go alone. I don't like the idea of her being exposed to her sister by herself. And I don't want to spend a whole weekend away from her. I don't know how long I'll be here; a weekend apart feels like time wasted, when we could be getting to know each other.

"I'm not sure," she says. The disappointment must show on my face. "Not because I don't want to be with you," she adds quickly. "I'm just not sure you're ready for my family, and their friends, en masse. They're terrifying."

"I'm not that easily scared."

"Lucky you. I am."

"Then let me come with you. I'll keep you safe… I promise." She doesn't respond. "Why don't we get up off the floor and make the coffee, then we can go find somewhere more comfortable to sit."

She nods her head and goes to pull away, but I drag her back. "Please think about it," I say to her. "About the weekend, I mean… what you want me to do. I'd like to come with you. I want to be there for you, but if you'd rather go alone, I'll understand. I'll miss you, but I'll understand."

We sit in exactly the same positions as we did last night, with Holly resting in between my legs on the sofa. This time, she doesn't make a joke about us being in the same city, although she must be able to feel how aroused I am by her. Instead, she just curls up on me, her head on my chest and I stroke her hair gently.

"That feels nice," she whispers.

"It does," I reply. "But everything about you feels nice." Is 'nice' a good enough word? No, not really. "I like being here," I tell her. "I feel relaxed."

"More relaxed than in Boston?" she asks.

"No, but I do feel relaxed. I miss my friends, but I don't miss my job. I don't miss the pressures of it: the type of work I have to handle, the type of people I deal with… or carrying a gun all the time…"

"Is carrying a gun a pressure?"

"Yes. When you know what it can do, it is." She sits up a little, looking at me.

"You've shot someone, haven't you?"

"I've shot a few people." She stiffens. "I guess that's a bit alien to you. Gun crime isn't as common here, is it?"

"We have it, obviously, but it's not something I've come across… not yet."

"I hope you never do… I'd be terrified at the thought of you being anywhere near a gun."

"Do you feel like that because of what happened to your dad?" she asks.

"I'd be terrified because of how I feel about you," I say. Is that too much? She blinks at me, and tilts her head, like she doesn't understand, but she doesn't say anything. "But… yeah," I continue, "I guess it's also to do with my dad, and because of the things I've done myself."

"Do you want to talk about it?"

"It's hard…"

"You don't have to," she says.

"No, I mean it's hard to know where to start."

"How many times have you used your gun?"

"Fired it, or used it? There's a difference. Usually just the threat is enough."

"Have you killed anyone?" she asks.

"Yes… Two people." I pause, remembering them both. "Does it bother you?" I ask her. "That I've done that, I mean?"

She shakes her head. "No. I'm sure you had good reason."

"Both times, it was to save someone's life, so yes, I did. But it was still hard to come to terms with, especially the first time."

"Why?" she asks.

"It isn't something I've talked about for ages," I tell her, pulling her close so she can't see me. "I had some therapy afterwards, but then I tried to leave it behind."

"Then leave it behind. You don't have to tell me."

"I want you to know all about me though," I tell her. "I want you to trust me completely and know I'm not keeping things from you."

"Even so…"

"No." I take a deep breath. I'll keep it brief. "It was a while ago…" I begin. "I was still in uniform. It was a robbery gone wrong in a liquor store. There was a guy who'd held a woman hostage. He was high… waving his gun around. The manager of the shop reached for something under the counter, and the robber shot him… so I shot the robber. He died instantly. The hostage was okay, scared to death, but okay."

"Then you saved her life."

"He was sixteen years old."

She sits up, breaking free of my hold. "The robber? Sixteen?"

"Yes. I didn't know that at the time. He was wearing a hood; I couldn't see his face."

She sighs. "He still shot the manager… Did he survive?"

"No. He died too. That doesn't make it any easier. That kid was some woman's son."

"So was the store manager." She's right, I know she is. I spent months going through this. "What about the second time?"

"That was more recent… and more personal."

She turns over, so she's lying on her front, on top of me, looking up into my face. "More personal?" she prompts.

"It was to do with Matt…"

"How come?"

"I don't think I mentioned that Grace is British?"

"No, you didn't."

"Well, she is. They met a couple of years ago, when Grace started designing the web site for Matt's company. He came over here, they met, and he fell in love with her straight off. Just like that." I click my fingers. I get how that could happen now, although I don't say anything. "Her husband had just died, so he held back, and waited, but after a few months, they started seeing each other."

"A few months?" I can tell she's surprised.

"Well… it turned out Grace's marriage wasn't what it seemed to be. Her husband had a mistress, and a baby on the way when he died. And he used to beat Grace… badly." I leave out the fact that he raped her. Grace doesn't like people knowing about that. She struggled with all of us finding out, but we had to if we were going to help her.

"Then I'm surprised she waited that long to get together with Matt."

I smile at her. "I guess because of her past, she needed to learn to trust again… It seems that's a common theme with you British women." She smiles back, lowering her eyes. "Anyway, not long after, she started getting threatening texts, which seemed to be coming from her dead husband."

"I'm sorry? How can a dead person send text messages?"

"If they've faked their own death they can. Grace was terrified of the guy, so Matt asked me and Will to look into them."

"How could Will help?" she asks.

"He used to work for the government. He never talked about what he did, but I think he was basically James Bond, but with a computer, rather than a Walther PPK. He's got his own security business now. Well, we both have, being as I own half of it... but that's a whole other story. Anyway, Will started trying to work out who was hacking into Grace's phone. I worked on finding out whether her husband was really dead."

"And was he?"

"Very. It wasn't him at all. It turned out to be a crazy ex-girlfriend of Matt's... She managed to get Matt out of the way, by telling him Luke had been in an accident, then she got Grace to let her in to their place, tied her up and waited for Matt to realize it was a hoax and come back home again. She knew Matt wouldn't let her get near Grace, you see. He worked it out when Will called him. He wasn't at the hospital; he was at home, with Luke and Luke was absolutely fine. Will's quiet, unassuming and very shy, but Luke's a useful guy to have around in a fight, so he said he'd go to Matt's and he got Will to call me... and... and that's when I screwed up." My voice fades. I hate even remembering this part of the story, let alone talking about it.

"How?" She senses my anxiety and puts her arms around me. It's comforting.

"I'd left my phone on my desk because I was having a conversation with my captain. That meant I took a while to pick up Will's call. Those few minutes nearly made all the difference."

"Why? What happened?"

"Luke and I arrived at the same time. Although I had further to travel, and I left after him, I had the advantage that I'd taken my motorcycle to work that day... and I could break every traffic law in the book... but Matt had still got back there first and had left all the doors open for us, so we let ourselves in. His ex... Brooke... she'd decided that she wanted Matt to have sex with her in front of Grace on their kitchen table, and then she was going to kill him."

"What?"

"I did say she was crazy. She gave him two options… that was the first one."

"And the second?"

"She was going to kill Grace in front of Matt, but let him live."

"So he had sex with her?"

"Hell, no," I reply quickly.

"What? He chose to save himself?" She's shocked.

"No… of course not. He took the first option, but he was bluffing. He had no intention of having sex with Brooke. He'd never have done that… he was playing for time because he knew Will had called me. He knew I'd get there. They were both still fully clothed when Luke and I arrived. Matt had his back to me, so I couldn't see much, but I think he knew I was in the room. It was weird. His whole demeanor changed. I saw it in his shoulders… I just said his name and he moved, so I could get a shot at Brooke, but she was too fast. Both our guns went off at the same time. Matt dived in the way of her bullet, which was aimed at Grace. Mine killed her outright."

"And Matt?"

"She caught him in the stomach. It looked bad at the time, but he made a full recovery."

She pulls herself up my body a little further, so she's facing me. "And you?" she says.

"I took a while to forgive myself," I tell her.

"What for?" She seems surprised.

"For getting there late; for nearly getting it wrong."

"It sounds like you saved Grace's life… and Matt's as well."

I hold onto her. "Yeah. They said that too. But Luke has to take the credit for saving Matt… except he never does."

"You've got a lot in common then."

"Me and Luke? I don't think so. Not really."

I feel her arms come tighter around me. "You like protecting people, don't you?" she asks.

"I like protecting the people I care about." I kiss her forehead and she looks up at me. "Let me come with you this weekend," I add.

"So you can protect me?"

"Yes."

"Why?"

"Because I care about you."

"Like your friends?"

"No... not like my friends." I stare at her. "Let me be there for you."

Holly

I don't answer him, but I hold onto him instead. I'd love to have him there with me; I don't want to spend the weekend on my own, away from him. I'd love to feel protected and safe with him. And, if I'm being honest, a little part of me would love to gloat and show off this gorgeous man, especially to Ellie. And while it's tempting to just say 'yes' to him, the fear lingers. The fear that Ellie will take one look at him and decide he's her next target, and that he won't be able to resist. How could she not want him? Or he her, for that matter? He tightens his grip on me and I know I can't lose him to her as well... I think it'd probably break me completely.

"Do you realise we've spent the whole morning just lying on the sofa?" he says.

"Do you realise I don't care?" He chuckles at my reply. He doesn't seem too worried that I haven't given him an answer about the weekend. I'll think about it a little longer. It's the coward's way out... but I'm a coward at heart. "We should probably do some work," I say, going to sit up.

He pulls me back down. "There's no point. I need to speak to Adam again first. It'll wait until tomorrow."

"So, what are we going to do?" I ask.

"Given our current positions, I've got a couple of ideas..." He smirks at me. I'm sure he has... and I have to admit I'm not immune to the temptation, especially as I can still feel his erection pressing into me. I think he's permanently hard. I wonder for a moment if it's uncomfortable for him… but I'm not going to ask. "Why don't we sort out the bedrooms?" he suggests.

"It's a lot of work," I tell him. "I should just pull myself together."

"It's not a lot of work," he says, running the back of his finger down my cheek. "And you don't have to pull yourself together at all." He changes position so we're lying side-by-side, me with my back against the rear of the sofa, his arms tight around me, and he brings a leg around me too, so I'm wrapped up in him. "I kind of get that you might be able to forgive Jason." He pauses. "Actually, if I'm being honest, I don't get that at all, but either way, I want you to forget him. I want you to put him in the past," he says. "If moving the beds around helps, I'll do it a dozen times."

"A fresh start?" I say, losing myself for a moment in his molten chocolate eyes.

"Yes. Well, the beginnings of a fresh start, anyway."

"Okay… but I'm warning you, my bed is heavy."

"That's fine," he says. "I need the exercise. I haven't been to the gym in days. It'll do me good to get a bit of a workout."

"You carried me to bed last night… that's got to count for something."

He squeezes me tighter. "You don't weigh anything," he says. And to prove it, he sits up and then, in one move, stands, and takes me with him, in his arms. "See?"

"And where are you planning on taking me?" I ask. I know I'm teasing… and I like it. I think he does too.

"Planning?" he replies. "You think I'm planning any of this? I'm making this up as I go along, baby." I love it when he calls me that. He doesn't do it all the time, but when he does… the effect is liquifying. He starts walking along the hallway, like I weigh nothing, and goes into the guest room. From a reasonable height, he drops me on the bed, and I bounce. I can't help giggling as he quickly flips me round so I'm facing him, looking up into his volcanic eyes. He leans over, his hands gripping mine, either side of my head, one knee resting on the bed, between my legs. I'm pinned down beneath him… No-one has ever held me like this before… It makes me feel wanted and a little helpless – in a good way – because I know he won't hurt me… "I'll go strip off the sheets in the other room. You can do this one," he murmurs. "If we're both in the same room for much longer, it won't be the bed I'm stripping." Oh my God, the look in his eyes…

He releases me, then stands, stares down at me for a moment, shakes his head and walks away.

I lie on the bed for a while, wondering if I should chase after him and ask him to strip me anyway. But I'm still not convinced I've got any kind of future with him; especially since the idea of him with Ellie has now firmly settled in my head. I can flirt and tease… but anything else…? I'm still not sure yet.

I get up and start pulling the bedclothes off the bed. Why am I letting her dictate my happiness? Even when she's not sleeping with my boyfriend, she's still dominating my thoughts, and actions. If I only had more confidence in my ability to make Todd happy, to keep him happy, I'd run through to the other room and leap on him.

"Don't take it out on the sheets," he says and I jump out of my skin, and turn to see him standing in the doorway, looking at me. "Whatever's wrong, it's not their fault." He pushes himself away from the doorframe and comes in, gathering up the pillowcases that I've flung around the room. I didn't even realise I was doing that. "Let me help." He pulls the sheet out from under the bed and dumps everything inside it, gathering it up in his arms. He walks past me on his way to the door. "You were thinking about your sister," he says.

"How did you know that?"

"Lucky guess?" He stops for a second. "Don't sweat it," he adds and leaves the room. What does that mean?

He comes back a few moments later. "I think we should move your bed out of your room first, and put it in the hallway, on its side. Then we can move all the furniture around in your room to where you want it, and put this bed in there… and then put your bed into here. How does that sound?"

"Very organised."

"I can do organised," he says and turns around to leave.

"What did you mean?" I ask him.

"When?" he replies over his shoulder.

"When you said 'don't sweat it'."

"It means don't worry about it," he calls out.

"I know that…" I follow him into my bedroom, for a more detailed translation, to find he's already lifted the mattress off the bed frame.

"Coming through," he says, and I move back out of the way so he can carry it into the hallway. It's hard not to notice the way his muscles flex and ripple… On his way back, he stops by me. "You okay?" he asks.

"Confused, but yes."

"Why confused?"

"Because I still don't know what you meant."

"Think about it, Holly," he says and goes back into my bedroom, kneeling on the floor by the bed. "I'm assuming this frame comes apart," he adds.

"It does, but we're going to need a screwdriver."

He looks up. "Please tell me you have one."

I smile down at him. "Of course I have one." It's under the sink in the kitchen, so I fetch it, and hand it to him.

He makes short work of dismantling the bed frame and stacking the pieces in the hall by the mattress; including the high wooden headboard, which two men had to bring in when Jason and I bought the bed about eighteen months ago… and even then they struggled.

Within an hour or so, we've re-arranged the furniture so the guest bed is in my room, but it's no longer in the same position. It's now under the window, with the dressing table and chest of drawers straight ahead as you come into the room, and the chair in the corner. The wardrobe is built-in, so we couldn't move that.

"Let's just re-build your bed next door," he says, "and then we can put clean sheets on them."

"I can do that," I tell him. "I don't feel like I've contributed much. You've done all the work."

"I'll make a start on the frame," he says, "if you want to make up the bed in here?"

By the time I've finished putting on the clean sheets, he's already re-built my bed in the guest room and is sitting on the edge of it. I stand in the doorway, looking at him.

"Very impressive," I say.

"I'm not him," he replies, his eyes meeting mine. "That's what I meant. You don't need to sweat it, about me going with you to your parents' place, because I'm not Jason. I'm not going to look twice at your sister, and I'm sure as hell not going to fall into bed with her." He pauses. "That's what you were thinking, wasn't it?"

I nod my head. "I can't help it. You haven't met her."

He gets up slowly and comes over to me. "I don't need to," he says. "She hasn't got anything I want."

"You don't know that. You might meet her and be overwhelmed by her… you can't say—"

"Yeah… I can." He traces the outline of my mouth with his fingertip and I shiver. "You're everything I want, Holly."

"Come with me… at the weekend. Please."

A frown crosses his face. "Why?" he asks.

"Does it matter?"

"Yes… I mean, I'll come with you anyway, but I need to know why you want me there."

I sigh and take his hand, leading him back to the unmade bed, and sitting us both down. I decide on the truth, because I have to be honest with him. "I don't trust her," I tell him. "I never will. And I'll be as nervous as hell the whole weekend. I know I'll feel inadequate and I know I'll be reminded of what she did with Jason, and it'll probably be a backward step for me… in terms of getting over him… But it's my dad's birthday, and I have to go and I'd rather be there with you than on my own. I like the sound of being protected by you, Todd. I don't want to spend two days away from you. And… if I'm being honest…" I look up into his eyes and smile at him. "I quite like the idea of showing you off and gloating a little."

"Gloating?" he queries, smiling slightly.

"Oh, trust me… you in a tux… they'll be falling over themselves."

"Who will?" I notice he's blushing.

"Um… just every woman there, I would imagine." I feel my shoulders drop. "But then, as much as I'll enjoy the bragging rights, that's part of the reason I worry so much… It's not just Ellie. It's all of them, looking at you and wondering why on earth you're there with me…" I've let him see my insecurity now… all of it. He continues to stare at me, then, just when I'm thinking he's not going to reply, he pushes me down on the bed, on my back, and straddles me, leaning over, my hands clasped in his, just above my head this time. God, this feels so good.

"I'll be there, Holly, because being with you is the only place I want to be," he whispers.

"You can't say that," I reply. "We've only just met. We don't really know each other. You could walk into the party on Saturday night and meet the woman of your dreams."

He bends forward, his lips almost touching mine. "No, I couldn't. There's only one woman in my dreams," he says, smiling. "I've already met her. I'm just starting to get to know her. I'm getting to understand that she's not very confident. People have treated her badly; people she thought she could trust, and she's struggling to get her faith back again – especially in men. I get that. She needs time, and I'm gonna give her that. I'll wait for her… and I'll keep waiting until she's ready, no matter how long it takes, or how many backward steps there are along the way, because she has absolutely no idea how beautiful, sexy, warm, funny and compassionate she is… and that any guy would be lucky to have her. And in case you're still having doubts, I'm talking about you, Holly… okay?"

"I think plenty of others would disagree with your description," I tell him.

"I don't care. That's their problem." He pauses. "I'll say it again, and I'll keep on saying it until you believe me… You are all I want," he whispers. He lets his lips touch mine. It's not really a kiss, just a coming together of our lips. "Thank you for asking me to accompany you," he murmurs. "You won't regret it, I promise."

Chapter Nine

⚮

Todd

I'm not entirely sure how I dragged myself off of Holly, but I did and we made up the bed together, and I moved my clothes back into the guest room.

I can still remember the feeling of my lips on hers, even now... and it's nearly twenty-four hours later. It wasn't a kiss, not in the proper sense, even though I wanted it to be, but I didn't want to push her. She needs time still. She's not there yet... and I need her to come to me, not the other way around. She knows that. She knows I have to be sure it's me she wants, not just that she's trying to prove a point – either to herself, or him, or her sister.

At least she's asked me to go with her at the weekend. I really didn't want to stay here by myself, worrying about her. She seems to think the women attending this weekend will be impressed by the sight of me in a tux. They must be a bit starved of male company, is all I can say, but if she thinks they're that easily impressed, I'm sure I can give them a few things to think about when it comes to Holly. It might just boost her confidence to have a few jealous eyes on her for once.

Adam revealed this morning that pretty much everyone at the club has access to the computer in the main office, which isn't password protected, so anyone can see the membership details, which is why the list he provided was so extensive. This doesn't really help very much; it doesn't isolate who we're looking for at all. He also told me that the Watsons won't be at the club tonight, or Monday. They've gone away for a long weekend, flying out of Gatwick to the south of France yesterday evening, and they're booked on the Tuesday morning flight back. The only advantage I can see to all this is that it means I'll probably have to stay here even longer, which makes me smile to myself. Going home is inevitable, but I'm not thinking about that yet, not until I know what Holly wants. If she wants me, we'll find a way to make it work. If she doesn't… well, I'm not gonna think about that.

We've still got an hour or so before we have to start getting ready for tonight's visit to the club. Holly's ordered in a Chinese take-out and we're sitting on the couch, with it spread out on the coffee table in front of us.

"Can I ask you a question?" she says, crossing her legs and balancing her half-empty plate on them.

I turn to face her. "Sure."

"I've told you about Jason… and he was my only serious boyfriend. Can I ask how many girlfriends you've had?"

"I haven't really had any serious girlfriends," I tell her. It's the truth.

She drops her fork onto her plate with a clatter. "You mean… you mean… you're a virgin?"

I roar with laughter. "No, Holly. I'm not a virgin. I'd have thought that much was obvious, even if only because I told you my embarrassing story."

"Which one?"

"About women faking their orgasms." .

"Oh… I'd forgotten about that. But, in that case, I don't understand."

"And that, baby, is why you're so adorable." I put my plate down on the table and move across to her, my arm along the back of the couch, behind her head. "I've never had a serious girlfriend; I've never been in a proper long-term relationship; I'd never lived with anyone until I moved into your apartment on Sunday. But I have slept with women, on a casual basis."

"How many women?" she asks, staring at me.

"I've got no idea."

Her eyes widen. "What are we talking about? Ten? Twenty? More than twenty? More than thirty?"

"I don't know." I do have a vague idea. She's not far off with her last guess. If she added a few more, she'd be around the right number, I think. But she doesn't need to know that.

"More than a hundred?"

"No. Not more than a hundred."

"So somewhere between one and a hundred."

"Don't do this, Holly. Please."

"I want to know."

"No you don't. It's the past. Whatever I tell you, you probably won't like it, and it's not important. All that matters is the present, and the future. And I want you in both, more than anything. I don't want anyone else, not any more. Whatever I've had with other women, and however many times I've had it, I've never had that feeling before, I've never wanted to let anyone into my life… until now. Not once."

She looks at me. "I—I don't think I like your past." she says, tears filling her eyes.

"I don't like yours either." I take her plate and put it with mine, then pull her across to sit on my lap. "But you've got a lot less to worry about than I have." She twists and looks up at me.

"How do you work that out?" she asks. "I've only been with Jason. You've been with countless women."

"It's not countless women, it's some. And it's not about quantity, Holly. I didn't love any of the women I slept with. I didn't feel anything for them at all, and I certainly didn't wait for them. I never met anyone worth waiting for. But you loved Jason, and love is so much more important than sex. I've got a lot more reason to be jealous of your past than you have of mine."

"And are you?" she asks.

"Hell, yes." *Especially as you don't seem to be able to let it go…*

She rests her forehead against mine, then brings her arms up around my neck. She doesn't say anything, but she clings onto me for a long while. Her lips are resting against my cheek and it feels so damn good.

It's good enough, for the moment at least, to stop the thoughts of her past from invading and tearing me apart.

I think the red dress looks better on her than the black one did. It goes with her dark hair better, although I still prefer her in jeans and a top, or – better still – her pajamas, curled up on my lap, her head on my chest, my arms around her…

As we sit in the back of the cab, she squeezes my hand. I haven't let go of hers since we left the apartment. "I want to try and be of more use tonight." she says.

"Okay." I turn to her. "What do you have in mind?"

"I don't know, but I can't just keep sitting on your lap the whole time. Anyone looking at us will think it's odd."

"Don't you like sitting on my lap?" I fake a pout.

She smiles a kind of shy smile. "Yes," she says.

"Good." I grin back at her. "I like it too."

"Do you think I could try facing the stage a bit more?"

"Even if there's a performance going on? You don't have to, if it reminds you…"

"You said changing the bedrooms was the beginning of a fresh start, didn't you?" she says, and I nod my head. "I slept in my own room last night for the first time in six weeks. This is the next step."

"You don't have to do all the steps at once, not if you're not ready."

"And I won't know if I'm ready unless I give it a go."

That feels like a big leap forward for her, but also for us, so I tell her we'll try it. "Let me know if it's a problem," I say, and I bring her hand up to my lips and kiss her fingers.

When we arrive, we have our champagne in the bar, which helps loosen us both up, and then we go upstairs. We know the Watsons won't be here tonight, which means we can concentrate on watching the employees, and I think it's about time I let myself be a little more 'American' around them. Maybe we'll order some drinks and I'll try to get into conversation with the waiter, or something. We've got to tempt this guy out somehow.

I find us an empty booth and lead Holly into it. The performance on the stage is in full… thrust, for want of a better word. I doubt it'll be long before a new couple replaces these two. I sit Holly at the back of the booth and lean across her, pretending to kiss her neck so I can whisper in her ear, "Do you want to sit on my lap for a while, and then swap over."

She nods her head. "I think I need some time to get used to being here again."

"Okay. Just give me a few minutes. Close your eyes if you don't want to watch anything." I glance up and she's already got them shut, her head rocked back and her face a picture of ecstasy. I'd like to think she's not acting, but I'm not sure. I kiss my way down her neck and, as I did on Wednesday, I breathe across the top of her breasts, just letting my lips make the slightest contact with her soft skin. She groans and I feel her hands come up, holding my head in place, her fingers in my hair. I pull back and look at her. Her head falls forward and she opens her eyes.

"Sorry," she murmurs, looking a little shame-faced.

"Hey… Don't be. It felt good."

"Yes, it did." She smiles. "But not here."

"No." I sit back next to her, leaning against the seat. "Time to work," I whisper in her ear, nuzzling her neck. And I turn and lift her onto my lap. Just like on Wednesday, I grab the back of her skirt as I sit her down, to make sure it hasn't ridden up… and my already hard cock becomes like steel. I can't feel any underwear down there… The material of the dress is quite thin and I'd stake my life there's nothing but flesh beneath it. What's she doing coming here like that? Is she insane? Or just trying to drive me insane? Either way, this is a really risky thing to do. I keep my hand where it is and lean back in the seat, pushing her away from me and looking up into her face. "What's going on?" I say to her, my voice a little gruffer than usual.

"How do you mean?" She leans into me, her arms around my neck, getting ready to enact her part, but I'm no longer interested in our roles and I push her back again and glance down between us. The skirt has split open again and I can see the tiniest scrap of black lace. So she is wearing something. Thank God for that. Relief washes over me... relief that quickly turns to need. Even in this light I can see through the lace that she's shaved... and beautiful. I didn't think it was possible to get any harder than I was without exploding, but I guess I was wrong. Despite that, I still think it was a dumb idea.

"What the hell are you wearing?" I ask her.

"A dress... You bought it."

"I mean under the dress."

"Underwear."

"You call that underwear?"

"Yes, I do. What's wrong with it?"

"There's not enough of it."

She laughs. "I never thought you'd complain about that," she says.

I'm not laughing. "I wouldn't, if we were at home." I put my other hand – the one that isn't holding her ass, and her dress, in place – behind her head and drag her closer so I can whisper in her ear, "What do you think you're doing, Holly?"

"I don't see what the problem is. No-one can see me, except you." She pulls away from me and bites her bottom lip, and I think her eyes are glistening. Did she do this for me? And have I blundered in like an idiot? "Have I done something wrong?" she asks.

"No," I say quickly. I don't want her to be offended, or think I don't like what I see. "It's just... well, what if the dress had ridden up at the back? Anyone could've seen you..."

"I knew you wouldn't let that happen," she says. "I trust you to look after me when we're here."

That one sentence makes me feel more hopeful, than I would have ever believed. Actually, it makes me feel like a fucking God, and I know that's ridiculous, but it does.

"Just here?" I ask her.

"I'm getting there with the rest," she says, and lays her forehead on mine. "It's just... I'm—"

"Don't worry about it." This is not a conversation I want to have here.

She leans back a little and looks at me. "So it's okay?" she asks. "The thong, I mean?"

"It's a little better than okay. Sorry I overreacted. I've just gotten used to you wearing your cotton panties when we're here, that's all."

"You mean my boring period knickers."

"'Period knickers'?" I can't help smiling.

"Period panties, if you like. I only wear them during my period. It's finished now."

"And you wear this kind of thing the rest of the time?"

"Yes. All the time." So her sexy underwear isn't just for my benefit then. Oddly I'm now disappointed. It seems there's no pleasing me tonight. Except... I wonder if maybe this is who she really is... sexy, and not ashamed of letting me know. Hmm, I kinda like that. "I prefer thongs to knickers," she adds. "I think they're more comfortable... Now, I think you should stop moaning and start working, before someone wonders what we're doing."

"Moaning?" I smirk and lift her ass off me and, making sure her skirt stays in place and she's covered, I pull her firmly back down onto my erection, then flex and grind my hips into her core so she can feel my whole length against her. She groans loudly, shuddering... and I know I've hit that sweet spot. "Who's moaning now?" I say into her ear and I trail slow kisses down her neck and back up again. "If we were at home, baby," I whisper, "we'd be in your bedroom. I'd have stripped you out of this excuse for a dress, and I'd be pulling those panties off you right now... with my teeth." She gasps.

"Did you say...?"

"Yeah... my teeth." I take a breath... A thought crosses my mind. It's not something I've ever considered before, but I wonder how she'll react to this... "And then I'd spank your ass for coming out tonight with so little on," I growl.

"Oh, God... yes... please," she breathes and shivers, grinding down onto me even harder. Well... I didn't expect that. I can feel her breasts heaving against my chest as she sighs into me. There's no doubt about it, she likes that idea almost as much as I do. She's turned on... and so am I. And now either I'm going to embarrass myself, or I'm going to die trying not to. I really didn't think this through…

She starts to rock on me, pushing herself hard against my cock, putting more into it than she has before, her head against my shoulder, her breasts pressed against my chest, her arms around my neck. It takes every ounce of my willpower not to undo my zipper and release my cock, pull her thong to one side and enter her right here and now, but I focus instead on the room around us. The performance on the stage has just reached its noisy climax, which has covered our short conversation, and nearly all the booths are busy. There are more waiters standing around tonight, but they're not paying particular attention to anyone. Basically, it's the same scene as I've watched on our previous two visits. The couple leave the stage and are immediately replaced by another. A tall, really muscular guy, with dark, cropped hair, and a slim blonde woman disrobe. She climbs onto the bed and gets on all fours. There's clearly no foreplay with these two.

We've been sitting like this for about twenty minutes. I put my mouth next to Holly's ear. "Do you want to try changing position? Or do you want to leave it?" I whisper. The guy on the stage has started grunting, quite loudly.

"What's going on?" she asks me. She's breathing hard, panting, her voice is a little shaky, and I'd say she was close to coming. I'd love her to… but not here.

I look over her shoulder. "You want me to describe what they're doing?"

"Just… just in vague terms," she says, her head dropping to my shoulder, as she slows her movements, sucking in breaths and trying to calm herself. Her thighs are trembling. She *was* close… really close. But I think she's deliberately holding back, and I hope it's just because of where we are, and isn't anything to do with me. God, I wanna watch her come…

"Okay." I pull myself back to the scene before me. Where do I start? "The woman's on the bed, on all fours… He's behind her… You get the picture?" She nods her head, now much calmer. "We can stay like this, if you want," I tell her. It might kill me; I think it might kill her too, but...

"No, I'll try," she whispers. I guess maybe she needs a break too.

"I'll lift you off." I place my hands on her hips and move her onto the seat, quickly pulling her skirt across to make sure she's covered. She looks at me and mouths, 'Thank you,' straightening herself out a bit more. I lean across her. "You're welcome." I have to move down a little if she's going to get decent view of the room, so I kiss the tops of her breasts again, my hand resting on her leg, just where her skirt splits.

She's really tense, so I caress her soft thigh gently with my fingertips to try and get her to relax. She does, and parts her legs slightly, her breasts heaving as she starts to breathe more erratically. She's turned on... really turned on... and I like that. I move my hand up a fraction and she slides down in the seat, just a little, parting her legs even more. I glance down. Nothing's visible. Her dress is still covering her panties... just. She wants this. I know she does and I think, in the heat of what we're doing, she's even forgotten where we are. I need to be careful. We're gonna get carried away... both of us. The grunting on stage stops really suddenly, there's a pause and then I hear the woman let out a high-pitched cry. It makes Holly jump and she clamps her thighs together, my hand clasped between them. It takes her a full minute to start to relax again, just as the woman on the stage begins moaning, really loud, and telling the guy to go 'deeper' and 'harder'.

I move back up to Holly's neck, planting firmer kisses there. Her breathing is slightly more normal now, and maybe that's a good thing... I think we were both in danger of doing something we might well have regretted. All of a sudden, I feel her tap hard on my shoulder, twice. Something's wrong. I stop what I'm doing and sit up, facing her, pulling her close. "What is it?" I say, keeping my head in front of hers, our eyes locked.

"Them," she says.

"The couple on stage? What about them?"

"You told me the women were strangled... right?"

"Yes." Where's she going with this?

"He's strangling her now..."

What? I don't bother about moving Holly with me… I flip in my seat and look at the stage. She's right. The woman is on her back now. The guy is inside her, fucking her real hard… and he's got his right hand around her throat. Her eyes are wide and bulging, but she's moaning, loudly.

I don't need to think twice. I take Holly's hand. "Let's go," I say to her. She gets up, straightens her skirt and lets me lead her out of the room. We go quickly down the main stairs and out onto the street. I hail us a cab and we climb in the back, after I've given the driver Holly's address.

"We're going home?" she says, surprised.

"Yes. Where else would we be going?"

"We left so suddenly, I assumed… well, I don't know what I assumed."

"I need to call Adam, that's all." I pull the phone out of my jacket pocket and call up his number. He answers on the third ring.

"What's happened?" he asks by way of greeting.

"Nothing. I know it's not our scheduled time, but I need you to check up on one of the performers at the club before Monday… and we're going away for the weekend."

"You are?" he says. I can hear the smile in his voice.

"Yeah. Holly's got a family thing going on. We're meant to be married, remember?"

"If you say so." He coughs. "What do you need me to do?"

"There was a guy there tonight. We haven't seen him before. He came on stage at just after ten-thirty, with a slim blonde. He's around six foot one tall, probably about thirty-five years old, dark brown cropped hair, long face, lots of muscles. I'd have said brown eyes, but I wasn't that close to him. Into erotic asphyxiation, maybe?"

"Seriously? That's kinky…"

"Well, either that, Adam, or he's our guy. He was choking the woman on the stage with him. It could just be part of the act… but it's worth checking him out."

"I'll ask the management who he is, based on your description, and get a full background check, and send it over to you for Monday morning."

"Keep it quiet," I tell him. "I don't want him picking up on this."

"I will. Good work, Todd," he says.

"It wasn't me. It was Holly."

"Really?" Christ... Does no-one have any faith in her? I wonder, just for a moment, if I can help out with that... maybe let Andy know how invaluable Holly's been, get them to see she's not just window dressing.

"Yeah, really," I reply.

"Well... that's great." I can still hear the doubt in his voice. Yeah... I'm definitely gonna have to do something about that. "I'll e-mail you the information over as soon as I get it," he continues.

"Thanks. Unless you've got anything to report, I can't see the point in me calling you on Monday. Nothing's gonna change for us over the weekend. We won't even be here."

"Okay. I'll hear from you on Tuesday then, after you've been to the club again."

"Yeah."

"Have a good weekend." He's chuckling as he hangs up. *Asshole.*

I put the phone back in my pocket and turn to Holly. "You gave me the credit," she says.

"Because you deserve it. You noticed what he was doing and put it together with the case."

"But you think it might just be an act... this erotic... what did you call it?"

"Erotic asphyxiation... It's possible. But it's still worth finding out about him."

"What is it anyway?"

I look at her. "Basically, it's a dominance thing. The guy chokes the woman while they're having sex."

"Just to dominate her?"

"Not *just* to dominate her, no. It heightens her orgasm, and him having that much control over her makes the whole thing more intense for both partners."

"You've *done* it?" She's shocked at that thought... really shocked.

"Er, no. Whatever gave you that idea?" I'm staring at her, and I think my surprise must be obvious, because now she's blushing.

"I—it's just you seem to know a lot about it and, well… you said earlier about… spanking me…"

"Oh… and you assumed I was into that whole scene?" She nods her head, just once. "No, Holly," I whisper. "I've never tried anything like that before. Wanting to spank you, that was a spur of the moment thing. That's not something I've done or wanted to do before… but there are quite a few things I wanna do with you that I haven't done before."

"Things?" She's wide eyed, echoing my words. "What kind of things?"

I lean toward her. "You'll find out… if you want to, when you're ready." My voice is a low hum and she lets out a sigh. "And if you don't want to, then that's fine too. I'd never make you do anything you weren't completely comfortable with…"

She looks up at me. "And if I do want to?" she whispers. God, she's full of surprises.

"Then I can think of so many ways to pleasure you, baby…" Her eyes widen even further, and she stutters out a breath.

"And how do you know about… the um…?" she asks, a little incoherently, after a moment's pause.

"How do I know about erotic asphyxiation?" She nods again. "I attended a case years ago where the woman died. The guy was devastated. He thought he knew what he was doing; they'd done it before, but this time he got it wrong… badly wrong. I did some research afterwards. It's incredibly dangerous."

"Sorry." She's blushing even more now. "You sounded like you were speaking from personal experience."

"Well, I suppose I was… but not in the way you were assuming." I need to stop thinking about all the things I want to try with Holly. "What I can't see is why this guy would use it on stage, not when you understand the point of the act."

"I'm not with you."

"You remember I told you the women at the club are faking it?" I say. She nods her head. "Well, the main point of erotic asphyxiation is to heighten the woman's orgasm, so why bother, if she's faking it?"

"Oh… I see what you mean. Do you think that makes it more likely he's the killer?" She's gone pale.

"I don't know… Maybe I'm just hoping he is."

"Hoping?"

"Yeah. I want to catch him, Holly."

"Even though he's so dangerous?"

"That's why I want to catch him."

She shifts across on the seat and leans against me and I put my arm around her. "Just don't let him catch you first," she says. "I remember the photographs… what he does to his male victims."

I rest my head on hers. "I won't. If you recall, I told you I'm quite attached to that part of my anatomy."

She sighs again, and nestles into me.

Holly

I'm so tempted to tell him that I'm getting quite attached to that part of his anatomy as well, but I don't. I'm not ready to take things further yet. Who am I kidding? It was all I could do not to come when I was on his lap just now. His cock felt so good. I suppose I should feel embarrassed for behaving like that… especially for the way I was when he was touching me, but I don't. I don't feel embarrassed at all. I feel sexy… really sexy, and turned on. And wanted. When I felt his hand on my thigh, it was instinctive to part my legs, to offer myself to him. I couldn't help it. It was the most natural thing in the world. If he'd tried to do more, I'd have let him, I know I would… I wouldn't have been able to stop him; he does something to me that takes away all my self control. I didn't care about being in the club. I'm not even sure I was aware of where we were. I wanted Todd too much to think about anything. I wanted him to go further. I wanted him to feel the soaking lace of my thong, to feel how wet I was for him – I still am. I wanted to lie back and let him touch me, let him pleasure me… I've never had thoughts like that before. Never… And as for the idea of him pulling my knickers off with his teeth, and spanking me… nothing like that has ever even crossed my mind, but when he said those words, I wanted him to take me, there and then, more than I've ever wanted anything. The problem is, I know, deep down, that's all just physical. Emotionally, I've still got things to sort out. I'm taking small steps, and sometimes it feels like I'm making progress, but other times I feel like I've still got mountains to climb. One of those mountains seems greater to me than all the others… greater even than Jason having cheated, and me needing to learn to trust again. Todd lives in Boston, and when this assignment is over, he'll go back there… and then what'll happen? If we get together now, how can we hope to sustain a relationship if we're three thousand miles apart? I keep trying to tell myself it'll work out. But it won't. I know it won't. And I so want it to… I really do.

"Are we driving tomorrow?" he asks me, making me focus on something other than my currently wayward thoughts.

"Yes," I manage to say, dragging my mind away from having an ocean between us, or – even more distracting – being held down by him while he spanks me. Oh, God…

"How long will it take, do you think?"

"It's usually about an hour and a half, depending on the traffic."

"Okay. And when are we leaving?"

"The less time I spend in Ellie's presence, the better, so not until after lunch… probably around three. Why?"

"No reason. I just wondered."

The taxi pulls up outside the flats and Todd opens the door, getting out first and then helping me. He pays the driver and we go inside and take the lift to my floor.

The first thing I do once we're inside is kick off my shoes. They're killing my feet. I switch on the light and move down the hallway a little, leaning back on the wall by the kitchen door.

"You look tired," he says, coming to stand beside me. "Did you sleep okay in your own room?"

"Yes. How did you get on? I forgot to ask this morning…"

"I was fine. I can sleep just about anywhere."

He undoes his tie and top two buttons. I think this is when he looks most sexy… apart from when he's not wearing anything, of course.

"I'm sorry about earlier," he says.

"Earlier?" I don't understand.

"The panties thing…"

"Oh, that." With all the other excitements of the evening, I'd forgotten all about it.

"I overreacted."

I smirk. "You did a bit."

"I can't help it," he says.

"Can't help what? Overreacting?"

He turns and stands in front of me. "No. Wanting to keep you safe."

"But I was safe. I knew that. You were there. If I hadn't felt safe, I'd have worn the boring period knickers, and to hell with feeling comfortable."

"You really find thongs more comfortable?" he asks, his head tilting to one side.

"Yes."

"It's not something Jason got you to do?"

"No. This is my choice."

"Sorry," he says. "I didn't mean to question your decisions."

"I know." I can't blame him for doubting my ability to choose my own clothing after what I told him about the dresses.

"So… now would probably be a good time to tell you that Matt and Luke own a company that makes some of the sexiest lingerie in the world. They'll do me a very, very good discount."

"You're joking."

"No."

"What's the name of their company?"

"Amulet."

"Oh my God." I can feel myself blushing.

"You're not wearing…?"

I nod my head and he laughs out loud, throwing his head back.

"Just wait until I tell them."

"Don't you dare."

"Okay, I won't tell them you were wearing one of their thongs tonight, but I'll tell them you like their stuff… Is that alright?"

"Yes, that's fine." He starts down the hallway, then turns, and continues walking slowly backwards, his eyes on me.

"I'll say it again, just so we're clear," he says. "It's not about whether you're wearing a short skirt, or jeans, or the biggest *knickers* – as you call them – or the tiniest lacy thong… or even nothing at all. It's just about you, Holly. All of you. I want you relaxed. I want you comfortable. I want you focused… on me, and no-one else." He stares at me as he crosses the threshold into the living room and turns to pick up his laptop from the table, coming back along the corridor and passing by me with it in his hand. We're close… really close. I can feel the heat from his body. "I want you my way. And I want you here… nowhere else. Certainly not at the club," he murmurs as he opens the door to the guest room. "I'll see you in the morning. Sleep well, baby." And he closes the door behind him.

It's all I can do not to slide down the wall and settle in a puddle on the floor, but I manage to open the door to my room and go inside, grateful that at least he didn't say anything about my behaviour at the club, or the things we said in the taxi… I'd have been mortified. But maybe he worked that out…

I'm awoken by someone ringing the doorbell and the sound of Todd's voice, and I check the time… It's just gone ten o'clock and I jump out of bed in shock, then sit down again, feeling a little light-headed. I've slept for over ten hours. I can't remember the last time I did that. I stand again, and go out into the hallway. Todd suddenly appears from the kitchen, looking gorgeous as ever.

"Good morning, sleepyhead," he says, smiling at me.

"Hello. Who was at the door?"

"It was for me," he says. "Nothing to worry about."

"Oh." That's odd. "Okay. How long have you been up?" I ask him, leaning back against the wall by my bedroom door.

"Since seven. I went for a run earlier. I left you a note in case you woke up, but you were still asleep when I got back."

"I feel guilty for sleeping in. I should be up… looking after you."

"Looking after me?" he says, smiling. "I'm a grown man, in case you haven't noticed. I live alone when I'm at home. I can look after myself."

"No. I mean, you're my guest."

"Oh… we're doing this again, are we? I'm not your guest. Your boss and my boss got together and decided you could provide me with somewhere to stay. I'm taking advantage of your hospitality. You don't have to do anything for me." He crosses the hallway towards me. "Well, except maybe…" he grins at me but leaves the sentence unfinished and that familiar heat flickers.

"What?" I may have only just woken up but, after last night, I'm in the mood for flirting with him already.

"I think you know what," he says, taking a few more steps.

"I must have forgotten." He's only a couple of inches from me now.

"So you'd like me to remind you?" His eyes have darkened, but I can't take mine away from his lips. I nod my head and he moves closer, although he doesn't touch me at all. "The one thing I want you to do," he says, his voice vibrating across my skin, "is to let me in. Let me show you how good we can be together, and let me make you safe and happy. I'd really like that… more than anything."

I let my head fall forward until it rests against his chest. "I'm so nearly there."

"I know, baby. I know." He cups my face in his hands and raises it, so we're looking at each other. We're not flirting anymore… not at all. This is serious. "I'll wait," he says. "You're worth it."

"You don't know that."

"Yeah. I do." He leans forward and gently kisses my cheek. "I do," he whispers, and then he lets me go and stands back, staring down at me. "And in the meantime," he says, "I'll do my best to make this weekend as easy on you as possible."

"Thank you." With everything that's happened lately, and my fears about the parties, and his kindness, I'm finding it quite hard not to cry.

He takes another step back. "Now, why don't you shower and I'll make you a coffee and some breakfast, and we can pack? I wasn't sure what to take... apart from my tux, of course. What's Sunday all about?" He smiles down at me and I'm grateful to him for breaking the tension... I was in danger of breaking myself just then... and I think he knew it.

I cough to clear the lump in my throat. "They're planning a barbecue, if the weather holds."

"Smart-casual. Not jeans, I'm guessing."

"You've obviously met my mother already."

"Call it a lucky guess," he says. "You go shower. I'll fix you some toast."

We've both packed. I've loaned Todd a small holdall, and used another myself and we've put my long dress and his tux in the suit carrier the dry cleaners brought his tux back in. At least it'll all fit in the car. We had a late lunch and, being as it's gone three o'clock, I suppose we'd better leave.

"C'mon," he says, picking up the bags from the hallway. "We can't put it off any longer."

"I know."

I lock the door behind us and we go down in the lift and out of the back entrance.

"What the hell?" I say. "Who's parked that there?"

Someone has parked a black Mercedes convertible in front of my car, blocking us in. I know I don't want to go to my parents' house, but this could take hours to sort out and get towed away... and Ellie will give me hell for being late.

"That would be me," Todd says and I flip my head around to face him. He's smiling at me. "Well, not technically me. The guy from the car rental company left it there... but I told him to. That was who called around this morning. You didn't actually think I was going to sit in your car for an hour and a half, did you? I'd have been incapable of walking properly by the time we arrived... If you were looking for bragging rights over your sister, as you put it, that wouldn't really have helped."

"You hired a car?"

"Yes." He pulls a key from his pocket and presses a button to open the doors. "Are you mad at me?" he asks.

"Mad?"

"Angry…"

"No. I'm not angry." I think it's sweet of him. "But who's driving?" I ask him.

"Me," he says, opening the boot and putting in the holdalls. He lays the suit carrier on the tiny back seat, then opens the passenger door and waits for me. I walk over to him.

"So you've driven a right-hand drive car on the left-hand side of the road before, have you? In central London?" I ask him. He takes my hand and lowers me into the seat, closes the door and walks around to the driver's side, getting in beside me.

"No," he says, a grin forming on his lips. He starts the car and revs the engine a few times. "But it'll be fun. I mean, how hard can it be?"

"Oh, dear God." I put my head in my hands as he selects 'drive' and pulls away smoothly.

"See, it's easy."

"We're in the car park, Todd." He gets to the entrance to the flats and drives out into the road, the right way, thank goodness. "Why didn't you get it in my name?" I ask him.

"Well, a couple of reasons." He checks the mirrors and speeds up a little. "Firstly, I did this late last night. You'd gone to bed and I didn't want to disturb you to get all your details. Secondly, I felt like driving… it's something I enjoy doing. Thirdly, I'm a firm believer that we should live a little. I've never done this before – so why not try it? And finally… I wanted to surprise you."

"You've managed that," I tell him.

"Good surprise?" he asks, glancing at me.

"I'll tell you when we get there in one piece."

We stop at red lights. "Trust me," he says, looking at me. "We'll get there in one piece. I'd never do anything to put you at risk."

Once we're on the A3 and have got beyond Guildford, which is always busy, the traffic clears a bit and I feel more relaxed. Todd's very at ease behind the wheel.

"I meant to say to you earlier," he says, glancing at me. "We should take off the wedding rings, don't you think? We don't want your parents to think we eloped and got married without you even telling them."

"Oh heck. I'd forgotten all about that." I take mine off. Todd does the same and I take them both and put them in the pocket of my jeans. "That was close."

"What am I supposed to be this weekend?" he asks.

"How do you mean?"

"Well, I'm not your husband any more, sadly. Not until Monday, anyway. So what am I?"

"Um… my boyfriend?" I look at him out of the corner of my eye.

"You don't sound too certain."

"Only because I don't know if you want to be my boyfriend."

"Baby," he says, seriously, "I know I've been your husband for nearly a week, so this is gonna sound weird, but I'd be honoured to be your boyfriend." He pauses. "I've never been *anyone's* boyfriend before, but you know it's what I want, more than anything." I can feel myself blushing at the sincerity of his voice, and his words. "And what kind of boyfriend would you like me to be?" he continues, lightening the tone. "You get to choose… I'm undercover, so I can be anything you want."

And there it is. My worst fear – or at least one of them – that this is all an act; that none of it's real for him.

He glances across at me. "Hey, what's wrong?" he says. I shake my head, because I can't speak. I can't tell him how scared I am that this is all just a big fake as far as he's concerned. He reaches over and places his hand gently on my leg. "Holly, what I meant was, what kind of boyfriend do you want me to be in front of your sister and your parents, and their friends? For them, I can put on an act, if you want me to, but with you…" he pauses for a moment, "with you, I can't do that… well, except at the club, but that's the job."

Oh God, he saw right through me. I swallow hard. "I want you to be yourself."

"That's what I just explained, or tried to, anyway. I'm always myself with you—"

"I mean, all the time."

"You want the real me?" he asks. "And you want them to see that too?"

"Yes, I do." I really do.

He grins, and gives my thigh a squeeze. "You got it, baby." Then he checks the mirror, pulls out into the fast lane and floors the accelerator.

Chapter Ten

∽

Todd

It's a great car. With the windows up, it didn't even mess up Holly's hair.
She looks beautiful when we arrive her parents' house… or should I say,
her parents' mansion. It's huge, very elegant and reeks of money. I had
no idea Holly came from this kind of background.

"How many rooms are there?" I ask, driving slowly down the long,
tree-lined driveway.

"Nine bedrooms in the main house, plus there are two in the
annex… I don't know how many rooms in total though," she says, as
though everyone lives in a house like this. "Just park anywhere," she
adds as we get into the courtyard. There are so many cars parked out
front, I just pull up next to one – a Jaguar – and hop out, going around
to Holly's side and opening her door.

"Holly?" I hear a voice behind me and turn. A woman, probably in
her mid-fifties is approaching us. "Is that you? We thought you'd got
lost." I help Holly from the car.

"Yes, it's me, mother." Holly sounds almost bored. It's not a tone of
voice I've heard her use before. I close the door and hang back a little,
leaning on the car and watching Holly and her mother embrace stiffly.
This woman is what I would call primped. Her brown hair is swept back
in a tight bun behind her head; her make-up is perfect; the cream
colored suit she's wearing fits her figure and, I imagine, cost a fortune.

She's looking at me over Holly's shoulder.

"And who have you brought with you?" she asks, plastering a fake smile on her face.

Holly turns and beckons me forward. I push myself off the car and approach them. "This is my boyfriend," she says. God, that sounds good and I can't help my genuine smile as I offer my hand to her mother.

"Pleasure to meet you, Mrs King," I say.

"Yes," she says absently. *Well, that's a different response.* "An American." I wonder if she could have said that with any more distaste. Holly looks at me, her face suffused with embarrassment, but I smile and shrug, and head back to the car to collect our bags. I've just popped the trunk open, when I hear another voice from behind me.

"About time," it says. I don't even have to turn, or be introduced to know this is Holly's sister. I recognize her voice, and her tone, from her telephone message. "I told you to be here this afternoon," she's saying. "It's nearly evening now."

"It's only just gone five," Holly replies. "We got held up at Guildford."

"Then you should have allowed for it. You know it's always busy there. You're the last of the overnight guests to arrive. How does that look?" Her sister isn't going to let it rest. I haul the bags from the trunk and grab the suit carrier off the back seat before turning to face them. "You'll only just have time to change before the party now. I was about to go up myself... The other guests are arriving at sev—"

She stops talking mid-word when she notices me, and her mouth drops open, in an almost cartoonish fashion. It's hard not to smirk, but I manage it. In terms of build and coloring, she's very similar to Holly, but other than that, they're quite different. Where Holly's eyes are warm and sparkling, there's a cold conceit to Ellie's, like she's judging whatever's before her, and finds it wanting. She's got higher cheekbones and thinner lips, which are painted bright red to match her taloned nails. Her pale blue designer-looking dress tells me she doesn't mind being uncomfortable, as long as she can let people know she can afford to buy whatever she likes. Personally, I prefer Holly's faded jeans, white blouse and black leather biker jacket... and her full smile, which seemed to fade as we drove down here and disappeared completely when we pulled into the driveway.

"Who's this?" her sister asks, the tone of her voice changing completely. The shrewish whine has been replaced by a throaty purr, which makes the hair on the back of my neck stand on end. I don't think I've ever reacted in quite this way to any woman before in my life... or to any person, male or female, come to that. Pretty much every nerve in my body is telling me to grab hold of Holly, get back in the car and get the hell out of here. Her sister is trouble... big trouble.

I move forward, until I'm next to Holly again.

"This is your sister's latest boyfriend," her mother explains, and I can't fail to pick up the word 'latest'. "He's an American." She turns back to Holly, and continues, "But I don't think you introduced him properly did you, dear? You didn't tell me his name."

"Sorry... This is Todd Russell," Holly says and turns to look up at me. "Todd, you've met my mother. And this..." She faces her sister. "This is my sister, Eleanor."

"Ellie," her sister corrects, taking a step toward me.

"Hi," I say, but make no attempt to approach her, or shake hands. She falters, and decides to stay where she is.

Mrs King looks at Holly. "I wasn't expecting you to bring anyone," she says. "Not this soon after... well, you know. All the rooms have been allocated already, so you'll have to share. Still, I'm sure you'll be fine with that." *Excuse me?* I open my mouth to defend Holly.

"What about the annex?" Ellie asks before I can say anything. "Todd could sleep in there, couldn't he?"

"No," her mother replies. "We're having it decorated. Don't you remember? I told you all about it."

"But we can make room for him over there, surely?" She's persistent. What's that about?

"No, Ellie. The decorators have left all their equipment lying around. There are dust sheets over everything. It's not possible."

"Oh." She deflates.

"We'll be fine sharing," Holly says. We'll be better than fine. "I assume we're in my old room?"

"Yes, dear."

"Lead the way," I say to her. I desperately want to get away from these two women. They're bad news.

Holly takes me across the courtyard and through the wide front door. I assume her mother and sister are still behind us, probably talking about her... and me. The hall is not a disappointment. It's double height and has a stone floor and walls. There's a big fireplace on one side and a circular table in the centre, with a flower arrangement in the middle. We turn toward the massive staircase, just as a man appears at the top, holding the hand of a child, I'd say roughly three years old.

"Hello, Holly," the man calls down. "I didn't know you'd arrived."

"Hi, James," she says. "We just got here. And how's my best nephew?" The little boy lets go of the man and comes trotting down the stairs and runs up to her. She kneels and hugs him tight, and he puts his arms around her neck, planting a wet kiss on her cheek.

"Hello, Aunty Holly," he says.

"Hello, Oliver."

The man joins us just as Holly stands up, her hand on Oliver's head.

"This is my boyfriend, Todd," she says, turning to me. "And this is my brother-in-law, James." He holds out a hand and I drop one of the bags to shake.

"Nice to meet you," he says. He's probably around five feet eleven tall, good looking, with salt and pepper hair, I'd guess around forty to forty-five. I'm very confused now. I didn't know Holly had another sister, but then I'm coming to realize I don't know much about Holly's background at all.

"You too," I reply.

"Welcome to the madhouse," he adds. "We were just looking for mummy, weren't we, Oliver?" The little boy nods his head.

"She's outside with mum," Holly replies, nodding toward the front door. Holy fuck... Ellie's married? She's got a kid. I revise my earlier assessment. She's more than trouble. She's certifiable. "I'm just going to take Todd up to our room," she says. "We'll be back down later."

"I'd take your time," James calls, leading Oliver out the front door. "Come down fashionably late. I think you two could make quite an entrance." He turns and grins. I like him… Why the poor guy married Ellie is beyond me.

I pick up the bags again just as Holly grabs me by my jacket and pulls me toward the staircase. She runs up, so I take the steps two at a time to keep up with her and, at the top, we turn to the left and into a broad oak-paneled hallway, with five doors coming off of it. We go along to the last one on the right and Holly opens it, passing through and holding it open for me.

"She's married?" I say as soon as she closes the door.

"Yes."

"And she's got a child?" I drop the bags on the floor, standing right in front of her, my hands resting on her hips.

"Yes."

"And she slept with your ex?"

"Yes."

"I take it her husband doesn't know?"

"None of them know."

"You didn't tell them?"

"No. Well, I told them Jason cheated and that I'd thrown him out, but not that he cheated with Ellie."

"Why not?"

"You've seen them, Todd. Oliver and James, I mean. They're lovely. I can't be the one who breaks them up."

I pull her into my arms. "You wouldn't be. She did that."

"I still can't do it." She leans back and looks up at me. "And neither can you. Whatever happens, you have to keep my secret… Promise me?"

I stare down at her. "Okay," I say.

"Say it."

"I promise I'll keep your secret, even though I think your loyalty is seriously misplaced. James is probably better off without her, you know that, don't you?"

"And Oliver? Is he better off without his mother? Or without his father? I can't do it, Todd." She rests her forehead on my chest and I stroke her hair.

"Okay." We stand still for a while, until she pulls away and walks over to the bed, flopping down on it and lying back, staring up at the ceiling.

"Do you think that could have gone any worse?" she asks.

"Probably, but don't worry about it. We've got an entire weekend. I'm sure there's a helluva lot more ways we can screw up yet."

"I apologize for my mother," she says, sitting up again and looking at me. "She was awful to you. Anyone would have thought being American was a disease."

I laugh and look around the room. It's large, decorated in different shades of green and cream, with two windows, a small one looking over a swimming pool, and a wider one with a view over the gardens, which are immaculate. There's a couch under the bigger window, with dark green and cream throws. The four poster bed is set on a raised platform and rest of the furniture is oak, and looks old. "Nice room," I say. It's an understatement… a big one. "I had no idea you came from this, Holly."

"Does it make a difference?"

I go and sit beside her. "To how I feel about you? No." Is that too much of a hint?

She leans into me. "Good… Because if you run out on me now, and leave me to do this by myself, I'll never forgive you."

I hold my hand on my heart, like I'm swearing an oath. "I promise to stay here with you… and if I can't, I promise to take you with me when I run away." She laughs.

"That's better," I tell her. "You should laugh more often when we're here. It differentiates you from your sister. And speaking of your sister, why was she so keen to get me into the annex?" I ask. "Because that was weird… And what was with that comment your mom made about you being okay sharing a room with me? That was not a very nice thing to say. She was implying you sleep around, wasn't she? Or did I misinterpret that?"

She leans forward, putting her head in her hands. "No, that was her implication, and it's kind of connected with the annex," she says.

Wait a second... I feel a cold chill creep down my spine. Holly's maintained all along that Jason is the only guy she's been with... but now I'm starting to wonder, especially after the way her mom introduced me to Ellie as Holly's 'latest' boyfriend. "Holly..." I keep my voice quiet, and low, "is there something you're not telling me?" I don't care how many guys she's slept with – I can hardly judge – but I don't like the idea that she's lied to me.

"No." She turns and looks at me. "I've been completely honest with you about my past. But they'll try and have you believe otherwise."

"Can you explain?" I ask her. "Because right now, I'm confused."

She lies back down again and I go with her, so we're side by side, both looking up at the ceiling. I take her hand in mine, entwining our fingers and giving her a light squeeze.

"About six years ago," she says, "Ellie and James got engaged and my parents threw them a big party here. Ellie worked for a PR company in London at the time, and James was – well he is – something in the City. Anyway, a few of their work-mates came to the party and there was one guy in particular... Tim, his name was and he worked with Ellie. He was her boss, I think, but I'm not entirely sure. I didn't really pay much attention. As far as I knew, he was staying over in the annex and that was that. I got up the next morning, slightly hungover, and went downstairs and all hell broke loose. My mother and Ellie were waiting for me in the kitchen and accused me of spending the night with Tim... lowering the tone of the party, being disreputable... you name it, they threw it at me. It seemed my mother hadn't slept well and had gone into her bathroom in the early hours. She'd looked out of the window and, without her contact lenses in, had seen a figure creeping back to the house from the annex. She'd – quite rightly – thought it was Ellie and had confronted her, but Ellie had lied and said it wasn't her, it was me, and told my mother she'd mistaken the two of us. My mother believed her, and I was painted as the loose woman of the family... It's a badge that's stuck ever since."

"And Ellie wanted me in the annex...?"

"I guess so she could repeat the experience she had with Tim, and probably countless other men at different parties over the years. Even if you don't fall for her charms…"

"Which I'm never going to," I interrupt.

She hesitates and I wonder for a moment if she doesn't believe me. "Either way," she continues, "if you'd been sleeping over there, she'd have found a way to sow seeds of doubt in my mind as to what might have gone on between you, in the hope of causing trouble between us, maybe breaking us up… Not that she could break us up, being as we're not together in reality, but you get what I mean."

I turn onto my side and prop myself up on one elbow, looking down at her.

Aren't we together? I thought we kinda were… but I guess I'm the only one who's already on that page. She still needs to catch up with me, and I guess I have to help her do that… especially while we're here. There must be so many reminders.

"Don't doubt me, Holly," I tell her gently. "Your sister leaves me cold."

"I saw the look on her face. She's interested in you, and she's tenacious, Todd. She won't give up."

"Then she's gonna be disappointed."

She sighs deeply. "I'm sorry about all this," she says. "I'm afraid my family are showing themselves up."

"Don't worry about it. That's what I meant when I said about choosing your friends."

"Even they might prove difficult tonight… and tomorrow."

"Your friends?"

"They're not my friends; they're my parents' friends… well, mainly my mother's. And Ellie's."

"And they'll be difficult because…?"

"The few of my dad's friends who're actually here will be fine, although they can get a little boring when it comes to golf. But my mother's friends… They'll probably keep mentioning Jason, and they won't worry about doing it in front of you."

"Why?"

"We were together quite a while. People expected us to get married. My mother had virtually bought the dress, booked the reception, and ordered the flowers, even though we were never actually engaged. I'm sure she'd discussed it among her friends and I think they'll be surprised…"

"That you're here with someone else so soon…?"

"Something like that. I mean, I know you're not my real boyfriend or anything, and I know you're faking our relationship for their benefit, and mine…"

"I'm not faking, Holly." She needs to know this… she may not be there yet, but I think she needs to know that I am. "I'm waiting for it to be a reality. And I'll wait as long as I have to for you. You wanted the real me, and that's what you're getting… I don't care about your mother's friends, or anyone else for that matter," I tell her. "I'm not interested in their opinions of me, or you, or your ex." I run the back of my finger down the side of her face. "The only person whose opinion matters is you. I want *you* to be over Jason. *They* can pine for his presence as much as they like. I couldn't care less."

"Thank you for saying that," she says, closing her eyes and leaning into my touch. "It's just… it might be difficult for you, having to hear about how wonderful he was, when you know the truth."

I kneel up next to her, and pull her up so she's facing me. "See these?" I say to her pointing to my shoulders.

"Yes." She looks confused.

"They're kinda broad."

She smiles. "Yes, they are."

"They can take it."

At least I hope they can.

Holly

"What's happening tonight?" Todd asks me, getting off the bed and going over to the window.

"I'm not entirely sure. Ellie's been in charge of organising a lot of it. She's booked a DJ and the food's being catered by a local company. It's a buffet, thank goodness, or I'm sure she'd find some way of being seated next to you."

He turns. "And I'd find some way of ignoring her."

"For an entire meal?"

"For an entire lifetime, if necessary. The gardens are pretty."

"I'll show you around them tomorrow. It'll give us an excuse to escape from the barbecue." I check my watch. "If we're due downstairs by seven, I suppose we'd better start getting ready. We've only got just over an hour."

"How do you want to do this?" he asks. "We hadn't anticipated sharing a room, had we?"

"I can change in the bathroom," I say. "It's just through there." I point to the door in the corner of the room.

"No. You change out here. Do you want to shower first?"

"That probably makes sense. Then you can have the bathroom to yourself."

"Okay. I'll wait out here."

I take off my jacket and go into the ensuite. There are two fluffy white towels on the heated rail. I'll need both of those – one for my hair. I go back out to the bedroom.

"Is something wrong?" Todd asks. He's sitting on the sofa by the window and stands as I re-enter the room.

"We need more towels," I say and go out into the hallway and along to the cupboard where they're stored. I take two, just in case, and return to him. "I won't be long."

I'm not. The shower isn't as good as the one in my flat, so I don't hang around to enjoy it. I come out into the bedroom, with one towel wrapped around me, under my arms; the other in a turban on my head. I'm carrying my clothes and Todd stands again.

"I'm gonna take my shower," he says, his lips twitching upwards. "It'll be a cold one."

I can feel myself blushing as he passes me and goes into the en-suite, closing the door behind him. I pull myself together and do my make-up first, then dry my hair, using a little more mousse than normal to give it more curl and body. I've just turned off the hairdryer when I hear a knocking coming from the bathroom. I go over and open the door, my breath hitching as I take in the sight before me. He's wrapped a towel low around his hips, water is dripping down his toned chest and he's leaning against the doorframe, looking sexy as hell. "Is something the matter?" I manage to whisper.

"Yeah… I forgot my clothes," he says. "You distracted me when I was on my way in here, and I didn't want to come out there unannounced, in case you weren't wearing anything. I didn't want to have to take another cold shower. Although you're still not dressed, so…" His eyes move down my body and his smile makes everything below my waist liquefy. I swallow hard and stand to one side so he can pass me, and he comes into the bedroom. He opens the suit carrier and takes out his tux, then goes to his holdall and takes what he needs from there, and goes back into the bathroom. "Call me when you're dressed," he says, "I can't do this again," and he closes the door, and I hear the shower turn back on. I'm not sure what he's doing, but time's passing; I need to get on.

I cover my hair with spray wax and tease it into a styled messy look. Now all I've really got left to do, is put on my underwear and dress. I open my holdall and delve inside to find a thong. I brought a really nice, comfortable black one to wear tonight. It's by Amulet, which makes me smile. It has a completely see-through mesh panel at the front, with lace edging and tiny bows. I undo the towel, letting it fall to the floor, then pull on the thong, adjusting it, and stand in front of the full length mirror next to the wardrobe. It's very sexy – even I have to admit that. I know it would look a lot nicer on pretty much anyone else, but I really do enjoy wearing underwear like this. It makes me feel better about myself. I wonder if Todd's friends know their products have that effect?

As I stand, looking at myself, I hear the water in the bathroom being turned off again and I wonder if Todd really needed a cold shower… the thought makes me blush as I imagine his reaction if he were to come through the bathroom door right now and see me standing here like this. I wonder if he'd go back into the bathroom again, or if he'd come to me, pick me up, carry me to the bed, lay me down, hold my hands above my head, like he did before, and take me. Oh God… In the mirror, I can see my nipples have hardened at the thought. I need to calm down and get dressed, just in case he really does come out of the bathroom. I know he said I should call him, but what if he forgets? I'd be mortified if he caught me standing here virtually naked, flushed and fairly obviously aroused.

I turn and take my dress from its hanger and step into it, doing up the side zip. I don't often wear a bra when I'm not at work, but it's not possible anyway with this dress. It's strapless and the back is far too low. The navy blue bodice is embroidered and beaded, and leads down to a straight, fairly tight, floor-length skirt, with a split at the side which comes up to the middle of my thigh. I'm not wearing tights, because my legs are still quite tanned from my holiday.

"I'm decent!" I call to Todd. I've still got my shoes to put on, but there's no need for him to wait around in the bathroom any longer.

"That was quick," he replies from the other side of the door. "Be there in a minute."

I sit on the edge of the sofa and put on my shoes. They're high-heeled, strappy blue sandals and I've got a matching clutch bag, which I throw onto the bed. I stand, once more, in front of the mirror, feeling considerably calmer than I did a moment ago. I'm not wearing a designer outfit – it came from a high street store – and the whole thing cost less than Ellie would spend on a manicure, but it's comfortable. No doubt she'll be wearing some eye-wateringly expensive concoction tonight, designed to draw everyone's attention to her… and that's fine by me.

I go over to the bed and start folding my clothes, and as I shake out my jeans, the wedding rings fall out onto the floor. I bend and pick them up, holding them in my hand. We can't afford to lose these. I'm still holding onto them when Todd comes out of the bathroom.

"Jeez, Holly. What are you trying to do to me?" he says.

He throws his clothes on the bed alongside mine and stands behind me, his hands resting gently on my hips.

"I'm not trying to do anything to you." *Although I'm not sure what might have happened if you'd been five minutes quicker.*

"Well, there's a lot of skin on show back here," he says. "And I don't have time for a third cold shower now."

I turn to face him. "You really had two cold showers?"

"Yeah." He looks down at the front of my dress and sighs. "They were necessary." He lets me go and runs his fingers through his still-damp hair. "You look… beautiful."

I can feel myself blushing. "Do you practice saying things like that?" I ask him, because – as ever – I'm embarrassed by his compliments, I genuinely have no idea why he says things like that, and I want to divert his attention away from me.

He looks confused, and a little hurt, I think. "No, Holly," he says, his voice serious. He puts his hands on my shoulders. "None of this is rehearsed." He moves a little closer. "But you clearly have no idea how to take a compliment, do you?" I don't respond. "Do you?" he repeats and I shake my head. "Well, you just need to say 'thank you'…"

He makes it sound so easy… it isn't. "Thank you," I mumble.

"You're welcome. Now get used to it."

I'd really rather not.

"I need to put these somewhere safe," I tell him, trying another diversion and opening my clenched hand to reveal the wedding rings. "They fell out of my jeans when I was folding them."

"Do you want me to take them?" he offers.

"My clutch bag has a zipped pocket," I suggest. "That would do for now, and then we can put them back on when we get home."

"Okay."

I pick up my bag from the bed and put the rings inside, zipping up the pocket to keep them safe, ready for when we become Mr and Mrs Sanders again.

"We should probably go down." I say, and I'm unable to keep the disappointment out of my voice. "It's already gone seven."

"Must we? You sure we can't have our own party up here?" He smirks.

"Don't tempt me." And it is tempting... very tempting, for all kinds of reasons.

He leans forward, and whispers, "I'm gonna do so much more than tempt you, Holly. This is me, tonight. All me. No Mr and Mrs Sanders; no club; no distractions; no job. Just me... and you." He takes my hands in his and kisses them gently, one at a time. "And no-one else... C'mon," he says, pulling me towards the door.

"Please don't be swayed by her games," I blurt out, my feet rooted to the spot.

He turns back to me and holds me in his arms. "Never."

"I know she'll try something, and I couldn't bear it, not again..."

"She can try, but nothing's gonna happen. You have to trust me."

If only it was that easy. "I want to. I really do."

"What's stopping you?" he asks.

"Memories. The sight of them together, being here with her... the past. All of it."

"I'm not your past, Holly. I'm not Jason... and I won't be tempted by your sister, or anyone else. Please believe me."

I really want to believe him... but getting those images of the two of them in my bed out of my head is easier said than done.

"Ready?" he asks.

"No, but we have to go."

"Trust me," he says. "This will be better than you think."

Chapter Eleven

Todd

We walk together down the hallway and back down the stairs. At the bottom, there are a few couples gathered, who seem to have just arrived and are being greeted by Holly's mother and a man I presume to be her father. To be honest, he looks every one of his sixty years. He's probably around five feet ten, with silver gray hair, steel rimmed glasses and looks like a little exercise wouldn't hurt.

"I'll introduce you to my dad," Holly says as we descend the stairs. He turns as we approach and breaks away from the couple he and his wife have been speaking to.

"Holly!" He seems genuinely pleased to see her, which surprises me, given the reception she received from her mom and sister.

"Dad." Her smile tells me the feeling's mutual.

She lets go of my hand and they hug. It's good to see that someone in this house is on her side… or at least it appears that way. "And who do we have here?" Mr King turns to me.

"This is my boyfriend, Todd Russell," Holly says and I step forward, holding out my hand.

He gives me a firm shake. "Good to meet you, sir."

"An American…" He's interested, rather than dismissive.

"Yes, Dad. An American."

"Whereabouts are you from?" he asks me.

"Boston, sir."

"Please, call me Alan." He smiles. "This party is making me feel old enough, without you calling me 'sir' as well. I went to Boston once," he continues, "just after I finished university... in 1978, I suppose it would have been. I stayed there for a few months in the end." He turns to Holly and lowers his voice. "It was before I met your mother." He looks back at me. "I had a great time." He winks at me. "Met the most incredible blonde..."

"Dad!" Holly cuts in.

He laughs and I join in. "I'm sorry, darling," he says. "Why don't you take Todd through. Drinks are in the small sitting room; food in the dining room and... well, you'll find the dancing by yourselves, I imagine." He turns to me again. "Pleasure to meet you, young man."

"Pleasure's mine, Alan." He smiles at me again and Holly takes my hand, leading me away.

"I like your dad," I whisper in her ear.

"So do I," she replies. "He kept me sane... when he was here." There's a hint of sadness in her voice, and I imagine her as a child growing up here in this enormous house, with the company of her cold mother and bitchy sister, longing for her dad to come back from his job and make everything better. Suddenly I feel very lucky that my folks were always there for me when I was younger, and my friends are there for me now. I put my arm around her shoulders and pull her close.

"I'm here now."

She looks up at me and a slight smile forms on her lips.

We enter into an enormous room which is devoid of furniture. The track currently blaring out is Madonna's *Vogue*. A bit retro... "This is normally the drawing room," Holly says, "but all the furniture's been moved out to make way for dancing." She points upwards, to where there's a balcony overlooking the room, with a DJ set up. "I hope you like music from the '80s and '90s," she adds.

"Not especially."

"Shame. Because that's all you'll be getting tonight."

"I can hardly wait."

"Let's get something to drink." She drags me across the room, and through a door in the far wall. This room is considerably smaller, although it's still bigger than my living room at home. A long table has been set up, running the length of one wall, behind which are four men dressed in white shirts and black bow ties. We go over and Holly asks for two glasses of champagne, which are promptly poured and handed to her, and she gives me one.

"Cheers," she says, clinking her glass against mine. She's so on edge, she's likely to fall over the precipice.

I lean down and whisper, "Relax," in her ear, but I'm not sure she even hears me… Her eyes are darting all over the room, which is filling up with guests. I know she's looking for Ellie.

"C'mon," I say, taking her hand. "Let's move out the way."

We go back into the drawing room, where a few people are now dancing.

"Do you dance?" she asks.

"Not if I can avoid it."

She smirks and turns her head, just a fraction, and her face falls. "Dear God, what isn't she wearing tonight?" I follow her gaze.

Ellie has just come into the room from the hall, and she looks as though she seriously expects either a drumroll, or that, at the very least, everyone should stop what they're doing and turn in her direction, and perhaps applaud. A few people do at least look and she laps up the attention. Her hair is longer than Holly's but she's wearing it up tonight. And her dress… Well, let's just say it leaves nothing to the imagination. It's bright red and has a plunging neckline that ends a good six inches below her breasts, just above the waistband, and then flows down to the floor. I hope to God she's stapled that thing to herself, because if she so much as turns around too fast, we're all going to get a good view of her assets. I'm sure she thinks she looks alluring. Personally, I think she looks trashy.

"She probably paid more than a month's salary for that dress," Holly says, just loud enough for me to hear above the music.

"Then she wasted her money."

"I think most of the men in here would disagree."

I look around the room, and sure enough, there are a lot of male eyes feasting on Ellie.

"More fool them."

The party's in full swing now. It's nearly nine-thirty and we've spent most of the evening talking with Alan, James and some of Alan's golfing buddies, in the dining room. These are definitely more my kind of people. I like James. He talks to Holly and me like he's genuinely interested in what we've got to say, which is fairly unusual around here. It turns out he studied for a year at Harvard back in the late nineties – something Holly didn't know – and he shares some of his memories of that time with us. I get the sense he remembers it fondly.

"So, this is where you all are…" Ellie's voice cuts through the conversation, and she comes and stands between me and James, interrupting us, mid-sentence. I expect her to turn to her husband, but she doesn't; she faces me, cutting him out. "I hope you're having a good time," she says.

"Yes, thanks."

"Did you check on Ollie?" James asks her.

She huffs out a sigh and turns to him. "No," she replies. "I thought you were going to."

"I put him to bed," James says, his lips becoming a thin line. "I asked you—"

"I was just going to the bathroom," Holly puts in helpfully. "I can go and check on him, if you like."

"Would you?" James replies.

"It's no problem." She puts her hand in mine and gives me a tug. "We'll be back in a minute."

"You're going too?" Ellie says to me.

"Yes," Holly and I both reply at the same time and I lead her out of the room and into the drawing room. Cher's *Believe* is belting out now and a lot of people who are old enough to know better are attempting to dance. I pull Holly closer to me as we make our way through the room… there are too many flailing arms for it to be considered safe in here. Holly's hips move in time with the music, and for the first time in my life, I wish I did dance.

"She's not exactly subtle, is she?" I say, once we're in the relative peace of the entrance hall.

"No."

"Surely James notices… I mean, it's hard to miss."

"I don't know. Maybe he doesn't care. Or he loves her too much to rock the boat…"

"That's not my idea of love." It isn't. I hold onto her for another moment.

"You don't have to come upstairs with me," Holly says. "Just wait for me somewhere around here."

"Okay." I watch her climb the stairs, and I'll admit, I'm finding it real easy to forget her family and admire the view. Once she's turned the corner at the top, I move away and lean against the doorway into the drawing room.

"Hello." A sultry voice whispers against my neck and I tense. The woman sure didn't waste any time. She must've been following us, waiting to catch me on my own. I feel a hand snake up my arm and I pull away instinctively. "They're real then."

"What?"

"The muscles." *Is that really the best she can do?*

"Of course they're real." What does she think I am, inflatable, or something?

"You seem a little uneasy," she purrs. "Perhaps I can help you out with that."

"I wouldn't have thought so." I don't think my voice could be any colder.

"You'd be surprised what I can do."

"Not a lot surprises me."

"Why don't we go and find somewhere quiet and I'll show you…"

Not a chance. I go to move away, but she grabs my arm. "Let. Me. Go," I growl.

"Or what?" She simpers. She thinks I'm playing… flirting with her?

"Or I'll make you." I glare at her.

"Hmm… sounds like fun." A simpering smile forms on her lips. "What are you going to do? Take me over your knee?"

"No." That's a horrible thought.

"Oh, how odd…"

"What's odd?"

"I had you down as a man who likes his women to be submissive… and I'm happy to oblige. Well, I am for someone like you, anyway."

Submissive? She wouldn't know where to begin… I mean, not that I'm into the whole Dom/Sub thing… but, I have to admit, since meeting Holly, I've thought of little else other than all the different ways I could take her… that is, when I'm not thinking about keeping her safe, holding her in my arms, waking up beside her, sharing my life with her, and all that other new stuff I've never even contemplated before, but that I want more than anything now.

"So?" Ellie whispers. "What do you say?"

The best answer with women like Ellie is to say nothing that could come back and bite later, so I ignore her comments. "Get your hands off me. Now." I raise my voice just a little.

"Well, Holly really has got you wrapped around her little finger," she says, sulking a little and removing her hand from my arm at last. "Not that you'll be getting what you want – or need – from my little sister, I imagine. Still, don't worry about it. If you don't get bored, she soon will. It never did take her long to flit from one man to the next." She makes an annoying fluttering motion with her fingers. "I can't imagine Jason's side of the bed was even cold when she slipped you in between the sheets."

I lean down just a little, while still keeping a distance between us. "You should know," I say, loud enough for her to hear me clearly. "Being as you were helping him keep it warm." Her mouth drops open.

There's no sign of Holly yet, but I've just had an idea… something I think she might like. It's certainly going to give her 'bragging rights', if it works, and I push myself off the wall, leaving Ellie staring after me.

I cross the room, and go up the steps that lead to the balcony, where the DJ is standing behind his kit.

I tap him on the shoulder and he removes his headphones.

"Can I help, mate?"

"Yeah. Well, I hope you can. I've got a favor to ask… I need you to play a particular track for me… I'm… I'm trying to get a message across to someone." I think that's the best way of putting it.

"Okay. What's the track?"

I tell him and he smiles at me, giving me a knowing look. "You're here with the sexy dark haired woman in the blue dress, aren't you?"

"Yes." He's noticed her, and I can't say I blame him. So long as all he does is look, that's fine.

"Okay. I'll keep an eye out for you and I'll play it when I see the two of you together. The rest is up to you."

"Thanks."

He gives me a wink and puts his headphones back on as I go down the steps again. It dawns on me as I descend that if Matt or Luke were here, they'd be laughing their asses off. Especially Matt, considering how hard a time we've all given him for using song lyrics in his pursuit of Grace… And I'm about to do that right now – in public – to prove to Holly how much she means to me. Considering I don't really dance, this could go badly wrong. I must be insane. Or in love… But then I'm beginning to think maybe they're one and the same thing.

Holly is just coming in through the entrance, and I go straight to her.

"I couldn't find you," she says. I put my hands on her waist.

"Sorry. I wanted to speak to the DJ."

"Why?"

"I had a request."

She laughs, putting her hand to her mouth. "Really?" If she thinks that's surprising, she needs to wait and see what's gonna happen in a minute.

"Yeah. Oh… and your sister took advantage of your absence and came to see me." It's best she hears it from me.

Even in the dim light, I can see her skin pale. "What happened?"

"She just made a few comments about Jason. Nothing I couldn't handle."

"Did she try to…?"

"She made the offer, yeah. I told her I wasn't interested." Holly looks over her shoulder to where Ellie is still standing, glaring at us.

I glance up at the DJ and he gives me a 'thumbs up'. Once the current piece of music finishes, I know I'll have just over three minutes to either get the message across to Holly, or screw up royally, in front of around fifty, maybe sixty people… So, no pressure then. Out of the corner of my eye, I notice Alan, James and Holly's mom come into the room. Oh great… an even bigger audience. This just got better.

I vaguely know the track that's playing now. It hasn't got long left, and I can't blow this. I take Holly's hand and lead her out onto the dance floor. "What are you doing?" she asks as I turn her to face me. "I thought you said you didn't dance."

"I'm making an exception."

Holly

I think the track playing is by Whitney Houston. It's not really my thing and I'm fairly positive it's not Todd's either. He pulls me in close and we sway in time to the music, but I can tell he's not comfortable.

"We don't have to do this," I say to him.

"Wait," he replies.

"What for?"

"Just wait."

The track comes to a crescendo and ends, and there's a moment's pause. Then he smiles, and steps away, so I'm at arm's length, still holding his hand. What's he doing? I hear a dramatic introduction, but before I can register what's going on, I feel Todd tug me hard, back into his arms, right up against his solid chest, just as a woman sings 'Hold me, hold me…' and then he places one hand on my waist, the other in the small of my back, his feet either side of mine, our bodies pressed really close together, and he rotates our hips first one way, then the other, in a gloriously slow, sexy figure of eight. I move my arms around his neck and go with him. He's just using his body against mine, in the most sensual dance imaginable. The woman's now singing, 'Thrill me, thrill me…' Our lips are almost touching and I can feel his arousal pressing into me as he continues to roll our hips. 'Kiss me, Kiss me…' she sings and he moves back, just a little, looking down at me, his eyes piercing mine. The singer repeats the phrase, and he tilts his head slightly, and places his lips on mine, just gently, holding them there and continuing to move our bodies, as the song fades.

As it does, he slowly pulls away and I grab his shoulders, because if I don't, I think I might slide to the floor. He brings his arms around me and I'm vaguely aware that, while other couples have been dancing, a space has cleared in the area nearest to us. People are looking – no, they're staring… and among the faces is Ellie, her mouth open, her eyes wide. James is smiling… Oh God, when did my dad come in here? Did he just see Todd doing that with me? And my mother looks like she swallowed a lemon… whole. Seeing her expression, it's hard not to laugh. I look up at Todd and he smiles at me.

I assume he did that to show Ellie that she needs to back off. I really wish it had been about me, and not her, but it's a nice gesture anyway, and very sweet of him.

I keep my arms around his neck and hang on to him and, as the next piece of music starts, he just sways me in time with it, letting me rest against him. And we stay like that for a long, long time.

I'm already in my pyjamas, and in bed by the time Todd comes out of the bathroom wearing shorts… and nothing else.

"I didn't bring a t-shirt," he says. "Sorry… I wasn't expecting to share a bedroom with you."

"It's fine."

"I'll sleep on the couch."

"You'll never fit."

He looks at it and shrugs. "Well, the floor then."

"I think after everything that's happened in the last few days, we can safely share a bed."

He smirks. "You might think it's safe," he says, pulling back the duvet on his side. "I'm not so sure, but I'll try and behave myself."

I turn towards him as he settles down and pulls the covers back up. "Thank you for tonight. You made it bearable."

He looks a little crestfallen. "Only bearable?"

"Well, okay… that dance was a little more than bearable."

"Nah..." he says, grinning, "it was nothing." He turns to face me, his head resting on the pillow. "I hope I didn't embarrass you too much."

"I don't think anyone is ever going to look at me in quite the same way ever again."

"Well, I think that might be a good thing."

"I was surprised," I tell him. "I didn't have you down as someone who'd like that kind of music."

"I don't," he replies.

"But you seemed to know it so well. You knew when the beat was going to change, and everything."

"That's because it was a favourite of my parents." He lowers his eyes. "I was practically conceived to that piece of music."

I can't help but laugh out loud. "Seriously?"

"Yes. Well, not that version, obviously. That's a nineties cover. But my dad took my mom away for a long weekend when Vicky was two years old. She was a horrible toddler, evidently and my mom needed a break, so my grandmother took care of her while he took my mom to a place up in Vermont. They went out to a bar, heard that piece of music... and the way my dad told it to me, years and years later, they didn't make it back to the hotel. He found somewhere quiet and parked up... and one thing led to another."

"You're joking."

"No, I'm not. You're looking at the result. Anytime that song came on the radio, they'd go all dopey over each other. And when that version we danced to tonight came out, my mom liked it even more than the original. To be honest, I'm amazed they didn't have more kids."

"How on earth did you remember it, if you haven't heard it in so long?" He told me his dad died thirteen years ago. That's a long time to remember a song you don't even like.

He moves a little closer to me. It's hard not to be distracted... but I try to stay focused on what he's saying. "When my dad died," he says, "my mom didn't cope well, so I gave up my apartment and moved back in with her for about six months. For the first three months of that, she played that damn piece of music day and night, pretty much non stop. It drove me crazy, but I let her do it. I knew she needed to. She lay on her bed, listening to it, refusing to speak. It scared the hell out of me. But, in the end, that was how I knew she'd finally turned a corner… when putting on that track wasn't the first thing she did in the morning."

"It must have been so hard for you."

"Seeing her like that was the hardest thing I've ever done. She'd always been so strong… and she was broken, just completely broken."

"I meant, you were grieving too. You'd lost your father."

He looks at me, his eyes darkening a little. "Yeah. He was my hero, as well as my dad, but I had to hold all that in, in front of her, anyway. I could never let her see what I was going through."

"I suppose at least you had your sister to help… to share it with."

He laughs, but there's no humour behind it. "Vicky?" he says. "Help? No, she didn't help, or share. She came up to Boston for the funeral, made a big fuss, because she was pregnant at the time, and then went back home. When Ethan was born, nearly six months later, she called my mom and told her she couldn't handle it… the baby coming on top of dad's death was too much for her." He pauses, and takes a deep breath. "My mom sold up and moved down there."

"And you?"

"What about me?"

"Well, did no-one ask how you were? Whether you were coping?"

"Yeah. Matt did. He got me through it. He was there for me. Don't get me wrong, I love my mom, and I get it was hard for her… and for Vicky…"

"But?"

"It would've been nice if one of them had asked how I was, that's all."

"Well, I'm sorry you had to dance to a piece of music that brought back unhappy memories."

"Hey…" he says, reaching out and touching my cheek with his fingertips. "That was my choice. No-one made me do it." He smiles at me. "I wanted to." He leans a little closer and hesitates just for a moment before kissing me gently on my lips. It's a brief kiss and I don't have time to respond before he pulls away again. "I wanted to do that too."

I return his smile. "I suppose it's getting late. We should probably go to sleep." I'm not sure I want to. But I'm not sure about anything at the moment. There's part of me that's very tempted to kiss him back… and maybe, just maybe even see where that leads us. But I don't want that to happen here. And I want to be absolutely certain about my own feelings first. That's never going to happen while we're here… not with Ellie just down the hallway.

"Okay," he says. He looks as uncertain and, perhaps as disappointed as I feel.

"Sleep well."

"I seriously doubt it," he mutters, and turns onto his back.

Chapter Twelve

∞

Todd

I wake up with Holly's head resting on my chest, her hand low on my stomach, and one of her legs wrapped over mine. My arm is around her and her top has ridden up in the night, so my fingers are touching her bare skin, all of which makes it no surprise that I'm as hard as nails.

I don't want her to be embarrassed, so I ease myself out of the bed. She stirs, moans gently and turns over. The sounds she makes and the fact that the covers have been pushed down, revealing her barely covered ass, makes my cock twitch. I need to get out of here, before I forget I ever promised her I'd wait.

The shower is still set to cold, so I drop my shorts and step right in, turning it on. It works well, making me forget everything except the freezing needles puncturing my skin. I turn the heat up to wash, shave and shampoo my hair, then get out and towel myself dry, wrapping myself up before I leave the room, to find Holly's now up. She's bending over the holdall, fetching out her clothes… and at the sight of her, it seems all my good work in the cold shower was for nothing.

"Good morning," I say to her.

"Hi," she replies, standing and turning to face me. "You got up…" I'd like to think she's a little downhearted about that, but maybe that's wishful thinking.

"Yeah. I kinda had to. I needed another cold shower." Her eyes drop to the bulge in my towel. "Not that it did much good, it would seem."

She laughs. "Well, I'll get out of the way, shall I?"

I want to suggest she hangs around, but I don't and she takes her clothes with her into the bathroom.

Only once I've heard the shower turn on do I drop the towel to the floor and start getting dressed. I put on tan colored pants, and a white button-down shirt, with deck shoes, and no socks. As I roll up the sleeves of my shirt, I go over to the window and look outside. Beneath me, a team of men are setting up tables and chairs. These people don't do parties by halves, I'll say that.

While Holly finishes up in the shower, I pack the rest of our things, so we can be ready to leave later on this afternoon.

When I hear the door to the bathroom open, I turn and – yet again – she takes my breath away. I wonder if this will ever stop; if I'll ever get used to the effect she has on me every single time she walks into a room. Somehow I've got my doubts. She's wearing a pale pink sundress. The skirt flares out from her hips, to just above her knees, but for some reason, the top isn't sitting right.

"Could you zip me up?" she asks, looking shy. *That explains it.*

"Sure."

I go over to her and she turns… and it's all I can do not to let out a groan. The back of the dress is open, revealing perfect, smooth, soft skin from her shoulders down to just below her waist. And no bra… again. I've rarely known her to wear one and I really like that. I reach forward and notice my hand is shaking as I grasp the zipper and slowly pull it up, reluctantly concealing her. "You're all set," I manage to say, leaning forward and kissing her shoulder. She shivers. She actually shivers, then turns to face me again. "And you look lovely."

"Thank you." She blushes a little, then looks away, embarrassed, I think. She really is crap at taking a compliment, but at least she said 'thank you' this time, rather than questioning whether I meant what I said… that made me kinda mad last night. "I need to dry my hair and put on some make-up and we can go down for breakfast… unless you want to go on ahead without me?" *Hell, no.*

"No. I'll wait." I want to stay with her, ideally as close to her as possible. I don't want to face her family – or, more particularly, her sister – without Holly at my side; and I'd quite like to watch what she does. I sit on the couch as she applies her make-up. She just uses mascara on her eyes, a little blusher and some pale lipstick. To be honest, she doesn't really need any of those; she looks beautiful just as she is.

Then she puts some kind of mousse into her hands and runs it through her hair and, to my surprise, bends over, tipping her head upside down, while she blow-dries it, scrunching it up between her fingers at the same time. I'm naturally engrossed by the sight of her bent over in the way she is and the temptation to walk up behind her to see if I can distract her, is almost too much. But I'm fascinated by what she's doing. Her hair has gone from being fairly straight when it was wet, to exquisitely curly as it dries. She shuts off the hairdryer and, in one move, stands and throws her head back. She teases a few loose ends into place, then unplugs the hairdryer and packs it away.

"Is that natural?" I ask her.

"What?" She turns to face me.

"The curls."

"Oh… My hair has a slight curl. The mousse enhances it."

"And why do all of that upside down?"

"It gives it more body, evidently."

I stare at her. "Looks good." It does. She looks a little flushed, and real sexy… real fucking sexy.

I would say there are probably somewhere close to a hundred people here, scattered over the lawn.

"That was not my idea of a barbecue," I whisper to Holly. We've had lunch and, to escape her mother and sister, she's been taking me on the promised tour of the gardens. We've been gone for around an hour, I suppose and have just passed through an archway and into a more formal area, with boxed hedges on either side of us. We're walking hand-in-hand and are nearly back at the house, which is a shame. I've enjoyed the break from the crowd, and the time alone with her.

"What are you used to?"

"Back home, Matt and I would be arguing about how rare the steaks should be, Will and Luke might be in the kitchen making salads, and baking potatoes… or it might be the other way around. We tend to take it in turns. Grace, Megan and Jamie would be sitting on the deck drinking wine… except Megan doesn't drink and, at the moment Grace is breastfeeding, so they'd be having soda and Grace would be looking longingly at the wine… but that gives you a reasonable picture."

"So the men do all the cooking?"

"Mostly… at our barbecues anyway. We like to give the ladies a break."

"And whose house is this at?"

"Matt's, usually. He's got the biggest deck and the nicest garden. It leads down to a lake."

"It sounds lovely."

"It is, especially in the spring and summer, so we tend to hang out there when the weather's warmer, and then take it in turns the rest of the year."

We round a corner and we're back on the edge of the lawned area.

"There you are, Todd!" Ellie's voice carries a long way as she approaches out of the crowd. I could almost believe she was looking out for us… well, me it would seem, since she's ignoring Holly. Didn't she get the message last night? Judging from the hungry look in her eyes, it would appear not. Her inappropriately short dark red fitted dress would look more at home in the club than it does here and that thought brings a smile to my lips, which I have to check, in case she thinks it's for her benefit.

I feel Holly shrink into herself beside me, trying to pull her hand from mine. She has nothing left inside to fight her sister with; she's all in… and something snaps inside me. She needs to know how much I want her, not her damn sister; how gorgeous she is by comparison and how there's no need for her to surrender like this, because she's got nothing to fear. "I'm so done with this," I murmur and turn to her, bringing my hands up onto her cheeks. I lean forward and brush my lips against hers, just gently. And I honestly think I would have kept it gentle, if it hadn't

174

been for the slight moan Holly gave off as I stepped closer and held my lips against hers. That simple noise vibrates through my whole body, making every nerve quiver, and very slowly, I run my tongue along her lips. Her gasp gives me the opening I need to taste and explore her, to discover her. She's delightfully soft, sweet and fragrant and nothing else exists as our tongues twirl perfectly together; not the crowd behind me, nor her sister, nor the job, nor the club… not anything except her lips and mine, locked together.

Holly breaks away first and now she's looking at me, all doubtful – breathless yes – but definitely doubtful. And I want to hold her and kiss her again, to show her I meant every single second of that, and that I want to keep doing it every day for the rest of our lives. I really do…

"Everyone's looking," she whispers. She can see the crowd of people behind me.

"So what?"

"Well, I think you proved your point."

"Did I?" I'm not entirely sure I did. In fact, looking at the uncertainty in her eyes, I'm fairly damn sure I didn't.

"Judging from the look on Ellie's face, yes."

"I don't care about Ellie's face."

She snorts out a laugh. "You should. It's quite a picture." Her laugh brings a smile to my lips and I turn just slightly. She's right. Ellie's face is a picture… a picture of green-eyed resentment, anger and disgust. I turn back around again and lead Holly toward the house. "They're going to be talking about this for weeks," she sighs.

"Does it matter?"

"Yes." *Why?* I'm confused.

As we pass through the door, I pull her into my arms. "You asked me to be myself, Holly… I offered to be anyone you wanted in front of your family, but you said you wanted the real me… and that's what I just gave them…"

"I… I just don't like being talked about," she murmurs.

"Look at it this way: would you rather be talked about for being cheated on, or for being wanted… being kissed?"

"Being kissed." At least she answered that without hesitation. The difficulty is, she's not being specific as to whether she wants it to be me doing the kissing.

∽

Holly

His lips were soft, and hard at the same time. I've never been kissed like that before; with so much heat and passion, and tenderness, all at the same time. It was impossible not to respond, even though I knew he wasn't doing it for me. Well, he was… he was doing it to help me out with Ellie; to score points and to show her that he's not available to her and to keep away. So, I guess really, he was doing it for himself, as much as anything, so she'd let up in her pursuit. And it worked. I've never seen her look like that before – totally defeated, resentful and enraged, all together. But the point is, I wasn't about me. Just like everything else in my life, it was about Ellie… and that's what hurts. For as long as I can remember, all my life, it's always been about Ellie.

Now, I'd just really like to go home. Being here, this person I become when I'm with my mother and my sister, it isn't me, anymore than I'm Mrs Sanders, the woman who inhabits the club. But I think I even prefer being Mrs Sanders, at the club, to being who I am when I'm here.

"How soon can we leave?" Todd asks, his voice low and echoing my thoughts. We're sitting in the garden on one of the low walls, slightly apart from the main crowd of people. It's dusk and the trees surrounding the lawn have been decked with lights. In other circumstances, I'd say it looked like a fairy tale… except I don't believe in fairy tales.

"What's the time?" I ask and he checks his watch.

"Nearly seven-thirty."

"We could start saying our goodbyes now," I tell him. "It'll take us at least half an hour, probably longer to go around them all… and then we'll be home by about ten."

He stands and holds out his hand to me. "Let's go," he says.

It actually takes nearly an hour to go around all the various people and say goodbye and make small-talk for the umpteenth time. Ellie barely acknowledges our existence, but James and a very tired Ollie come with us to the car, along with dad, and James gives me a hug goodbye.

"You found a good man there," he whispers in my ear. "Much better than Jason ever was. Don't let him get away." I have to blink back the tears. If only he knew...

As he drives out onto the main road, Todd must have noticed me wiping my cheeks, even though I've turned my face toward the window, hoping the darkness will shield me from his view.

"Holly, what's happened?" he asks.

"Nothing."

He pulls over to the side of the road, but leaves the engine running. "Tell me," he urges.

"It's just something James said."

"What did he say?" He turns in his seat to face me and I hear the concern in his voice.

"He told me not to let you get away." I glance across at him.

"Then you should listen to the man, instead of crying." He's smiling.

"I'm crying... well, I'm trying not to cry, because it's made me realise that I don't have a hope, do I? James is right. I did let Jason get away. It'll be the same with you, won't it? I've been blaming Ellie for everything, telling myself she took Jason from me, when really it's entirely my own fault. It's my fault that he slept with her in the first place."

"And how the hell do you work all that out?"

"If I'd been enough for him... if I'd been *good* enough for him... he'd never have strayed."

"It's not your fault, Holly. It's his... and hers."

"But he wouldn't have wanted her in the first place if I'd been enough, would he? And it'll be the same with you. I know it will." I feel the tears trickle down my cheeks.

"Not all guys are like that, Holly," he says, and he puts the car into drive and takes off down the road again.

It's a long, silent ride home, but I appreciate the quiet after the last two days of noise and bustle; two days of feeling as inadequate as I usually do whenever I'm with my family… well, my mother and sister, anyway. Todd's made it tolerable – no, that's not fair. He's made it enjoyable in places, and special in others. The dance last night, the walk this afternoon, and that kiss… that was very special. He's made polite conversation all day, put up with my dad's boring golf friends and my mother's inquisitive tennis friends, without a word of complaint.

On the bright side, at least it's over with now and I don't have to see any of my family again until Christmas, unless I'm really lucky and they do what they did last year, and decide to go skiing for the festive season, which enables me to use work as an excuse not to go with them. Fingers crossed…

Todd parks the Mercedes behind my car at just after ten and climbs out, coming around to my side and opening the door. He offers his hand, which I take and he helps me from the car, before letting me go and fetching the bags from the boot. He doesn't make eye contact, but starts towards the apartment building. He's never done that before. We usually walk in together.

I catch up with him at the door, which he's holding open for me.

"Is something wrong?" I ask him as we get into the lift.

"No." *Could've fooled me.* There's an emotion I haven't seen before in his eyes. I'm not sure what it is, but I don't like it. Is he angry with me?

We ride up to my floor in silence and, once the lift door opens, ever the gentleman, he waits for me to exit first, and follows me to the door to my flat, which I open. As soon as we get inside I switch on the lights and he puts the bags down on the floor and turns to face me, that look still filling his eyes.

"Something *is* wrong," I whisper, slightly scared of what his reply might be.

"It's nothing." It clearly isn't nothing, but I get the feeling he's not going to talk about it. It's probably easier to change the subject… and I'm all for taking the easy option.

"I haven't thanked you."

"What for?" He runs his fingers through his hair, sounding confused and impatient, I think. I guess maybe he did want to talk about whatever it is that's annoyed him. Well, he only had to say…

"The weekend," I continue, quietly. "You made it special."

He's taken aback by my reply. "Special?" he whispers and his eyes clear a little, and I see the warmth of a more familiar Todd slowly returning. Thank God for that.

"Yes."

"How special?" His lips twitch slightly, grabbing my attention, as he comes to stand in front of me.

"Very."

"Very," he repeats softly, and he brushes his hand against my cheek. "Very special indeed." He looks into my eyes and leans forward until his lips touch mine. He holds them there for a second, and then his hands are on my waist and he's walking me backwards until I feel the wall behind me. He shifts his feet to be closer to mine, his hips flexing so I can feel his arousal hard against me. He brings his hands up, his fingers in my hair, his tongue delving deeper into my mouth. He intensifies the kiss and I respond to his touch, his tongue, his lips. I move my arms up around his neck, and I hear a growl in his throat which echoes through my body and settles at the pit of my stomach, where it's joined by the aching awareness that I want him… right here, right now. I don't want to think, or feel, or analyse. I don't want to mull things over… and I don't want to wait. I just want him.

Chapter Thirteen

Todd

I don't care that she hasn't told me she's over him. I don't care that she hasn't told me she wants me, or that she trusts me. I don't care that we haven't got anything straight between us. I don't even care that she hurt me… she really hurt me, and she made me a little mad, when she started talking about not being good enough for him… or me. Why does she have to assume I'll behave like him at every goddamn turn? I know we should probably talk that through… but, like I say, I don't care.

What I do care about is that her lips feel incredible, her tongue is playing with mine, her arms are around my neck, my fingers are knotted in her hair, her breasts are crushed against my chest, and… oh, fuck… she just moaned into my mouth.

I move my hands around behind her to the zipper of her dress and lower it, feeling her bare skin beneath my touch. She gasps and I feel her arms come down and her hands tugging at my shirt, pulling it from the waistband of my pants. She fumbles with the buttons, undoes one, then groans and wrenches the shirt open. I'm vaguely aware of buttons pinging off the walls as she slips my shirt down my arms and I release her, just for a second to throw it to the floor. Then I pull the straps of her dress from her shoulders and she leans back a little, to shrug it off. I push it down below her waist and it drops to her feet. For a moment, I stand back and just look. She's wearing a white lace thong, which conceals pretty much nothing and her breasts are rounded and firm, her nipples already proud pink peaks waiting for my touch. I lean down and capture one between my teeth, biting gently and she holds my head in place, letting out a low cry. I kiss my way back up her neck and take her mouth again, reaching around and cupping her ass in my hands, her silky soft skin molding to my touch.

I can feel her hands between us, struggling with my belt, so I let go of her and undo it, and the button behind, and she takes over with the zipper, lowering it and pushing down my pants. Without breaking the kiss, I kick off my shoes, then step free of my clothes.

I need to be inside her. Now.

"Where?" I whisper into her mouth.

"Bedroom," she breathes back.

"Which one?" She has to choose. She's the one with the memories of this place.

"I don't care." Good. That's promising. At least I think it is, it means… no, I'm not gonna think about that, not right now.

We're right by the door to my room, so I open it, my mouth still on hers, and I lift her into my arms. She instinctively wraps her legs around my waist – *fuck, that feels good* – and I carry her into the room, laying her down on the bed. Between the light from the hallway and the moonlight coming from outside, I can see her clearly, and she stares up at me, her eyes filled with heated want.

I'm out of my boxers in a second and she lowers her eyes to my cock, licking her parted lips as I kneel on the bed and push her legs apart with my hands. I pull aside the drenched scrap of lace which is doing a poor job of screening her from me, and I can't help but let out a gasp. Her shaved pussy is already glistening wet, and I run my finger up and down her folds, circling her clitoris repeatedly, until she's breathless and moaning loudly, her hips rising to meet my touch. "God, you're so wet, baby," I whisper and I move down a little, and slowly insert my middle two fingers inside her. She suddenly stills and quietens, like something's wrong, and I look up at her face.

"That was so good. Please touch me again… I was…" she murmurs, panting. "Stroke me, Todd… please. I can't. I can't…"

She can't communicate, that's for sure. "You can't come this way?" I think that's what she's trying to say. "You think the only way you can come is if I stimulate your clit?"

"No. Normally I can only come if *I* stimulate my clit... but I was close..." She closes her eyes, seemingly ashamed. *Why?* She's got nothing to be ashamed of... Jason, on the other hand... I smile to myself.

"Look at me, baby," I say. She opens her eyes, fixing them on mine and, without withdrawing my fingers, I move, so I'm kneeling alongside her. "Lift your legs a little, spread them wider," I murmur. She does, opening herself to me, and I lean down real close. In one move, I rip off her panties, tearing through the seams. "I'm gonna make you come so hard," I whisper, "and I'm not going to even touch your clit... not with my fingers, or my tongue, or my teeth. Hell, I'm not even gonna blow on it." She sucks in a breath and then, very slowly I circle my fingers inside her, resting my other hand low on her belly, applying just a little pressure right above her mound. "Relax," I tell her. And I start to make 'come hither' motions with my fingers, against the front wall of her vagina, while moving my hand up and down inside her. She moans, and bucks her hips into me, rocking her head back. I use my other hand to hold her still, as I find a steady rhythm and stick to it, not letting up. She writhes beneath me, squealing, groaning, and arching her back to get more of the sensations that I'm fairly sure are slowly starting to overwhelm her body.

"Todd..." She clasps my arm – the one that's holding her still – and looks at me, wide-eyed, breathless and just a little afraid, I think.

She may not be able to tell me she trusts me, but she's gonna have to show me she does, and put one hundred percent of her faith in me if this is gonna work... because I've got complete control of her body right now. "Don't be scared," I tell her. "Let it happen. Let it take you, baby. Trust me with this... and just let go."

And she does. She throws her head back and lets out a piercing scream as she tightens around my fingers. Her whole body convulses, shuddering and completely out of control, while I hold her steady, keeping up the movements inside her, as she comes all over my hand,

and the bed, her orgasm going on and on, relentlessly, until the spasms slowly start to subside, her breathing slows and she calms back down again, sighing quietly.

I give her a moment, but no longer, then withdraw my soaking fingers from her and move between her legs, parting them a little further. I place the head of my aching cock against her drenched entrance and, without taking my eyes from hers, I push deep inside her. She's lets out a loud gasp at the penetration of her swollen, sensitive core, and I still for a moment – just so I can get my brain around what I'm doing – and try to hold on.

"You're so tight," I mutter, bringing my hands down on either side of her head, my body raised above hers. I'm almost losing it, she's so tight… but every instinct I have is telling me to move, even if it is only slowly at first, pulling out and sliding back in, feeling her clenching around me. She lifts her legs up around my waist, letting me go deeper inside her with every stroke, right to the base of my cock.

"More," she whispers, "please, more, Todd… Harder…" and with those words, I'm gone. I grab her hands, holding them by her head, pinning her, and I give her what she wants. I start to pound into her, deep and fast, beads of sweat forming on my chest and back as I take her hard and make her mine.

Even in the haze of my own building orgasm, I sense a change in her breathing and she tightens around me, bucking against me and screaming out my name in her renewed ecstasy just before I explode, filling her over and over, pulsing into her, my whole body contracting as the built-up, agonizing wait and the pent-up love that I can't yet express bursts out of me. It overpowers me and I collapse to my elbows, just keeping my weight off of her. What's happening to me? It's never been like this. Ever. I can't take her in… she's too much.

Even as I begin to recover, I know I'm not done yet… I need more. I give myself a just few seconds to catch my breath, then raise myself off of her and kiss her neck with a feather-light touch, working my way down her body, stopping at her perfect, erect nipples, licking and capturing each one between my teeth and nipping them gently. Then

I move further down, across her flat stomach and lower, to her shaved, wet pussy. I lie between her legs, resting on my elbows and run my tongue along her swollen folds, swirling around her clitoris. Holly lets out a sigh, parting and raising her legs again, giving me easier access to her. I can see now that she's still wearing her white high heeled sandals and the thought of them wrapped around my waist a few minutes ago makes my cock twitch back to life. She reaches behind my head, holding it in place and rocking her hips as I flick my tongue across and around her, tasting her… and me. I swirl my tongue over and over her, sucking her hard nub into my mouth until she starts to moan more loudly, her climax approaching once again. Fuck, she's good. She's more than good. She's perfect. Why have I never known it could be like this? *Because you've never been in love before, that's why…* I increase the pace, the pressure, the intensity, as she tips over the edge, her legs clamping behind my head and I hear her cry out my name yet again, through breathless gasps.

Once she's calmed a little, I kneel back and slowly undo her sandals, flinging them, one by one, onto the floor, before taking each of her feet in my hands, and licking from her instep up her calves, and her thighs, to her core. I move back up, settling naturally in the cradle of her thighs and press my erect cock against her.

"Again?" she murmurs, heavy-lidded.

"Yeah… again." I stare down at her as I push inside her once more, taking it slower this time, enjoying the feel of her skin against mine, her soft wet flesh enveloping my entire length. Then I withdraw, almost all the way out, so just the tip of my cock is still inside, before pushing back into her. With every slow, repeated plunge, she lets out a groan, each one becoming louder, until her guttural cries fill the room. I don't increase the speed this time around. I keep it slow, steady, unremitting, taking her long and deep, ensuring that each stroke of my hard shaft rubs against her aroused clitoris.

She utters a stuttering breath. "I can't. Not again. It won't work… I'm too…"

I'm not listening. "Yeah, it will. Come on, baby." I swivel my hips as I enter her again and again and she stares into my eyes, just before hers flutter closed, and I watch as she finally grips me, sucking in a breath, and then letting it out in a wild howling scream of utter pleasure. Seeing and hearing that is enough to push me to the brink and I tense, throwing back my head and crying out her name as I release inside her once more.

I'm completely exhausted and I really need to collapse onto her, but I don't. I don't even move… I want to stay connected a little while longer. I look down into her just opened, glazed eyes. "It's probably a little late to be asking this, but are you on birth control?"

"Yes," she replies, nodding slowly, a light smile touching her lips.

"I should've checked first," I say, leaning down and kissing her soft, swollen lips. "I'm sorry, Holly. I should have been more considerate. I can only plead that I got carried away with the moment, and with you."

"It's fine." She reaches up and touches my cheek. "Don't be sorry. I knew it was okay. I would've stopped you if it wasn't." She was capable of stopping? Hell, I wasn't.

"In case you're wondering, I'm clean," I add, just to reassure her.

"So am I." She pulls her hand away and looks toward the window, a shadow crossing her eyes. "I got tested after Jason slept with my sister, just to be on the safe side. Jason might have only strayed the once, but I know what Ellie's like…" The sadness in her voice cuts through me, but more than anything, I really wish she hadn't mentioned them, well, *him* to be more precise. It more than takes the edge off, hearing his name right at this moment, and I pull out of her, and flop down on my back beside her.

Holly

I've never felt anything like that. Never. Not once… let alone four times over. And each time was different from the last. How did he do that? I don't think I'll ever forget the shattering, consuming, uncontrollable, peak of his fingers, or the wholly connected bliss of that final time, with him so deep inside me. Just when I thought I couldn't handle any more, he got me there. And then, in between, there was his tongue… what he can do with his tongue. My God. I'm still breathless and in awe of that. As for being held down like that. He was strong, dominant, forceful… and I loved every second of it. It was just what I needed.

I'm not sure how much time has passed since he pulled out of me, but I'm still lying spread-eagled on the bed, unable to move, or even think straight.

"Do you want something to drink, or eat?" he asks after a while. His voice is quiet, but I imagine he's probably as spent as I am.

I turn slowly, my muscles aching. He's on his back beside me, staring up at the ceiling, breathing hard still, and I rest my head on his chest, listening to his heartbeat. "Maybe some water," I murmur.

"Okay. Nothing to eat?"

"I don't have the energy to eat. I'll do that tomorrow… or maybe the next day."

I hear him chuckle softly and feel him kiss the top of my head. "I'll fetch you a glass of water," he says gently and moves me to one side so he can get up. His weight shifts off the bed as he stands and I hear him padding out of the room, returning a few minutes later.

"Can you sit up?" he asks.

"I don't think I can do anything," I reply. My words are slurred. I sound drunk… drunk on him. I hear him place something – presumably the glass of water – on the bedside table and then I feel the bed dip under his weight and his arms come around me as he lifts me, effortlessly, and moves me up, so I'm lying with my head on the pillow.

"There," he says, and sits down on the edge of the bed, leaning over to hand me the glass of water. "Take this… or do you need me to help you?"

"I think I can raise a glass to my lips… just." I take a sip. It's ice cold and perfect. He takes the glass back and returns it to the bedside table. I feel drained… like I could sleep for a week.

"You okay?" he asks, his voice soft and concerned.

I nod my head. "Hmm. Just tired… well exhausted, to be honest."

"Not sore?"

"No… not sore." I smile up at him. He grins back.

"Do you…" He hesitates. "Do you want me to carry you to your room?"

I turn to face him. "Do you want to?" *Doesn't he want to sleep with me?*

"Well, are you capable of you walking?" he asks. Now I'm really confused.

"I don't know."

"Then I'll carry you," he says, and I feel him get up again.

"Don't… don't you want to sleep with me?" I ask him, feeling shy, embarrassed that we've done so much, but he seems to be rejecting me.

"Of course I do," he replies. He looks down at me, then realisation dawns in his eyes and he says, "Oh. You thought I meant I'd carry you to your room and then I'd come back here?"

"Well… yes," I whisper.

He lets out a half laugh. "No, baby. That's not what I meant at all." He pulls me across the bed and lifts me into his arms. "You came… all over the sheets," he explains. "They're kinda damp, to put it mildly."

Oh God… how embarrassing. "I'm sorry."

"Hey… don't be sorry. You looked beautiful. I've never seen anything as crazily beautiful as you coming, but I'm too tired to change the bedding now, so I thought we could spend the night in your room… if you're okay with that?"

I'm so relieved. "I'm more than okay with it," I murmur, resting my head on his chest as he carries me out of the room and along the hallway, into my bedroom.

He lays me down gently and then lies next to me and I put my head back on his chest again. I feel his his arm come around me as I rest my hand on his stomach and he brings his over, entwining our fingers. The exhaustion, the sound of his rhythmic heartbeat, and the satisfied afterglow of our lovemaking quickly lulls me into a deep sleep.

I have a strange feeling of being half awake and half asleep, and not knowing which is which, like I'm in a dreamworld. My eyes are closed, and I can't hear anything at all, and yet in this blurred reality of lost senses, I'm aware of something very intense and arousing. It's a touch... at least I think it is. Yes, it is... it's a very gentle, intimate, touch. Something is rubbing against my clitoris. I'm lying on my left side, but I twist slightly onto my front and bring up my right leg, wanting more, knowing – yet not really knowing – that my movement will heighten the sensations, deepen the pleasure. I'm right; it does. The pressure increases, I'm aware of something entering me... and I'm awake. And I'm moaning.

"Hmm, that's good," I hear myself whisper.

"Relax." Todd's voice is low, soft and right next to my ear. "Just relax and let it take you, baby."

I need a moment just to take on board what he's doing. I'm lying on my front and he's beside me, his hand is between my parted legs, his fingers on my aroused nub, and his thumb now inside me. Whatever he's doing with his thumb, it's pushing me to the limit, and I grab the pillow as my orgasm builds.

I'm barely awake and yet... "I'm going to..." I breathe.

"Go on..." he urges, and the light explodes behind my eyes, in millions of fractured rays, the pressure building from within, coursing out through every muscle and fibre of my body as the waves and waves of pleasure wash over me. He doesn't let up, but keeps his movements going through my writhing orgasm, until I'm begging him, "I can't... please, I can't take it." My breath hitches in my throat.

"Yeah, you can. You really can... This is you, baby. This is who you are." He quickly withdraws his hand, then I feel him kneel up between my legs, parting mine even further. I'm so exposed. He raises my hips off the bed, so my backside is in the air and he enters me. Hard.

"Argh!" I let out a cry, clasping the pillow between my fists. "That's deep."

"It's meant to be." He stills, but only for a moment. "Want me to stop?" he asks.

"No." It feels so good. "No... please don't stop. Don't ever stop." Then he pulls out and slams back into me again.

"You want more, baby?"

"Yes," I whisper between gritted teeth. "More... Give me more."

"You got it." And he starts to plunge into me, deep and hard, his hands on my hips, pulling me back onto him with every powerful thrust. It's glorious, relentless… and I love it.

It feels urgent, like there's some desperate need in him to take me, right now, right this very minute. It's the most incredible sensation.

"I want more of you, Holly," he mutters. *How's that even possible?*

He runs his hands up my back, resting them on my shoulders, and pulls me onto him even harder still, increasing the pace and force of every movement. *Okay… it's possible.*

He begins to grunt with each thrust and I feel him expand inside me. He must be close…

"Holly," he mutters. "Please… Please come with me."

"I c-can't," I stutter out. "I can't do it again." I'm too tired; he's drained me.

"I need you," he pleads. "Now." He moves his right hand down, in front of me and starts to circle around my clitoris, while his left hand moves to my right shoulder, clasping tight onto it. The sensations are overwhelming as he pulls me down onto his shaft, forcing his length even deeper into me. I let out a cry.

"You feel so good," he says. "You're so tight on my cock." His need, his want, coupled with my own, and the way his fingers are working me over and over… it's too much. "Come on, Holly!" he yells. "Now!"

"Oh, God… Oh yes…" I hiss between my teeth. He's pushing me over the edge and then I'm screaming, "Todd… Please! Oh… yes!" I want to tell him to stop, that it's more than my body can handle, but the pleasure is too much and I know I don't really want it to end… not ever. He cries out, a harsh, anguished howl, which comes from deep in his throat as I feel him spill into me yet again.

It takes us both a few minutes to come back down, and for our breathing to calm, and he pulls slowly out of me and I collapse down onto the bed. He lies beside me and and turns me so I'm facing him.

"You okay?" he asks, still a little breathless.

"Hmm."

"Is that a yes?"

"Hmm."

I've lost the power of speech. If I could talk, I'd tell him I've never experienced anything that good, or that intense in my whole life. I'd tell him that he's changed me. I've never been like this before; never been so vocal, so passionate, so heated, so desperate for more. I know, deep down, we should talk. I haven't told him any of the things he wanted – well, needed – to hear. Most importantly though, I haven't told him I've fallen deeply in love with him... but we can do all that in the morning. Right now, I really need to sleep...

Chapter Fourteen

Todd

She's drifted off to sleep again, and I hold her in my arms, listening to her deep, even breathing, feeling her soft, delicate skin beneath my fingers and remembering how sensational she just felt. Waking up in the middle of the night with a hard-on is not that unusual; what I just did with Holly – the passion, the heat, the frenzied, desperate, urgency – that's something else. That was new to me, very new. I've never felt anything like that kind of consuming desire, that compelling, obsessive need to have her, right then. Sure, I offered to stop, but I'm not entirely sure I could have done. I wasn't really in control of anything, and that's never happened to me before. I half expect that to make me feel uneasy… it doesn't.

I've been hard and turned on around her for days, since the moment I met her, really, and I've kept control. I've even slept with her, woken up with her, and managed to restrain that urge… but not this time. I wish, in the heat of the moment, she'd told me how she feels. But then I guess I haven't told her either. I haven't told her I'm in love with her, or that I'm starting to dread the thought of going home, of having a whole ocean between us, and not seeing her every day, or even knowing when I'll see her again. I've held back on that, even if I haven't held back on much else in the last few hours, because I really need to know how she feels first. I have to know she's not still thinking about Jason… that I'm her world now, like she is mine. I may have always shied away from love and relationships, but to hell with that. I'm quitting the force as soon as this case is over. I won't be doing a dangerous job anymore. And I want her in my life… No, I *need* her in my life, because I simply can't imagine my life without her in it.

My eyelids are starting to close and I pull her tighter to me. She moans in her sleep. God, I love her. *Please, even if she doesn't love me yet, let her tell me there's no-one else in her head… let her tell me I've got a chance.*

I wake with a start, and turn over. It's daylight, and the bed's empty. The sense of disappointment is almost overwhelming.

Did I dream it? No. I can't have done. It was far too real to have been a dream, or a figment of my imagination.

I climb out of bed. Where is she? I want her back in bed, in my arms, underneath me. I want to fill her again, before the day has to start and encroach on our time together.

"Holly?" I call, leaving the bedroom.

She appears from the living room and we face each other; me naked and aroused, just because she's there; and her in a knee-length, dark blue fluffy bathrobe… *Okay.* I know I said I didn't care what she wore, and I don't, but I kinda hoped she'd be wearing nothing… or at least something that offered me a few reminders of last night, other than the ones in my head.

"Good morning," she says, her voice a little high-pitched, a little unnatural and forced. She's staring at the floor between us, but not at me. She won't make eye contact with me, or look at me in any way. Why not? She's seen me virtually naked before, and has seemed to enjoy the view. And after last night, she's seen all of me, she's certainly felt all of me… in great detail. *What's wrong? What did I miss?*

"Is everything okay?" I ask.

"Yes," she says, still with that weird, overly-happy, too bright tone of voice. She bites her bottom lip. Is she embarrassed about what we did? Is that it? I hope that's all it is; I can handle embarrassment. "Everything's fine. How did you sleep?"

"I slept just great." I smile at her, hoping to put her at ease, and lean back against the wall. "Sorry I woke you in the night."

"I didn't mind." Excuse me? She didn't *mind?* I made her come… twice… She was screaming my name, for Christ's sakes… and she didn't *mind?* "Do you want a coffee?" she asks.

"Not especially. I want you to talk to me, Holly. Something's wrong. What's happened?"

She clears her throat, awkwardly. "Nothing. But you're right, we should talk." I'm getting worried here. I'm not so sure she is embarrassed. This feels more like regret. Like she wishes we hadn't done all the things we did last night. "Do you want to put some clothes on?" she says.

"Not particularly. Why? Do you want me to?" *Please tell me you don't want me to, or that, if you do, it's just because you're embarrassed, that you don't regret the best sex I ever had in my life.*

"I just think it would be easier…"

"For whom?"

"Both of us." I don't like the sound of this.

"What are you trying to tell me?" I fold my arms across my chest.

Her eyes dart up to mine. "Just that I think it would be easier to talk if we both had some clothes on, that's all." Her voice has changed; it's a barely audible whisper.

I take the few steps down the hallway and stand in front of her. "Why?" I repeat, keeping my voice low. She doesn't answer me. Instead she closes her eyes, and I can feel the air being sucked from my lungs. She doesn't want this. She doesn't want any of it. She wasn't ready. I moved too soon and I've blown it. "I'm sorry," I mutter. "This is my fault. I said I'd wait. When we got back here last night, I should never have taken you to bed. We should have talked."

"But, I don't…" she whispers, opening her eyes and staring at me. She looks so hurt. What have I done to her? "What do you mean?" she asks.

"This isn't what you wanted, is it?"

"Did I say that? I—"

"You didn't have to say it, Holly. It's written all over your face."

"Can I speak?" I'd probably rather she didn't, but I nod my head. "I didn't say I don't want this… I didn't say that at all. But I'm scared, Todd."

What? "What the hell are you scared of?"

"Being hurt again."

I reach out and run my finger down the side of her face. "I'll never hurt you."

She lets out a half-laugh. "That's easy to say now, when we're standing here, like this. But what about when you go home, when you're three thousand miles away, and you're surrounded by beautiful women, making you offers you can't refuse... The temptations..." she continues, her voice trailing off.

"There are no temptations. I don't cheat, Holly. Ever."

"Yes. And I didn't think Jason would cheat either."

Hearing his name, the contempt in her voice... it's like a switch flicking inside my head. "For the umpteenth fucking time... I'm. Not. Jason." She cowers and takes a step back from me. *Oh no, baby.* She clearly needs a reminder that I'm not him; I'm nothing like him. I thought I proved that last night, but I guess it wasn't clear enough. I pick her up, my hands just above her waist, and I carry her across the room, slamming her up against the wall next to the window, my body crushing hers. I claim her mouth, hard, and run my tongue along her lips. She opens to me first time, with a sigh, her fingers twisting into my hair, and I delve deep inside, taking her. My hands move up and down her body, feeling her through the thick material of her robe, until my thumbs snag on the tie that's binding her, which I yank undone, pulling apart the fleecy material, exposing her nakedness and moving closer, so she can feel my rock hard cock against her bare hip. I cup her breasts, squeezing her nipples tight, pinching them between my thumbs and forefingers, and she squeals into my mouth. I want her... right now. I pull the robe off her shoulders and let it fall to the floor, then take her hands and raise them high above her head, holding them both there with one of mine, while I move the other down, cupping her pussy, inserting two fingers into her soaked entrance. "You're so fucking wet." She's breathing hard, moaning loudly, her breasts heaving into my chest, as I pump my fingers in and out of her. "Who were you thinking about?" I ask, between hard, bruising kisses. "When I was deep inside you last night, when I was fucking you, when I was licking you, making you come...

Was it him?" I start to twist and circle my fingers inside her. She pants loudly, her hips bucking, trying to take me deeper. "And now, when you're so wet, you're soaking my hand… Who are you thinking about now, Holly? Me, or him?" She doesn't reply, but I hear a choked sound, and it's like a slap to the face, an instant cold shower. What the fuck am I doing? She made it quite clear already she doesn't want this, not with me. Okay, she didn't push me away, or say 'no', and I might even be tempted to say she's enjoying it, perhaps. But her words before, and her lack of words now tell me everything I need to know. Sure, she responded to my touch, and she's soaking wet, but that's a basic reaction; that's a need, not a choice. Her *choice* was to get out of bed before I woke up, and put some distance between us. Her *choice* was to ask me to get dressed so we could talk. Her *choice* was to take a step back from me when I got too close. It was a step back I ignored, because I wanted to prove a fucking point… and whatever I might want, need or hope, she isn't mine and she doesn't want to be. And yet I'm all over her. I pull my fingers from her and release her, drawing in a deep breath. Her arms fall back down to her sides. "I'm sorry, Holly. I'm so sorry. I shouldn't have done that. I apologize. That was inexcusable."

"No, please…" she whispers, but I can't bear to look at her.

I walk toward the door, but stop on the threshold, bracing myself with my arms against the top of the door frame. I don't turn around. "I don't know who you were thinking about last night, Holly, or who's in your head right now, but it was my name on your lips. It was my name you screamed every time I made you come. If you don't believe me, or you don't remember, we can go ask your neighbors. Hell, I think the whole damn street would have heard you." I can feel a lump rising in my throat, but I cough it down again. "I've got no idea what you want and, if you're honest, I don't think you do either. The only thing you're clear on is that you think I'm the same as him. You think I'd cheat on you, which just goes to show, you don't know me at all. You still don't trust me, and you probably never will, not entirely… and that's it for me. This was all a mistake. A big fucking mistake. I'm sorry for what I just did to you. Truly sorry. It was unforgivable. But I think, for both our sakes, it would be better if we just pretended like none of this ever happened, none of it – not last week, or the weekend, and especially not last night, and this morning. We'll do our jobs, we'll catch this guy, and then… and then I'll go home."

I don't give her the chance to reply; I walk down the corridor and straight into the bathroom. I lean back on the closed door, and then fall to my knees, clenching my fists. I haven't cried since my dad died… I'm not going to now. I'm not. Except the room's a blur, and there's a pain in my chest like nothing I've ever felt before.

Holly

Everything I wanted to say to him came out wrong… spectacularly wrong.

I only wanted him to get dressed – or at least put some shorts on – so I wasn't tempted to jump on him. He's always exuded masculinity and sex appeal, even before last night, but now I know what he can do; how he can make me react so quickly, so intensely and feel so deeply. I want more… I want a lot more. But we needed to talk first…

I wore the very un-sexy blue bathrobe and deliberately got out of bed before he woke up, so neither of us would be tempted to start the morning with more sex, rather than the conversation we both know we needed to have. A talk was necessary, to get everything out in the open, so he could understand that I'm over Jason, that I want him and no-one else, *but* that I'm also really scared about how we're going to make this work when we live so far apart. I've got used to having him around and I don't know if I can handle him being three thousand miles away, and not seeing him every day. If he'd let me finish what I wanted to say, I was also going to tell him that I was nervous… that I *am* nervous and I'm scared I'll get hurt, because I'm so in love with him and I've got no idea how he's going to react to that. I don't know how he feels about me – he hasn't said – and now I'll probably never know, being as he's decided – unilaterally – that it was all a mistake… that we should just forget the whole bloody thing. How do you forget something like that? How do you forget someone who bought you ice cream just to make you feel better? Or held you while you fell asleep on him and carried you to bed? Or let you swap rooms with him in the middle of the night, just because you were too scared to sleep in your own bed? Or danced with you and kissed you, just to teach your sister a lesson? How? And how do you forget the most intense sexual experience you're ever likely to have?

I feel the first tear trickle down my cheek. No-one's ever put me first like that… no-one, except him. And he thinks it was all a mistake.

It's hard to trust people when you've been lied to and cheated on. I know I probably shouldn't have brought up Jason, or even mentioned his name, but I thought that was the whole point. He said he wanted to know that I was over Jason… and I was getting around to that, if only he'd let me finish, instead of second-guessing what I was going to say, and then flying off the handle at me.

I pick up the robe and pull it on, wiping away the tears on my sleeve and pulling it closed around me, then doing up the tie again. I go along the hallway, and I can hear the shower running through the bathroom door. What would happen if I went in there now, and got under the water with him, held him, kissed him? Would he want me, or would he reject me? Can I take the risk of finding out? I think I have to. Apart from anything else, I think I need to apologise for hurting him, because he did sound hurt… but I need also answers. I need to know what he meant when he said this was a mistake. Why does he want to pretend that none of it happened? Did he ever want me in the long-term or was it just about the sex? Was he lying and faking it all along? And why won't he even listen to me, for crying out loud? I carefully try the handle, but the door's locked. I'm on the outside, and I wonder if he's trying to tell me something…

I go to my bedroom and close the door behind me. My mind is filled with memories of his eyes, his hands, his lips, his body against mine… that intensity of need when he woke me in the early hours. That urgency

– I've never known anything like it. And now I'm not sure I ever will again… because he wants us to forget it all.

I was expecting him to take me, right there in the living room just now, up against the wall. I was breathless with anticipation. I wanted it so much. It was exciting, intoxicating to inspire such want in someone else, especially in someone like Todd, who could have any woman he wants. It was almost too much… I was struggling to control my feelings, choking back the tears, partly because his need, *his* emotions were so overwhelming, but also because I couldn't understand how he could even imagine I'd be thinking about Jason, while he was making love to me in the way he did… So why did he have to stop… and then apologise? *Apologise?* Was I not making it clear enough by my reactions that I wanted him? Well, obviously not.

It's things like that which make me realise I'm right. I'm not good enough for Todd… or Jason. Whatever I do isn't enough either. Todd clearly can't get away from me fast enough now he's had me and, like Jason, he'll no doubt look elsewhere for someone more satisfying. Maybe he's right. We are better off ending it now, before we get in too deep. What a joke… How much deeper does it get than giving your whole heart to someone who doesn't want it?

I sit on the edge of my bed. God, this hurts. I love him. And I know now that I didn't love Jason… not if this is what love is. Because this is so much more.

Apart from being so obviously useless in bed, where did I go wrong? I suppose saying Jason's name didn't help. That seemed to be the catalyst… and come to think of it, I may have said his name last night as well… not in the throes of passion, but when we were talking about me getting tested. *Not very subtle, Holly, reminding him of your ex after you've just had sex for the first time, and such incredible sex, too. No wonder he was questioning who was in your head.* But that didn't stop him from holding me while we fell asleep, or from making love to me… wildly, desperately, in the middle of the night. So, can that really have been so much of a problem?

I lie back on the bed, staring at the ceiling. Why… why does this have to be so confusing, so complicated?

And why can't he just listen to me, let me speak and finish a bloody sentence? If he'd only do that, we might be able to understand each other. Instead, he's made his mind up already. And it seems I don't get a say. We'll finish the job, and he'll go home. Really? He thinks it's that simple? Maybe it is for him... being as he doesn't love me. But how on earth am I supposed to sit on his lap at the club tonight and pretend I don't want him and love him? I can't do it.

The shower shuts off. He'll be out in a moment. And we'll have to face each other again. Well, whatever he thinks, I'm not going to just let him walk away from this. It's too important. I'm going to talk to him. No... No I'm not. First, I'm going to give myself a little longer to calm down and think it through; work out exactly what to say to make him understand. I'll shower, I'll get dressed and we can sit down in the living room, fully clothed, like civilised people, and talk this through... and this time, I'll make him listen, because, whatever he thinks and says, *I* can't just forget everything that's happened between us. I love him too much.

Chapter Fifteen

Todd

I've tried hot water, and cold… and neither's working.

I'm still hard, and I still feel like a complete shit. It doesn't matter how many times I tell myself she had her fingers in my hair and her tongue in my mouth, or how many times I remember her gasps and moans of pleasure, or how wet she was. I know I shouldn't have done what I was doing. I was too rough, too demanding. It was a juvenile way of proving a point… staking a claim. I made it about ownership and possession, not love. And it was all wrong. All fucking wrong.

I shut off the shower and step out, wrapping a towel around my hips. I avoid looking in the mirror while I brush my teeth – I'm not too keen on the idea of my own reflection right now. I've been an asshole. And not just for mauling her when I should have been talking to her, but for not listening to her either.

The thing is, I wasn't sure I wanted to hear her answers, so I shut them down, just in case. I sure as hell don't want to hear Jason's name – ever again – or know that he still occupies any part of her mind, or her heart. I don't want her thinking I'm going to cheat, just because he did. And I really don't want to hear that she still has any doubts about me, because if she can't trust me to love her more than life itself… if she doesn't know by now that I'll defend her to my last breath, and that she can depend on me to always – *always* – put her first, then we don't have any kind of future.

Future? Who the hell am I kidding. She doesn't want a future… at least not with a guy who lives three thousand miles away, in a world filled with uncertainty. She wants someone who's close by, who can spend time with her, be with her, devote himself to her. And why shouldn't she? She's worth that, and more. She's worth so much more. I wonder if she'd consider being with me, giving me another chance, if I made the commitment and moved here? But could I do that? Could I give up everything I've got back home for a woman who won't even tell me how she feels about me? *Oh, for Christ's sake, Todd. Stop giving yourself false hope. If she wanted you, she'd have said so. She'd at least stop mentioning Jason's name, and making comparisons; and she'd tell you how she feels.* It's hopeless.

I come out of the bathroom and glance into the living room. She's not there. I check the kitchen, which is also empty. Her bedroom door's closed, and I don't feel like knocking. She might yell at me, or she might be crying and I'm not sure I can handle either of those. But just in case she's run off somewhere, freaked out, or scared by what I did to her, I go along the hall, and breathe a sigh of relief. Her keys are on the hook by the door. She's still here, thank God.

I shut the door of my room behind me, drop the towel and find some clothes out of my case, dressing quickly. Then, I hear her going across the hallway and into the bathroom.

This assignment is going to be tricky as hell if we're not going to talk to each other. We're supposed to be going to the club tonight as Mr and Mrs Sanders. The thought of her on my lap, writhing and grinding on me, knowing that I love her and can't have her… How on earth is that supposed to work? We have to sort everything out – somehow – one way or the other… and we have to do it today.

I don't want to sit around in my room waiting for Holly to finish in the bathroom, so I go into the living room and fire up my laptop. I may as well see if I've got any new messages.

While I wait for my mail app to load, I realize I haven't had any coffee at all yet. It can wait, I guess, until Holly comes out. Maybe we can be civilized with each other over breakfast. No, that's not fair – she's never been anything but civilized with me. It's me who's behaving like a goddamn caveman. A jealous, unreasonable caveman.

There's an e-mail waiting for me from Adam, from yesterday.

In it, he explains that the performer at the club... the one Holly noticed on Friday evening, is a French national, named Pierre Durand. There's an address for him in Boston, and one here in London, but no French address, which seems odd. We'll have to look into why that might be. He's got no criminal record, either in Europe, the UK, or the US, but we all know that doesn't make him innocent; it just means he's never been caught. He's worked at various clubs in New York, LA, and Vegas for the last three years, as well as doing some movie work, and he started working at the club in Boston in October, so two months before the first murder, before shipping over to England in March. The timing is perfect. I could almost smile, if I wasn't feeling so miserable. He's single, but has had a string of short-term relationships. I think the first thing I need to get Adam working on is speaking to some of Durand's ex-girlfriends... see if he's ever been violent and whether his interest in erotic asphyxiation is something he confines to the stage, or uses at home as well.

I must've been absorbed in reading Adam's message, because the bathroom door's open. Holly must have finished her shower and gone through to her room without me noticing.

We need to talk. Now. There's nothing in Adam's message that can't wait an hour.

I go along the corridor and knock on her door. "Can I come in?" I call.

"Yes."

I go inside. She's facing me, wearing her silk robe now, rather than the blue one and, with the window behind her, I can see right through it. I try to focus on her face, rather than her body and what I'd like to do to her.

"We need to talk," I manage to say.

"Yes, we do." She looks a little doubtful. "Do you mind if I get dressed first?"

"No. Go ahead." I wait for a moment. "I guess you want me to wait outside?" She nods her head. "Holly, I'm—" The doorbell rings. I ignore it. "I'm sorry… about earlier. About what I did…"

She doesn't respond, other than to bite her bottom lip. "Just let me get dressed," she whispers, "and we'll talk."

"Okay." The doorbell rings again.

"And can you get that?"

"Sure."

I go along to the front door, press the entry phone button and speak. "Hi," I say into it.

"You really need to answer your fucking phone," replies a voice through the speaker.

"Who is this?"

"Adam. Let me in."

I press the buzzer. "Come on up."

"Who is it?" Holly calls, and I remember her door's still open.

"It's Adam," I reply walking back to her room. "He's on his way up. I'll close your door." I look up. She's pulled a t-shirt over her head, and is wearing a bright red thong… and nothing else. God, I want her. I want her so fucking much.

"Christ, yes. He can't see me like this."

"Put a bra on, Holly," I tell her. "That t-shirt's too revealing."

She looks at me. "Is it?"

"For me, no… For him, yeah."

"Oh." She blushes. "Okay." She whips the t-shirt back off, even though I'm still standing there. I can't help the groan that escapes my lips at the sight of her, and it's all I can do to tear myself away.

"I'll let him in," I say.

"Be there in a minute…"

I close her door, catching a last glimpse of her, and go back to let Adam in.

He's just exited the elevator as I open the front door.

"What's wrong?" I say to him.

"The shit's hit the fan, that's what's wrong."

"Care to elaborate?"

He comes inside and I close the door.

"Did you read my e-mail, about this Pierre Durand character?"

"Yeah. I read it this morning."

"Well, there's been a development."

My cop's instinct goes into overdrive; my stomach flips over, my skin tingles, I'm suddenly more alert. "What development?"

"I hope you're packed." *Why would I be?*

"What?"

"You're going back to Boston…"

"When?" I can feel the panic rising inside me.

"Now."

What the fuck? "Why?" I ask, but I don't get an answer because Holly comes out of her bedroom at this point, and looks from Adam to me and back again.

"Hi," she says to him, moving forward to shake hands. Of course, they've never met before.

"Holly." He smiles at her and lets his eyes roam down her body. I want to punch him. "It's good to meet you at last. I've heard a lot about you."

"Really?" She seems surprised… and maybe a little worried.

"Yeah. Jason Bishop is a friend…"

"Oh." She blushes and lowers her eyes. Great. He had to mention Jason, didn't he? Had to remind her. "W—What's going on?" she manages to say, stuttering slightly.

"I've come to relieve you of your lodger," Adam replies.

"You have?" She turns to me.

"Don't look at me," I tell her. "I've got no idea what's going on."

"It's Durand," Adam explains, finally giving us some details. "It seems he had a girlfriend over here, one of the other performers… a blonde?"

"Who's Durand?" Holly asks.

"The guy from the club," I explain. "He's French." I turn back to Adam. "Tell me about this blonde…"

"She turned up beaten, half strangled, in hospital in the early hours of this morning. Uniform were called out to interview her but we weren't informed until about four hours ago. It took a while to make the connection between her and him… We went round to his place, but he'd already left, taking everything with him. We checked at the club, but he wasn't there, so we alerted the airports, and ports and…"

"And what?" I already know what he's going to say.

"He left on the eight-forty flight this morning."

"Headed for Boston?"

"Yes."

"What time does he land?"

"Eleven-twenty local time."

"Are Boston PD going to pick him up at the airport?" I ask, although I've got a feeling I know the answer to that one too.

"No."

"Why not?"

"Your boss thinks you should be there. He wants to go over the evidence with you and for you to pick him up yourself tonight. He's worried about the crowds at the airport – so he says. He's going to have Durand watched from the moment he lands."

"My boss is fucking insane." He's been the bane of my life for the last two years, and it doesn't look like he's going to give me a break now, either… "Why can't they just pick up Durand somewhere away from the airport, if he's so worried about there being too many people there, and I'll get back tomorrow to question him?" I need more time here with Holly. We're not done yet. We're nowhere near done.

"Don't shoot the messenger, Todd, okay?" He's pissed. "It's not my decision. I've just been told to drive you to the airport. You're booked on the next flight. I've got to come with you so I can get you through security. Being as you didn't answer your fucking phone all morning, you're going to be late for check-in."

I ignore his tone. I've got more important things to think about. Much more important things. "And we have to leave right now?"

"Yeah. That's why I asked if you're packed."

"Why the hell would I be packed? I didn't know I was going anywhere."

"Then I suggest you get packed – fast." He looks at his watch. "We've got ten minutes."

"Ten minutes?" I can barely speak. I look up at Holly, but she's staring at the floor.

"Yeah. Time's ticking, Todd."

"Fine."

I go through to my room and start throwing my things into my bag. How can this be happening? All I wanted was to sit down and talk with her, to explain about what happened this morning, to ask her to forgive me, and beg her to let us try again... and instead, I'm gonna have to leave without even getting to speak to her alone.

I take my tux out of the suit carrier, fold it roughly and put it on top of everything else in my bag, then zip it up and go back out into the hallway. Holly's standing there, with Adam. She's holding my messenger bag.

"I packed up your laptop," she says, holding it out to me.

"Thanks."

"Is that everything?" Adam asks.

"Yeah."

Holly turns to me. "You haven't left anything behind?" *Apart from you and my shattered heart... no.* I shake my head.

"We'd better be going. Your flight leaves in two hours." Adam's voice intrudes.

"I'll come down with you," Holly says, slipping on some trainers. She grabs her keys, pulling the door closed behind her.

We get into the elevator, in silence, both still shocked, I think. It's all happened so fast. Then, as the doors close, I remember the hire car and I reach into my pocket, pulling out my keys.

"The car rental company will be round later to collect the Mercedes," I tell her, pulling the key from my keychain. "Can you deal with it?"

"Of course."

"And... and here's your spare key too." I hand the car key to her, together with the spare one to her apartment. "I won't be needing it now, will I?" *Please tell me to keep it. Tell me you want me to come back. Give me a reason... a glimmer of hope, and I'll be here.*

I see her swallow hard, and she glances at Adam, blinking back tears. "No, I don't suppose so."

And I guess that's all the answer I need.

∽

Holly

I wish he'd tell me he'll come back. I wish he'd make the offer… say it first, and give me a reason to hope. But he doesn't.

If he's waiting for me to say something, he'll be waiting a long time… I can't do that in the lift, in front of Adam. Surely Todd realises that? I'm not confident enough. Adam knows Jason… and I have to work with him. It'd be all round the office before lunch. I can't be everyone's gossip. I've been humiliated once too often before and I can't do it again.

He's given me back his key now as well. And that feels like the final goodbye. Why didn't he ask to keep it? All the hope of our one perfect night is just… lost.

They've loaded Todd's bags into Adam's car and he's in the driver's seat, with the engine running.

"I have to go," Todd says, going to the passenger side and opening the door.

I can't speak. I have no words. Nothing. It's been too quick.

"I'm sorry I rushed you," he says. I don't want him to be sorry, not for anything, except perhaps for leaving me – and even that isn't his fault. I shake my head; I still have no voice. "Yeah, I am. I'll always regret that." He grabs hold of me and pulls me into him, hugging me close, his arms tight around me, his body against mine for what I fear is the last time. "I think if I'd waited until you were really ready, and let things take their natural course, we might have stood a chance, but I had to be a jerk and rush you. And I'm sorry… Will you do something for me?"

207

"Yes." I manage to speak at last.

"If you do ever think about me… if you do remember me… please, please don't think about the man I've been this morning. I'd hate for you to remember me like that."

"But, I…" He puts a finger gently on my lips, so I can't tell him that I liked the man he was this morning – well, except for the part where he said it was a mistake. I liked the rest though. All of it.

"Please, try and remember me as the other guy. The one you danced with, the one you fell asleep with, ate ice cream with, the one who slept with you, talked with you, laughed with you, kissed you…" *Oh my God… his memories of the good times are exactly the same as mine.* He hesitates and clears his throat, his finger still on my lips. "I want you to remember me as the man I really am… the man who made love to you last night, and please try and forget what I did to you this morning."

"Why do you want me to forget it?" I've got so many questions, but there isn't time. I want to tell him that I liked what he did, so I'm damned if I'm going to forget it, but instead I just ask, "Why didn't you want me?"

He looks confused. "I did want you. But, it was for all the wrong reasons. Please, I beg you to forgive me for what I did. It was wrong." *Why?* Adam revs the engine, letting us know they need to be going. *No, please, not yet. I'm not ready.* Todd runs a finger down my cheek and I feel the tears welling in my eyes. "Don't let anyone ever tell you you're not good enough," he whispers. "You are. You're the best," and he climbs into the car, and before he's even closed the door, Adam pulls away.

I manage to get back upstairs and inside the flat before the tears start. I slide down the back of the closed door, onto the floor and hold my head in my hands.

He's gone. That was so final, like he was really saying goodbye. He's got no intention of coming back. I was deluding myself. Maybe I should have tried to stop him… but if he wanted me, he wouldn't have ended it, not like that. He'd have given me some hope, wouldn't he?

Chapter Sixteen

Todd

"You got your leg over, didn't you?"

I ignore him.

"You lucky bastard."

I stare out the window.

"Can't say I blame you. I mean, what the fuck was Jason thinking of, banging her sister, when he had that at home? Still, that's his loss and now she's available, I wouldn't mind giving her one myself—"

"Shut the fuck up, Adam." I turn in my seat to face him. "I don't wanna hear Jason's name, and neither does Holly. And don't even think about going near her, you hear me?"

"Okay, okay—"

"I mean it. If I hear you, or anyone else has done anything to hurt her, I'll come back over here… and I'll bring my fucking gun with me."

"Calm down," he says, keeping his eyes on the road. "Jesus. She really got to you."

"Yeah, she did. Now, for the second time, shut the fuck up."

We carry on in silence for a while, and then he just says, "Sorry," his voice real quiet. I don't know if he's sorry for what he said, or because I'm hurting and he knows it… and I don't care. Either way, I really don't want to talk about it.

He helps me through security, being as I'm late for check-in, his badge enabling us to waive some of the usual red-tape. Then, when we're done and I'm about to go through to the departure gate, he turns to me.

"I'm sorry things didn't work out for you," he says.

"Not your problem. Just leave her alone, okay?" He nods his head, looking more than a little contrite.

"Let us know how you get on with Durand."

"I will."

We shake hands and I go through to catch my flight back home... Home. Where the hell is that now? I know where I'd like it to be. Anywhere Holly is, that's where.

I stare out the window at the clouds below. Not that I really notice anything... all I can see is Holly's face. That's all I've been able to see since we took off, and I'm now about an hour out of Logan.

I know I was too rough with her this morning, but she still wouldn't tell me how she feels about me. It wasn't like I was asking her to love me; I just wanted to be the only man she thought of when she woke up in the morning and before she went to sleep at night... and every moment in between. I guess that is love though, isn't it? So, I guess I wanted too much.

And she didn't ask me to stay, or give me a reason to come back either, so I guess she doesn't want me to. I was kidding myself all along. Maybe I was just an itch that needed scratching; proof that she can pull another guy after Jason; and now she'll find the man she really wants to be with... That thought makes me feel physically sick.

It's just before two-thirty local time when we land, but the last seven hours feel like a blur – a blur of confused thoughts and images. I need to get my head straight and focus on what I've got to do. I can think about Holly later tonight... and tomorrow and then every day, for the rest of my life.

I take a cab to the precinct, and leave my bags by my desk. It feels odd being back here and I'm already glad that I'm going to be resigning at the end of this case. I can't face the prospect of *this* being my future... I've got to stop thinking about the future. It just reminds me of Holly, and of everything I don't have anymore.

Chris isn't at her desk but I guess she's out watching Durand, so I go straight to the captain's office, knocking on the doorframe and walking in. He's at his desk, the top of his bald head pointing in my direction. He looks up, over the top of his glasses as I sit down opposite him, uninvited.

"You're back."

"Yeah." *Well done. We'll make a detective of you yet.* "What's happening? And why the hell hasn't someone picked this guy up already?"

He stares at me for a moment. "I'll put your attitude down to tiredness… jet lag."

"Put it down to whatever you want. Why is he still out there?"

"Because I want to go over the evidence with you first."

"Why?" I'm not sure we actually have any. It's a hunch… but it's a good one.

"I'm not sure you have any." Damn. I thought he was too stupid to notice.

"What? And we never pick someone up without evidence?"

"This case has been ongoing for nearly six months, Russell. I'm getting pressure from upstairs to come up with something."

"It isn't six months, sir," I say, trying to sound respectful, even though it's dawning on me that my boss can't even count. "It's just over four."

He glares at me. "The length of time is irrelevant…" *Why bring it up then?* "What matters is that we need something concrete."

"Then bring the guy in… and let me get something."

"But we can't afford to get it wrong."

"We won't be. I know it's him."

"You know it's him… Great. How reassuring. Do you have any evidence against Durand, or are we just basing this on your gut reaction?"

I might as well be truthful. "Gut reaction, mostly. He was in the right places at the right times, he's into erotic asphyxiation, and he beat and strangled his girlfriend last night in London. Apart from that…"

He stares at me. "Okay. Jefferson is watching his apartment—"

"On her own?" I interrupt him.

"Yes, until you get there. Durand only got in from London himself a couple of hours ago." He scribbles something on a piece of paper. "This is the address Jefferson called in from." I glance at it. It's different to the one on Durand's file. That's odd.

"How did he get from the airport to this address?" I ask. Maybe he's staying with a friend and they collected him from the airport.

"He took a cab."

There goes that theory. I get to my feet. "I'm gonna bring him in," I say.

"Just for questioning. I don't want you to arrest him yet." *Like I give a shit what you want.*

After what he did to that woman in London, I'm hoping Durand resists... just a little. I don't reply, but go back out to the squad room, grab my bags and head downstairs, where I hail a cab and give the driver my home address.

I let myself in. My apartment feels empty without Holly, which is the weirdest thing, considering she's never been here – but then very few women have. My mother, my sister, Grace, Megan, Jamie... That's it. How can I miss someone who's never been here? That's not possible, so I guess what I mean is my life feels empty without her... That'll be it.

I shrug off my leather jacket and dump my bags in the living room, then go through to the bedroom, and into the bathroom, where I take five minutes to freshen up. I still can't look in the mirror. I'm unsure how I'll feel about what I see there.

I dry my face with a towel, which I throw on the bed when I come back out. The safe is in the closet and I punch in the combination, waiting for the door to pop open, so I can retrieve my gun and extra ammunition. I collect my holster, put it on, grab my jacket and keys and head back out again, down the stairs and around to the garage block.

I open my garage and stare ahead of me. Car or bike? I haven't ridden the bike for a while, but I'm kind of in the mood for it today. I check the address. I know the street. It's in a rundown district in the north of the city, about a twenty-five minute drive away in Monday afternoon traffic, or fifteen minutes on the bike, if I push it a little… Decision made. I pull on my crash helmet and mount up.

I park up behind Chris's car, dismount and remove my crash helmet, going around to the passenger side and getting in. I put my helmet on the back seat.

"Hi," she says quietly, glancing at me. "How was London?" Chris has short blonde hair, and always dresses smart… way too smart for a cop. Normally she wears contact lenses, but today, her blue eyes are peering at me through rimless glasses.

"Don't ask." I give her a look that I hope is enough to stop her from pushing. "What's happening?"

She nods her head slowly, while still looking at me. I think she gets it. "Nothing," she says quietly. "I followed your man back here from Logan, and he's been here ever since."

"Did he let himself in?"

"Yes."

"So the apartment's his?"

"No. It's registered to someone called Paige Bailey."

"And who the fuck is Paige Bailey?"

"She works at the club in Boston…"

I turn to look at her. "Great. So she could be in there too?"

She shrugs. "I haven't seen anyone else, but I guess so… Are we waiting for back-up?" she asks.

"I wasn't offered any. Carpenter just wants him brought in for questioning."

"Well, let's go ask him nicely, shall we?" She grins across at me.

We get out of her car and cross the road, entering the apartment building. "Number eight, yeah?" I whisper to her. She nods her head. "Second floor."

We climb the stairs and go along the hallway until we find the door marked eight. I put my ear against the door, but there are no sounds coming from inside. If the guy's as tired as I am, he's probably sleeping… and hopefully Paige Bailey isn't here.

"Shall I?" I ask.

"Sure. You look like you could do with kicking down a door," Chris replies as she pulls her gun. I follow suit, then, taking a step back, raise my right leg and kick open the door.

"Police!" I shout, entering first and taking in the layout of the apartment.

There's a dark hallway, with doors coming off of it to both left and right. Chris indicates she's going to check the ones to the left, so I move forward and push open the first one on my right. It's the kitchen… and it's empty. I check behind the door, just to be sure, then come back out, looking across to Chris, who shakes her head. She's found nothing yet either. I go further down the hallway. The next door is closed. I turn the handle, and slowly push it open…

The pain is instant, sharp… and blinding. The sound is deafening, which is surprising, considering it's not the first time I've heard a gun being fired, not by a long way. I'm propelled backwards, hitting the wall behind me – hard – and landing awkwardly, although I manage to take in the image of Durand, kneeling on the bed, his arm around the neck of a woman, her naked body held across his, shielding him. Looking up at him from my position on the floor, I can see now why the force of the bullet was so great… he's pointing a Smith & Wesson .44 Magnum at me, and it's one powerful revolver. I keep hold of my gun, still aiming it at Durand's just visible head, despite the throbbing in my left shoulder.

"Let her go," I mutter, even as I feel the blood dripping – well, pouring – down my chest, and pooling into my lap. This isn't good… That's a lot of blood. That's way too much blood.

"Fuck off, bastard." There's just the barest hint of a French accent in his voice.

"I don't think so. Let. Her. Go."

He stares at me and I hold his gaze. In my peripheral vision, I'm vaguely aware of Chris moving down the hallway toward me. She's a good shot… better than me, especially from this angle. If I can keep Durand talking and focused on me, Chris might be able get a shot at him.

"Why should I?" Durand says, smiling. "All I have to do is wait. You'll bleed out in a few minutes." He laughs. "I guess I'll have to make an exception in your case…" I'm not sure what he's talking about, but he soon makes himself clear. "I'll cut your dick off and feed it to you *after* you're dead."

I'm tempted to say 'over my dead body', but that's kind of his point. "I'll kill you before that happens," I manage to say.

"I'll bet you already feel light-headed, don't you?" I wonder, just for a moment, why he doesn't finish me off, but then I realize he's enjoying this.

"Not yet," I lie, but I think I sound convincing. I daren't look to see where Chris is, or what she's doing. I can't afford to distract Durand.

"Yes, you do," he says. "The light is starting to fade. I can see it in your eyes. You'll lose consciousness soon."

"Not planning to. For the third fucking time. Let. Her. Go."

He laughs again, and relaxes, just a little and, right at that moment, Chris steps into the doorway in front of me, blocking my view, and I hear another loud gunshot, a split second of silence and then a woman screams… and screams.

"Shut up!" Chris yells, and she moves into the room. The woman stops screaming, and starts whimpering. I keep my gun raised while Chris checks Durand for signs of life, but as she holsters her weapon, I let my arm drop, my head falls to one side and my eyes drift closed.

I feel a tapping on my cheek and open up again, the light seeming less intense than it was a moment ago. "Stay with me," I hear Chris say. I look up into her face. It's kinda blurry, indistinct. "I've called the paramedics." She looks down to where I know the blood is pooling beneath me. "Fuck," she whispers under her breath. "Hang on, Todd. They'll be here real soon. Just hang on. Please…" Her voice starts to fade.

"Holly," I whisper.

"What?" she says.

"Tell Holly… I'm sorry… I…" I can't manage any more. For a moment, Holly's beautiful face is all I can see; her sparkling eyes, her glowing soft skin… her full lips… Then I close my eyes and welcome the darkness.

∽

Holly

Todd's been gone less than twenty-four hours, but the flat feels so empty without him. It's like he was always here; like there was never a time before him. His physical presence still fills every room and every space has a memory of him. All of them are good… even the ones that he asked me to forget. I won't, of course I won't. I don't want to. I don't want to forget any of it. And how could he even doubt that I'll ever think of him? I'll never think of anyone but him.

I wandered around aimlessly yesterday after he'd left, and then spent the night on the sofa. I can't sleep in either bedroom yet. The memories are too raw still.

I wasn't really sure what to do today. I'm obviously no longer needed to work undercover, so I'm at work, riding up in the lift. I imagine I'll be made chief coffee maker and filing clerk for the next few weeks, which is pretty much what I'd expected when I joined CID.

I get out of the lift, go along the corridor and enter the main office. Everyone's looking busy.

"Ahh… Holly," Andy says. He's standing by the door into his office. "Good to see you again." Is it? It doesn't feel good to be back here. Actually, it feels alien, but then I suppose I've never worked here. I stare at him and he takes a step or two towards me. "We've got two robberies, a suspected arson, and a possible murder case – although it's looking more like suicide at the moment – Harry and Rob have both got flu and Alice started her maternity leave yesterday. Your timing is immaculate." He turns to the man who's sitting by the window. I don't know his name. He's probably thirty-five, good looking, with black hair, and stubble. He smiles at me. It's a nice smile, I suppose. "Sam…"

Andy says, "Holly's new, but she's good. She worked with Todd – the guy from the US – on that murder case. Can you bring her up to speed? She'll help you out." He turns back to me again. "Sam's working the arson case… at the moment, on his own, so he could use some help." And with that, he starts walking back towards his office.

"Andy?" I call after him. He spins around.

"Yes?"

"Have we heard what happened in Boston? Whether they picked up the Frenchman?"

"I had a message this morning. He took a woman hostage and one of the police officers shot him. He died." He shrugs. "Saves the American taxpayer some money, I suppose."

"Oh. Nothing else? I mean, they didn't tell you anything else?"

"No. It was just a short message from Todd's captain… Carpenter, I think his name is." I don't care what his name is. But I suppose he would have said if anything had happened to Todd.

I turn back to Sam, who's now standing. He's a little shorter than Todd, but most people are. "Good to have you here," he says. "Take a seat." He offers me a chair at the end of his desk and I perch on the edge of it. "Here's the file." He pushes a thin folder across the table towards me, and I notice his wedding ring. "Take a look while I make some coffee. White? Black?"

"White, no sugar, thanks." He smiles at me before walking away.

It's seven o'clock and I'm still at work… and, thankfully, the day has passed quickly. I've been so busy, I haven't had time to dwell on Todd for too long… only when I've been on my own, or not concentrating. We started off the morning going over Sam's notes, which weren't great. They weren't as organised or meticulous as Todd's. Then we went out and interviewed three witnesses, each of whom gave us completely different descriptions of what happened two days ago, when the factory they clean each evening burned down. Two of them were lucky to get out alive. The man who owns the factory wasn't so fortunate. He didn't die, but he's still in hospital. One of the cleaners gave us a description of a man they'd seen hanging around outside the entrance, but it's so nondescript, it could be anyone.

"This is looking more and more like insurance fraud, if you ask me," I say to Sam, yawning, stretching my arms up and leaning back in my chair.

"I'd agree," he replies, "except the owner had no insurance. And, don't forget, he was in the building at the time. He was the one who was badly burned. He'd hardly set light to the place if he was still inside."

"He had no insurance? None at all?"

"No. He couldn't afford the premiums, so he let it lapse."

"And you're sure? He's not just telling you that?"

"No. I checked it out."

"So, he loses everything?"

"Yes."

"Including his company?"

"Yes."

"He might be avoiding being wound up by a creditor, I suppose."

Sam stares at me. "It's a bit elaborate, isn't it? If he's in financial trouble – which he clearly is – he could just wind the company up himself. Go for voluntary liquidation."

"Maybe he can't afford it."

"Sorry?"

"It's not free, you know."

He leans forward. "Tell me more."

"Well, you'd have to speak to an insolvency practitioner; I don't know how much it costs, but I know it's not free, that's all. And the creditors have to agree to it. Maybe he knows they won't."

"And how do you know all this?" He stares at me, his blue eyes boring into mine, until I start feeling a little uncomfortable.

"Because my dad worked in the City. I listened."

He jots down some notes on a pad. "I'll check it out in the morning. I guess if he's flat broke, this might have seemed like the only way out. It does feel a bit drastic though… He's still in intensive care."

"Maybe he wanted a way out for himself as well…"

"What? Suicide?"

I shrug. "Don't dismiss it. Let's face it, nothing else is fitting."

He looks at me. "Andy was right. You're good." He smiles. "You're really good, especially considering this is only your second case."

"I was lucky…" I whisper, almost to myself, "I worked with the best on my first."

Sam stands and looks around the office. There are still quite a few people working at their desks. "Fancy a drink?" he says. It's the last thing I want. But should I go along, just to be polite? I don't want my new colleagues thinking I'm aloof, not willing to be part of the team. I get up too.

"Don't you have to get home… to your wife?" It seems like a good excuse and would get me out of going.

"No. She doesn't notice if I'm there or not these days." He glances at the clock on the wall between the windows. "She'll probably be shagging my next-door neighbour right about now."

"I'm sorry?" I can't keep the shock from my voice.

"They've been banging each other for a few months. I can't blame them… I had his wife first, at a Christmas party we all went to together. He threw her out, and now my missus goes round there every Tuesday and Thursday, regular as clockwork. They think I don't know, but I'm not a bloody detective for nothing." He's been so easy to work with all day, I was even starting to like him… but now, he's like a different person.

"And you're still married?" I can't believe I'm hearing this.

"Yeah, but probably not for much longer. Now, what about that drink?" I feel his hand on the small of my back, and I see red.

"Don't touch me." I pull away.

He smirks. "I haven't touched you… not yet."

"And you're not going to."

He looks at me, his brow furrowing, and folds his arms across his chest. "I used to work at Westminster up until a couple of months ago… with Jason Bishop." *God, does he know everyone?* "I still meet up with him for a drink every so often," Sam continues. "If you froze him out like this all the time, I'm not surprised he shagged your sister…"

Jason told him? How could he? I have to work here, for God's sake.

I grab my bag from the back of the chair and run, and I don't stop running until I reach my car.

It's probably not wise to make momentous decisions when you're two thirds of the way through a bottle of red wine… and it's even less wise to actually type out your resignation letter, but I don't care, I've done it anyway, and I've printed it out, and put it in an envelope, in my bag, ready to give to Andy first thing tomorrow morning. I know Andy will probably throw a fit and I know I'll have to work out a month's notice, in an office where at least one person knows my secret – and he'll probably spread it around, now I've rejected his advances… but what does it matter? What's a little more humiliation?

I'm sitting on the edge of my bed, cradling the rest of the bottle, and my half-empty glass, tears pouring down my cheeks. To think, I was ever stupid enough to compare Todd to Jason… or any man for that matter. There's no comparison. Not only would Todd never have cheated, but he'd never talk about me behind my back – well, certainly not in an unfavourable way, anyway. He's far too honourable. Even if he does tell his friends about us, I instinctively know he'll only tell them good things about me, and probably bad things about himself. And that just makes me feel worse. What the hell was wrong with me? Why did I just let him leave without saying something? Why did I throw it away?

What Jason did to me hurt. What Ellie did to me really, really hurt. But being without Todd… It's like a tear in my soul.

But that's not his fault. I've done that all by myself.

Chapter Seventeen

Todd

I try to move, but nothing works. How odd. Not even my eyes will open. I'm awake… or at least I feel like I'm awake. I feel conscious. But my eyes won't open. This is weird.

"He's going to be alright, isn't he?" That's my mom's voice. "He's my only son." Her voice is trembling. She sounds scared. *Don't be scared, mom. I'm okay.* What's she doing here? Come to think of it, where is 'here'? Where am I? What's going on?

"Yes, Mrs Russell. He's through the worst." I don't know whose voice that is. It's a man; he sounds serious, but kind. Well, I guess that's good news. I'm going to be alright. What happened? The worst of what? "We got the bullet out; he lost a lot of blood, but he'll be okay. He just needs time now." I'm guessing he's a doctor and I'm in the hospital, but I've got no idea why.

"Why won't he wake up?" Good question, mom. That's exactly what I was going to ask… at least I would if anything was working.

"Like I say, he needs time. He's very weak."

He's not wrong, if even my eyelids won't work. That's pathetic. Wait, he said 'bullet'. Oh yeah… I was shot, in the shoulder.

"But you're sure he's okay?"

"Try not to worry, Barbara. He's getting the best care, I promise." Matt. Matt's here? And he called my mom Barbara. He's always called her Mrs Russell before. I'm starting to think I've entered a parallel universe.

"I'd better call Vicky," my mom says. "Her number's on my phone… somewhere."

My mom is useless with phones. In fact, she's useless with technology in general. She'll probably end up calling a complete stranger.

"Why don't I do it for you?" Hell… that's Grace's voice, I'm sure it is. Is everyone here? "Give me your phone and I'll call her while I go and get some coffee. You stay with Todd… You and Matt."

"Oh, that's very kind. Thank you, thank you so much." I hear my mom's voice crack, and then a sob. Shit. I need to hug her, but I can't. I need to tell her everything will be okay. I feel useless. She shouldn't be going through this alone.

"Hey, come here," Matt says. And I know that he's holding her, and I know then that she's not alone.

"Are you okay?" Grace asks after a while.

"Yes, I'll be fine." My mom's voice is a little stronger.

"I'll go and get the coffee, and phone Vicky, and I'll be back as soon as I can."

"Take care, baby," Matt says. I can hear a concerned note in his voice. What's that about? Is something wrong with Grace?

"You two should get home to your little boy," my mom says, sniffing and blowing her nose.

"George is fine. I'll try and persuade Grace to go back later. For now, he's okay with Luke and Megan. Will and Jamie are helping out." Wait a second. Did he just say Luke and Megan? My mom's talking again…

"But you've been here for so long…"

"I'm not leaving here, not until Todd comes round." There's a pause. "You're exhausted," he says. "I can get Luke or Will to come and fetch you. You can go back to our place and rest for a while, and they'll bring you back later."

"I should stay here."

"I'll be here. I won't leave him, and I'll call you as soon as he wakes up. You'll be doing me a favor, Barbara. We might be able to persuade Grace to go with you, to keep you company. She needs to rest too. She's hardly slept since I got the call, apart from a few hours here and there."

"You haven't even had that, Matthew."

"I'm fine. And please call me Matt." His voice sounds like he's asked her that a hundred times already.

"Would it be okay, do you think, if I went? Now I know he's going to be alright, I'm just so tired."

"I'll call Luke."

"And you'll let me know…?"

"The moment he wakes up… yes." There's another pause, and the tone of Matt's voice alters. "Hey," he says. "No, there's no change. But can you drive down and pick up Todd's mom, and Grace… and take them home. They're both exhausted." He waits. "No. I'm staying. Yeah, I know you could, but I'm staying. I want to know you're there, looking after Grace, and Barbara and the babies." There's another pause. "Okay, see you soon."

"He's coming?" my mom asks.

"Yes. He'll be here in under an hour."

"How is he?" That's Luke speaking, so I must have drifted off to sleep again for a while… well, at least an hour. This doesn't make sense though. He's supposed to be in Italy, with Megan. They're on their honeymoon. Am I dreaming this? I'm starting to think I must be, but…

"The same. He still hasn't woken up," Matt replies, "but the doctor says he's gonna be okay. It's just a matter of time."

"I'm happy to stay, if you want to take Barbara and Grace home," Luke says. It's definitely him. "You can take my car… get some rest. I don't even want to think when you last slept."

"Sunday night." That's Grace again. What day is it now then? Man, I'm so confused. I need to wake up, so I can work out what the fuck is going on.

"No. I have to stay." Matt sounds weary.

"Are you sure you'll be alright?" Grace asks. "I'm not happy about leaving you here by yourself."

"I'm not by myself, baby," he replies. "I'm with Todd."

"You'll call?"

"I'll call. Text me when you get back home. Give George a hug and a kiss from me."

"I will."

There's a movement in the room, but I can't work out what it is. Then Matt speaks again.

"Take care of them for me."

"I will. You take care of yourself, Matt." That's Luke again.

"I'm fine."

"Yeah, right."

I hear the door open and close.

"I can stay." It's Grace's voice.

"No. Please. I want you to go home. I'm worried about you. You're exhausted, and you need to see George. I know you're missing him."

"But I'll miss you." I hear the emotion in Grace's voice.

"And I'll miss you too."

I think I can hear them kiss… I've heard and seen them kissing many times before, so why does that sound – that thought – make my chest hurt all of a sudden? I've never reacted like that to them, or anyone else, kissing in my presence. Why now?

"He will be okay, you know," Grace says, her voice real quiet.

"I know he will, but I have to stay. I can't leave him. I owe him everything."

"Yes, I know." They kiss again, and then I hear the door open and close once more.

Silence descends and I sense… no, I know it's just Matt in the room. Matt, and me.

And that pain in my chest is still there. If anything, it's getting worse. What's that about? I've never felt anything like it. Wait though, have I? It is familiar, now I come to think about it. I felt something like it recently. Oh yeah, when I was shot. No… that was in my shoulder, not my chest. I can't feel my left shoulder at all right now. I'm probably dosed up on painkillers, I guess. This pain in my chest… this is different. It's like a crushing, numbing, completely overwhelming pain and it feels like it's gonna go on forever. It feels like a part of me is missing and I'm never going to get it back.

What the hell happened to me? It must have been something before I was shot… I need to remember. *C'mon Todd… think back.* I remember

224

getting off a plane. So, where had I been? Above the clouds, looking out the window. Oh, yeah, London... a car ride... saying goodbye... Holly... *Oh, God, no*... holding Holly. That hurts... that really fucking hurts.

"Holly!" The cry comes from deep inside me, unlocking the pain in my chest, releasing it, so it fills my whole body.

"Todd?"

"Holly. P—please. Please..."

"Wait. I'll fetch someone."

"No." I open my eyes. Matt's looking down at me, right above me, his eyes red rimmed and filled with concern.

"Let me get the nurse."

"Not yet," I croak. His hand is right beside me and I grab it. "Pain..." I manage to say. "Please, stop this fucking pain."

"Just stay quiet," he says, and he disappears from my sight, pulling his hand from mine.

The doctor has been to see me, together with two different nurses. I'm wired up to a monitor, with an IV tube in my right arm, and now the morphine's wearing off a little, my shoulder's starting to ache... but that's okay. It's nothing compared to the other pain.

"What time is it?" I whisper. My voice isn't working properly.

"It's just after midnight." Matt's sitting on a chair beside me. He called my mom within a few minutes of me waking. At Matt's suggestion, they've decided to stay at his place until the morning to get some rest.

"What day?" I ask.

"Thursday, but only just."

"I flew back on Monday... I think."

"Yeah. You did. Thanks for letting us know, by the way."

"Sorry about that. I had something that needed doing."

"Getting shot, evidently."

"That wasn't part of the plan." I reach to get some water, but wince in pain and Matt leaps up and brings it to me, putting the straw into my mouth so I can take a sip.

"Enough?" he asks, and I nod. He puts the beaker on the table and I settle back onto the pillow.

"Is something wrong with Grace?" I ask, once he's sat back down again.

"No, not really. She's just tired. She'll sleep better tonight."

"And that's all it is?"

"Yes. Why?"

"I could hear you talking... before I woke up. You sounded worried about her."

"I am. She's hardly slept since Monday afternoon, when we got the call."

"From what I heard, you haven't slept at all. You can go home now, Matt. I'm okay. Go be with Grace and George. I know you don't like being apart." I get it now. I never used to, but I really do get it.

"I'm not going anywhere. Not just yet."

"I'm okay."

"Sure you are." He looks at me and takes a deep breath. There's an expression behind his eyes I've never seen before – not on Matt's face, anyway. "I knew I'd be the one to get the call... if anything ever happened to you. I knew you wanted to protect your mom from that... I just never thought it would happen."

"Neither did I. Who called you?"

"Chris. Chris Jefferson. She's been in and out of here ever since, checking up on you. She told me what happened and that you were on your way to the ER."

"And you called my mom?"

"No."

"No?"

"Well, the whole point of me being notified first was to protect her from getting a phone call about you, so I flew down there."

"You flew to Atlanta?"

"Yeah. I'll admit it was a little chaotic. I was in a meeting, which I ran out of. I called Grace and Will on the way to the airport. Will and Jamie drove straight here from their office and Grace came down with George... but it all got a bit much for him, so Jamie took him back to our place." He stops for a moment. "Grace didn't want to leave until I got back," he explains. "Will stayed with her until I arrived with your mom, then he went back to help Jamie."

"And Luke?" I look at him. "I'm sure I heard him, or did I dream that?"

"No, you heard him. Will called him to let him know what was going on and he booked them on the first flight back. They landed late Tuesday afternoon. He took Megan and Daisy straight to our place and then drove down here. He stayed for a while, but he was exhausted, so I sent him back to our place to be with Megan and the babies… Everyone's been camped out there ever since. It was easier to do that than for anyone to go home."

Hell. They all just stopped their lives… put everything on hold. All of them. For me? And Luke? He and Megan just ended their honeymoon. I don't know what to say. "It sounds like you got a quick turnaround… with the flight back from Atlanta, I mean…" I can't put words to how I really feel, so this is a good diversion.

"I chartered the plane. The pilot was waiting for us on the tarmac."

"You did what?" My voice comes out a little louder, and I cough. Matt offers me more water and I sip.

"I needed to know I could get your mom back quickly. Telling her was one of the hardest things I've ever done."

"How was she?" I'm not sure I want to hear, but thinking about that distracts me from what everyone's done for me, *and* how much money this must have cost Matt.

"She broke down on me. I think she thought you were already dead. To start with, I couldn't convince her you weren't… and then she was certain you'd die before we could get back here. I was damn glad we weren't flying on a commercial airline. It meant there was no waiting around, and we talked all the way back here."

"So that's why you're calling her Barbara now?"

"Yeah." He smiles. "Mrs Russell felt a bit formal after the first hour or so."

"I owe you so much," I whisper.

"No. If you remember, you saved Grace's life. I'll always, always owe you, Todd. Everything."

I close my eyes for a moment. When I open them, he's still staring at me.

"Sorry, did I fall asleep?" My voice is working a little better.

"Just for a while."

"You really can go, Matt."

"I will… soon." He leans forward, his elbows resting on his knees. "Who's Holly?" he asks.

The pain intensifies, cuts a little deeper. "How… How do you know that name?"

"Chris told me it was the last thing you said before you blacked out… and it was the first thing you said when you woke up earlier. Don't you remember?" I remember saying her name, I just didn't realize I'd said it out loud. "And just now, when you were sleeping, you kept saying it too, over and over." He waits. "Who is she?"

"A woman."

"Yeah… I kind of worked that much out for myself."

"I met her in London."

"She's British?" He smiles and I know he's thinking of Grace.

"Yeah. She's British. We worked together. We were married."

"What?" He leans forward even further, his face frozen.

"Only for the purposes of the job. We were working undercover together; we had to pose as a married couple."

"Oh." He looks at me. "But I'm guessing it wasn't all an act for you?"

"No, it wasn't." I expect him to crow. He's always said that when I lost my heart, he'd laugh his ass off. He's not laughing.

"But… something went wrong?" he asks gently.

"Yeah."

"What with? The job?"

"No… with me." He doesn't say anything, but raises an eyebrow.

"Wanna talk about it?" he asks.

"Not now."

"But she's okay?" he asks, concerned. "I mean… from what you were saying, it sounded like something might have happened to her."

"No. Nothing happened, except that I fucked it up."

He lets out a long breath and in that one simple action, I can see he won't crow.

He leans forward again, putting his hand on my arm. "Let me know when you wanna talk about it."

                            ∞

Holly

As I expected, I've got to work out my notice, so I'll finish work in four weeks' time.

I didn't actually hand Andy my letter of resignation this morning, but left it on his desk and, once he'd read it, he called me in.

"You mean this?" he asked me, looking serious, and a little disappointed.

I just nodded my head, which was probably a mistake, because the hangover was far worse than I'd expected.

"Why? You don't really explain…"

"I can't work here anymore."

"Why? I'm sorry, Holly, but your letter doesn't make sense." *Probably not, but then I was really quite drunk when I wrote it.*

I knew he wasn't going to let me off easily. And the truth is usually the best policy… Holding back never pays. I've found that out to my cost lately. "I can't be the butt of gossip."

"Gossip?" He looked out over my shoulder, through the glass partition. "What's Sam said. The guy's a dick, you know that, don't you?"

"Even if he is, he's going to spread it around the office."

"Spread what?"

"Jason told him… about what happened with my sister. Sam wasn't exactly subtle. I don't need it, Andy."

"I can get you a transfer to a different station, if that helps."

"Jason doesn't even work here and the gossips are talking. He knows so many people. How do I know who else he's told... or will tell?"

"I don't know who he's told. But I don't think he'll tell anyone else. I think even he realises it was a mistake."

"You can't know that."

"I was there when he told Sam. There were a few of us there that night. Jason was very, very drunk and he was having a hard time coming to terms with what had happened... and before you bite my head off, I know it was his own fault. But he was completely wrecked, and it just kind of came out."

"And how do you know he won't tell anyone else?"

"Because I know he regrets saying it. I mean, he regrets that it happened in the first place, but he regrets telling everyone. He spoke to me." Andy sighed and put the letter down on his desk. "Look, I can't change your mind for you, but I know you're good at this job and I don't want you to throw it away over something trivial. Don't give up your career, not if you think there's even the slightest chance you'll regret it later."

"How do you know I'm good at the job? I've only done a few days' work – and none of it here."

Then he opened a file that had been sitting in front of him. "Todd e-mailed me." He looked up at me. "He knew it was your first case, and he sent me a brief report on your work at the end of your first week. I didn't ask for it, Holly... he provided it. He speaks very highly of you and your abilities. He says here that you're adaptable, quick-thinking and insightful, among other things. He recommends you for future undercover work."

"When did he write it?" I asked him that because I'd have been willing to bet it was after we made love. Andy took out a piece of paper and checked the date and time at the top of the message.

"Friday night... late." I recalled Todd taking his laptop into his bedroom... I'd assumed it was just to book the hire car, but it seems not. Andy laid the piece of paper down again and looked up at me. "I'm not going to persuade you, am I?" I shook my head. "What are you going to do?" he asked me, closing the file.

"I don't know."

"I'll put you on another case for now, so you're not working with Sam."

"Thank you."

He stared at me. "I'll be sorry to lose you, Holly."

Now, in my flat, half way through another bottle of wine, I've got nothing to look forward to, nothing planned and no prospects, but I know I've made the right decision.

I just have to decide what to do with the rest of my life; and how to do it without Todd.

Chapter Eighteen

∞

Todd

A week in the hospital was more than enough for me.

I've been at home for six days though and I'm already going crazy. Matt dropped me off, with my mom, and she's fussing. No, I'm being unfair. She's trying to help, but I'd rather be left alone, even if I know that's a dangerous place for me to be at the moment.

She's said she's going to stay until I'm better. I don't know how long that'll be. If we're talking about my shoulder, a couple more weeks should see me fine. If we're talking about the rest of me… God knows. Probably never.

"What's wrong?" I'm sitting in the chair by the window in the living room, which is what I do every day. It's *all* I do every day.

"Nothing."

"Todd. I may not see you very often nowadays." *Who's fault's that?* "But I'm still your mother. Something's wrong. And I'm not talking about the fact that you got shot. It's more than that."

I look across at her. She's sitting on the couch, looking concerned.

"I met someone," I tell her, staring out the window again. "It didn't work out."

"You've met a lot of people," she says. "It's never worked out and it's never bothered you before."

"She was different." My mom's waiting. "I thought… I thought I could have something with her."

"Really?"

I turn to look at her. "Don't act so surprised, Mom."

"Why? You've never even spoken about any of your girlfriends, not once… Of course I'm surprised if you're thinking about having a relationship with someone… maybe settling down."

"Well, I'm not. Not anymore."

"But you were?"

"Yes."

"And something went wrong?" she asks.

"Yes."

"What?"

"Me. I got it wrong."

"And you can't go back to her and make it right? When you're better, I mean."

"No."

"So you're just gonna give up?" She sounds a little disappointed.

"It's complicated. She's not free."

"She's married?"

"No, Mom. She was with someone else before me… it didn't end well and she's not over it yet. The timing was just real bad."

"Then let her get over it and go back."

"I wish it was that easy."

"It's never easy, Todd. That's the whole point. It's worth having… so it's worth fighting for."

We sit quietly for a while and I think about Holly. It's Saturday today. I wonder if she's shopping at the store. I can picture her, pushing the cart around, picking up her groceries. She'll have no-one to carry her bags… At least, I hope she doesn't. I wonder, just for a moment, if she's met someone else, or maybe got back together with Jason. Would she do that? I guess anything's possible. She said she could forgive him… The pain in my chest intensifies the more I think about it.

"Why have you always been alone?" My mom's words cut into my thoughts and I turn to her.

"Sorry?"

"You've never had a serious relationship. Why?"

"I couldn't. Not while I worked on the force."

"Is that why this one was different. You felt you could make that commitment, because you knew you'd be leaving soon?" I've really already left. I got Matt to prepare my resignation letter and I signed it as soon as I was able, while I was still in the hospital. I officially leave the force on June 15th, although I won't be fit to work before then anyway, so it's all a formality.

"No. She was just different... special. Even if I hadn't already decided to leave, I think I'd have left for her." I know that now.

"She really was special then. But what difference did the job make? A lot of cops settle down. Your dad was a cop; it didn't stop him from getting married and having a family."

I look away again. "That's the whole point, Mom."

"I don't understand."

"I couldn't put anyone through what you went through when he died."

"Really? That's it? That's the whole reason you've stayed single all these years?"

"Yes." I turn to face her again. "I watched you grieve for him. I couldn't be responsible for doing that to someone else."

"So you think it's been better not to have had someone in your life at all?"

"Well, I've never met someone I wanted to share my life with... until Holly... so it's not really a relevant point."

She gets up and comes to stand in front of me.

"Sometimes I think I did the wrong thing moving down to Atlanta. I think I should've stayed up here with you."

"Why?"

"Because, I sometimes think you need me more than your sister ever will."

"How do you work that out? Vicky always needed your help more than I did."

"Yes, son, that's very true. You're much more independent and self-sufficient. I worried a little about you when I left, but I knew you'd be okay. I knew you'd cope. Vicky's not good at coping… never was, never will be. She's a drama queen. But it strikes me right about now that you need someone to knock some sense into you." She moves away and leans back against the wall beside the window. "Your father loved his job, and I'd never have asked him to give it up for something that kept him safe. Even though it took him from me, I'd never have asked him to change a single thing about what he did, or who he was. I wouldn't change a single day of my life with him."

"His death broke you, Mom."

"Of course it did. I'd lost the man I loved. But at least I'd loved." She comes and stands in front of me again, putting her hands on the arms of my chair and leaning over. "And so have you now. Whatever happened with this woman, if you really love her, find a way to work it out, son. You'll regret it for the rest of your life, if you don't."

Like I don't already know that…

∽

Holly

"Can you come in here a minute?" Andy calls me over from his office door. It's nearly time to go home for the evening. I don't exactly relish going back to my empty flat, but I'm not enjoying being here either. Being in the police force was all I ever wanted… but now I can't wait to leave. That's something else Jason's taken from me. Or has he? If I was stronger, I guess I could face up to the gossips and stay on. So it's not his fault really. It's that I'm not good enough to be here either…

I've spent the last four weeks generally helping out on various cases, which has suited me fine. I didn't want to get into anything important, knowing I'd be going soon, and tomorrow is my last day. The month has gone surprisingly quickly, and I've still got no idea what I'm going to do with my future. There's nothing on the horizon, except staring at the walls of my apartment, and missing Todd.

"Sure." I get up and go into his office.

"I've just been doing some clearing up," he says. "Not my strong point... And I've noticed that the wedding rings Todd Russell was given for your undercover op weren't returned with the file he gave to Adam. Do you know where they are? And please tell me he didn't take them back to the States with him..."

"No. I've got them. They're at home in my bag."

"Well, can you bring them in tomorrow?" he says.

"No problem. Was that it?"

"Yes."

It doesn't take more than five minutes to find my bag and the rings, still zipped in the inside pocket, precisely where I put them that Saturday night at the beginning of May... when everything was still so perfect. Before it all went wrong.

I don't want to think about all that. I only managed to stop drinking so heavily a couple of weeks ago. I can't go back there again.

I put the rings into my jacket pocket ready for the morning and go through to the kitchen to prepare my dinner.

Even now, so many weeks later, every room in my apartment reminds me of him. In my bedroom, I think about the night he changed rooms with me, and the day we moved the furniture around, and he pinned me to the bed for the first time... and sleeping with him... and being woken by him in the middle of the night. In the guest room, I think about how he made love to me... how he made me come so hard. I sleep in there all the time now, just so I can feel closer to him. In the kitchen, I can still recall him singing to Bruce Springsteen, and holding me while I sat on the floor crying about my sister; and in the living room, I think about watching movies, falling asleep on him... and that last morning, and how intense he was when he pushed me up against the wall. I can still see the look in his eyes...

There are no bad memories. None. Even as he was leaving, he tried to make it okay. And I did nothing. I said nothing to make him stay, gave him no reason to come back to me. And I can't forgive myself for that.

I've wondered, on and off, over the last few weeks, whether he'd change his mind and come back. I've lain awake at night, fantasising about him knocking on my door, telling me he can't live without me and asking if we can try again. It's not going to happen, I know that. He asked me for one simple thing – to trust him – and I couldn't do it. So why would he come back to me?

Chapter Nineteen

❦

Todd

The knocking at the door wakes me.

I've got no idea how long I've been asleep, or why I didn't hear the doorbell, but I get up and go across, adjusting my sling en route, then pulling the door open.

"Hi," Grace says, her voice a little subdued.

What's she doing here?

"Hi," I reply, not standing aside to let her in. It's rude. I know it's rude but I don't give a damn.

"Can I come in?" she asks. I stare at her. For Christ's sake. I've been ignoring text messages and phone calls from everyone since I came out of the hospital. Can't they take the hint? "Todd?"

"What?"

"I said, can I come in?" she asks again.

"I'm not really in the mood…"

"Oh." God, she looks kinda crushed. I hate doing that to her.

"The place is a mess," I add, by way of an excuse.

"That doesn't matter."

"Okay… don't say I didn't warn you." I reluctantly step to one side and let her pass me, then close the door.

When I turn, she's standing there, looking around my normally tidy living room. It's horrible. There are half-empty take-out cartons and pizza boxes everywhere, beer cans and bottles on the floor. Clothes are scattered on the couches. I've basically been living in here for the last week, since my mom left. I've ordered in food, but not always eaten it; I've been drinking too much and I sleep – when I can sleep, that is – in the chair by the window. It's hard to believe, looking around, that this is only a week's accumulation of crap.

I stand, looking at her. I've got no idea why she's here, but I wish she'd just tell me… and leave.

"I came over to invite you to a barbecue on Saturday," she says quietly, still looking around the room.

Really? And she couldn't call, or text… so I could ignore her? "I'm not sure I'm up to it," I lie. Physically, I'm more than up to sitting on the deck at Matt and Grace's house.

"I know you can't drive yet, so Matt would come and get you," she offers, "or I could arrange with Will for him to pick you up."

"My shoulder…" I start to say.

"Is getting better," she interrupts, turning and looking at me. "Todd, you need to get out of here." Judging from the expression on her face, I'd say I look about as bad as my apartment, but then I still haven't been able to look in the mirror – not properly. I run my hand across my chin, feeling the week-old beard… yeah, I must look pretty rough.

She walks further into the room and puts her purse down on the end of the couch.

"Why don't I have a bit of a clear-up for you?" she says and, without waiting for me to answer, she starts picking up boxes from the floor, carrying them through to the kitchen.

"Grace…" I need to stop her, to get her out of here… "You don't need to do that."

I look up. She's tapping something into her cell phone. "Sorry?" she says, looking over at me. "That was Megan. She's looking after George for me. Did you say something?"

"Yeah. I said you don't need to tidy my apartment."

"Have you looked around lately?" she replies.

"What I mean is, it's not your job."

"I know that, but I'm here, so I might as well." She comes back and grabs some of the clothes. "Why don't I do some laundry?" she suggests.

"Because I'm not incapable?"

She turns and raises an eyebrow at me. Okay, I know it looks like I'm incapable, but I'm not… I just don't give a fuck.

"At least let me stay and have a coffee with you." She sounds a little desperate.

"I'm not sure there are any clean cups…"

"Then I'll wash some."

She's not gonna let up.

Twenty minutes later, she's cleared some of the mess in my living room – at least enough for us to both sit down – and we've drunk a cup of coffee together, although we've barely spoken more than a few sentences to each other, and I haven't really given her an answer about this damned barbecue, even though she's suggested I could stay over as well. I don't want to go. I don't want to sit and make polite conversation with the guys. I want Holly… Just the thought of her makes everything hurt again.

The doorbell rings and I get up and answer it. Standing on the threshold are Matt, Luke and Will. I'm momentarily reminded that I haven't thanked any of them properly for what they did when I was shot… and especially Luke, for cutting short his honeymoon. Still, I can't think about that right now.

I hold the door, barring their entrance and turn back to Grace.

"You called them?" I'm mad at her now. She looks a little wary, but I take a few steps toward her anyway.

"No. I texted Matt," she whispers. When did she do that?

"So it wasn't Megan?" She shakes her head. "You lied." She stares at me. "Why?" I ask her.

"Because you're hurting, Todd. You need your friends."

"No, I don't." I need Holly.

"Yes, you do. You need to talk. I'll leave, if you want me to, but you need to talk to them." She nods in the direction of the door. I look around to see Matt, Luke and Will standing behind me, the door closed. Matt's got a look on his face… I know what it means. I wouldn't hurt Grace and, deep down, he knows that, but he's letting me know his friendship has its limits. If I do anything to her, we're through. I get it... I feel the same about Holly.

"Look, guys... I'm fine." I turn to them.

"Bullshit," Matt says.

"Yeah, you look fine," Luke adds, shaking his head. "You look a fucking mess. And so does your apartment."

"I got shot," I say, trying to sound as normal as possible. "Keeping house isn't a priority."

"What's wrong?" Matt asks patiently.

"Nothing's wrong. I told you, I'm fine."

He takes a deep breath, letting it out slowly. "This is about Holly, isn't it?"

"You fucking asshole," I whisper. How could he?

"Isn't it?" he pushes.

Something flips inside me. "Yes!" I roar at him. "Alright, it's about Holly... I'm sure you've told everyone else, and had a good laugh that Todd finally fell in love after all these years... after all these years of saying he was immune... *and* that Todd fucked it up. So, now everyone knows, perhaps you'd all like to leave?"

"No." Grace comes over and stands next to Matt. "He didn't tell anyone – not even me. And if he didn't tell me, you can bet your life no-one else knows. I've got no idea who Holly is or what you're both talking about, but whatever's going on, you can't keep doing this. You have to tell someone what's wrong... Because the way you're going, you're about to self-destruct and we're not going to just sit around and let you. W—we all love you too much."

I stare at her. God, I really wish she hadn't said that. And I really wish her voice hadn't broken on that last sentence. And more than anything, I wish she didn't have a British accent. It only reminds me of Holly. Again. And I don't need any more reminders. Her voice – her words – they cut through the searing pain and bring me to my knees – quite literally. Matt catches me, just as I'm about to hit the floor.

"Okay, I've got you," he mutters, and helps me to the nearest couch. He sits down beside me and waits... and waits. When I look up again, Will and Luke have cleared the couch opposite of all my shit, which they've piled on the floor, and are sitting, facing us, Grace is on the chair by the window.

"I can't do this," I whisper. "It hurts too much."

"Tell us," Matt urges. "We may not be able to help, but talking can't make it any worse."

I know he's right. What I'm doing now isn't getting me anywhere. Grace said it perfectly… I am going to self destruct soon. I'm not sure how much detail I want to give them. Some of it's too personal. It's between me and Holly, and no-one else. I take a deep breath. "I met someone in London. Her name's Holly…" I say simply.

"And?" Luke asks. I stare across the room at him. He stares back.

"And I fell in love."

"And?" he repeats.

"And I fucked up. Okay?"

"You already said that. How?"

"I—I don't know…" I do, but I don't know how to tell them.

"You must know." Luke's persistent. What's his problem? "If you know you're the one who fucked up… you must know what you did."

"I rushed her."

"And?"

"And… she wasn't ready."

"And?"

God, it's like he's interrogating me… pushing me. I don't want to fight with him. I take a deep breath. "There was a guy before me… a boyfriend," I murmur. "He cheated on her, but she wasn't over him. I told her I'd wait for her, but… I didn't. I think she regretted what we did."

"You say you *think*… But you don't know?" he says.

"No… I don't know. Not for sure." That's the first time I've really thought about that. I don't know for sure that she regretted it. I've assumed it, but she never actually said she regretted any of it.

Luke stands up, takes off his jacket, throws it on the couch and puts his hands in his pockets, then walks over to me. Everyone else sits back into their seats and lets him take over. Did they plan this? It sure feels like it, but I can't see how that's possible – they didn't know this was going to happen, or what I'd say.

"Did you tell her you loved her?" he asks.

"No."

"Did you two talk at all? Or did you just take her straight to bed?"

"No. I didn't take her straight to bed, Luke. I'm not you." He doesn't even blink at the insult, the reference to the way he lived his life, before he met Megan. "And yes, we talked."

"Just not about the important stuff, evidently."

"We talked… We talked a lot, about all kinds of things."

"Then how come you don't know anything?"

I stand up and face him. I'm starting to feel like I could fight him now. He's pissing me off. We're just inches apart. We're about the same height and build… and right now, he's really making me mad.

"What the fuck are we doing here?" he continues.

"Excuse me?" I get a little closer to him. "I didn't invite you, remember?"

He sighs. "It seems to me you've done pretty much everything *except* talk to her, Todd. You should be telling her you love her, and seeing what she's got to say about it."

I know that. "But, what if she doesn't… love me, that is?" It's the thing I'm most afraid of.

"And what if she does? You're sitting here, day after day, wrecking your life, beating yourself up, dwelling on stuff that might not be true, wondering where you went wrong. And she could could be sitting in London, wondering why you haven't gotten back in touch with her, whether she meant anything at all to you, or whether you're like every other guy she's ever met and it was all about the sex, and you're just full of shit." I stare at him. "So… was it just about the sex? Are you full of shit? Or do you *really* love her?"

"Luke, I'm gonna fucking hit you in a minute. Real hard."

"Go ahead, if it makes you feel any better." I move a step closer. He doesn't flinch.

I take a deep breath. Hitting him isn't going to make me feel better. Only Holly can do that. "Yeah… I really love her." I say quietly.

"Then why the fuck have you given up on her?" Luke says.

"Because I more than fucked up…"

"How?"

"I told her it was all a mistake, and we should forget it ever happened."

"Nice… Why the hell did you do that?"

"Because she kept comparing me to her ex, she didn't trust me; she wouldn't tell me how she felt… and it fucking hurt," I yell the last four words at him.

"Oh, I see. And you wanted to hurt her back. Is that it?"

"No!"

"Then why say it?"

"Because I was hurt." Is he even listening?

"And so was she, after you'd said that." He takes a deep breath and runs his fingers through his hair. "Here we go again…" he mutters, kind of under his breath – almost to himself. Then he looks up at me. "Okay… I'm gonna guess you made love to her – and that was the bit you rushed into – and either during or after that happened, you wanted her to tell you how she felt about you… and when she didn't, or couldn't, for whatever reason, you told her to forget the whole thing, and that it was all a big mistake. Because you're really… what? Fifteen? Way to go, Todd. I bet she felt pretty fucking amazing about herself after that. Is that what you wanted?"

"No, of course not." I feel like even more a jerk, hearing it put that way.

"So, did you get a chance to explain why you'd said those things?"

"No. We were gonna sit down and talk it through, but I had to leave; a guy from Holly's station turned up unannounced to take me to the airport… I had about ten minutes."

"Ten minutes with Holly?"

"No… ten minutes to pack and leave."

"And did you tell her you'd go back to her?"

"No."

"Why the hell not?"

"Because she didn't give me a reason to…"

He glares at me. "Christ… You really did want her to do all the work, didn't you?" he mutters. "This guy from her department, was he there the whole time?"

"Yeah."

"And you still expected her to tell you how she felt about you? In front of someone she has to work with?" He stares at me. "Would you wanna do that, Todd? You know what squad rooms are like… I imagine they're pretty similar in England. You wanted her to spill her guts to you and then face the gossips the next morning…?"

"No," I mutter. *What the fuck was I thinking? I wasn't thinking. That was the problem.*

"And how was she when you left?"

"She was upset. Really upset…" I can still remember her eyes brimming with unshed tears.

He smiles, just a little, for the first time since he stood up. "Okay. Well, that's something…" he mutters, under his breath again. He squares his shoulders and looks at me. "You wanna make it right?" he asks. I nod my head. "Then you need to tell her how *you* feel, tell her you were wrong, that it wasn't a mistake, and you're a jerk for having said that. Apologize to her; tell her you love her… and don't keep dumping it all on her. And if she's mad at you and won't listen the first time, you go back, and you keep going back, and you keep telling her you love her. You keep trying, and you never stop, no matter how much it hurts…"

"And if I can't do that?"

His smile drops, he looks at me and shrugs. "Then you don't love her."

I take another step toward him and raise my clenched right fist. He doesn't even blink. "You have no fucking right to say that," I growl at him.

"I have every fucking right," he shouts. "If you love her, you'll go through hell for her. You'll go through worse than hell… you'll rip your own heart out for her. So don't fucking tell me you can't." As he says the last word, he jabs me in the chest with his forefinger. I stare at him for a very long moment and then slowly lower my arm.

I turn and look from him to Matt. "What he said," he murmurs, nodding to Luke. "All of it. Every word. He's good at this stuff. He made me realize when I was being an idiot over Grace… so listen to him. And then get your ass on the next available flight to London. I'll even pay the air fare if it helps." He pauses for a moment, then stands and comes over to us. "When you woke up in the hospital, you asked me to stop the pain. But you weren't talking about the pain in your shoulder, were you?" I don't answer him. "I can buy you all the medical care in the world, but I can't make this pain better," he says. "Only you can do that. Only you can make this go away, Todd."

I don't know what to say to them – not yet. I've got too much to think about.

Luke moves away, his head lowered. "Did you guys plan this?" I ask, because it still feels like they did.

"No," Luke replies, turning back to me. "But you'd shut yourself off," he explains. "I don't think any of us knew how we were gonna get through to you." He pauses for a moment. "Matt said on the way over here that getting you to talk was gonna be like getting blood from a stone. We knew you'd get mad about us turning up – and you did – I just figured that if I could get you *really* mad, you'd talk." He smiles. "It was the only way I could talk about Megan when we broke up. Matt'll tell you. I got mad at him, and it all just came out. I'm sorry I was so aggressive. It was the only way I could think of breaking through your wall."

"Why you, though?" I glance from him to Matt.

Matt shrugs, like he doesn't know either, and Luke looks at the floor. "I guess because part of me thought you might get mad enough to wanna hit someone – and it was always gonna be better if that was me. There's no way I was gonna let you hit Will, and you'd have felt real bad if you'd hit Matt…"

"I wouldn't have felt great if I'd have hit you," I admit. "Especially if you'd hit me back." Most people don't get up again when Luke hits them.

He smiles. "I wouldn't have hit you back," he says. "There aren't many people I'd take a punch from and not retaliate – and they're all in this room… but you and the big guy have history. Besides, Grace is here, so there was no way I was gonna let the two of you come to blows in front of her…" His voice fades and he sighs. "In any case, I know better than Matt how you feel. I nearly lost Megan… twice. I know what you're going through. But the answer's in your own hands, man. You can sit around, feeling sorry for yourself, regretting what you *think* you did wrong. Or you can go and find out how she really feels about you. Take the risk… because the prize is worth it, believe me."

"And if I lose? If she rejects me?"

"We'll be here." His voice softens to a whisper, and he places a hand on my shoulder. "We'll always be here."

"I'm sorry," I say quietly.

"Why are you apologizing?" Luke asks.

"What I said earlier," I reply, "about not being like you. That was wrong of me. I know you're not like that anymore."

"But I was – once. What you said was perfectly true, and completely justified."

We stare at each other for a minute. I've always been closest to Matt – I remember telling Holly that – but at this moment, I feel a connection to Luke I've never had before.

"It's different, isn't it?" I say.

"What?"

"All of it."

"You mean when you fall in love? Hell, yeah." He's really smiling now. "None of the others even come close. It's like brilliant, warm sunshine after the longest, darkest storm."

He's right. He's so right. "She's amazing, Luke. I mean, *really* amazing." For the first time in weeks, I smile too. "I can't even think about being with another woman now."

"Then go find her. Tell *her* that, tell her you were wrong, tell her you love her and you want her back, and then bring her home, so we can all meet this amazing woman of yours."

Mine? Is she mine? God, I hope so…

"I think I owe you," I say to him.

"No, you don't," he replies. "I'm getting used to giving these little pep talks now." He glances at Matt, and then at Will. "Admittedly I don't normally do it in front of an audience, but…"

"I wasn't meaning that," I interrupt. He looks confused. "I meant cutting your honeymoon short. I owe you…"

He shakes his head. "No," he says quietly. "We weren't gonna sit in Italy worrying about you… We had to come back." They were worried? "And anyway, you'd have done the same thing for me, if it'd been the other way around…"

He's right, I would. I nod my head.

"Which means you just have to get your ass over to London, win her back, and marry her, so I can find some way of interrupting your honeymoon." He grins at me.

Will stands. "I hate to ruin the moment, but I really think you should wait… at least until you're a little better. You're not fit enough to travel yet. Spend a couple more weeks concentrating on getting well, and then you can focus on Holly."

"He's right," Matt says. "I know I said you should get on the next flight, but Will's got a point. You really shouldn't be traveling yet. Take a bit more time, and then go and get her. Bring her back here… and then we can all tell her what a loser you really are."

"She knows that already," I reply.

"Oh, I seriously doubt that."

Grace is still sitting on the chair, by herself. I go over and crouch in front of her, although I can feel Matt watching me closely. "I'm sorry," I whisper to her.

"What for?"

"Being an ass when you got here."

"You're not an ass," she murmurs, "or even an arse – as both Holly and I would put it, I'm sure." I smile at her. She's right. Holly would say 'arse'. "You're just in a bad place," she continues.

"Yeah." I hesitate before speaking again. "I hope I didn't scare you."

"No. I'm never scared of you, Todd. You're a good man, and I'm sure Holly knows that too." She leans forward and kisses me on the cheek.

"And that's enough of that," Matt calls over. "My sympathy wears a little thin when my wife starts kissing other guys." He's grinning as he walks across to us and sits down on the arm of the chair beside Grace, pulling her close to him.

"Have you changed your mind about the barbecue on Saturday?" Grace asks me as I stand and go over to the couch, sitting down again.

"Yeah, sure. I'll come over."

"At last," Matt says. "He returns to civilization."

Luke and Will take their seats again too. "Well, we have to rehabilitate him somehow," Luke adds. "He's going to see Holly soon. We can't have her thinking he's incapable of surviving without her."

"Even if I am?"

"Yeah." Luke smiles at me.

"Why don't we get Megan and Jamie to come here tonight and order in some food?" Grace suggests. "Megan can bring the babies with her."

"Sounds like a good idea," Luke replies.

"Um… there's the minor problem that my place looks like a dump?"

"There are five of us here. I'm sure we can clear it up between us," Luke says.

"While you take a shower, and have a shave, my friend. You're looking a little bit wild," Matt adds, taking off his jacket. And it's only now that I register he and Luke are wearing work clothes. I check my watch. It's four-thirty in the afternoon… and it's a Thursday.

"Shouldn't you guys be at work?" I say to them.

"Yeah," Matt replies, rolling up his shirt sleeves. "But the best thing about being the boss – as you'll find out if you ever get your sorry ass in to work with Will – is that you get to do whatever you damn well please."

Holly

"Here you go." I hand the white gold rings to Andy.

"Thanks." He takes them and puts them in the top drawer of his desk. "Have you decided what you're going to do yet?"

"No."

"It's not too late to reconsider, you know. Even if you don't want to stay on here, I can still get you a transfer."

"No, but thanks for the offer."

"So, no plans?"

"No."

"You could travel." He looks at me, with a peculiar gleam in his eye. "I hear Boston's nice this time of year."

"Boston?"

"Yes, Holly. You and Todd were good together, in all kinds of ways."

"You didn't see us together."

"Yes I did. I was right here when you met."

"That was only when we met."

"It only takes a moment for some people to know they've met the person they're meant to be with. With others – like my wife and I – it takes months and months of dogged pursuit." He smiles.

"I didn't know you were married." I glance at his bare left hand.

"I don't wear a ring, but I'm still married," he says. He takes a deep breath. "I know something happened between you and Todd... and I know it went wrong." He looks up at me. I guess my expression must give away my confusion. "Adam isn't renowned for his discretion," he explains.

I feel my shoulders drop. "Great."

"I told him to keep his mouth shut. As far as I know, he has done."

I can't deny, I haven't been the butt of any jokes, or gossip, not to my knowledge, anyway.

"Look," Andy continues, "I don't know what went wrong between you and Todd, and I don't want to, but whatever it was... well, most things are fixable; if you want them to be."

"And what if Todd doesn't want to fix it?"

"I'll bet he probably does – unless he's clinically insane." He smiles and looks up at the clock on his wall. "Your shift officially finished five minutes ago, Holly, so I suggest you get out of here. And that maybe once you get home, over a glass of wine, you check out the flights to Boston… What would you rather do? Spend your whole life wondering what might have been? Or risk getting a little more burned finding out? If he doesn't want to work it out, you'll be no worse off than you are now… Honestly, Holly, how bad can it be?"

His words ring in my ears all the way home. It's Friday, and the traffic's heavy and I should go to the supermarket, but I can't be bothered.

I let myself in, eventually, and kick off my shoes. It's not dark enough yet to need the lights on and I flop down on the sofa, staring at the ceiling. I'm not hungry – I'm rarely hungry these days. I eat because I know I should, rather than because I want to. It's hot tonight, so I'll make a salad later. I'll have a shower first… when I've had a think.

It feels like the future – well, my life, really – is stretching in front of me… but I can't see it. Everything's obscured by my indecision. Andy may be right – perhaps I should go to Boston, and see whether Todd wants to try again; see whether he's prepared to forgive me for not trusting him, for doubting him and constantly comparing him; whether he can try and love me. Would it last? Would I be good enough for him? I've got no idea. But how would I feel if I didn't even try? Like this? Hollow, empty and alone… forever?

I sit up. I guess there's only one way to find out.

The problem is, I've got no contact details for him. We never needed them. I don't know his address, or his phone number, or even an e-mail. Great… so I've managed to make the decision to go and now, I've got no idea what to do when I get to Boston, or where to go, or how to find him.

This is ridiculous. I put my head in my hands. Andy said I was a good detective and I can't manage something as simple as working out how to contact the man I love.

I imagine there's a phone listing, like there is here, but like most police officers, I also imagine he's unlisted. His mum and sister live in Atlanta, but I've got no details for them either. I feel like I'm going round in circles, missing the obvious. There must be something. How can he be impossible to contact?

I get up and go through to the bathroom. I'm hot. I need to cool off if I'm going to think straight. I peel off my top and trousers until I'm standing in my underwear... and stop dead. Of course. I'm being dense...

I go back into the living room, grab my laptop and set it up on the coffee table, and wait for it to come to life, tapping my fingers impatiently on the sofa.

Eventually, I go to a browser and to a search engine, and type in *'Amulet lingerie contact details'*. A listing comes up and I click on the one that looks most helpful, then wait while the page refreshes.

Sure enough, there's a phone number.

I'm suddenly nervous. What am I going to say? Will they help me? I've got no idea. I take the laptop with me into the kitchen, setting it on the work surface and pick up the landline, dialling the number before I have time to stop myself.

"This is Amulet, how may I direct your call." The female voice is a little high-pitched... a little annoying.

"Can I speak to Matt, or Luke, please." I don't know their surnames.

"Matt Webb?" she asks.

"Yes." I hope so. What if there's more than one person called Matt?

"May I ask who's calling."

"My name is Holly King, but he doesn't know me."

"Please hold. I'll see if he's available." Somehow I have a feeling he won't be. And I'm going to have to explain to the woman with the high-pitched voice who I am, and why I need to speak to her boss.

I wait, and wait... and then... "Hello?" His voice is just slightly deeper than Todd's, but soft, friendly... kind.

"Hello. Um... I'm sorry to trouble you. You don't know me." I'm gabbling. I pause for a moment. "My name's Holly. Holly King." That's better. I sound a little calmer.

"Yes," he says, and I wonder for a moment if he's smiling. It sounds like it. "How can I help you, Miss King?"

"Call me Holly, please. This is um... awkward," I tell him. "I... I know a friend of yours... Todd Russell... I met him when he was here in London."

"Yes."

"And... and, well, I'm trying to get to see him."

"Right." Again, it sounds like he's smiling.

"I'm going to try and fly over there tomorrow. And I wondered if you could help me."

"How?" he asks.

"I don't have any of Todd's contact details."

"You want me to let him know you're coming?"

I think for a moment. What if he doesn't want me there? What if he never wants to see me again? I think I'd rather see him face-to-face and find that out, than have him call me and tell me not to come. At least if I'm there, in person, I'll get the chance to explain. If he sends me away, even after that, I'll know I tried. "No," I say quickly. "Can you just give me his address? Would that be alright? I'll get a taxi there from the airport."

"I'll go one better than that," he says. "How about I pick you up at the airport and take you to his place?"

"Oh..." That's unexpected. "No, really, there's no need. I don't want to put you out. I'm quite happy to take a taxi."

"It's no trouble. You won't be putting me out. I'm sure Todd would want me to collect you. Or he'd want to collect you himself, if he could."

"I think it's best if he doesn't know I'm coming."

"Oh?" He seems surprised.

What should I tell him? The truth I suppose. "Um... Todd and I," I say, wishing I'd never started this conversation, "we... I don't know how to put this... we were together for a while, when he was here. I'd like to see him again. There are things I need to explain to him. Things I got wrong. Things I said, or rather didn't say... I think I hurt him. Well, I know I hurt him. I want to see if he can forgive me. I want to see if I can put it right."

"I see."

"I sound like a crazy woman, don't I? But I promise, it's nothing like that. I'm quite safe… I'm even quite sane, most of the time."

"You don't sound like a crazy woman, not at all."

"So, can you give me his address?"

"I'd really be happier collecting you. Tomorrow's Saturday. I've not got any plans until the evening, and even they're quite flexible. What time's your flight?"

"Really… You don't know me."

"I know Todd. I know what he'd want. What time's your flight?" The man's persistent.

"I haven't booked it yet. I needed to be sure I could find Todd first."

"Okay… well I'll give you my cell number and you can text me the details of your flight once you've booked it. And I'll collect you and take you to his place. He doesn't live that far from the airport."

"Are you sure?"

"I'm positive. Have you got a pen?"

"I've got my mobile… I'll put your number straight into it."

"Okay." He gives me the number and I add him to my contacts lists.

"This is very kind of you," I tell him.

"Not at all."

"And you won't tell him?"

"No. Not if you don't want me to."

"Thank you."

"Text me the details. I'll be there."

Matt seems really kind, and very considerate. I'm not surprised he's Todd's best friend. Now, all I've got to do is book the flight. I stand in the kitchen, still in my bra and thong, and go online. The best flight I can get, which doesn't involve me either landing in Boston really late, or having to get up at the crack of dawn, is the one-fifteen, from Heathrow, which lands at Logan International at three-thirty local time. That should be okay for Matt. He definitely said he was free all day, and only had plans for the evening. If Todd lives quite close to the airport, he should have dropped me off in plenty of time for whatever he's doing later on. I just need to decide how long I want to stay there. Apart from my dad, I've got no reason to come back here at all, but I can't book a one-way ticket… that's too presumptuous. I don't even know if Todd wants to see me, let alone if he wants a future with me. But how long? A week… two? If he doesn't want to see me, two weeks is a long time to spend over there, doing nothing. After twenty minutes weighing up the pros and cons, clicking on the various dates and then back again, and waiting for the page to refresh each time, I decide on ten days, as a compromise. I'm grateful that my visa is still good from that awful trip to Las Vegas I had to endure with Jason last autumn. That's one less thing to worry about. Then I call up a local taxi company and book a cab for nine o'clock in the morning, to take me to the airport. That should get me there by ten, which is fine… just over three hours before the flight. Perfect. And finally, I text all the details to Matt. Now all I have to do is pack… oh, and have that shower I was going to take nearly an hour ago, before I started all this.

I wander into the bathroom and look at my reflection in the mirror. Am I insane? Very probably.

I slept better last night than I have since Todd left. I guess that's because I'm going to see him very soon now. Well, I hope I am. No… I know I am. Even if he slams the door in my face, I'll at least get to see him first. But he won't slam the door in my face. He's far too polite, too decent to do that. He might tell me he wants nothing to do with me, though… No, I can't think like that. I have to hope for the best.

I finish packing my last few things and check I've closed all the windows. The taxi's due in fifteen minutes, and I'm ready. I wonder if I should wait downstairs. It's probably wise.

I leave my case by the door and check around the flat one last time, making sure everything is switched off in the kitchen, just as I hear the sound of someone knocking on the front door.

It must be one of my neighbours. No-one else can get into the building without the passcode. What on earth can they want? I don't need any hold ups now. I run down the hallway and pull open the door… and my heart stops.

"You?" I manage to mutter, even though I feel light-headed and I'm struggling to breathe.

Chapter Twenty

Todd

Everyone spent the whole evening at my place.

I showered – as instructed – and shaved, and generally cleaned myself up. I still avoided looking at myself in the mirror. It's too soon for that. I need to know Holly's forgiven me first.

By the time I came back out into the living room, Matt, Luke, Will and Grace had already worked wonders on my apartment. Jamie must have arrived while I was in the shower and she was helping out too, and Megan came along with the babies a little later. Grace helped me put my sling back on and we ordered in Chinese and sat in the living room, spread out on the couches and the floor, eating and talking – and even laughing – all evening.

I apologized to all of them again for my behavior, which I know has been appalling and, frankly, out of character. I can be a bit grouchy, but I'm never normally rude… and I've been horrible. They were very kind, very sympathetic and, during the course of the evening, I told them a little more about Holly. I explained how we met, that we worked undercover… I even told them that we'd had to pretend to be married, which caused some amusement, especially for Luke. He enjoyed that, and I let him. I owed him that, and a lot more. The guy made me see sense better than probably anyone else could have done.

I didn't tell them about the club, or the case, or any other details about mine and Holly's relationship, but it felt good talking about her. I wish I'd done it a while ago, instead of shutting myself away. It was dumb of me to do that, when I've got friends who care about me. I don't think I realized how much they care about me until they all just turned up – putting their lives on hold for me. Again.

When Matt and Grace left, he reiterated his offer to pay for my air fare once I'm ready to go to England. I don't need him to do that – I can pay for it myself – but I appreciate the sentiment. And they all repeated the fact that I need to wait, to get better, and then go over there. On that point, we disagree, but I didn't say anything to them about it. I just nodded my head.

Once they'd all gone home, I went to bed – in my bedroom – and I slept properly for the first time in ages. And I woke up this morning feeling better than I have since I got out of the hospital. It'll be four weeks on Monday since I got back here, four weeks since I got shot, four weeks since I saw Holly. And for the first time in all that time, I actually know what I'm doing…

I'm going to see Holly. I'm going to speak to her and we're going to deal with things. And, most importantly, I'm going to be honest with her about how I feel, not put all the pressure on her to be the first to make a commitment. I love her. She needs to know that. I think she felt something for me and, if it isn't love yet, maybe it can be. She said she needed more time, not that she couldn't see a future for us. I don't know how she'll react to seeing me, but I do know that my mom's right… if I don't try, I will regret it for the rest of my life, and I can't do that, because what I've got now isn't any kind of life worth having.

I've made the decision, so I have to go. I can't wait, like the guys suggested. I have to go now. This morning, I went and got a haircut. If I'm going to see Holly, I don't want her seeing me looking wrecked. What am I saying, 'if'? I'm *going* to see her. I'm definitely going to see her. Well, I am, providing she lets me in to her apartment, of course.

So, now I've just got to book the flight. I'm going to get a one-way ticket for now. Then, when I get there, I'm gonna tell her straight out that I love her. I'm gonna tell her I want to be with her and, just like Luke said, I'm gonna keep telling her that until she says it back. And then I'm gonna ask her to come back here with me. If she agrees, we can book our flights back together. If I book a return, she may not be able to get on the same flight… and I'm not coming back here without her. I'm not giving her the chance to change her mind. If she doesn't agree – if she doesn't want to leave England – well, then I guess I'm gonna be working out how I can move over there. Because we're staying together from now on… whatever happens.

I smile to myself as I tap my credit card number into my laptop. Ironically, I know the guys would try and talk me out of this now, if they were here, but I'll be fine. I'll take my sling off, so no-one will know there's a problem with my shoulder; it'll avoid any questions at the airport.

I'm booked on tonight's flight, which lands at Heathrow at ten tomorrow morning, which is good. Tomorrow's Saturday, so she shouldn't be at work and I can go straight to her apartment and see her. If she's not there, I'll just wait for her… for however long it takes.

The flight was good, although it seemed to take forever, which is probably just because I'm impatient to see Holly. It felt like it took a long time to get through immigration as well, but eventually, I get a cab and give the driver Holly's address. I'd prefer to hire a car, but I can't drive yet, so a cab it is.

It's good to be back in London, and finally on my way to see her. My mood's already lifted, just being back here, where she lives.

It's nearly one o'clock by the time the cab drops me off at Holly's place and I go around the back to see if her car's there. It is, so I guess I can be fairly sure she's home… unless she's gone shopping, in which case I shouldn't have too long to wait. I pause, just for a moment, my hand over the security pad. Should I use the passcode, or buzz her apartment? If I buzz up to her and she doesn't want to see me, she can just tell me where to go… but if I'm standing on her doorstep, she'll at least have to see me… okay, so she could slam the door in my face, but that's a chance I'm just gonna have to take. I input the four digit code and I go inside, catching the elevator up to the third floor.

My sling's in my bag, and I haven't bothered to put it back on yet, but I'll need to soon. My shoulder's starting to ache and I could do with some painkillers too, but I know I don't have long to wait. Holly has some in her bathroom cabinet; I remember her taking them when she had period pains. I get to Holly's floor, and go along to her apartment and ring the bell. All my nerves, which have been present since I left home last night, have gone. I've got no idea what kind of reception I'll get, but I'm suddenly not nervous anymore.

The door opens, and I feel my blood turn to ice… I even feel a little sick, and I know, without any doubt, that I'm looking at Jason. This is my worst fucking nightmare, standing right in front of me. She forgave him? She really forgave him…?

We stare at each other for a moment. He's maybe two inches shorter than me, blond, very good looking, more athletic than muscular, wearing jeans and a dark blue t-shirt. And I've seen all I need to see. They'd look good together; I know they would… and they can carry on doing just that. I'm out of here.

Without saying a word, I turn and start back down the corridor.

"Are you Todd?" I hear him call, but I don't stop. "I said, are you Todd?" There's a little more urgency in his voice, so I turn.

"Yeah."

"I thought so." He comes out of the apartment. "You're looking for Holly?"

"Yeah, but don't bother her. I'm clearly too late." I turn to go again.

"Yes, you are. She's not here. She left a few hours ago." I stop and look back at him. He checks his watch. "She's about to get on a plane."

"A plane?" I feel my skin tingle. "Where for?"

"Boston. She's gone to find you."

"You mean… you mean she's not with you?"

"No, I already said, she's not here… Oh… you mean *with* me, with me? Why would she be with me? Why would she take me back after what I did to her?" He motions toward the apartment. "Come inside for a minute. I'd rather not have this conversation where the neighbors can hear."

I hesitate, just for a moment, then follow him into Holly's apartment. He closes the door and we stand together in the familiar hallway. I try hard not to remember kissing her here, or stripping her out of her dress that night, before I carried her to the bedroom… not when I'm standing face-to-face with her ex. The ex who became a specter between us.

"I'm Jason," he says, holding out his hand.

I shake it. "Todd," I reply.

"So I gathered."

"If you don't mind me asking… If you're not back with Holly, what are you doing here?"

He shuffles from one foot to the other. "I needed to see her," he says. I take a step back and he looks at me. "It's not what you think," he continues, holding up a hand, like he thinks I'm going to hit him. "I needed to get something from her. My… my dad died, last week…"

"I'm sorry," I say, kind of automatically, but I mean it because I know how that feels.

"Thanks." He pauses. "Anyway, Holly had taken some photographs on her phone, at a family party last Christmas. It was the last time the whole of my family were together and I wanted to see if she still had them, and if she could let me have them."

"And you couldn't call her?"

He looks at me. "No. She blocked my number after… well, after what happened. I went to see her at work yesterday evening, but she'd already left, and Andy warned me off. So, I called round this morning, just as she was about to leave for the airport. I… I was lucky to catch her, although I think I scared the living daylights out of her."

I don't like that idea, and I take a step toward him. "How?"

"I let myself in." He looks sheepish… so he should.

"In here?"

"No. Into the building. I wasn't sure she'd give me the time of day if I rang up from the street, so I used the passcode."

I need to tell Holly to get that changed. "Is she okay?" I ask him.

"Yes. She was fine by the time she left. She still had the photographs and she's sent them to me."

"So…"

"Why am I still here?"

"Yeah."

"I had a camera, which I can't find. I thought I might have left it here. It might have some more photographs on it. My mother doesn't have many of him, so I'm just trying to see what I can find for her. Holly didn't have time to look, because she didn't want to be late for her flight, so she said I could stay and look for it."

"Any luck?"

"No. I've tried all the places it could be, although I see she's moved the bedroom around... but I don't think it can be here."

I look at my watch. It's nearly twelve-thirty. "What time's her flight?"

"I think she said one-fifteen."

"Damn."

"You couldn't have caught up with her anyway."

"No. I'll have to get a cab back to the airport and catch the next flight home."

"You could do that. Or you could let me give you a lift. It'll be quicker."

"Um... thanks, but I think I'll try and find a cab."

"Why? Because you think it's odd taking a lift from me?"

"Frankly, yes."

"So what if it is odd? My car's right outside. I can get you to the airport in less than an hour. Or you can wait around and try and find a taxi. What's more important? Your pride, or Holly?"

"Holly." I don't even hesitate.

"Exactly. Let me fetch my jacket and lock up." He goes through to the living room, returning with a denim jacket over his arm. "As you're going to be seeing her, you can give her back her keys. I was going to put them in her mailbox, but that's not very secure."

"No, it's not."

He locks the door and hands me her keys, and I put them in my pocket.

His car is a BMW, and he makes quick work of getting through the London traffic.

"Andy told me you worked with Holly," he says after a while.

"Yes. She helped me on the case I was working."

"And you… got together?"

"Yes." I don't want to discuss our relationship with him.

"Did you meet her family at all?"

"Yeah. I liked her dad."

"Alan's a good guy. Her mother's a bitch. And as for Ellie…"

"I know about you and Ellie," I tell him.

"I thought you might." He sighs. "I threw away the best thing I ever had," he says, changing lanes and speeding up a little, "for a quick, and not very good fuck." I turn to look at him. Well, I guess that was one way of putting it. He sighs. "Ellie came to the flat one evening, when Holly was working, claiming to have had a row with James, her husband…"

"I met him. He's a nice guy."

"Yes, he is… far too good for Ellie. Anyway, she claimed he'd hurt her and turned on the tears, and I was comforting her, because she seemed to be genuinely distraught. But then she started touching me, and… one thing led to another."

"And you didn't think to back off? You didn't think about Holly?"

"No. Holly had been working nights for ages. We'd barely seen each other, let alone…" He doesn't need to finish that sentence.

"Oh, I see." My voice is overloaded with sarcasm. "So you were feeling neglected, just because of Holly's work commitments. And you thought that made it okay to bang her sister?"

"No, it wasn't like that."

"Then why did you do it?"

"Because I was stupid."

"And Ellie wasn't great?"

"Compared to Holly, no."

"So, you were having such a terrible time fucking Ellie, you didn't even notice Holly standing there watching you?"

"She told you that?" He glances across at me.

"She told me everything."

"No," he says, "I didn't notice her. Neither did Ellie… or if she did, she didn't say anything. Holly threw me out, there and then. It was weird. She didn't even raise her voice. She didn't say much at all…" He pauses, like he's thinking, or remembering. "I think it was her silence I found most unnerving. It was like she'd given up."

She had, you dick, on herself. "Did you try and get back with her?" I ask.

"Of course, but she cut me out of her life."

His tone is sad, and I know he's still missing her. And I know how that feels.

I decide to give him a break, and we continue in silence until he pulls up outside the terminal.

I turn to him. "Thanks for bringing me," I say to him. "I just wanna know one thing…"

"What's that?" he asks, keeping his hands on the steering wheel.

"Am I going to be spending the rest of my life looking over my shoulder for you?"

He shakes his head. "No," he replies quietly. "She'd never take me back. She doesn't love me anymore. And after the way I behaved, I don't blame her."

"Okay," I say, and I climb out of the car, opening the back door and retrieving my case. I walk around the back and up to his open window to thank him again.

"One thing though," he says, before I get a chance to speak. "If you ever hurt her, you won't have to worry about looking over your shoulder… I'll be standing right in front of you."

He drives off before I get the chance to tell him I'll never hurt her. Never again…

Holly

There's a man, standing in the arrivals hall, holding up a card with my name on it. It's odd. I've seen that in films and on television, but I never thought it would happen to me. I go over to him… God, he's tall. He's even taller than Todd.

"You're Holly?" he says, looking down at me.

I nod my head. "Yes… And you must be Matt?"

"Sure am." He's smiling, like he knows me. I wonder if Todd's told him about us… about me. And I wonder, if he has, what he's said. "Let me take your bag," he says and leans over to take it from me.

"Just like Todd," I say, without thinking.

"How's that?" he says, as we start walking towards the exit.

"He never let me carry the shopping, or a suitcase, or anything."

"Why would he?"

"Because I have arms?"

"You sound just like my wife."

"Grace?" I say.

He turns to look at me. "Yes. She's British too. I can see the two of you are gonna get along just fine."

He's assuming that we'll meet, that we'll get to know each other… which presumes Todd will want to see me.

We get to his car, which is an Aston Martin DB9.

"Nice car," I say as he opens the boot and puts my bag inside.

"Are you sure you haven't met my wife?"

"I'm guessing she appreciates your car?"

"Only so's you'd notice." He opens the passenger door and helps me in, before coming around to the driver's side.

"It's a bit impractical with a baby, isn't it?" I ask, as he closes the door and starts the engine.

"Has he told you everything about us?"

"No. But he told me you'd just had a baby… The car's lovely, but…"

"Yes, it's impractical. We have a more sensible, family car too." He revs the engine.

"I'll bet it doesn't make a noise like that though."

"That's it…" he says, grinning. "Now I know you've met Grace."

I laugh. "I haven't," I reply. "Honestly."

It takes about fifteen minutes to drive to Todd's apartment, during which we talk about his son, Grace, the car and a little about London, but not about Todd.

He pulls up at the roadside and gets out, coming around to my side again to help me out.

"Todd lives there." He points across the street to a gated property. "You can only drive in if you've got a card. But we can walk through the side gate." He puts his hand gently in the small of my back and we cross the road together, then he holds open a wrought iron gate, allowing me to pass through. "He's in this block," he says, guiding me to my left. There are three separate buildings, arranged around a central courtyard, each two storeys high, all red-brick, with large windows. We go in through a main entrance and up a flight of stairs, then along a hallway until we reach a door, numbered six.

And suddenly, although I've been calm all day, I'm nervous.

"Go ahead," he says, standing back.

I ring the doorbell, and wait. Nothing happens.

I try again, but still there's no reply and I turn to face Matt.

"Wait a second," he says, "I'll call him. He might be asleep."

Asleep? In the middle of the afternoon?

He presses a few buttons on his phone, then holds it to his ear for a second or two.

"Odd," he says, "it's gone straight to voicemail." He doesn't leave a message.

I feel really deflated, having flown three thousand miles and built this moment up in my mind, that he's not even here. And if I'm honest, the thought that he's not here, and his phone's off, makes me wonder where he is… or rather *who* he's with. I can't say it hasn't crossed my mind that he'd have found someone else in the month that we've been apart, but I'd banished the thought… until now. I don't want to say any of that to Matt, though, so I just look up at him.

"I guess the best thing for us to do, is for me to take you back to my place," he says. "I can hardly leave you here…"

"But…"

"Well, I can't."

"Where do you think he is?"

"I don't know."

It's no good. I have to ask him. "I'm sorry to ask you this, but… is there someone else?"

"Another woman, you mean?"

I nod my head. "It would explain his absence and his phone being turned off."

"There's no-one else."

"How do you know?"

"I know."

He sounds certain, and I don't want to labour the point. I'll sound desperate, and insecure. I don't mind Todd knowing how scared I always was of losing him, but I draw the line at his friends seeing or hearing me like that.

"I'll take you back home," he says. "You can meet Grace and George… Todd will turn up."

It's nearly six-thirty by the time we pull up in the driveway of a grey, wood-clad house and Matt helps me from the car, getting my bag from the boot and leading me around to the side of the house, where there's a raised deck and a lawn, leading down to a large lake. Todd's description didn't do it justice. It really is a beautiful property.

"You have a stunning home," I say to him as we climb the steps leading up to the raised deck.

"Thank you," he replies.

"Todd told me you often have barbecues here."

"We're having one tonight."

Oh. "Well, hopefully, I'll be out of your hair by the time your guests arrive."

"Hello." At that moment, I look up and notice a beautiful woman sitting on a sofa to one side of the deck. On the floor next to her is a crib, and I can just make out a baby, who seems to be playing with his feet.

"Honey, this is Holly." Matt goes over to her, leans down and kisses her, then helps her to her feet and they both come across to me.

"Hello, Holly," the woman says. It seems odd to hear an English accent here.

"Hello… Grace."

"Sorry," she says, "I didn't introduce myself."

"It's fine, baby," Matt replies. "Todd's told Holly all about us."

"Oh dear, has he?" She's smiling. "I dread to think what he's said."

"It was all complimentary, I promise."

"Speaking of Todd…?" Grace questions, looking confused.

"We can't find him," Matt explains. "He wasn't at home and he's not answering his cell."

"I've been thinking, could he be at work?" I ask.

"He's not working, not at the moment," Grace says. She looks a little worried.

"Why?" I ask.

"Well, he resigned soon after the case he was working on was concluded," Matt says.

"Yes, I knew he was planning on doing that," I reply. "But surely he has to work out his notice?"

"Well, ordinarily, he would have done, but he's not been fit enough."

"Fit enough?" What is he talking about? "What's wrong with him?"

"Oh…" Grace turns to me. "You don't know, do you?"

"Know what?" Suddenly everything's a little blurry. Grace takes my arm, leading me back to the sofa. "Know what?" I repeat, looking at her as she sits beside me. Matt perches on the coffee table in front of us.

"He was shot," Grace says gently.

"No. Oh, God… no." It's all I can manage as tears form in my eyes.

"He's okay." Her voice is soft and calm, and she reaches across and holds my hands in hers. "I promise you, he's okay."

I turn to her, and see sadness and concern in her eyes.

"What happened?" I ask.

It's Matt who speaks, although Grace keeps hold of my hands. "He went to pick up the suspect…"

"The Frenchman?"

"I guess so… the guy from the case in London."

"That's the Frenchman."

"And he… the Frenchman, that is… he had a woman with him. He used her as a shield and shot Todd in the shoulder."

"Oh, God."

"Chris, Todd's partner, was there with him, and she managed to shoot the Frenchman, but Todd lost a lot of blood… a helluva lot of blood."

"It was touch and go, as to whether he'd make it," Grace continues, and I hear her voice crack.

"But he did," Matt adds quickly. "He's been home for just over two weeks now."

"Then where is he?" I ask, feeling frantic. "Is he even well enough to be out by himself?" They exchange a worried glance. "What aren't you telling me?"

Grace nods at Matt and I turn to him.

"It's just that he… well, he kind of let it all get to him," he says. "We all went to see him on Thursday and…"

"He was in a bit of a state," Grace finishes his sentence.

"Then it sounds like he really shouldn't be out by himself."

"I wonder…" Grace murmurs.

"What?" Matt asks.

"Do you think he might have gone to Will's. They're coming here together later. He may have gone over there early to save time?"

"I guess…" Matt doesn't sound convinced.

"Try calling Will," Grace suggests, but Matt already has his phone in his hand. He gets up and goes to the other side of the deck.

"Try not to worry," Grace says to me. "I'm sure he'll be fine."

I wish I had her confidence.

Matt comes back a few minutes later, shaking his head.

"Will and Jamie haven't seen him or heard from him since Thursday. Will's supposed to be picking him up in half an hour, so hopefully, wherever he went, he'll have gone home by then."

"I'm sure he will have done," Grace replies, although I notice them exchange another glance.

"Let's have a drink, shall we?" Matt suggests, and I'm not about to say no.

He goes into the kitchen and returns with a glass of white wine for me, an orange juice for Grace and something that looks like water for himself. I'm surprised to find I'm the only one drinking alcohol, but I remember Todd telling me Grace is breastfeeding… still, that doesn't stop Matt… unless he thinks he might need to drive somewhere later on… maybe to look for Todd.

A little over half an hour has passed when Matt's phone rings.

I look up at him, but he shakes his head. "It's Will," he says and connects the call, getting up and going inside the house. I'm on tenterhooks, wondering why Will's called, and it doesn't take long for Matt to return.

"Todd's still not at home," he says, coming back outside.

Neither Grace nor I respond… For myself, I can't think of anything to say and I'm scared that, if I open my mouth, I'm going to cry.

"I've told Will to come on over here," Matt continues. "There's no point in him and Jamie hanging around at Todd's place. I'm just gonna leave him a message." He presses the screen of his phone a few times, then holds it to his ear.

"Hey, buddy," he says. "I guess you forgot the barbecue tonight. Will's on his way here, so when you pick this up, just get a cab and come over. We've got a surprise here for you." He looks at me as he hangs up.

Grace takes my hand in hers again. "Where do you think he's gone?" she asks Matt.

"He could have just gone for a walk," he replies. "Or to do some shopping."

"Then why turn his phone off?" I ask.

"He might have had a sleep earlier, and turned it off and maybe forgotten to put it back on," he offers, but I sense he's clutching at straws. "I'll send him a text message as well, and tell him you're here. We can be sure he'll turn up then."

"Really? What if he doesn't want to see me."

He turns to me. "He wants to see you, don't worry about that—"

"Hey guys." We all turn at the sound of a male voice, but I know it's not Todd – and so do Matt and Grace. A couple walk around the side of the house. The man is tall and blond, impossibly handsome, with a broad smile and muscular build. He looks relaxed in grey shorts and a white t-shirt, which accentuates his muscles, and reminds me of Todd. Beside him is a stunning woman with long, wavy hair and a slim figure, carrying the most beautiful baby girl I've ever seen... which isn't surprising, looking at her parents.

"Luke... Megan." Grace says, like she'd forgotten they were coming.

"Is everything alright?" the man called Luke asks, coming up the steps onto the deck. He bends and kisses her cheek.

"No. We can't find Todd."

"Why are we looking for him? He's meant to on his way here with Will, isn't he?"

"Yes, except he isn't." Grace turns to me. "Sorry... This is Holly," she says.

"Really? You're here?" He smiles at me. "Well, I'll be damned..." Luke comes over. "Sorry," he says. "It's nice to meet you. We've... well, we've heard a lot about you."

"Oh?"

"Yes. All of it good... I'm Luke." He motions to the woman he arrived with. "And this is my wife, Megan and our daughter, Daisy."

"Hello, Holly," Megan says. Her voice is soft, quiet. Up close, she's even more beautiful. "When did you get here?" she asks.

"Just a couple of hours ago. I wanted to surprise Todd... but..."

"But he's disappeared?" Luke asks.

"So it would seem."

"We should probably think about the food," Grace says, scratching her head.

"We'll order in," Matt replies. "It'll be easier. We can barbecue tomorrow. I'm not in the mood for cooking now anyway..."

I get the impression they're all more worried than they're letting on... or than they're prepared to say in front of me, anyway.

By seven-thirty, Will has arrived, with his fiancée Jamie, but without Todd. Considering that Will is Luke's brother, they look nothing like each other. Will has longer, dark hair, wears glasses, and seems more serious than his brother. Jamie is blonde, very pretty, and seems like she'd be fun to spend time with… except I'm really not in the mood for fun right now. The one thing they all have in common that I can see, is their concern for Todd, who still hasn't made contact, even though Matt sent his text and has left two messages now.

"He'll turn up," Grace whispers in my ear as she tops up my wine glass. "And if he doesn't arrive tonight for some reason, you can stay here and we'll find him tomorrow."

"But where can he be?"

"I don't know, but I'm sure there's a good explanation."

Really? I wish I had her confidence. Right now, I'd sell my soul for just the sight of him, even if he rejected me straight away and told me to catch the next flight home. I'd give everything I have just to know he's safe.

Chapter Twenty-one

Todd

The earliest flight I can get doesn't land until eight o'clock, well, just before... which means Holly will have been in Boston for around five hours by the time I get back. I've realized while I've been sitting here at the airport, that she's got no contact details for me; she has no idea of my address, or phone number, or which precinct I work at, or worked at, because she doesn't even know I've resigned... So what's she going to do? Wander the streets looking for me?

And how am I going to find her when I get back? She could be anywhere. I'm trying real hard not to panic, but the idea of her on her own in Boston, not knowing what to do or where to go is really getting to me. I should be with her, taking care of her... If I'd just flown here one day sooner, none of this would be happening...

Waiting here seems to be taking forever, but they finally call my flight. I don't know why I think it'll make a difference if I hurry, but I do, even though my shoulder is more than painful now. I want to get home. I want to start trying to find her, although I've got no idea where to look. I don't know her number either. This is so damn stupid. Even Jason's got her number... and I don't. Why didn't I get it from him when I had the chance? I guess because I'm really fucking lousy at taking my chances...

Despite my fear and my impatience, I manage to get a couple of hours' sleep on the flight. I told them I had a headache and the flight attendant gave me some painkillers, which helped for a while... long enough for me to close my eyes, anyway. I don't even want to think about what time my body thinks it is… the jet-lag from today is going to be a bitch.

When we land, as with everything today, the baggage seems to take a lifetime, but eventually, I'm through and out into the arrivals hall and on my way to find the first cab I can lay my hands on. My best bet, I think, is to head for home, in the hope that she's somehow managed to discover my address, although I don't now how, as all my details are unlisted. If she's not there? I'll need to think… well, take some more painkillers and think.

I jump in the first taxi and give him my address, then reach into my back pocket and pull out my phone, and turn it back on. There's are two missed calls from Matt… Oh yeah, I was meant to be at the barbecue tonight. Well, I'm sure they'll have fun without me. I've got better things to do right now. And there's a text message… also from Matt. God, the guy's impatient. So… I'm missing a barbecue? So what? I click on the text message, and it blurs before my eyes. I'm really tired and in a lot of pain, but I manage to read it.

*— **Holly's with us, at our place. No idea what's happened to you, but suggest you get your ass over here. M***

She's at Matt's place… How? All kinds of questions roll around my head, but there are no answers – not yet, anyway.

I lean forward and tap the driver on his shoulder.

"Change of plan," I tell him, and give him Matt's address.

I'm only a half hour away from her now. It hardly seems real when I've waited so long for this…

Holly

I check my watch for the hundredth time.

"It's just before ten," Matt whispers. "It's still early." He's sitting next to me, and Luke's on my other side. We're around a large circular table and have finished eating a take-away Chinese, which I'm sure was delicious, except I really couldn't taste anything. There's a lot left-over… I don't think anyone really had much of an appetite. The only person missing at the moment, is Megan, who's taken baby Daisy indoors to change and feed her.

"What if something's happened to him?" I ask.

"Then we'd know," Luke replies. "Well, Matt would." I turn to him.

"He's still officially employed by Boston PD for another week or so. If anything happened to him, they'd notify Matt."

"Matt?"

"Yes."

"Not his mother?"

"No," Matt says, and I turn back. "He set it up, so I'd be notified first in the event of anything happening to him. He didn't want his mom getting a phone call, or a visit from a cop. A long time ago, his dad—"

"I know about his dad," I interrupt him.

"You do?"

"Yes, he told me."

He raises an eyebrow, and I wonder if he's surprised. "Then you'll understand why he did it." I nod my head. "All the while my phone doesn't ring," he says, "I know he's okay."

I feel a little relieved, but only a little.

Megan comes out through the patio doors. "I've put Daisy down to sleep in our usual room," she says, looking at Luke.

"Okay," he replies and she goes to sit by him. He takes her hand.

"I thought you'd want to stay," she says quietly.

"Thanks." He leans over, kissing her gently.

"We'll stay too, if that's okay," Will says, from the other side of the table.

"Of course," Grace replies.

I get the impression this wasn't planned, but they're staying because they're worried about Todd, and my earlier relief evaporates.

"So, Holly," Matt says, "what was it like being married to Todd?"

I twist in my seat to face him. "He told you about that?"

He smiles at me. "Yeah... he said it was part of the job you were doing?"

"It was." I glance around and see that they're all watching me.

"We've heard Todd's version" Luke says, grinning. "But knowing him, he missed out all the good stuff. I think we need the whole story. And who better to tell it than his wife?" I can't help but smile, and I suppose it can't hurt to tell them a few things... it'll distract us and kill some time, anyway. And I'd like to talk about him.

"It was part of our cover, although neither of us really wanted to do it, but we needed to pose as a couple to get into the club where the murderer was working. He was targeting Americans, so Todd had to be kind of obvious about his nationality, and I just had to pretend to be his wife..."

"What kind of club needs you to be a couple, just to get in?" Will asks, leaning forward.

I can feel myself blushing. "It was a sex club."

"Holy shit!" Luke laughs. "A sex club? That must've been..."

"Uncomfortable," I offer. "And awkward, especially with someone you've just met... But Todd was incredible." I play with the hem of my blouse, feeling self-conscious and wishing I'd never told them this part. "I was very embarrassed by the whole thing, but he put me at ease and was a perfect gentleman."

"Sounds like Todd," Matt says, and I turn to him.

"Yes," I reply. "He was... very good to me. He made an amazing fake husband, for the short time he was there."

"I'm sure you deserved it," Grace says.

"Oh, I don't think so. I put him in some very difficult positions."

"At the sex club?" Luke asks, and I turn to see him grinning again. He's very mischievous.

"No." I have to smile. "Not at the club. At my parents' house."

"You took him to meet your parents? Todd didn't mention that. Sounds serious…" He's still grinning.

"It wasn't like that, well not really. He… he came with me to a party at my parents' house and… he danced with me."

"Todd?" Luke's beside himself. "Todd danced? Oh, please tell me there are pictures of this."

"No. There were a lot of people there, but as far as I know, no-one was taking pictures."

"Damn. I'd have paid good money, just for a sight of those."

"I think we all would," Matt joins in.

"You're both horrible to him," Grace says.

"No, we're not," Matt replies. "Well, no more than he is to us, anyway." He turns to me. "Can you describe it?" I sense they're enjoying this.

"Well, he was wearing his tux…"

"Oh, this just gets better," Luke says.

"And I was in a long, blue dress…"

Chapter Twenty-two

✎

Todd

The cab pulls up outside Matt and Grace's house and I pay the driver, grab my bag and climb out.

Although it's gone ten, it's really warm, and I'm fairly certain they'll be on the deck still, so I go around the side of the house. Sure enough, I can hear voices, and laughter… lots of laughter. I can't see them though, so they must be sitting at the table, on the far side, by the doors.

I'm about to put my foot on the first step, when I stop dead.

I can hear Holly's voice. It's like a soft, gentle breeze washing over me. It's like the most peaceful, calming sensation, but at the same time, sets all my nerve endings on fire. She's really here. The others are talking, but all I can think about is that she's really here. I start to climb the steps, and then I freeze again.

"Can you describe it?" Matt asks, and I hear a humorous, almost mocking tone in his voice. What are they talking about?

"Well, he was wearing his tux." That's Holly's voice.

"Oh, this just gets better." And that's Luke. Like Matt, he sounds like he's enjoying the conversation.

"And I was in a long blue dress…" Holly speaks again. Wait a minute… a tux, a long blue dress. The party… "And he danced with me." *Now would be a really good time to stop talking, sweetheart.*

"To what kind of music?" Grace asks.

"It was a song he chose." She seriously needs to stop talking. I take another step and glance to my left. I can see them now. They're sitting around the table, as I thought. Holly's got her back to me, with Matt to one side and Luke on the other, and Megan's beyond him. Will and Jamie are opposite and Grace has her back to the house, on Matt's right. It looks like they didn't bother with the barbecue... the table is littered with take-out containers, plates and glasses.

"What was it?" That's Matt again.

"I don't know the title, or the singer. It was something personal to him."

"Doesn't sound like Todd... It wasn't Bruce Springsteen then?"

Holly laughs, throwing her head back, and shivers run down my spine. God, I've missed that sound. "No," she says, "it definitely wasn't Bruce Springsteen. It was a woman who was singing."

"And he definitely danced?" Luke again... *Yeah, I danced. So what?*

"Yes, he did, but it was only to prove a point." Wait a second... She knew? She knew what I was trying to get across to her with that dance, and she didn't say anything? That doesn't make sense. Why wouldn't she let me know she understood? They're all looking at her. I can just imagine her cheeks flushing. "My sister was there," she says. "She'd been flirting with Todd all evening. He wanted to get her to back off. Dancing, like that, with me... it was a good way of doing it. It worked, anyway." Yeah, it worked, but that wasn't why I did it.

"That's what you really think?" They all turn as one at the sound of my voice as I reach the top step.

"Todd!" Holly leaps off her chair and runs at me. I just manage to drop my bag as she throws herself into my arms. It hurts like hell, but I catch her, and she wraps her legs around my hips, her arms painfully around my shoulders... and I don't care. I just hold her, burying my face in her hair, smelling her scent. She's home... I'm home.

"You're here," she whispers.

"So are you."

She nods her head. She feels good. She feels really good, but I can't do this. My shoulder really is hurting now, and I'm only holding her up with my right arm... I'm scared I'll drop her. I let her go, lowering her to the floor. "Sorry, but I have to..." I mutter and she puts her hand to her mouth.

"Oh, God," she says, her eyes filled with concern, and tears, as she starts leading me slowly back toward the table. "I'm so sorry… Your shoulder."

She knows? "It's fine."

"It's not fine. Which one is it?"

"My left." She moves to my right side, so I can put my arm around her, and for the first time, I look up, and see six pairs of eyes watching us. They look concerned, worried, relieved… I'm not sure why, and at this point I've got more important things to deal with. I stop a couple of feet from the table and turn toward Holly.

"You really think I danced with you to prove a point to your sister?" I ask her.

"Why else?" she whispers.

I close my eyes. I guess it could have seemed like that. It's another misunderstanding to add to the list. I reach into my pocket and pull out my phone.

"I can't believe I'm gonna do this here, in front of these guys, but have you ever actually listened to that song? I mean *really* listened to it?" I say to Holly, still holding her close.

"No. I was a little distracted during the dance." She smiles up at me. "And I didn't get a chance once we got home again… we were kind of busy, if you remember?"

I smile down at her. "Yeah, I remember."

"And the next day… after you'd gone, well, I didn't want to be reminded."

"Okay…" I understand that. I call up my iTunes and find the piece of music, which I surprised myself by downloading the day after I came out of hospital. "Listen, baby," I say quietly, turning up the volume. "Listen to the words." I hold the phone between us and let it play. The memory of that evening comes flooding back and I picture us dancing, so close, so tight, her hips against mine, our bodies locked. Gloria Estefan finally finishes singing *Hold Me, Thrill Me, Kiss Me*, and Holly looks up into my eyes, her own filled with tears.

"Do you get it?" I ask her, sliding my phone back into my pocket. She doesn't reply, but she blinks and a single tear falls from each eye, down her cheeks. "It was about *you*, not Ellie. I could have dirty danced with you to anything if I'd just wanted to prove a point to your damn sister. This is all about you, baby… It always was."

"Are you saying you…?"

"I'm saying I love you. I loved you from that very first day."

"You did?" She's wide-eyed and, seemingly, incredulous.

"Of course." I lean down and very gently kiss her, feeling her soft lips against mine. I don't care if she doesn't love me yet… She's here. She's in my arms. I can wait – and this time, I will. I keep the kiss brief, because I know everyone's looking. I pull away, and look down at her. "And I'm so, so sorry that I said it was a mistake, and that we should forget it happened. I didn't mean it… I only said that because I was hurting." She tilts her head to one side and I smile, because I know exactly what that expression means. "I thought you were thinking about Jason," I explain.

"No. I was thinking about you… just you," she whispers. "And I'm sorry I hurt you. I'm sorry I didn't tell you how I felt."

"Why didn't you?"

"I was trying to, but you wouldn't let me. You wouldn't listen. And then, later, when I'd thought we'd get the chance to talk… to explain… Adam arrived, and it was all so fast, and I couldn't say what I wanted to say in front of him."

"What did you want to say?" I ask. "Tell me now. I promise I'll listen, and I won't interrupt."

I look down into her eyes. They're sparkling, but not with tears… this is something else. "I wanted to tell you that I love you," she murmurs. And I feel my heart swell and expand to fill my chest, where all that pain used to be.

Holly

"Really?" he asks.

I nod my head and he glances across at his friends, then, after just a moment's hesitation, he grabs hold of my hand and pulls me towards the house, through the patio doors and into the kitchen. He brings me in close to his body and, running his hands down my back, leans forward and kisses me with such desperation, his tongue finding mine as he walks me backwards across the room until I come up against something hard behind me. His hands are on my waist and, with a loud groan, he lifts me and sits me on the work surface.

"Careful," I mutter into his mouth. "Your shoulder."

"To hell with my shoulder." He leans back and looks at me, his hands now on my thighs, parting them so he can stand closer. "I want you."

"I want you too."

"No, I mean I want you… now."

"What? Here?"

"Yes."

God… He really means it. He takes my mouth with his again and I bring my arms around behind his head, fisting his hair and pulling him closer. He lets out a groan, which shudders through my body, and I feel his fingers undoing the button of my jeans, then pulling down the zip. He pulls away, then stands back for a moment, looking down at the triangle of white lace material that's barely covering me.

"Fuck, Holly," he whispers. "I need you."

His hands come up, undoing my blouse, exposing a matching white bra.

"A bra?" he smirks. "Since when?"

"Since you pointed out that what's underneath is just for your eyes," I say.

"Damn right it is."

"And this is a plain white blouse," I point out. "You can pretty much see through it in the right light. I didn't think you'd want me to be that exposed."

He looks down at me. "No. I don't. You're just gonna have to not wear plain white tops from now on," he smirks.

"Or I could start wearing a bra instead…"

"No." He pulls the lace down, exposing my breasts and pushing them upwards. "No bra," he orders, then he leans down, taking one of my hardened nipples between his teeth, biting gently. I hold his head in place and suck in a breath.

"God, that's good."

"Hmm… and it's gonna get so much better." He stands up and runs his hands down my back to my behind, pulling me forward, so I'm right on the edge of the work surface and then he brings his right hand around to the front, under my lacy thong, until he's caressing me intimately. I can't help but part my legs a little wider, and let my head roll back. "You're so wet," he whispers, inserting two fingers into me. I gasp, then start to rock back and forth onto him. I want more… now…

"Todd…" The voice from outside makes us both still, and I sit up straight. I'm not sure who's speaking… maybe Matt? "If you're having sex on any of my kitchen countertops, you're buying me new ones."

We both stop and chuckle, his forehead resting against mine.

"Damn," he whispers, and pulls his hand from inside my jeans. "Later?"

I nod my head. "Yes… please." He doesn't move straight away, but brings his glistening fingers up to my lips and inserts them into my mouth, not taking his dark eyes from mine. I can taste myself… and I start to suck. Hard.

"Oh fuck…" he mutters. He slowly pulls his fingers from my mouth and steps back, his eyes wandering over me. He shakes his head just for a moment, then he straightens my underwear, and I jump down from the work surface, doing up my jeans and re-fastening my blouse.

"C'mon," he says, taking my hand. "Let's see how much I can humiliate myself in front of these guys… and then I'm taking you to bed." He leads me back outside and everyone turns to look at us… We go over to the table and, although Matt stands and offers his chair, Todd sits in the one I'd been using and pulls me down onto his lap, holding me tight. It's like he doesn't want to let go… and I like that. A lot.

"So, am I looking at new countertops?" Matt asks, smiling at Todd.

"No. Nearly, but not quite," he replies, smiling back. "I think it would've taken a little longer than that."

"Oh, I don't know," Luke says. "You're miserably out of practice."

"I'm not *that* out of practice," Todd growls, although he's still smiling.

"Nice song by the way," Luke continues, grinning.

"Be quiet," Todd replies.

"And you dirty danced to that?" Luke isn't giving up.

Before Todd can get in a response, Will leans forward. "What is dirty dancing exactly?" Everyone looks at him, but Luke quickly comes to his rescue.

"It's about as close as you can get to having sex, on the dance floor, with your clothes on."

Will turns to Todd. "And you did this, in front of a bunch of strangers?"

"Yes," Todd replies. "I don't care how much you guys laugh at me, if it gets Holly to realise what she means to me... any amount of humiliation from you three is worth it."

No-one says anything though. Todd and Luke stare at each other. Luke's smiling, and there's something in the look they exchange; it's meaningful... significant. I have no idea what it's about, but I'll ask Todd later.

Matt turns his chair towards us. "So, where the hell have you been?" he asks Todd. "We've been worrying about you all afternoon and evening. You weren't at home when I brought Holly over, or when Will came to collect you."

Todd tightens his grip on me. "I've been to London."

"What?" Matt, Luke and I all speak at the same time. Everyone else just stares at him, open-mouthed.

"But we only saw you on Thursday night."

"And? I flew out yesterday evening, and landed in London this morning – at least I think it was this morning. It was this morning in London."

"But… you've only been out of the hospital two weeks… Come to think of it, where's your sling?" Grace asks. She sounds a little cross.

"It's in my bag. I took it off, to avoid any awkward questions from the airline."

"So you were vaguely aware you probably shouldn't really have been flying?"

"Yes. But that didn't matter."

I twist on his lap, turning to him. "Yes, it did."

"No, it didn't. I needed to see you, to talk to you and explain. That was more important than anything else."

"Including your health?"

He nods his head. "I'm okay, aren't I?"

"You're more than okay," I murmur, and he smiles.

"And it didn't occur to you to tell any of us that you were going?" Matt says.

"No. Well, yes, but you'd have just tried to persuade me to wait, and I didn't want to." He holds me tighter. "I was gonna send you a message once I'd caught up with Holly, but she wasn't there. She was here, or at least on her way here." He looks down at me. "You didn't have my contact details, so how did you end up here?"

"I called Matt," I tell him.

"Okay… and how did you track down Matt?" He seems a little hurt that I managed to find his friend, and not him.

"I was standing in the bathroom at home, wracking my brain, trying to work out how to contact you… and I remembered you told me that Matt and Luke owned the company that made the underwear I was wearing." I can feel myself blushing. "So I went online, looked up the company, and phoned him."

"And I had one of the weirdest conversations of my life," Matt adds, smiling.

Todd nuzzles into me. "I always knew you were a damn good detective," he says.

"With excellent taste in lingerie, evidently," Luke puts in, with a glint in his eye.

285

"We've gone off topic," I remark, desperate to get the subject away from my underwear. "You were telling us about your trip to London."

"Yeah," Matt says, "so, what happened?"

"I went to Holly's place."

"You did?" I'm feeling a little sick all of a sudden.

"Yeah." He's looking at me.

"And when Holly wasn't there, you just got the next flight back? How did you know she hadn't gone out shopping? Or to visit friends?" Will asks.

"Because there was someone at her apartment." His eyes are boring into mine now.

"He was still there?" I whisper.

He nods his head. "Yes."

"Who?" Matt asks.

"Jason. Holly's ex." I can feel them all looking at me. "It's not what you think, guys," Todd says quickly, defending me. "He called round to collect some photographs from Holly. His dad just died, and he knew she still had these pictures of him."

"You talked?" I say. I can't quite believe this is happening.

"Yeah… we talked."

"And?"

"And… well, I didn't hit him. And I didn't have my gun with me, so I didn't shoot him either."

"But if you'd had your gun…?"

He shrugs. "Maybe… maybe not. I felt kinda sorry for him." He gives me a squeeze, resting his head against mine.

"You felt sorry for him?" Did he really just say that?

"He misses you and he's still in love with you, Holly. I know how that feels."

"Well, I'm not in love with him. I'm not sure I ever was. Not really. But either way, I'm very, very over him."

"You're sure?" Todd pulls back just a little, so he can look at me. "Seriously?"

"Yes. I think it took losing you to realise how over him I was. It was so much harder losing you… even after what he did."

He leans down and kisses me gently.

"Stop kissing for a minute and tell us what happened." Matt urges.

"Oh," Todd says, pulling back again. "Well, Jason explained that Holly had flown out here, and then he gave me a ride to the airport."

"He did? Why would he do that?" I know Jason, he always has a motive for everything he does.

"I think he wanted a chance to explain. To put his side of the story… maybe so I'd tell you. I don't know."

"You don't need to tell me. I've heard his side of the story before… Let me see… My sister came round, pleading she'd had a row with her husband, and how hurt she was. Jason was commiserating and, somehow, all their clothes fell off and he ended up clamped between her legs, on our bed—" There's a collective gasp around the table.

"Well, I guess everyone's heard the story now," Todd says, grinning.

"Oh… yes." I look at his friends.

Luke leans over towards me. "You seriously had to think about being over this guy?" he asks. When he puts it like that, it does sound ludicrous that I wasted more than a minute thinking about it.

"I know," I say. "I was stupid."

"He's not stupid though," Todd adds. "He's still got the passcode for your apartment."

I shake my head. "No. I sent a text to the building supervisor and asked him to change it." I can feel Todd let out a sigh. "It'll be done next week, once he's notified the other tenants. I didn't want Jason just turning up whenever he felt like it."

"Good." He leans into me again. "I've also got your keys. He gave them to me to pass on to you."

"Oh, okay. I'm sorry you had to meet him and go through that," I tell him.

"It's fine," he replies, then smirks. "He gave me a warning, can you believe?"

I twist to face him. "He did what?"

"He told me not to hurt you."

"That's a bloody joke, coming from him, especially considering he'd told just about everyone I worked with that he slept with my sister."

Todd pulls back just a little. "Oh, I seriously wish I'd known that."

"Why?"

Luke leans into me. "Because he'd have definitely hit him."

I can't help laughing as I turn back to Todd. "In that case, I wish you'd known too."

"How could he do that to you... after everything else?"

"Because he was a waste of space?" I suggest. Todd's lips curve upward. "I'm sorry I compared you to him so much." I reach up and touch his cheek with my fingertips. "There's no comparison. You never gave me any cause to doubt you. Not once. And still, I... still, I..." I can hear my own voice cracking.

"Hey... it's in the past now," he says softly. And his lips meet mine once more.

We're standing in a magnificent bedroom, in the attic of Matt and Grace's home.

"This is beautiful," I say, looking around. The walls are a deep cream, the curtains a soft blue, and the vaulted ceiling slopes above the super-king sized bed in the centre of the room.

"Not as beautiful as you." Todd comes over and stands in front of me.

"Or you." I run my hands up his arms and rest my head on his chest. "You're sure your friends don't mind me staying here?"

"I stay here all the time," he says, kissing the top of my head. "They're delighted you're here."

I lean back. "And you?"

"Don't I seem delighted?" He smiles down at me, flexing his hips into mine, so I can feel his erection. "Or do you think this is just because we're in the same city again?"

I can't help but laugh. He shrugs off his jacket, carefully, to avoid hurting his shoulder, and throws it onto the chair in the corner, then starts undoing the buttons on my blouse. I bring up my hand and place it on top of his.

"Sorry," he whispers, staring down at me. "I thought you wanted to. I mean, in the kitchen..."

"I do want to, but there are a few things I need to know first. Last time, we made the mistake of going to bed before we'd talked. We're not doing that again."

"Okay…" He looks concerned.

"Well, you're too distracting, and there are things I need to ask you."

"I'm distracting?" he smirks.

"Yes, but stop changing the subject."

"Hey… you brought it up." I take a deep breath. "What do you want to talk about?" he asks.

"That last morning…"

"Yeah?" Now he sounds worried.

"Why did you stop what you were doing? I didn't understand… I still don't. I mean, you said you wanted me, so why stop?"

He closes his eyes and, just for a moment, he looks like he's in pain. "I told you," he says, opening his eyes again. "I was doing it for all the wrong reasons."

"Yes, but what did that mean? What were the reasons?"

He takes my hand and leads me to the bed, sitting us both down. Then he turns to me, his eyes dark and intense. "I was jealous," he says.

"Of Jason?"

"Yes, of Jason. I woke up and you weren't there. That was such a disappointment. I wanted to make love to you again… and then you were being a bit weird. I thought you regretted what we'd done. I thought he was still in your head. I thought you still wanted him, and the idea that we'd spent the night together and done all the things we'd done and you'd been thinking about him the whole time… It drove me a little crazy—"

"I wasn't thinking about Jason," I interrupt. "You were the only thing… the only person in my head."

He smiles. "I didn't realise," he says. "I thought…"

"Well, you thought wrong."

"Evidently. I guess… I guess I was trying to prove to myself – and maybe to you – that I was the man you'd been thinking of, even if I wasn't. I knew I was being rough and overbearing. I… I went too far.

I forgot to pay attention to what you wanted. I didn't listen. It was dumb, selfish, childish. I still feel bad about it."

"Well don't. You weren't rough." He raises an eyebrow. "Okay, maybe you were a little. But, I liked it."

"You did?"

"Wasn't that obvious?"

"I guess so. But you stepped back."

"Only because I thought we should talk first," I explain.

"And you choked. It seemed like you were about to cry."

"No. I was emotional, but only in a good way. What you were doing was very intense. It was hard not to respond."

"And you didn't mind what I was doing?"

"Mind? Um… no. You'd shown me a whole new side to myself that night. I wanted more. I was ready for more. I thought you were going to take me there and then, up against the wall."

"I was… I wanted to."

"I wish you had. That would have been another new experience for me." He tilts his head to one side. "Pretty much everything you did was new to me. It's never been like that. It was exciting." This is embarrassing, but I need to tell him. We have to be honest. "It… it seems I quite like being taken like that; being, um… d—dominated in the bedroom… at least some of the time."

His lips twitch upwards. He's not even remotely embarrassed, damn him. "Oh really? And when did you work that out?"

"When this man I know pinned me to the bed, held me down and made love to me, and… and then woke me up in the night, because he wanted more. And then slammed me up against a wall…"

A slow smile forms on his lips. "And which man would that be?"

"A tall, handsome, American I met recently."

"And which tall, handsome American is this?"

"Um… I only know one."

"I think you'll find you know four now."

"Well, only one of them has been in my bed."

"And that's how it's going to stay." He pulls me closer. "You're mine," he growls, then kisses me. Hard.

"This being dominated…" he says, breaking the kiss, his eyes wandering over my face, like he's seeing me for the first time, "is it limited to the bedroom, or are you interested in trying it out in other places too? I mean, I guess we kind of tried the living room already, but we can take it a lot further than that. And what about the kitchen, and the bathroom… or outside?" He leans in and lowers his voice. "If you want to restrict it to the bedroom, that's fine with me, but I'd really love to take you in the shower… and I've got a motorcycle at home. We could go somewhere real quiet… real secluded…" He shudders. "Oh God, the things I could do to you…"

I shiver at the thought. "I'll try anything you want, anywhere you want," I whisper. "As long as it doesn't hurt."

"I'll never hurt you."

"I know." His eyes widen, and I feel a pool of heat settle deep inside me.

"We're gonna have so much fun, baby." He leans down and claims my mouth. When he pulls back, we're both breathless.

"The way you take me like that," I whisper, "the look you get in your eyes, it makes me feel so wanted… so needed."

"Oh, you're wanted, and needed, Holly, trust me."

"I do. I do trust you, Todd."

"Finally! It's about fucking time." He grins, and kisses me again, pushing me down onto the bed and lying alongside me. He breaks the kiss and raises himself up his elbow, his injured arm resting across my stomach.

"I'm sorry it took me so long," I whisper.

"And I'm sorry too. I should've told you how I felt, not put all the pressure on you to come to me."

"No. I should have said something to make you stay – or at least given you a reason to come back. I was so in love with you, and I should have said so…"

I nestle closer to him. "I think," he says quietly, "that we need to learn to communicate a little better. Whatever else happens, can we promise we'll always talk to each other, no matter what?"

"Promise," I murmur. "On which note, can I ask you a question?"

"Sure."

"It's about you and Luke…"

"Okay, that's unexpected. What about us?" he asks.

"You told me Matt was your best friend, but I saw you and Luke giving each other a look earlier at the table. What was that about?"

He pulls me closer. "He talked me into going back to London to find you."

"You needed to be persuaded?" I feel a little disappointed by that.

"No, not exactly. I… I thought I didn't have anything to go back for. I thought we were over. I missed you so much, baby, I was slowly fucking up my whole life. I was pushing all my friends away. To quote Grace, I was self destructing." I hold him a little tighter. "So, the guys sat me down and Luke gave me a good talking to."

"Just Luke?"

"Yeah. Everyone else was there, but Luke did the talking. He knew what I was going through, he knew how it felt to lose the person you love more than anything in the world." He leans down and kisses me again. "They all told me to go to London, find you and bring you back. Of course, they didn't expect me to go the next day. They told me to wait until I was better… but I didn't want to wait. I wanted you back in my life. Luke told me to stop being a dick and get myself back to you and tell you, over and over, how much I love you… because love means never giving up."

"I think I like Luke," I say quietly.

"Hmm," he murmurs. "As long as you don't like him too much."

"No, not too much." I kiss him. "And nowhere near as much as I love you," I whisper.

"I love you too." He deepens the kiss. "Now… can I ask you something?" he asks.

"Okay."

"What made you come over here? You wouldn't even give me a reason to come back to you, so what made you decide to take the chance on coming here?"

"Believe it or not, Andy… He was my version of Luke."

He leans back and looks at me. "Andy?"

"Yes. He told me I should try and fix things between us… And I'd regret it if I didn't."

"How did he know there was an 'us'? *We* didn't even know there was an 'us'."

"He said he worked it out while we were still in his office."

"On that first day? Before either of us had even thought about it?"

"Evidently."

"So, not the ass I thought he was then?"

"No. He turned out to be a good guy…"

"There are a few of us around." He falls silent for a moment, then his lips twitch a little. "And how long do you think this fixing things up between us will take?" he asks quietly. "How long can you stay?"

"I booked a flight back for ten days from now."

"Ten days?" He sounds disappointed.

"But… I don't have to use it… I can stay longer, or I can go before then, if you w—"

"I don't want you to go at all," he says, "and certainly not before you have to, but I get that you've got a job to go back to, so we'll work something out. Maybe I can—"

"I resigned. I don't have a job anymore."

He laughs. "Really? That's great news. I don't have a job anymore either… Well, I do, but not really."

"That's not at all confusing."

"Sorry. What I mean is, I resigned too."

"Yes, I know. Your friends told me."

"Okay… And do you remember I mentioned Will and I having a business together."

"Yes, vaguely."

"Well, that's the job I kind of have. I'm my own boss – with Will – but I haven't actually started working yet, because I needed to wrap up the case at work, and then I got shot. But I'll be starting work with Will soon."

"Are you well enough?"

"Probably not."

"So you could take some time off?" I run my hand down his chest and across his stomach, stopping at the waistband of his jeans. "We could spend it… fixing things…"

"I think I could speak to the boss." His voice is soft and low. "I know him quite well…" He leans over me. "I might even be able to persuade him to give you a job too… If you're interested in staying, more long-term."

I look up into his eyes. "You want me to?"

"More than anything, baby. And I think the boss can be persuaded. He kinda likes you."

"Only likes?"

"Okay… he loves you beyond words… more than life itself."

"In that case, I'll stay."

"You will?"

"Yes."

He grins and kisses me really gently. "Are we done talking?" he asks.

"I guess so… for now."

"Thank God for that." His eyes bore into mine. "I have an idea…" he whispers.

"Oh yes?"

"Well, when we were at the club, you spent a lot of time sitting on my lap…"

"Hmm?"

"So, how about we try that again… but without clothes this time, because I really need to be buried deep inside you… right now." His words make me shudder.

He kneels up between my legs and undoes my blouse. "I seriously hate you wearing a bra," he mutters. "It's another layer between us, and I don't like anything to come between us."

"Then lose it." He smiles as I raise myself up off the bed, and he takes off my blouse and undoes the clip, removing my bra and throwing it onto the floor behind me. Todd stands, quickly undresses and then leans over and unfastens my jeans, pulling them and my thong off. We're both naked, and he climbs back into the middle of the bed and sits down.

"Come here, baby," he murmurs.

I kneel up and clamber over, placing one knee either side of him.

"I think you remember how this works." He grins.

"I've only done it with my clothes on, though."

He pulls me closer and I wrap arms around his neck, feeling his hands come around behind me, my breasts hard against his naked chest, and his eyes burning into mine.

"But it's gonna be so much more fun without them," he whispers. "I've wanted to do this since that first time at the club," he adds. He leans forward and kisses me as I lower myself onto him, taking his length deep inside me. "I'm gonna make you come so hard," he murmurs, breaking the kiss.

"Hmm... I like the sound of that," I whisper as I start to ride him.

"Good, because I'm gonna keep doing it again... and again... and again"

"Until I beg you to stop?"

"You might beg me to stop," he says, stilling me. "But I know you won't want me to. You crave pleasure, and that's what I want to give you. That's what I'm here for. It's my purpose to give you all your pleasure, and all my love. And I know you won't ever want me to stop, baby, even when you think you do."

He's so right. I know he is. I lean back a little and look at him. "That's something I was going to say to you on that awful morning... the morning after our perfect night."

"What's that?" He looks into my eyes.

"That you changed me that night. You're right. I do crave pleasure, but I never realised it until that night with you." I stroke his face with my hand. "You made me into a more passionate, intense person."

He shakes his head. "I didn't change you at all, Holly. Deep down, you were always that person. You were always full of hot passion and need and desire. You just had to find someone you could trust enough to be yourself with." He smiles. "I needed that too, it seems. Luckily we both found what we were looking for... in each other." He swivels his hips and I feel his cock moving deep inside me. "Now..." He grins. "I think we should stop talking and you should start moving. I want you to take me, until you're screaming out my name… or I'm gonna have to spank that beautiful ass of yours."

"Can't we do both?" I murmur, moving myself slowly up and down the length of his erection.

"We can do anything you want, baby."

I shudder out a breath of anticipation. "Promises, promises…" I manage to mutter, leaning into him.

He kisses my neck, biting gently on my skin. "Yeah… and I *always* keep my promises."

Epilogue

Four months later

Holly

He stills inside me, and lowers himself down, supporting his weight on his elbows.

"What's wrong," I whisper. His shoulder hasn't given him any trouble for months. Why would it start now?

"Nothing's wrong," he breathes into my ear, holding completely still.

I move my hips up into him, wanting to feel him move again. I was close… I was really close.

"Wait, baby" he mutters softly. "Just wait a minute."

"What for?" He's never done this before and I'm so confused.

"I need to ask you something," he says.

"Now?"

"It's the best time I can think of."

"Okay."

He raises himself up, just a little, so he's looking down into my face, pushing a stray damp hair from my cheek, and studying me closely.

"You're beautiful," he says. "You're loving, sexy, intelligent, kind, giving… and I love you with all my heart." He shifts slightly, and I feel him move inside me. "Please, Holly… will marry me?" he asks.

"M—Marry you?" Is he serious? One look into his eyes and I know he is. He's staring at me, with such a look of need and longing. "You want to marry me?"

He nods his head. "Please, baby," he says. "It's all I want. It's the only thing I want."

"Then yes, I'll marry you." Because it's all I want too.

He covers my mouth with his, and slowly, tenderly, starts to move again.

This is only the second time everyone has come to Todd's apartment for dinner since I've been here and I'm nervous. The last time, we ordered take-away. This time, we're cooking. Todd's very relaxed, of course… but then he would be. He's very relaxed about everything, especially now we're engaged. He told me after he'd made love to me, when we were lying together curled up in each other's arms, how nervous he was about asking… How could he even doubt my answer? And today, we went and bought the ring… the beautiful emerald and diamond ring that's now adorning my left hand.

"Stop worrying," he says, coming up behind me and placing his hands on my hips, as he kisses my neck.

"Is it that obvious?" I turn in his arms so I'm facing him.

"Yes. You've re-arranged the table about five times. It looks fine. Although not as fine as it did this morning." He grins. "I can't think of anything I like to have laid out on the table more than you." He pulls me in close, running his fingers down my spine until he reaches my bottom, then pulls me onto his erection. "Want a re-run?" he asks.

"We can't. Everyone will be here soon, and it's taken me hours to get everything looking this good."

"Nothing looks as good as you… naked." His voice has dropped a note or two and his eyes are dark, intense… fiery. I love him when he's gentle, like last night… but I think I love him even more when he's burning hot, like this. That need in him hasn't diminished. If anything it's intensified. He takes my mouth, his tongue delving deep as he pushes me backwards until I hit the wall. Then he pulls my hands straight out to the sides, holding them there. "Don't move your arms," he murmurs into my mouth, as he releases me, moving one hand to cover my left breast, while the other cups my sex.

I gasp out a "Yes," between my teeth.

"Shh," he whispers, quickly undoing my jeans and pushing them down. "Step out," he says, and I comply. He does the same with his own, and his boxers. My thong is in the way still... but not for long. He rips through the seam and drops the shredded lacy panties to the floor, then lifts my left leg and, without hesitating for an instant, enters me.

"Fuck, yes," he mutters, as he starts to pound in and out of me, harder and harder. It only takes a few minutes for me to come and I have to move my arms, to hold onto him as the shattering waves wash over me. "You moved," he says quietly, stilling.

"I had to," I pant. And he picks me up, bringing my legs around his waist. I'm impaled on him, so deep, my arms clasped around his neck.

"You had to?" he murmurs.

"Yes." I nod my head. "You made me come."

"Well, I'm gonna make you come again." And he does...

"How do you do that?" I ask him.

"Do what?" he whispers. We're sitting on the floor semi-naked. I'm curled up in his arms.

"How do you know when I want gentle, sweet loving, and when I want you to just take me, hard and fast."

"It's an instinct, I guess." He smiles down at me. "It's not something I'm really conscious of."

"But you never seem to get it wrong. You always hit just the right spot."

"Good. I hope I always will." He leans over and kisses me. "If I ever get it wrong, baby," he says, "you have to let me know. I don't ever want to get it wrong with you..."

He kisses me again, for a long time. "Do you think we should get up and put our clothes back on," I ask him eventually. "Everyone will be here soon."

"No. I think we should call them and cancel. And I should take you through to our room, handcuff you to the bed and pleasure you... for hours..."

"Oh God." My breath hitches in my throat, and I can feel myself tingling at the thought. "I like the sound of that... but they'll be on their way, won't they?"

"Probably." He sighs and, with some reluctance, we both stand up. "Later?" he suggests.

I nod my head. "Oh… yes, please."

He leans down and kisses me. "We'd better stop this," he says, pulling away, "or I'm gonna have to take you again." I'm tempted to let him, but everyone will be arriving soon.

"Todd," I say as I pick up my clothes. "You've got to stop ripping my underwear off me… This is the fifth thong you've done this with." I hold up the torn piece of lace. "And it's an Amulet one. It cost a fortune."

He comes and stands in front of me. "I can't help it," he says, grinning at me. "You're too much… you always were." He kisses me. "But I'll speak to Luke. He'll let me pick you out some new things… at a very good rate."

"Hmm… And are you going to explain why you need to get me new underwear?" I smirk at him.

"Maybe…"

"So, you're going to tell your friend that you keep ripping my knickers off…"

"I might use the word 'panties'." He grins.

"You two are incorrigible." They are, but they're good fun too. He laughs. "Well, I suppose I'd better go and find another thong to wear tonight." I go to turn away, but he grabs my hand and pulls me back.

"No," he says, his voice dropping again. "I want you as you are."

"With no underwear at all?" I know my eyes have widened.

"Yeah. Just your jeans and your top. Nothing else. I want your wet pussy and your gorgeous ass available to me… all night. And only I'll know about it."

I lean up to kiss his cheek.

"You're getting kinkier, you know that, don't you?" I whisper.

"You bet." He grabs me and looks down into my eyes. "I also know how much you like it."

Once we're dressed and Todd has put my torn thong in his pocket, he takes my hand and leads me into the living area, which is probably my favourite part of his flat… apart from the bedroom, obviously.

There are two large black leather sofas either side of a big fireplace, with a low coffee table in between and, completely separate, over by the window, is a chair, which I often sit in to read. It's very peaceful in here, very calm and tranquil.

We've just sat down when the doorbells rings and he goes to answer it. Everyone arrives together, all piling through the door.

"It's turning cold," Grace says, kissing my cheek. She hands George over to me so she can remove her coat, and I instantly feel awkward. Grace and Megan both hand their babies around, and it always makes me feel… inadequate, I guess. I don't have that maternal instinct that they and Jamie seem to have. "You can keep George for a while, if you like," she says to me, handing her coat to Todd. "I'll have him back when he's… maybe twelve? He's just cutting another tooth, so he's grumpy."

I nod my head and smile, but I don't have an answer and she comes over and takes him back from me.

"I was only kidding," she says, winking. I think she's guessed that I'm uncomfortable. "I wouldn't expect anyone to have him at the moment… he's horrible." She kisses his pink cheek. "I still love him to pieces, though."

Everyone moves into the living room and sits down and Todd brings in drinks. We all talk separately for a while. Jamie and I discuss the dress she's ordered for her and Will's wedding, which is really why we're all here, as the big event is next weekend. She's collecting it tomorrow and wants me to go with her.

"What time?" I ask her.

"Twelve o'clock?"

"Absolutely fine. We could have lunch out at the same time. I'm sure Todd and Will can cope without us for a few hours."

We all get along working together really well. Todd and Will moved the business into purpose-built offices in the summer. It was never going to be practical for us to all to work out of Will and Jamie's home. Jamie's brother Scott has been working for the business since the end of August as well. He and his girlfriend, Mia, moved here a couple of weeks before that and they've just started renting a small apartment not far from the office. It's all worked out perfectly…

"I wanted to speak to you guys, while I've got you all together," Todd says, coming and sitting next to me, on the arm of the sofa. Everyone turns to him, me included. "Holly's agreed to marry me," he says simply. They all start congratulating us at the same time and, to be honest, it's a little overwhelming, being hugged and kissed and asked to show off the ring. I wish he'd told me he was going to make an announcement. I'm not entirely sure why he did. I look up at him, as he continues, "Ordinarily, I wouldn't have made an announcement, or even mentioned anything until after Will and Jamie's wedding. We don't want to take anything away from your day." He looks across at them, sitting hand in hand on the opposite sofa. "But, something's come up and I've got a favour to ask… I'm afraid it's a big one. A really big one."

What does he mean 'something's come up'? I turn to him. "Don't look so scared," he says to me, leaning down and kissing me. "There's nothing to be worried about."

He looks up at everyone else. "My proposal was… a little… well, impromptu." He smiles down at me. "To put it mildly." His smile becomes a grin. "And I didn't get around to speaking to Holly's dad until after she'd already said yes."

"You spoke to my dad?" I'm surprised.

"Yes, of course I did. I called him this afternoon, while you were preparing the dinner."

"So that's why you disappeared into the bedroom. I thought you were trying to avoid helping out."

"No, that was just a bonus." He smirks. "Babe, it wasn't a conversation I wanted to have in front of you," he adds. "What if he'd refused his permission?"

"I'm twenty-seven years old, Todd. I don't think he'd refuse."

"Well…" The tone of his voice makes me twist in my seat.

"He didn't, did he?"

Everyone seems to lean forward, just a little. "No, he didn't refuse."

"Am I the only one sensing a 'but' coming here?" Matt says from across the room.

"Hmm. It's a fairly big but..."

"What happened, Todd?" I ask.

"He's insisting on throwing us an engagement party."

I feel cold... really cold and I snuggle up to Todd. "No, I can't," I say quietly. "You... you told me not to be scared..."

"I'm sorry baby... I tried, really I did," Todd says gently, his arms coming around me. "But he absolutely insisted."

"When?" I say, feeling resigned.

"Two weeks from today... and you don't have to be scared..."

"What's the problem?" Luke says. "It's a party..."

"There's a bit of history with engagement parties," Todd explains. Luke looks at me. "You've been engaged before?" he asks.

"No, not Holly," Todd replies for me. "Her sister."

"The same sister whose clothes fell off a little too easily?" Luke says.

"That's the one... Ellie." Todd sits up a little, but keeps one arm around me. "She got engaged to her husband, James, about six or seven years ago but spent the night of the party shacked up with some guy in her parents' annexe. Holly's mom saw her returning to the main house the next morning, but to cover her tracks, Ellie blamed Holly and said it was her. At a distance, I guess they look kind of similar," he says.

"So my mother painted me as a slut, and Ellie got away with just being one... again," I conclude the story.

"Your sister sounds charming," Matt says.

"She's a piece of work," Todd replies.

"But... what's the favour?" Grace asks.

"If we have to go to this damn party, which we kinda do, being as it's our engagement... I really want you guys to be there. We'll need the moral support. It'd be good to have some people there who we know are on our side. I know it's a big ask, but..."

"When did you say it was?" Will says.

"Two weeks from today."

He turns to Jamie. "That works for us," she says. "That's the day we fly to England anyway. We were always going there for the second week of our honeymoon. We've booked the flights from Paris to London already…"

Will nods his head. "We're on the ten-thirty flight in the morning, aren't we?"

"Yes," Jamie agrees.

"So we can meet you guys somewhere, if you tell us where," Will suggests, turning back to the rest of us.

"Really?" I turn to them. "You'd do that? Even though it's your honeymoon?"

"Of course." Will looks across at me.

"We'll definitely be there," Matt says. "Grace will take any opportunity she gets to go back to England… even if only to shop."

"We can go, can't we?" Megan says to Luke.

"Sure," he says.

"What about work?" Todd says. "We've all got businesses to run…"

"Obviously Will and I were always going to be away then anyway," Jamie says, "but if you guys have to duck out for a few days as well, then Scott will just have to cope. It'll do him good to take some responsibility. And Mia doesn't start her new job for another few weeks, so she can always help out, if necessary."

"She won't object?" I ask.

Jamie laughs. "To the chance of spending more time with my brother? No… she won't object at all."

"And we employ over a hundred people," Matt adds. "If they can't function without Luke, Grace and me for a short while, then they shouldn't be working for us."

"So you'll come?" Todd asks.

"We'll come," Matt says.

I glance around the room. I really do understand why Todd places so much emphasis on friendship now. There's just one problem…

"Oh, God," I say, putting my head in my hands for a moment. "Ellie… She's going to have a field day." I look up at Todd. "Can you imagine what she'll be like with all four of you? She was bad enough when it was just you on your own."

"I think we can handle ourselves," Luke says. "Don't worry about your sister, Holly."

"But it'll be a black tie event," I say, feeling even more nervous. "I know how good Todd looks in a tux… I'm sure the rest of you do too."

"Nothing like as good as me, baby," Todd says.

"That's what you think," Luke replies.

"Either way, Ellie's going to think it's Christmas." I can feel the fear building. "Her tongue's going to be hanging out."

"Well, we'll try real hard not to fall over it as we walk past her," Luke says.

"But she'll think that you're all her own special presents, just waiting to be unwrapped."

"Like I say," Luke adds, "stop worrying. The wrappings will be on these presents far too tight for your sister to do anything about it."

"Oh, God…"

"Holly…" Todd's voice cuts into my thoughts. "Stop it. There's nothing to worry about."

I so wish that were true…

Todd's checked on the chicken, which needs another ten minutes, so he tops up the drinks.

"I've had an idea," Grace says. "Why don't we turn the trip to England into a holiday for all of us?"

"What do you have in mind?" Matt asks her.

She looks at Todd. "The party's on the Saturday, is that right?" He nods his head. "Well, why don't we all fly in on the Friday…? Then we could meet Will and Jamie on the Saturday lunchtime and drive down to Holly's parents' place… and then, when the party's over, we can take off somewhere. I can rent us a cottage or a house, or something. We could all do with a break."

"That sounds great," Luke says.

"I know," Megan adds. "What about the Lake District?"

"Brilliant." Grace is smiling. "Oh, Matt, it's so incredible there. I'd love for you to see it."

"It's fine with me, beautiful," he says. He looks around. "All agreed?" Everyone nods. "Even you two?" He looks at Will and Jamie. "It is your honeymoon… Are you sure you want to spend any of it with us? You can always go and do your own thing after the party… none of us will mind."

They look at each other. "We'll have had our romantic week in Paris," Will says. "And Luke's told me about the Lake District… I'd really like to see it."

"Me too," says Jamie.

"We could all hire separate cars, so we're not having to do the same things," Grace suggests.

"Even better."

"I'll take care of everything, shall I?" Grace says.

Matt turns to her. "Do you think you can find us a big enough place?"

"Yes. That won't be a problem. And I'll arrange the cars too, if you all tell me what you want. Maybe we should work out a budget for the trip, so I know what I'm looking at."

Matt leans over to her. "No budget, baby. I'll pay… flights, cars, the house… all of it."

"Oh no you won't," Todd says. "I got us all into this…"

Matt turns to him. "Call it an engagement present, if you want to. It isn't, but you can call it that, if it makes you feel better."

Todd stares at him. "Thanks," he says. He obviously knows there's no point in arguing. "And is there any chance you'll stop saying you owe me now?"

Matt shakes his head. "Nope. Never gonna happen."

Later, when everyone has gone home, Todd and I are lying in bed. I'm cradled in his arms, with my head resting on his chest.

"Can I ask you something?" he says.

I nod my head.

"Do you remember we said we'd be honest with each other and communicate?"

"Yes." I look up at him. This sounds serious.

"So, if I ask you something, will you be honest with me?"

"Of course."

He takes a deep breath. "Do you want to have kids?" Because my head is on his chest, I can tell he's holding his breath.

"Why do you ask?"

"That's not an answer, Holly." He turns us, so we're facing each other.

"I still want to know why you're asking."

"Because you're always… I guess, kinda awkward around George and Daisy." He thinks for a moment. "You were okay with Oliver though, so is it just babies you're uncomfortable with?"

I look up into his eyes. "No, I'm pretty uncomfortable around all kids. Between my own mother and Ellie, I don't have any great role models to base an idea of motherhood on. I think with Oliver, it's just that I've had a while to get used to him, that's all. And I feel sorry for him. Having a mother like Ellie, he needs all the sympathy he can get." I smile at Todd.

He nods his head. "I can understand that," he says, "but you still haven't answered my question."

"To be honest, I don't know whether I want kids or not. I do know that I'm not maternal, not like most women. I've never been able to picture myself as a mother and, when I see Grace and Megan with the babies, I genuinely can't imagine myself doing that." He nods his head again, more slowly this time, which has me a little worried. "If I said a definite 'no' would that be a problem?" I ask and it's my turn to hold my breath.

"No," he replies. "To be honest, I've never been entirely sure about kids myself. I guess because I never even wanted a relationship, having children wasn't something I considered."

"And have you considered it now?"

He looks at me. "Not really… it was just seeing you with George tonight made me think about it. And I decided it was something we should discuss."

"So, we're both on the same page?"

"If that's the *really not convinced we want children* page, then yeah, I think we are." He smiles.

"So it's just you and me," I whisper.

"Just you and me, baby." He leans down and kisses me, deeply. "Now..." he says, breaking the kiss, and flipping me onto my back, "where did I put my handcuffs?"

Todd

I feel like I've been here before... but that's because I have. The house is full, people are milling about everywhere and while I'd be the first to admit, Holly's parents know how to throw a party, it seems it's always the same party. The furniture in the drawing room has been moved out and people are dancing... badly... again.

Holly looks stunning. She's wearing a stylish ball gown that we picked up in Boston. As we were walking down the stairs earlier, I told her she looked like a brunette Grace Kelly, because she does. She's just so beautiful. Her reply floored me. She smiled at me, squeezed my hand and whispered right in my ear, "Hmm... that would be Grace Kelly with no knickers," and her eyes twinkled.

We're standing in the hallway with Matt and Grace. Luke and Megan are on the dance floor – more fool them – and Will and Jamie are upstairs. We're all taking it in turns to use checking on the babies as an excuse to escape the insanity. I'm not sure how much longer I can wait for it to be mine and Holly's turn and, judging from the expression on her face, neither can she. I'm so damn hard, knowing she's naked underneath that dress, I need to get her upstairs. I don't want to undress her, just lift up her skirt and bury my cock inside her. I want to take her so hard, she'll be screaming my name. Unable to resist all the bare skin on show, I run my fingers down Holly's spine and she shudders, letting out a slight moan. Oh, yeah... the smile on her lips and the look in her eye as she turns to me tells me she knows exactly what I'm thinking, and she wants it too, just as much as I do.

I look around, trying to calm down and find a distraction from my wayward thoughts. My eyes settle on Ellie – the human equivalent to a cold shower – who's staring at me from the doorway to the drawing room. Despite, Holly's fears, Ellie has left everyone alone – except me. She's followed me around all evening, like a lost dog. It seems Holly was right about one thing… Ellie wants whatever Holly has got. She's not getting it, but that doesn't stop her from trying, and I can see her efforts are making Holly feel nervous and insecure, even if she's got no cause.

Alan, and Holly's mom – who I've now been given permission to call Laura – come over and I introduce them to Matt and Grace.

I'm grateful that Matt was born into money, so these surroundings are nothing new to him, and Grace, being British seems to be able to fit in here. So far, within this conversation, we're not embarrassing ourselves.

"I want to talk to you, darling," Laura says to Holly, her voice dripping insincerity.

"Yes, Mother." As usual when she speaks to her mom, Holly sounds bored.

"As soon as your father and Todd had finished their phone call, I telephoned Amberley Castle and they've got several dates available in the New Year."

"Amberley? Are you serious?" Holly's dropped the bored tone and seems shocked.

"Of course I'm serious. It's the perfect venue."

"It's where Ellie had her wedding, Mother. I don't want mine there." Is her mom kidding?

"Well, I don't see why not. She and James are so happy together… You couldn't hope for anything better."

The temptation to tell this woman the truth about her elder daughter's supposedly perfect marriage is huge, but I don't.

"The castle is lovely," Grace says, her voice calm and serene. "But then there are so many beautiful wedding venues around here, you're spoilt for choice really, aren't you? I'm sure Holly's got plenty of ideas of her own…"

I know what she's trying to do, but it won't work.

Laura turns slowly to Grace, looks her up and down, and then turns away again. It's as though Grace didn't even speak. Matt raises his eyebrows, and opens his mouth to say something, but I shake my head. If anyone's going to take this woman on, it'll be me.

"Holly and I have discussed venues," I say, and I feel her stiffen in my arms at the lie. We haven't discussed anything at all, not yet. We've been planning Will and Jamie's wedding with them, and the trip over here. Between that and work, we haven't had the chance to discuss our own plans yet. "And we've got a short-list. When we've decided on one, we'll let you know."

"Young man," Laura says, her voice taking on an authoritarian note. "As Holly's parents, we will be paying for her wedding, so we will decide where and when it takes place."

I take a step toward her, keeping my arm firmly around Holly. "You will not be paying, Mrs King. I will. And Holly and I will decide everything. If Holly wants to get married in a castle, she can… but if she wants to get married naked on a beach on a South Sea island… then that's fine with me. She will have whatever she wants." I notice Alan raise his hand to cover his mouth and I know he's stifling a laugh.

Even beneath her heavy make-up, I can see the color of Laura's face change and her eyes widen.

"No daughter of mine—"

Alan takes her arm. "I think Todd is merely making the point, dear," he says calmly, "that Holly and he should be allowed to choose whatever they wish for their own wedding." She turns to him. "And I agree with him," he adds firmly. "It's me who'll be paying," he says to her, "not you, and I want Holly to have the wedding of her choice… of her dreams." Then he looks at me. "And I don't want any arguments from you about the money."

I shake my head. "As long as Holly can have what she wants, you won't get any."

"Then we're in agreement," he says.

"Oh, are we…?" Laura says, but he steers her away from us before we get to hear what she's got to say.

"Wow!" says Matt.

"I do apologize for my mother," Holly says to Grace. "That was inexcusable."

Grace puts a hand on Holly's arm. "You're not responsible," she says. "But I love your dad."

"I know." Holly smiles. "He's a sweetie, isn't he?" She turns to me, looking up into my eyes. "Naked on a South Sea island? Really?"

I shrug, grinning at her. "Well, it sounds good to me."

"And you wouldn't mind that being in front of all our friends?"

"You called them 'our' friends," I say, ignoring the rest of her question, as we both know there's no way I'd let her be naked in front of anyone but me. "That's the first time you've done that."

"You've witnessed the way my family behave and you're surprised I value our friends?"

"Not in the least…" I lean a little closer, resting my hand on her ass. "Now about that South Sea island…"

We got here three days ago, and I have to admit, nothing has disappointed.

The scenery is spectacular, and everything that Luke, Megan and Grace built it up to be.

The 'house' that Grace found for us is actually a grand hall, overlooking Ullswater, one of the northern lakes. Each of the bedrooms has a stunning view across the water to the hills beyond, and waking up to that each morning is something I'm getting used to. As is waking up next to Holly. We have more fun together than I would have thought possible; she never disappoints, and she really is willing to try anything… and I mean anything. She's so much a part of my life now, I wonder how I ever lived without her.

Holly and I walked quite a distance today, from Rosthwaite to Watendlath Tarn, and back, so when we got back here, we had a bath together… a very romantic and very intimate bath.

The others have done their own thing during the day, and now we're all sitting in the enormous living room. The wine's flowing, except for Megan, who's drinking hot chocolate. There's a log fire blazing at one end of the room. It's warm in here, so I've taken off my sweater and am

311

just wearing a t-shirt, with my jeans, although Holly's still got her thick check shirt on over her jeans... and no underwear. It's becoming a habit these days. It's a habit I'm really liking, especially after the party. We got to sneak off upstairs not long after our conversation with Alan and Laura, and the results were incredible, and really loud. By the time we got up there, we both needed the release, and it showed. It had other benefits too... I noticed, as we came out of the bedroom, while Holly was straightening my tie, that Ellie was standing by the window at the end of the corridor. True to form, she must've followed us upstairs and, judging from the sour looks she was giving Holly and me for the rest of the evening, I think she must have been outside the bedroom door the whole time. She'd have heard all the noise we made... my scolding Holly for being such a tease, and spanking her gorgeous ass while she bent over the end of the bed, her moans of delight and urgent pleas for more, her giggle and yelp of pleasure as I flipped her over and entered her, my softer words, telling her how good she felt, how tight she was, Holly's final screams of pleasure as she came and my yell of everlasting love as I exploded into her. It was just a frenzied jumble of sounds and words really, all things that are perfectly normal between Holly and me, but from the perspective of being able to demonstrate to Ellie that I love Holly with my whole heart, mind and body, and would never risk what she gives me for anything Ellie has to offer, the timing was immaculate. The thought still makes me smile now.

There are four luxurious sofas arranged in a square around a huge coffee table, and we've taken one each, and I'm sitting with my back to one end of ours, with Holly resting between my legs. Opposite us, Luke and Megan are curled up together, with Daisy between them. They're watching their daughter, their eyes filled with love. It wouldn't surprise me in the least if they had another baby in the not too distant future. I'm not sure Matt and Grace will. We all know there were worries at the beginning, and Matt was beyond terrified when Grace went into labor two weeks early. He's already told me he feels blessed to have what he's got... Still, who knows?

We've spent more time with the babies over the last few days than ever before and, watching them, I've been wondering if I could ever feel the kind of love Luke and Matt have for Daisy and George. I love Holly with everything I've got. Do I have enough love in me for anyone else?

All of a sudden, from the other side of the room, Daisy lets out a giggle, which goes on and on… I've never heard her laugh before and there's something real infectious about it. Soon we're all joining in. Holly giggles too, throwing her head back into my chest and, for a moment, our eyes connect.

She twists in toward me. "Can I ask you something?" she whispers, so no-one else can hear.

"Sure."

"How would you feel if I said I might be changing my mind…"

I sit up. "What about? Us? Getting married?" I'm suddenly real scared.

"No, you idiot." I heave out a sigh of relief. "About us having a baby together."

"Seriously?"

"Yeah." She lowers her eyes.

"Why?" I ask.

"Spending more time with our friends… with Daisy and George," she says. "I'm seeing things differently and I'm maybe not as immune as I thought I was." She looks up at me again. "If it's a problem…"

I look across the room to where Luke and Megan are sitting. They're holding Daisy, but they're staring at each other now and Luke whispers something to Megan. She smiles and he leans forward and kisses her gently… and, in him, I see that it really is possible to have it all.

"If it's what you want," I tell Holly, "then it's not a problem."

"There's no rush," she says. "It's not something I want to do straight away. I just wanted you to know that I might be changing my mind."

"Well, that's okay. I want you to myself for a while longer."

"And I like being your baby," she says, snuggling into me.

I raise her face to mine. "Hey," I say, "no matter how many kids we end up having, you'll *always* be my baby." She puts her arms around my neck and pulls herself up, and I kiss her deeply… and I don't care who else is in the room.

As I break the kiss, she whispers, "Maybe not just you and me, then?"

"Oh, no… It'll always be you and me."

I look up to find Luke smiling at us. It's like he knows what we've been talking about. Since our conversation before I went to find Holly in London, Luke and I are much closer. We may still make fun of each other, but I know I'd never have got to where I am without him. I think, when it comes to relationships, he's probably the most sensible of all of us. He'd punch me if I ever said that to his face… but that doesn't make it untrue.

"I give in," Jamie says, interrupting my train of thought. "I've waited long enough."

"Um… What for?" Will asks. He sounds worried. They're lying on the sofa to my right, with Jamie's head resting on Will's chest.

"I've known you quite a while now, Todd," she continues.

"Me?" I turn to look at her.

"Yes, you."

"What have *I* done?"

"Ever since we first met," she says, "I've been wondering about your tattoo. And now, I've just noticed, you've had an extra line added. There are three now, and there were only two."

Now everyone's looking at me.

"Oh yeah," Matt says. "I hadn't seen that. When did you get it done?"

"Just after Holly moved in with me."

"And not even I know what the new line means," Holly says. "He won't tell me."

"But you know the rest?" Jamie asks.

Holly nods her head. She twists and looks up at me. "Considering the amount of trouble everyone has gone to for us, don't you think it's time you told them?"

I realize she's right, and I look around the room at the people who mean most to me. "Okay," I say, and I show them my arm. "This line here." I point to it. "It's a kind of introduction. It says 'Blood makes you related'."

"Okay. And the next line?" Jamie asks. I look at Will, Matt, and Luke, in turn.

"That says 'Friendship makes you family'," I tell them. "It's about you guys."

They stare at me.

"You mean it was always about us?" Matt asks eventually. I nod my head. They all seem a little shocked, but Matt in particular. "But you've had it for so long," he continues. "You got that just a couple of years after we met."

"I know."

"And it's about us?" Luke says.

"Yeah. All of you. The point is, we may not be related, but as far as I'm concerned you guys are my family. You always were… always will be."

I catch Matt's eye just for a moment. Not for the first time, I remember that, apart from Grace and George, he doesn't have any family. I've got my mom and Vicky, and her kids, Luke and Will have each other… and we've all got the women we love, but Matt… He's spent a lot of his adult life alone… except he hasn't, because he's always had us. He and I know we're both thinking the same thing, and we both smile.

"What about the new line?" Holly asks me and I turn back to her and pull her a little closer to my chest. "Is that still about your friends?"

"Yeah… well, kind of." I tell her. "I wanted to get something added, specifically about my best friend." She looks across the room toward Matt, but he's looking at her now, not me. He understands. He gets it. "What does it say?" she asks.

"It says 'Love makes you mine'… And you can stop looking at Matt. It's about you, not him."

"I'm your best friend?" she whispers.

"Of course you are." She leans up and kisses me gently.

"Thank you," she whispers. Then she turns and looks around the room. "All of you, coming over here with us, it's made this trip so special. I find it hard to believe you'd do this… I mean, just drop everything and re-arrange your lives because we asked you to… but I'm very glad you did and that we're all here together."

That's a lovely thing for her to have said and I kiss the top of her head. "You'd better get used to it, baby," I tell her. "You're part of the family now."

The End

Keep reading for an excerpt from Suzie Peters' forthcoming book
Words and Wisdom
Part One in the Wishes and Chances Series.

Available to purchase from February 23rd 2018

Words and Wisdom

Wishes and Chances Series: Book One

by

Suzie Peters

Chapter One

✖

Four Years Earlier

Cassie

"Stop it." She moved his hand gently away from her hair. "It doesn't matter what you say, or do, I'm not changing my mind."

"C'mon, Cass." Jake's voice had that persuasive tone... the one that had talked her round so many times before.

"No, Jake. You know how I feel about this." She wasn't going to budge. Not this time. This was too important.

She stared at him until he looked away, but she knew this was no victory; the dark resentment in his eyes told her everything she needed to know. The argument was far from over.

"I'm gonna grab another beer," he said, getting up from his seat beside her. "You want anything?" She shook her head. "Suit yourself."

She felt like telling him to grow up, but what would be the point in that? Miracles never happened.

He moved through the throng of people toward Sean's kitchen and, looking at his back, she felt herself calming, just a little. Even from behind, he was gorgeous. Tall – a good head above most of the other people in the room – dark haired and muscular, Jake was stunning. His jeans hung perfectly on his hips, and his black t-shirt clung to his toned body. It was hard not to admire him, even when she couldn't see his face... the face that was usually so gentle, tender and caring, whenever it was looking at her. Except it wasn't at the moment, because Jake could also be childish and pig-headed… especially when it came to where they were going to live now that they'd graduated.

Cassie glanced around the room. As graduation parties went, this one was going… fairly badly. All she and Jake had done so far was fight – but then that was really all they'd done for the last three months. She hadn't even wanted to come here tonight in the first place: these were Jake's friends, not hers, and she felt really out of place. She'd wanted to go back to their apartment, finish packing and head straight home to Somers Cove, the small, coastal town in Maine where they'd both grown up together. She'd wanted them to settle down, maybe get a small place near to her mom, where she could write books, see her friend Emma every day and laugh over coffee with her. She'd wanted to stare out at the ocean, watch the sun rise and set over the still blue water, while the breeze played in her hair and Jake sat beside her, holding her in his arms… And she'd wanted Jake to want that too; maybe for him to work with his dad, Ben, fixing people's roofs and fences, helping out around the town, becoming as popular and loved as Ben was. And, one day, she'd hoped they'd get married, have kids and raise them in the quiet seaside resort she'd always loved and called home…

Except it seemed that wasn't what Jake wanted at all. Jake wanted them to take off for Boston. He had a friend there, who was happy for them to crash at his place until Jake could find work and then, he kept assuring her, they'd rent somewhere – maybe nothing much to start with – but they'd be together. And they'd go back to Somers Cove every so often to see her mom and his dad… and Emma could come to the city to visit with them. And it would be great… He'd made a point of smiling when he'd said that bit. He didn't want to work with Ben; he didn't want to be 'small town', as he put it. He wanted to make something of himself, to really *build* something; to create something more solid, more ambitious. Mending fences wasn't enough for Jake…

Clearly.

Cassie sighed. Mending fences had never been Jake's strong point. Busting down walls, and burning bridges... yeah, that was where his strength lay.

He wouldn't even think about going home with her for a few weeks over the summer while they worked out their future. She knew he thought that once they got back there, she'd never be willing to leave, and maybe he was right... but why couldn't he trust her enough to try it? It was asking too much to just take off to the city, with very little money, no prospects and no support behind them. Cassie wasn't that kind of risk taker. Even the idea of it terrified her, and Jake knew that... and that's what really hurt. He knew how she felt, but he didn't care enough to put her feelings first.

He came back into the overcrowded, overheated room and Cassie couldn't fail to notice that most of the female eyes in the room were turned toward him, following him as he crossed the room and sat back down beside her again. He looked at her, his green eyes darkening just a little.

"We seriously need to talk this through, Cass," he said, taking a swig from his beer. "I don't wanna go back there."

"Not at all?" She felt cold fingers of fear inching up her spine. "Not even for the summer?"

He gave her a withering look. "No."

She turned and faced him on the couch, trying to ignore the music that some idiot had just turned up a little louder. "How can we just go to Boston, Jake? You don't even have a job." At least he was listening this time, even if it was hard to hear what he was saying.

"I've already explained, Cass. It'll be fine. Pete is happy to let us crash at his place until I find work. It won't take long."

"You don't know that."

He looked at her, a furrow forming on his brow. "Well, thanks for the ringing endorsement."

"Sorry, I didn't mean it like that."

"Why can't you have a little faith in me?" *Right back at you*, she thought, but didn't say out loud.

"I do... I just..."

"What?" He sounded impatient, like he knew exactly what she was going to say – which he probably did, because they'd had this same argument so many times it was like déjà vu.

"You know I don't want to go…"

"And you know I can't live back there. Everyone has to know everything about you. It's so… claustrophobic."

"But it's where our families are." And there they were, back on the same old turf again.

"I'm not saying we won't see them, just that we don't have to live right in their back yard. I want my own life, Cass; not my dad's."

"And what about *my* life? What about what I want?"

"You can write anywhere…"

"Yeah, because what I want to do isn't as important as what you want to do, right?"

"I didn't say that."

"You didn't need to." She could feel the anger and resentment building again, and the argument degenerating into the usual tit-for-tat. She took a deep breath, trying to stay calm. "My mom hasn't got anyone else," she said. Cassie had no idea who her father was. Her mom never spoke about him and she never asked. They'd been happy together and she wanted that to continue.

"Your mom has the whole damn town, Cass. She belongs to so many committees and clubs, it's a wonder she has time to work."

She glanced up at him. "What do you want her to do, sit around doing nothing all day?"

"No, of course not. I'm just saying, she probably wouldn't miss you as much as you think she would."

Cassie felt the sting of tears in her eyes. "Well, thanks for that." She went to get up, but he pulled her back down again.

"I'm sorry. That came out wrong."

"Really?" She wondered if the truth was finally coming out in the heat of their argument.

They stared at each other for a long moment, until Jake broke the silence. "Do you love me, Cass?" he asked quietly, so quietly she struggled to hear his voice above the crashing music.

"Yes. You know I do."

"Then come with me."

"I'm scared, Jake," she whispered.

"What's to be scared of?" He raised his voice a little and smiled… the smile that normally had her melting from the inside out. "It'll be an adventure."

"I'm not feeling very adventurous." *I'm feeling scared that, if we go to Boston and you really are as fed up with me as you seem to be right now, we'll break up, and I'll be stranded… well, not stranded… Boston isn't an island, but it's not home either.*

He sighed. "What do you want from me, Cass?" he huffed out angrily.

"You know what I want. I want to go home."

"Christ, you sound like a baby…" He moved forward in his seat and looked back down at her. "A fucking selfish baby." And he got up and moved into the crowd, soon disappearing.

Cassie bit back her tears. Even in their worst arguments, he'd never spoken to her like that. He'd never called her names… but then they'd never been arguing on the eve of having to make the actual decision before. Tomorrow they were giving up their apartment, and they were going to leave – either for Boston, or Somers Cove. They'd packed up most of their things already. The only question was where were they going.

Except that wasn't the only question anymore. Because now, Cassie had to ask herself whether they'd be going anywhere together.

Jake

"What's up, man?" Sean's voice calling out from behind him cut into Jake's darkening mood.

"Nothing. I'm outta here."

x

325

"What about Cassie?"

Jake hesitated for a moment, then shrugged and strode on through the open front door, dodging the few people on the front lawn, before heading for his Jeep. He didn't glance back, didn't want to see if Cassie was standing watching him – mainly because he knew she wouldn't be.

He slammed the Jeep into drive and took off down the street, knowing, even as he turned the corner onto the main road, that he was abandoning the woman he loved – and he did love her – at a party she'd never wanted to go to, with people she barely knew, and no means of getting back to their apartment, other than calling a cab. He pulled his foot back off the gas. He should go back and get her. Leaving her there on her own was wrong… But if he went back, all they'd do is fight again.

"Fuck it," he said out loud, and smashed his hand down on the steering wheel as he floored the accelerator.

Ten minutes later, he parked up outside Joe's Diner, went inside and ordered a black coffee from Marilyn, who was on the late shift. Although nearly thirty-five, even Marilyn wasn't immune to Jake's good looks and she smiled sweetly at him as she poured his coffee.

"You okay tonight, hun?" she asked.

"Fine," he lied.

"We don't normally see you here this late… or on your own."

"No." He wasn't feeling very talkative. Marilyn gave up making conversation and moved back to the counter.

He was sitting in a booth near the back, away from the other customers – not that there were that many of them. It was gone eleven thirty, after all.

He stared through the misted window, at the haloed lights outside and sighed deeply.

Why couldn't Cassie understand? It really wasn't that difficult…

Ben Hunter, Jake's dad, was well known in Somers Cove. He was always there; always ready to help someone out whenever they needed him. Mending this, fixing that. And if they couldn't afford to pay him that month, well… he'd wait… and wait… and usually wait a bit more.

For as long as Jake could remember, everyone in the town – his dad included – had assumed that Jake would take over Hunter's Construction, the small building and repair business that his dad ran from the office above the family garage.

And nobody, but nobody, had really understood why, when he left high school, Jake had wanted to go to college.

"You don't need to do that," Mrs Adams, the coffee shop owner, had told him. "What do you need with an education when you've got a job ready and waiting for you?"

Jake had tried explaining to her that he wanted to learn construction engineering technology, so he could design and build houses and office blocks, hotels and shopping malls… but he knew he'd lost her halfway through his first sentence.

His dad thought he was going because Cassie was. She was going to study English, which made sense, considering she wanted to be a writer and his dad was happy for them to go together, being as they'd been inseparable since they were six years old. Cassie had always been his best friend… He remembered her being there when his mom died. He'd just turned nine and Cassie had been eight, and they'd spent that weekend sitting on the beach, while his dad made arrangements and cried quietly to himself in the bedroom he and his Jake's mom had shared for eleven years. Cassie had held his hand in hers and told him it would all be okay, and he'd believed her. And, eventually, it was – well, Cassie made it hurt less, anyway. So, when they turned eighteen, his dad said he understood that was why Jake was 'going with her' to college.

He took a sip of his cooling coffee and remembered that even Emma, Cassie's friend, who worked for Mrs Adams, had been surprised he was going. That had stung, because Emma had been going to college too – even if she had only lasted one semester before returning to work in the coffee shop again. It seemed it was fine for everyone else to want to better themselves, but not Jake…

The thought of returning to that suffocating town, the small-town ways and the small-town minds, filled him with dread. He knew Cassie wanted to go back there and she'd told him they should try it, just for the summer, or until he found a job in Boston. Except, he knew that once she got back there, he'd never persuade her to leave… and he'd be stuck there, drowning, forever.

He finished his coffee, paid Marilyn, who winked at him, and left.

When he pulled up at Sean's place again, the party was still in full swing. There were a few more people on the front lawn – he guessed it was getting too hot and crowded inside, and was proved right as soon as he tried to barge his way in. There were even more people here than there had been when he'd left.

He looked over the top of the crowd of heads, trying to see Cassie. She was fairly tall, at around five foot nine, so he should be able to see her, assuming she was standing up, of course. He searched for blonde heads, but there were very few there, and none of them were Cassie. He moved around a little more. She'd been wearing jeans – tight, sexy jeans – and a white camisole top, which showed off her tan, and her soft, soft skin… the skin he liked to kiss, and caress…

"You're back then?" Sean said, coming up behind him and tapping him on the shoulder.

"Yeah. Where's Cass?" he asked. "I can't see her."

"She's gone."

"Gone? What do you mean, gone?"

"Just that, man. She called a cab and took off, about ten minutes or so after you left."

"Where did she go?"

"How the hell do I know?"

"Was she alone?" He was suddenly gripped with fear that she'd left with another guy… but even as he asked the question, Jake wanted to kick himself for even thinking that. Cassie would never do that to him…

"Yeah. She sat outside and waited for the cab and then, when it arrived, she got in and left."

"And you didn't try to stop her?"

"No. Why the fuck would I do that? She seemed pretty mad."

"*She* was mad?" Jake couldn't understand why she hadn't just waited for him. She must've known he'd come back for her. "For fuck's sake." Jake turned and headed back toward the door.

"Where are you going now?" Sean called after him.

"Home." Not that he really wanted to. She was mad… he was mad. It didn't look good for resolving their differences.

Outside, he climbed back into his Jeep yet again and was just starting the engine when a tapping on the window made him jump out of his skin.

Standing on the sidewalk, looking at him, was Alice. She motioned for him to wind down the window, which he did.

"Hey," she said quietly. "You couldn't give me ride home, could you? I don't have enough cash on me for cab fare." She twirled her brown hair between her fingers, her big hazel eyes looking up at him through her long, dark eyelashes.

"Sure, jump in."

"Thanks, Jake. You're a lifesaver." She ran around the front of the Jeep, opened the passenger door, hitched up her already short skirt, and hopped up beside him.

"You live over on Westfield, don't you?"

"Yes. How did you know that?" she asked, smiling.

"Because you live in the same building as Mike and Steve… and I play football with them." It was hardly rocket science.

He pulled away and set off toward Westfield, which was only a ten minute drive away.

"What are your plans for the summer?" Alice asked, trying to make conversation.

"I don't know," Jake replied, trying to avoid it.

"I'm going home," she said.

Alice also lived in Somers Cove, but nowhere near Jake, or Cassie. Her father owned a car dealership on the outskirts of the town and, although they'd all attended the same high school, they'd not really known each other that well. She had hung out with a much bigger, louder crowd… the type of people Cassie tried to avoid.

"Really?"

"Well, I have to see my folks," Alice said. "Just for a few weeks… I'll probably stay until the fall, and then I'll try and get a job."

"Where?"

"Who knows? Maybe Portland... maybe Boston."

"You don't want to stay in Somers Cove then?"

"Hell, no. Why would anyone want to stay there?"

Jake felt a surge of relief. He wasn't alone. There was at least one other person on the planet who didn't think Somers Cove was the best place on earth and who saw the small town for what it was... Stifling. He took a deep breath. Okay, maybe he was overstating things. Most kids left Somers Cove because there wasn't enough work to keep them there. They moved to bigger towns and cities, where there was more going on. And that was exactly why he wanted to settle in Boston – with Cassie.

He pulled up outside Alice's apartment building, putting the car into park and relaxed back into his seat.

"This is kind of you, Jake," Alice said, placing her hand on his leg. "I'm real grateful."

"It's fine," he breathed. What the hell was she playing at?

"You know..." Her voice had dropped to a soft purr. "I've always liked you..."

What was he supposed to say to that? Her hand inched higher up his thigh.

She twisted in her seat, moved her leg to one side and, before he knew it, she was on his lap, straddling him, her skirt hitched up around her hips, revealing black lace panties...

"What the—" Her kiss interrupted his protest, her tongue delving deep into his already open mouth. The steering wheel at her back prevented him from pushing her away, so his only option was to lift her off of him. Just at that moment, she moaned into his mouth, and he became aware of her hands between them, fumbling with his belt, undoing it.

Oh, Christ. She was breathing hard, grinding into him with her hips.

There was nothing for it, if he was going to get rid of her, he'd have to touch her – even if she did misinterpret his intentions. He reached down and put his hands on her ass, then lifted her and dumped her back on her seat.

"What the fuck, Alice?" he said, glaring at her.

"Don't pretend you weren't interested," she murmured, peering up at him. "I could feel you."

"I don't know what you thought you felt, but I'm *not* interested."

"Oh, really?" She snaked her hand across and touched him… and he let her, just to prove that he wasn't aroused by her display. Not one bit.

"See?" he said. She pulled her hand away again. "Now get out of my car."

Embarrassed, she opened the door and quickly jumped down onto the sidewalk, running away into the building. She hadn't bothered to close the door and Jake leant across and pulled it shut.

He sat there, at the side of the road for a while. Nothing like that had ever happened to him before and he didn't really know what to think. The only girl who'd ever kissed him, or touched him, was Cassie, and he liked it that way. He liked – no, he loved – everything about Cassie and he couldn't imagine his life without her in it… except that meant he might have to face a life in Somers Cove, doing odd jobs and never realizing his own ambitions. He shook his head. He couldn't face it, he really couldn't… and, if he was being honest, he couldn't face Cassie and another argument either. He knew she'd be safely back at their little apartment on the other side of town by now. The inevitable argument could wait a little longer.

He pulled away from the curb, driving around aimlessly for a while. He wanted to forget about Alice, he even wanted to forget about Cassie, but only because he didn't want to think about what they were going to do tomorrow. They had to make a decision about whether they were going home, or going to Boston. They couldn't both win this argument, but losing meant either one of them being unhappy… or breaking up. After six years – well, a lifetime, really – could they break up over this?

He thought back over their time together. He remembered when everything between them changed. It had been a warm summer's day, they were both sixteen years old, and they were walking down the lane between his house and hers. His nerves had been jangling as he'd pulled her to one side, beneath the oak tree and asked her if she wanted to be his girlfriend. There was no point in just asking her out on a date, because they spent all their time together anyway, so he'd told her that he didn't want her as just a friend anymore, he wanted more... he wanted her to be his girlfriend. He remembered her reply, accompanied by a shy smile, that she would love to be his girlfriend, but that she would always be his friend. He'd leant in and kissed her then...

Now he *was* getting hard. Just thinking about Cassie could do that to him. Every. Damned. Time. She was like a drug... one he'd always been addicted to, ever since the day she and her mom had moved into the house right down on the beach and his mom had insisted they visit, taking a chocolate cake as welcome gift. Cassie'd looked at him with those wide, baby blue eyes and asked if he wanted to go swimming with her. He didn't really, because she was a girl and he thought she'd be a bit boring... but his mom had pushed him forward and he'd reluctantly agreed and they'd spent the whole summer together, swimming, playing on the beach, walking, laughing – especially laughing. He smiled and slowly shook his head. Cassie had a way of making everything better. Even the things that you never thought could get better... His mind wandered back again to the day his mom had died. She'd been ill for months... no years. She'd had breast cancer and, at first, she'd seemed to beat it and, for a while, everything had been okay, but it came back and very quickly claimed her. He recalled his dad, sitting him down on the edge of his bed and telling him that he had to be brave, and that his mommy wouldn't be coming home again; and how he'd run straight down the lane to Cassie's house, and found her playing on the porch and how he'd cried when he'd told her, and she'd silently taken his hand led him out onto the beach and sat there with him, watching the sun slowly fall into the ocean... He wondered if he'd loved her, even then.

He turned the car in the direction of their apartment.

He couldn't ask her to move to Boston with him... not when he had nothing to offer. But he could go there himself. He could get a job, find them somewhere to live... and then come back for her. He wondered if she'd accept that as a compromise...

She wanted to live in Somers Cove. He knew that. He just hoped she wanted to live with him more.

By the time he put his key in the lock of their apartment, it was nearly three in the morning. He hadn't realized he'd been driving around for so long. He opened the door quietly, so as not to wake Cassie, and went inside.

It was a small studio apartment, with everything, except the bathroom, in one room. He knew she'd be asleep in their bed in the far corner, curled up facing the wall as usual, so he tiptoed over in the darkness and leant across the bed.

"Hey, baby," he said quietly.

Something was wrong.

Even before he knelt on the mattress, he knew she wasn't there. He couldn't hear her breathing. He flipped around and turned on the lamp on the nightstand. Cassie was nowhere to be seen.

"Cass?" he called out, heading for the bathroom… but the door was open and the room was in darkness. The apartment was completely empty.

His heart racing, pounding in his ears, he went across to the small closet where they kept their clothes, and slowly opened the door to Cassie's side. Even as the hinges creaked, he knew… he knew it would be empty. He stumbled backwards to the bed and held his head in his hands.

What the hell had happened to her?

Well, the answer to that was obvious… she'd left him. She'd gone home. She was done arguing. She wanted one thing; he wanted another. They couldn't agree, so she'd gone.

But why couldn't she wait and tell him? Why just take off like that? They'd always been friends, always been able to tell each other everything… and they'd never argued about anything until they'd tried to work out where they were going to live and discovered they wanted different things from life.

Did she want her own way so much, she wasn't even prepared to sit down and talk it through? Wasn't she even willing to try and find a compromise? Clearly not.

Jake got to his feet and went over to the closet again, opening the door on the other side – the one containing his clothes. Then, grabbing his bag from under the bed, he started to stuff his belongings inside, moving quickly around the room.

Within an hour, everything was packed and he'd loaded his bags and three boxes into his Jeep. It was too early to call Pete – it was still only just after four in the morning – but if he set off now, he'd reach Boston by around seven-thirty. He could get some breakfast and then call his friend, and go around to his place... and then he'd turn off his phone. He had no intention of speaking to anyone, not for a while. Not until he'd calmed down enough to be civil... and he had no idea right now how long that was going to take.

To be continued...